SHINING SCABBARD

SHINING SCABBARD

A Story
by
R. C. HUTCHINSON

CASSELL
AND COMPANY, LTD.
London, Toronto, Melbourne
and Sydney

To
A. S. T. AND L. T.
IN GRATITUDE

First Edition	.	*September*	1936
Second Edition	.	*October*	1936
Third Edition	.	*October*	1936
Fourth Edition	.	*December*	1936
Fifth Edition	.	*October*	1945

PRINTED IN GREAT BRITAIN
BY JARROLD AND SONS LTD., NORWICH
F.745

I

"I am sure you will be glad," Madame Séverin wrote, "to hear that I have told your Father about your marriage. I chose the time very carefully, last Sunday evening, after Father had had his coffee. I had played some Chopin to him, he has grown very fond of Chopin, he has gone off Beethoven altogether. He has been much better this last fortnight, and I thought it would be best to use the opportunity, as he may have another bad turn at any time. He took the news very well indeed, only expressing a little surprise that you had not written to him yourself. I did not tell him all at once about your Renée, I brought it in by degrees that her parents had always lived abroad, and then that her great-grandmother on her mother's side had been a foreigner (that is right, is it not? I have not your letter with me at the moment). At that point Father rather startled me by saying suddenly (he is so very quick, you know, at guessing what you are trying to hold back): 'Not a negress, I hope, surely not a negress?' Of course I told him at once that that was absurd, only that Renée's great-grandmother had come, I thought (I wasn't quite clear, I said), from one of the great Warrior Peoples with whom we Latins have, in the past, been so closely allied, in friendship and in war. He seemed quite satisfied with that, he said, 'Well, I suppose that's all right,' and then I changed the subject altogether, but later in the evening he said again, as if he had been thinking about it all the time: 'Oh, well, I suppose it's all right.' I was rather worried when Father said at luncheon the next day in front of everybody, 'Is Pierre's wife quite black, or only brown?' (You know, darling, he didn't really mean that, it's just the blunt way he has of saying things sometimes.) Of course I just changed the subject at once. Then later on he said: 'Well, of course, my mother has Tartar blood, not very far back,' and that made your grandmother very indignant. I was very glad when luncheon was over and I was able to persuade Father to go to his room and rest. The north wind is very trying at present, and I am in hourly fear of another bad turn. . . . We look forward to seeing you again, darling, and I hope to hear from your next letter whether there is any chance of your getting leave in the summer, and if so, whether you can make arrangements to come home. I know you will understand me when I say that I think it wiser that you should not bring Renée on your next visit home, eager as I am to see her. I should like you to have a talk with Father first of all, and when he hears from your own lips—you are so much better at explaining than I am—how devoted you are to your

Renée, then I am sure that he will be more ready to take her calmly and to see her himself. You know, darling, that his illness makes him subject to prejudices which act in a curious way, and it is hard for him to take to new ideas such as people have nowadays. It was always his hope that you might marry a girl of our own acquaintance. I know you will not misunderstand my meaning. I want you to tell Renée how affectionate I feel towards my dear son's wife, and how glad we shall be to welcome her when Father is really better. Your Father . . ."

★

Pierre read the letter as he was dressing for parade. Tightening the laces of his boot with one hand, he stretched the other to turn over the large, thin sheets which lay on the floor at his feet. A bugle warned him that time was short, he laced the other boot, gathered the sheets together and threw them crumpled in a corner. Renée of course found them; Pierre was always throwing away something he meant to keep, things of particular importance. Renée smoothed out the letter, read it, and put it away among her own things. Returning in the afternoon Pierre asked casually "Did you see a letter? I'm not sure, I believe I left it somewhere, there was something I wanted to make a note of." "There was a letter all crumpled up," she told him, "I didn't think it was anything, I threw it away." "Did you? You threw it away? Oh, well, it doesn't matter, it was just gossip from my mother."

II

ARMAND spent his ninth birthday in bed. It was not surprising, the Colonel's wife said, now that the east wind had been blowing for a fortnight; the child looked delicate, he should have been taken home years before. The little girl was all right, she stood up to it like a native. "Home?" Renée said. "We've never had any. Oh, yes, my husband's people live at Baulon l'Epais, but they wouldn't want grandchildren. No, my father died two years ago; we used to live at Alger."

The doctor said the same thing. The child must be taken to Europe, it was insane to keep him in this climate. But it is doubtful if Captain Séverin would have paid much attention—he thought all doctors were frauds, especially army doctors—had he not received notice of transfer to Sigumbe. That meant separation; and he was not going to leave Renée among the patronizing she-cats at Djedoule. "There is only one thing to do," he said with finality, "you'll have to go to Baulon. Only for the time being, I shall get

6

moved again, I shall apply straight away for a post in Sonneger that would be better." Renée said: "But you know, Pierre, how I feel about Baulon. . . ." But already he was on the veranda, his back turned to her, and the orderly was waiting with his horse. He threw away the end of his cigarette and stooped to dust his boots with a handkerchief. "This evening, we'll discuss all that. . . ."

For most of the afternoon she was locked in her bedroom, for once deaf to the calls of the children. But when he came in the evening she had covered the traces of crying, and her mind was made up. It was no good talking any more, they had discussed it so often, this question of Baulon. It had become a fixed idea, that at Baulon she would be miserable. Perhaps she was all wrong, perhaps Pierre's people were kind and homely, Pierre never spoke of them except in a vague, impersonal way, it was impossible to tell. Certainly Armand must have a change, he was a constant worry to her. The question of schooling could not be postponed much longer. And soon Sophie . . . In any case, what option? "Yes, yes, Pierre, I have made up my mind, yes, I've quite decided, don't let's talk about it any more. We must think about arrangements."

Like her, Pierre wanted to get the matter settled. They distrusted themselves. And in the evening he wrote to his mother. ". . . they must, of course, be met at Marseille. Do you think Aunt Thérèse could manage it?—you will be too busy. The mail steamer leaves Congerisque on Saturday week, and is due at Marseille on the sixth of next month. . . ."

Up to that point Pierre was practical; and he did obtain useful information from the garrison transport officer. Thereafter his usefulness and his resolution failed together. He would not sit down, even to read a newspaper, he got up during meals and wandered about the room with his glass in his hand. He said a dozen times, "I've been thinking it over, I'm not certain . . . I might send you to a hotel somewhere, to Sonneger perhaps." "But, Pierre, the cost . . . and besides, we can't keep altering." "But you don't really want to go to Baulon?" He refused to do anything about the bungalow. "I can see to that when you're gone, there'll be time enough. I suppose the furniture will have to go to Congerisque, unless I sell it. I'll ask Debriel what he thinks. But I'm not sure, I'm going to see Malestroit again, I may still be able to get this transfer cancelled."

Renée still shared his hopes; but only with that part of her heart which the mind would not subdue. She made arrangements. She paid bills, ransacked the children's wardrobe for anything that would be suitable at sea, sent orders to Congerisque. Pierre was hard up at the moment, but they had an account at Congerisque, Maison Estophile would give her credit up to two or three hundred francs. It was hard to get everything done, with the children fretful and wanting her attention all the time, Marie-Noire too stupefied with grief to look after them properly. She curtailed her siesta, she worked furiously; almost mechanically, like a man dressing before his execution. They came to the last evening and Pierre was still faintly hopeful. Malestroit had written to Sonneger, Malestroit was not optimistic but it was still possible that a counter-manding order would come through in the morning. He wandered about lighting one cigarette after another while she took everything out of the trunk to find a doll of Sophie's that Sophie would want on the journey. He said, coming in from the veranda: "In any case I'm not sure that we couldn't arrange for you to go to a hotel at Alger. For the time being, anyway. I could get Debriel to cancel the reservation, he's frightfully thick with the fellow in the Agence Condé." "This one is ready," Renée said, "will you strap it for me? And will you see if Armand's still awake? Go quietly."

★

She woke feeling that she had not slept at all. Pierre was sitting by the bed in his night-suit, smoking. She asked: "What time is it?" "I don't know. I had a rotten night, you were snoring." He would hardly look at her; only in swift glances when her eyes were turned from him; he ignored the children, and went off to the mess directly after breakfast. Julie Velaillie came in with a bunch of flowers which she had had sent up from Congerisque, Julie was always so kind. There was nowhere to put the flowers, everything was in such a muddle. "If you could keep an eye on the children, Julie dear, while I get the packing finished off. Marie-Noire is no longer any use at all." "Darling, of course," But Julie remained at the door of the bedroom as if her feet were stuck to the floor, while the children sparred and tumbled in the salon, while Marie-Noire sat weeping in the kitchen. "You don't know, Renée, how dull it will be without you. And there's no one else to stand up to that awful Madame Malestroit." Pierre came back in a white temper. No, the order had only been confirmed, and Malestroit had read him a lecture on some futile point, "he talked to me like a father, just as if I'd been his youngest subaltern." And the result of all that—Renée would have to go down to Congerisque by herself; Pierre had meant to ask for special leave, he had forgotten, he was the Captain on duty that afternoon; but now, why, obviously it was impossible to ask favours from a man who spoke to you like a grandfather. He would telephone Maturin, Maturin would put her on board. He was sorry. "What's this woman hanging about for?" he whispered audibly. "Why won't she go?"

Marie-Noire had at last taken the children off to the kitchen, where she was feeding them according to her lights; her grief had blossomed into anger at Renée's refusal to let her dress them in their best for the journey. Julie departed at last, wistfully, and murmuring that she would be at the station—she had some pastries for the children. Regarding the living-room, where the boxes stood roped, where the portrait of Pierre had been taken down from the shelf, where everything was littered with newspaper, Renée saw that an epoch had ended. Two years they had been in that bungalow, they had never lived so long in one place before. It was familiar, the stir of decampment, but this was something new. Pierre was hunting for writing-paper; someone had been at his drawer, he said. "Let's take a walk, Pierre, we can spare ten minutes, there's no air indoors at all." "But it's hotter outside, and Debriel's sending a man for the trunks, I ought to be here to see him." "Come, darling."

They went past the married quarters and as far as the parade ground, walking so far apart that a man could just have passed between them. She said: "I'm afraid the place is in a frightful mess, Pierre, I couldn't tidy up with the boxes still about and the children all over everything. . . . I hate leaving you to clear up all the mess. (You won't forget Marie-Noire's wages, will you? Yes, on Saturday.) I hate the idea of your having to look after yourself." He smiled then. "But, my dear, I can look after myself perfectly. Besides, it won't be for long. I'll get shifted from Sigumbe in a month or two, I can work it somehow."

Glancing sidelong she saw that he was looking straight along the road as if he could see something invisible to her. His thin brown face was dry; he never sweated. He rolled a little as he walked, swinging each foot and placing it as if a narrow path were marked for him to walk on. His cigarette had gone out, but he still pulled at it, mechanically trying to revive the glow. "We must go back," he said, and swung about. "They'll all be watching us, you're always watched at this place, I shall be glad to get away from it." Then, "You'll like Baulon, all right. After a bit. It takes getting used to, everything does. Don't let them bully you." She moved closer to him, hoping that he would her take his arm. But he glanced apprehensively towards the bungalows, he always seemed to be aware of someone watching. They could have had this walk last night; why hadn't they? Pierre looked at his watch. "We reserve ourselves," he thought, "and time catches us out."

A native corporal saluted as he passed, and then the white road was empty. From the men's quarters, over to their right, came the noise of children brawling. There was no breath of wind now, the white dust hardly rose as they walked, the baked air made the distant houses quiver in the stillness. It was absurd, Pierre's fancy that someone was always watching; the trouble rather was that no one saw them. That the world was asleep while they went through this. For an instant she thought that she too was sleeping, that the sombre vision haunting her of Baulon would pass away when she awoke. A trick of light and scent had made the road appear to her as she had seen it in their first summer here. She had forgotten that appearance, seeing the township every day in drab familiarity. And slipping back into that former time she felt as if her happiness belonged there, an illusory sensation which she had outgrown and, could not quite remember. If she could spend another week at Djedoule, even another day, she might coax Pierre into his old, his settled mood. They could talk things over then, establish something, she would ponder carefully and find the sources of her old contentment. Another week with Pierre close to her, then she would be ready for a time of separation. But Pierre was walking faster, the time had gone now. She closed her eyes and tried to form a concrete vision of the station, of the road where it twisted, the serried huts, the iron armoury, the drooping tricolour. Already the picture was blurred in outline, in another climate she would not recover it. She wondered, looking at Pierre, if his thin face would become fainter also, if she would forget the way he walked, his trick of catching at an imaginary beard and jerking up his head at any sudden interruption, the odd, impatient way in which he slipped his shoulders from his braces.

Someone had got the trunks out on to the veranda, and there was Marie-Noire in furious argument with the soldier who had come in a mule-cart to fetch them. Pierre, in a burst of temper, sent the woman off to the kitchen. He said over his shoulder, as he strode into the living-room, "Get those things loaded, look sharp, yes, all of them." "But the woman told me——" "Don't argue, hurry!" "But, Pierre, I want to keep the valise with me——" "All right, give the man your own orders." Marie-Noire had set a meal, with tablecloth and manifold cutlery, in the living-room. The children, descended abruptly from their fever, were lying on their bellies in the carpetless salon, arranging a set of Persian chessmen in extended column. Renée went into the bedroom and Pierre followed her.

He asked: "Is there anything you want me to do, with the packing or anything? (You don't know what's happened to my writing-paper? It was in the middle drawer.) You do understand, don't you, about that cheque? Yes, at Marseille, yes, Banque du Sud." He took off his jacket to examine a pocket which had torn at the seam. "Yes, I did it on a nail in the armoury. It's always happening. Why the fools must put a nail there—oh, it's all right, I'll get Lardet to do it."

But she had her smaller sewing-box in the top of the valise. "It won't take a minute," she said.

He sat on the bed and watched her as she sewed. He said: "The money you've got with you ought to see you through. You'd better let the purser have it. You won't forget there'll be the stewardess to be tipped. The table steward—I should think ten would do. Two-fifty for the deck steward if he does anything —but make him earn it, make him keep an eye on the children. . . . You'll know Aunt Thérèse by her nose, it's like a horse's. A sort of disapproving look." Sophie was calling, "Mummy, is it time to go to the station?" Her eyes were fixed on her work, she saw only the shape of Pierre as he watched her. She said, "Tell them —tell them to go and say good-bye to Sergeant Mercier's collie." He shouted the message and locked the door. "There you are," she said, giving him the jacket.

He stood holding the jacket, looking at the pocket as if he were not quite satisfied, as if the jacket had been offered him for sale and he could not make up his mind. He said, "You're awfully quick, chérie, there's no one to beat you on that sort of job." He turned as he put his arm into the sleeve. "Any sort of job."

"I must get the children ready," she said. But he had taken the key of the door, and that escape was closed. She turned and saw that Pierre had thrown himself face-down on the bed. Something came into play then, a reserve of courage. She stood still, while the physical pain was at its worst, and then she lay beside him, holding his hand tightly, rubbing it with her thumb. He turned his head and thrust his face into her breast. He was crying like a child ashamed of tears, he was shaking so that the bed creaked. She locked her fingers with her hands across his neck, holding his head there. She felt nothing now except a wise compassion. Her mouth had dried, at first she found that the power of speech had left it. But presently she said, surprised how well her voice controlled itself. "It won't be long, chéri, not very long." The carriage had drawn up outside, and Armand was thumping at the door. Pierre sat up and stared towards the window. "What madness it is! What right has anybody got to interfere with us like this?" "The carriage is here," Renée said, "we must hurry now."

She wanted to look carefully at the bungalow, at the village as they went through; to create a picture in which her memory could clothe itself. I was happy at this place, she thought, forgetting what a worry Armand's health had been, how Pierre had chafed under Malestroit's sententious discipline. It was her sort of place,

Djedoule, with its hard shadows and its dry air, with brown soldiers tramping in the thick dust. But Sophie was worrying Pierre by threatening to fall over the side of the carriage, Armand said that his needs could not be denied until they reached the station, Pierre was giving haphazard instructions about the arrival at Marseille. Before she could collect herself the bungalow was out of sight.

At the station an orderly presented a message from Colonel Malestroit. The Colonel had observed that it was Captain Séverin's duty this afternoon; and being informed that Madame Séverin was leaving for Congerisque, where Captain Séverin would no doubt wish to see her off, he had arranged that Lieutenant Frigot should parade as substitute. "And who told him about my private affairs?" Pierre demanded, as soon as the orderly was out of hearing. "No, you needn't say it, it was his female. There's nothing but gossip in this station. . . . No, of course I can't accept favours of that sort, after the way he spoke to me this morning."

Julie Velaillie had brought the pastries folded in a paper napkin. The children seized them, Sophie with a bright smile, Armand without any acknowledgment at all. They sat opposite each other on the horsehair seats, munching. The carriage became strewn with crumbs and shreds of tissue paper. "You must say good-bye to Father," Renée told them. "Come, Armand, give your salute, your right hand." "But where is Marie-Noire?" Sophie demanded. "Isn't she coming?"

Julie stood back a little way, an uninvited mourner. Along the train the day-leave soldiers stood in groups, refusing to enter before the horn was blown. The sun came down between the train and the short platform roof; except for the murmur of voices there was utter stillness.

"I wish now," Pierre said, "that I had made some other arrangement. My family are strangers to you, it's a mad arrangement, I can't think why I even thought of it. . . . Renée darling, you won't believe anything they tell you about me? In one's family they say all kinds of things, you won't believe that sort of thing? Or anything you hear from anyone else—I do queer things sometimes, I'm not always quite myself when I'm lonely, people don't understand me."

He was interrupted by the station boy.

"Pardon, Captain, the conductor's compliments, he wants to know if the train may start.'

"What? Yes. No. What's the time? Yes, he'd better start. Tell him he may start."

"Come, children, you must say good-bye to Father. Armand, quickly."

"But isn't Father coming?"

"No, Sophie."

Sophie embraced her father, weeping. "It is enough to break your heart!" Julie said. Armand, still munching the remains of his pastry, perfunctorily gave his salute. Pierre kissed his wife on both cheeks quickly. She held his hands, she said:

"Pierre, if you feel——"

The horn drowned her voice. An orderly, saluting, said: "All the boxes are in the car of the conductor himself."

Pierre stood back. He bit his lip, he was thinking, there was something he had meant to say. He said:

"Your dress, Renée, you'll have to do something, somehow or other. The petticoat is showing."

The train jerked forward and he slammed the door.

She made herself look at him, trying to sharpen the last impression. Sophie was tugging at her skirt, asking something. She saw on his face a look she knew, of hopeless perplexity. He was still thinking, she realized, of something he had meant to say. Then he saluted and turned about and went briskly out of the station. She pictured him returning to the bungalow, wandering between the rooms, searching vaguely for his writing-paper.

"Armand, you must take your hands away from the window, the glass is dirty."

III

From time to time Madame Fleury would call the steward and ask him to shift her chair a little. She liked to have the sun on her legs, where it penetrated her petticoats sufficiently to give a pleasant warmth, but on her arms and face, no. And there must be no smuts. She lay there all day long, only going below for déjeuner if the sea was particularly calm. That way she was all right, she could almost enjoy the gentle roll. And the idleness was pleasant enough. Occasionally her husband would bring her a book; "You must be bored," he would say. "See, I have got this for you out of the library." And she would thank him, smiling distantly, and from then the book would lie open on her lap, and when she saw him approaching again she would turn over a few pages so that he should see she had made some progress. "It is very interesting," she would say, "it is about a young girl from Lyon who fell in love with a young man whom her parents detested." "Ah, yes, a romantic story, I know you like that kind of thing, I chose it for you specially."

Always B deck. It was the quietest; the noisiest flirtations were performed below and the most violent stretching of legs above. It was the children's deck, made specially safe for them. And Madame Fleury could compare the ones she saw with the grandchildren she knew at Nancy and with those she had never seen, but whose photographs she treasured, in America. That one, she thought, she would be the same age as Babette, and rather like her in the features, but not so well grown or so robust. . . . This voyage there were not many children, it was not the time of year when families would choose to travel. She dozed a good deal, as the elderly do when they are idle, and waking easily she called the steward and requested that he would move her chair back a little, here the sun was beginning to shine on her face. It grew a little cooler as they sailed northward, it was pleasant to feel that they were getting nearer to France.

It was soon after leaving Congerisque, where it had been so unbearable with no motion to cool the ship and with the heavy stagnant smell coming off the shore, that the boy whom she regarded with so much interest had made his first appearance. He had come shambling along the deck in his long, baggy, dungaree trousers, gesticulating with one hand like a political orator driving home an argument, mumbling one phrase again and again as if committing it to memory, his eyes on his yellow sandals. He had walked right into her, had murmured a ready-made apology, carefully rounded the obstacle, and proceeded in the same line. He had come back later to climb, as all the children did, upon the deck rails, turning his feet the same way and hoisting himself up to see above the canvas. She had cried a warning "Son! That's not allowed, it's dangerous." He had stared at her as at a very foolish person and slouched away.

Afterwards he came there constantly, and made a seat for himself, with a coil of rope between two stanchions. He sat facing her, his legs crossed, his hands folded: "a little Buddha," Madame Fleury told her husband. She took off her sun-glasses so that he would not be frightened of her, and presently he smiled, and would answer her greeting with a mumbled "'jour, Madame!" But for a long time their intercourse went no farther. He was full of his own thoughts, he would rest his eyes for a full quarter-hour upon her sun-hat, never meeting her glance, and suddenly would purse his lips and strike a fist as if a sudden attack had been launched upon him.

There was a little girl—his sister, Madame Fleury guessed, though so unlike him—who came sometimes, jumping and laughing to stand in front of him with one foot resting on the other, asking him questions in the rapid children's lingo that Madame Fleury could never quite understand; questions which the boy answered in careless monosyllables, often without looking, as one who had matured too far to concern himself with such trivialities. The little girl bore the treatment quite patiently; she was a good-tempered little thing, Madame Fleury thought, and quite pretty in her dumpy, flaxen way. Sometimes they would play together for half an hour or so, lying flat and throwing a coloured die, scoring very seriously. But at last the little girl would suddenly collapse into giggles, and the boy, rather offended, would stuff the die into his trouser pocket as she skipped away. Then he would make his way meditatively, a step at a time, to his accustomed seat, and for an hour or more till the bell rang for the children's meal he would sit quite still, unaware of the woman watching him, his pointed chin dug into the flesh of his long, thin arms, his eyes fixed and solemn. Madame Fleury asked him his name one day. He started, and said "Armand," and went away.

By degrees she persuaded him to be more friendly, at last to sit on the forepart of her chair.

"Your father," she asked one day, "is he a soldier?"

"Oh, yes. An officer."

"And are you going to be a soldier too?"

"No. No, certainly not."

"But why?"

"I have no interest in it."

"Then what are you going to be?"

"A monk."

"Ah, you are religious, then? You are interested not in soldiering, but in God?"

"No, not very."

"But why a monk?"

"I should like it. It's quiet. One gets away from women. No, I don't mean—you, Madame, have been very courteous."

Madame Fleury was anxious to see the parents, her eyes peered round the dining-saloon at every meal, it was amusing to speculate on their identity. But her table was in a bad position, she arrived only at negative conclusions. "It is curious," she said to her husband, "the boy always seems to be alone, except when his sister is with him. I have seen no one who might be the parents, but a nurse, surely, would spend more time with her charges. I'm afraid the parents must be selfish people who amuse themselves all the time." "Parents? Whose parents?" "Never mind, Georges dear, get on with your soup, it's getting cold."

But one morning a woman appeared on B deck, quite evidently in search of someone. She had been ill, Madame Fleury thought, her eyes looked tired. But a pretty woman, quite a beauty except for the colour of the skin, which Madame Fleury could not

15

altogether fancy. Italian perhaps. But no, the eyes were wrong; from the South, no doubt, and yet it was seldom that even Southerners had quite that darkness. If one lived abroad for a long time, and did not treat the skin with the care which Madame Fleury herself exercised . . . at any rate it was a very pretty figure, so slender, the breast so firm, the shoulders small and tidy. And the girl walked well, too, in spite of the unbecoming deck shoes she was wearing.

"You are looking for someone?" Madame Fleury asked.

She could see now, the expression was that of the little girl, although they were so different, the little girl quite fair and so very plump. It would be interesting to see them again in ten, no twenty, years, when the child was tall and fully breasted.

"Yes, have you by any chance seen my little son about? I thought I saw him go up to this deck——"

"You mean Armand?"

"Yes, that's the one."

It was the smile that was the same, the beautiful white teeth. Ear-rings, Madame Fleury thought, that would be an interesting experiment. And yet, no, no, too finished. The girl had taste of her own, her hair might be better arranged but it was done quite sensibly, her cotton dress was neatly made although it was of poor material. Really, it was a triumph to be so slender after two children, to look so young. It was a pity the skin was so very dark, but of course some people admired that nowadays.

"No, I haven't seen him recently. He was here about twenty minutes ago, but he didn't stay long. Wait, I'll help you look for him. No, I'm sorry, I can't stand up, I daren't walk about, only when the sea is very calm indeed. I'm so sorry."

Armand's mother was going away. Madame Fleury called her back.

"I must tell you, I really must, how much I admire your children. The boy, he is really very handsome, so serious, a perfect little Frenchman."

"You are very kind . . . but at present he is so unhappy, he misses his father. He's devoted to his father."

"Then he is not with you, your husband? How sad that is for you! Your husband is a soldier, no doubt?"

"A soldier, yes. We were obliged to leave him, he has been moved to another station, and it was time in any case to take the children to Europe. The little boy, his health is not too good. The doctor said that he must have a more temperate climate."

"Yes, yes, I know how it is. It's always the way. The children, they are the problem always. Myself, I have been in the tropics most of my life, I know what it is. . . . But I mustn't keep you—one of the stewards I'm sure will tell you where Armand has got to."

At luncheon Madame Fleury passed on the news to her husband. "Yes, I saw the mother this morning, the father is not with them. No nurse, as I thought—I should think their finances are not too strong. No, that's only my impression, the girl was dressed very neatly, but poor material, she should have got better stuff even in that part of the world. Wait now, I'll see if I can see her. Yes, very good-looking, an excellent figure. Ah, there—right over there, in the other corner. No, don't look yet, she's looking this way." Madame Fleury bowed. "Now then, quick, the way the handle of my knife's pointing."

"You don't mean that mulatto-looking woman?"

"No, it isn't fair to call her that. Her skin's dark, certainly, but she's entirely European, most intelligent. I thought the way she spoke was very intelligent indeed. Pretty eyes—you can't see her properly from here. The little girl's like her, not the boy. He probably takes after his father."

"We must invite her to coffee or something. The name you said——?"

"The name? I don't know, I hadn't thought of it: I must find out."

But why should Madame Fleury bother about the name of Armand's mother, or any other name, while the sun shone warmly and the ship's motion was enough to temper it? She saw her again, and they said "Good day" and exchanged civilities. The young woman was rather shy, Madame Fleury thought, and that was a pleasant feature in these days when girls had neither modesty nor discretion. It was a pity that she looked so worried—almost as if the children were not enough for her, as if she missed her husband. That was it, perhaps, Madame Fleury had met that kind of thing before and it was becoming more common, married couples in love with each other. It would be nice to take this girl to Paris and have her pretty figure dressed in the right colours, in the new mode but with a touch of the bizarre, something bright and Oriental to which the dark skin would give distinction.

Someone in sand-coloured alpaca was coming along the deck; it was Georges again, he was really becoming too attentive. "Yes, thank you, Georges, I am perfectly comfortable. No, I haven't quite finished the novel you brought me this morning, it is most interesting."

"I've found out the name for you," he said. "I asked the stewardess. Séverin."

"Whose name?"

"That woman."

" Oh, that woman. Yes, a nice-looking creature, I think, in spite of her skin. Séverin. Fancy that."

"Why? Is it a name you know?"

"No. I mean, it's quite common, isn't it?"

"I suppose so."

Rather disappointed, though he was careful not to show it, he went away. He repeated to himself, "Séverin."

The little girl appeared during the afternoon, and romped for a time by herself, unself-consciously, with a great display of petticoats. It was rather a boring little girl, Madame Fleury thought, though very good-tempered. The little Armand, he was different altogether. It was not shyness that made him silent, only his preoccupation with his thoughts. And there he was again, in his usual position, with his legs bent up beneath him, as still as waxwork. He had lost his blue cap now, or forgotten to put it on, and he looked still more enchanting with a lock of untidy hair falling down across his freckled forehead, his eyes as serious as a student's. "What are you thinking about, Armand?" she called at last. "About God?" "No, Madame, only about the sorrows of humanity." "You are a philosopher, then, as well as a theologian?" "I'm sorry, I must go now, my mother will be requiring me."

"I have been trying to remember," M. Fleury said at dinner. "Séverin, it recalls something, a long time ago, I can't quite remember."

"Then it's not worth the trouble, my dear. You have enough to do, remembering where you put your evening shoes, and to pay your taxes."

"Yes yes; still, one likes to get to the bottom of that kind of thing. It's like a piece of apple-peel in a hollow tooth."

*

Next day the clouds were gathering, Madame Fleury was obliged to get out her old travelling coat and to send the steward for more rugs. "That is the trouble," she complained, "you are no sooner out of the tropics than you are into the polar regions. There will be fog soon, and it will be difficult for the captain to steer the boat."

The wind, increasing, drove up the clouds until the sky was covered over, grey. Beneath the solid, homogeneous mass the lighter, tattered cloud blew fast, breaking and twisting. It had not begun to rain, but the air was loaded, the rails and deck were damp. The ship rolled increasingly. A young Norwegian and his wife were still on deck, watching the spray which the wind caught from the folded bow-wave, and carried upwards almost to their faces. They held hands, breathing deeply in the wet air. The other passengers were all below; "You can tell," they said to each other, sneezing, "that we are near to Europe now." The steam-pipes

18

had been turned on, there was a new, rusty smell in the cabin corridors. It was hot and close down there, the eternal throb, the hum, became unbearable. Madame Fleury went early to bed.

M. Fleury, turning in at eleven, undressed with the utmost care in order not to disturb his wife, using only the reading light above his own berth. But once between the sheets he leaned down, pulled aside the curtain of the lower berth a little way, and asked:

"Agnes, are you still awake? Don't move, my dear, don't wake up. I only wanted to tell you—Séverin, it's been puzzling me all day. But I'm beginning to remember. Are you awake, dear? Don't you remember—it was ever so long ago—a scandal of some sort, I don't quite know what it was, but there was a lot in the newspapers at the time. Surely you remember. Yes, it all comes back to me, a lot of gossip and so on in the newspapers, though I can't remember what it was all about. I'm sure it was a Colonel Séverin."

★

Long after the Norwegian couple had gone to bed, Renée locked the door of her cabin and went up to the boat-deck. She had lain awake, oppressed by the confinement of the narrow cabin, by the heavy air and the continuous vibration. She stood now with a travelling coat above her nightgown, her feet in canvas shoes, glad to suffer the cold wind for its freshness. Here, with no sound but the flush of water far below and the hiss of blowing rain, she was nearer to Pierre. A ship was so small, in the daytime you could not get away from people chattering, the high, twittering chatter of the tireless Paris women, the solemn drooling of the males. All the people seemed to know each other, they came from the smart places, they thought in unison, they measured value in notes of fifty francs. Even the children, Pierre's children, were a distraction which kept the image of Pierre away. She had written day by day a letter which was to be posted at Marseille—it was terrible to think how long it would take to reach him—but this evening, reading it again, she had felt it was a letter which any woman might have written him. She could go to the writing-room now and try again; perhaps, late at night like this, she would find it possible to put on paper a little of her longing for him. But someone might be there, old Madame Carliez who read and knitted half the night, it was better to stay up here, where only the dark waste of sea remained between them. She whispered, "Are you asleep, Pierre? Do you dream of me?"

To be alone relieved her loneliness. And now, with her face turned against the driven rain, she was strengthened by its cold attack. The trouble which possessed her in the daytime, of which she was conscious while she talked to fellow passengers, while she answered Sophie's questions, became like a blister on a runner's heel, a settled pain which fortifies his spirit. The anxiety for all that lay ahead, the dread of a new country and of strangers, was gathered up into the darkness through which the ship drove as if blindfold. There was nothing there, in the black distance, to which she could look forward hopefully. She moved, with every minute passing, farther from Pierre. Yet if you saw distance only as time to be endured, time moving, time slowly drifting behind, then you could feel that happiness lay forward, like summer seen from the first October frosts. That way, the winter was a challenge to endurance. Curiously, she had become more sleepy, here with the rain blown against her face. In her drowsiness she felt herself grown harder, the tangled country she must cross became more steady in her quieter vision. In daylight consciousness she suffered as a stranger, foreign to the splinter of Europe in which she travelled but now as she stood small and high above the tumbled seas, her mental eyes upon the whole of Europe's vastness, she knew the pride of strangerhood. It was in that spirit you should travel, close in yourself, observant, keeping aloof, relying on the difference of your blood for your defence. Pierre would approve of that. If she could have him now to talk it over, in this quiet place, if they could talk together for a moment only, his long arm round her shoulders. . . . The pain came back, with the bitterness of squandered opportunity. She had it all to do herself, days must go by before she even had a letter from him. "Pierre, my own, my darling, I am all alone. Are you asleep, Pierre, do you dream of me?"

*

She realized presently how cold she was; her feet and hands were numbed. Perhaps, in her warm berth, she would sleep now. She went down to the promenade deck where there was shelter from the drizzle and the broken wind came more gently. There she would have lingered, reluctant to give up her solitude; but she heard, or thought she heard, faintly, a child's scream.

It was dark in the corridor, her coat as she hurried caught on the cabin doors. She heard the high, sharp scream again, and knew she had been right. Armand. She reached the door of her own cabin, fumbled, and unlocked it. Switched on the light.

He was standing trembling on the floor, his eyes terrified. He threw himself into her arms, he held to her, neither speaking nor crying, but shivering violently. She asked, "What is it, Armand, what is the matter, has something frightened you?" But he would not answer.

Sophie was still asleep, curled at one end of the sofa-berth which the children shared. Renée picked up Armand and took him into her own berth; where he lay squeezed close to her, still shivering despite the warmth she gave him. Only when she stretched to put out the light did he stir, catching her arm. "No, no, keep it on, please, keep it on."

They lay both awake, Armand grew quieter. Sophie turned over and woke up. She had a pain in her stomach, she said, and must have a glass of water. Renée got up to give it to her, while Armand lay still, his hand stretched out to hold her nightdress, which he would not let go.

"Tell me," she whispered, when Sophie was asleep again, "tell me, Armand, what was it that frightened you?"

"I wasn't frightened," he said at last. "But a man came in, a man with a grey beard. He bent over me, I had to shout to make him go away."

"But, Armand, precious——"

He began to cry now. She could not tell whether it was from shame or because the terror was still vivid in his memory. She shifted, so that his head lay on her shoulder. She had his weight against her arm, pressing it against the sideboard till she felt it numb and pricking. But she would not move him till she was sure he was asleep.

IV

THE stewardess could not be sure, no one really knew, but she thought—as she took away the coffee—that they would berth at about nine that evening. Renée thanked her. Through the port-hole she saw the clouds low and running fast. In the angle of wind and tide the ship moved awkwardly, rolling broken-backed. Proud of her amateur sea-legs, Sophie stood swaying on a valise before the cabinet basin and industriously washed.

Armand lay on his front, waiting his turn, his bare feet waving. He said, with lazy interest:

"Have you seen the red spots on Sophie's chest? Sophie's chest is all covered with red spots. Lots of them. Six, I can see, seven, yes, eight. Ever so many."

Renée, already dressed, was counting the money which she had emptied out on to a smooth patch on her berth. "Ninety, and two fives, fourteen, fourteen-twenty. . . . Hurry, Sophie, Armand's waiting for the basin . . . fourteen-twenty-five, fourteen-fifty." Armand's words, repeated again and again, came slowly to her understanding. "Be quiet, Armand, while I'm counting . . . what are you saying? Oh, rubbish! Sophie, turn round, let me see you."

She turned on the light to see better. It was true. Tiny spots, bright scarlet, a colony in the centre of Sophie's chest with out-liers climbing sparsely towards her throat.

She asked, unguardedly: "Sophie, do you feel all right?"

"Yes . . . but I've got a funny feeling in my legs."

"A pain?"

"A sort of pain."

"Is it," Armand inquired, "like a red-hot needle drawn along the veins?"

Sophie admitted that it was much like that. "It's a kind of ache all over," she added, "going right up to my seats."

Renée scraped the money together and put it back in her purse; she would have to count later, when she had got the children out of the way.

"Sophie, you're talking rubbish. . . . Get dressed quickly now, if the Captain comes in and finds you're not dressed he'll send you back to bed again."

"I should like to go to bed again."

"Quickly! Armand, you wash now, hurry. Behind the ears. . . ."

Sophie could lie down in the afternoon if she really felt bad. With Sophie you never knew. This morning it was out of the question, she could never manage the packing in these cramped quarters with the children on top of her. It occurred to her to take Sophie's temperature; but the thermometer was broken—Armand had trodden on it—and you couldn't borrow another woman's thermometer without exciting curiosity. Besides, it was better sometimes not to know. The spots might be anything: the change in climate, something in the bedding—you never knew who had had these cabins last. A policy of blindness was best for the time being; so long as the spots did not spread to show above Sophie's dress. "You must wear your brown dress to-day, Sophie, it's warmer." It was higher in the neck.

Armand asked, tying his shoes: "Do you think Sophie's got some dread disease, a plague of some kind?"

"No, Armand, she gets those spots from eating too fast. And you do too, only yours are on the inside. Here, take this duster and go and polish your shoes on deck. Sophie, prayers."

At lunch-time Sophie complained of a slight headache in her stomach. There was a new spot now, right under her chin; but no one, Renée thought, would notice it.

*

They berthed in the half-light. It was raining. The immigration officers came aboad and opened business in the smoke-room, where an untidy and impatient queue wound slowly between the little tables. The performance was half-way through when the crowd of welcomers were allowed to thrust their way between the excited porters and find their friends on board. All the trunks had been stacked in the first-class entrance, there was nowhere to sit down. Renée had no idea where her own luggage had got to. She stood holding tightly to one child with each hand, her bag beneath her arm, while she watched the inward flow of relatives, trying to see the equine face which should be that of Aunt Thérèse. She had neuralgia, and she was not sure if she had under-tipped the cabin stewardess.

"Will Aunt Thérèse smell like Madame Velaillie?"

"I don't know. Yes, I expect she will."

"Pardon, Madame, the trunk on which your little girl is sitting——"

"Get up, Sophie."

"Why, Maman?"

"Maman, do you think Aunt Thérèse will be interested to see Sophie's spots? We showed one of them to Madame Fleury, she was very much interested."

The faces passed, peering: little men with legal beards and pince-nez, stout and cheerful Jewesses in furs, pale children. Now a tall woman: Renée stopped her.

"Excuse me—Mlle Séverin?"

"I beg your pardon? No, no, Platel."

"Oh, I'm so sorry."

"Was that Aunt Thérèse, Maman?"

"No, another lady."

The last of the welcomers had squeezed through the doorway and now the whole mob of passengers and friends was going round and round, chattering and continuously embracing, as the sweating porters chivvied them. There was a lively trade on little cognacs and benedictines. The under-purser picked his way amid the throng, curving his back to avoid the steward's tray as it was thrust against him, ducking neatly between a couple who held each other by the arms. "Papers," he repeated, "have you shown your papers—you, Madame, have you attended the examination?" Renée edged her way towards the door of the smoke-room, pulling the children after her. It would be fatal to let them separate. Possibly Aunt Thérèse was waiting down on the quay, in any case it would be wise to get the inspection business over. "Come, Sophie, yes I know you are tired, you'll have a rest soon."

The queue had halted. A passenger from the second class, a Sinhalese by his appearance, was giving trouble. His papers were not in order, he had not the medical certificate required for coloured passengers. "I am a Catholic," the man repeated, "I was baptized by the Jesuit missionary with water which had been slightly warmed." "But it's impossible for you to land without a medical certificate. You cannot even board a French vessel without a medical certificate. Technically you are still at the port at which you started." "But the Father told me it was all right, he baptized me, he said, 'Now, Josa, you are a Catholic.'" The queue edged forward half a yard, those who had reached a seat flopped down like players at musical-chairs. "It is now twenty minutes that I have been in this room," a man grumbled, "and I have to catch the early train for Paris." "I want you to explain," the officer said patiently, "why it is that you have no medical certificate." It was getting hotter and more smoky, the arpeggio of conversation had fallen to a drone. "Do you think," Armand asked, "that the man will complain about the spots on Sophie's neck?" "Be quiet, Armand, children are not allowed to talk in the smoking-room."

At last she reached the table on which the officers had spread their little bags and papers. She had her nationality-certificate ready.

The senior officer, tugging his moustaches, asked:

"You are Madame Pierre Séverin?"

"Yes,"

"Wife of Captain Pierre Séverin?"

"And you are travelling with two children, names Armand and Sophie?"

"Yes. These two."

A man in uniform had made his way into the room, he was calling something. He was close to Renée before she heard, at first half-consciously, that he was asking in a vague and pessimistic voice, "Sévérin?"

"And your husband is not travelling?" the officer pursued.

"Excuse me!" She turned. "I am Madame Séverin."

"A telegram for you."

"Thank you. Armand, hold my bag, be careful, don't lose it. Sophie, stay still where you are. Excuse me!"

"It is quite all right, Madame, pray read your telegram."

Those in the front portion of the queue craned forward. The situation had possibilities.

Renée read: "Much regret unable to meet you Marseille owing to indisposition. Thérèse Séverin."

*

They stood near the exit from the customs-shed, pestered by cab drivers. Sophie repeated that her legs were aching, the pain from her stomach had gone down and down; also she was cold. Armand was stoical. He stood apart a little, his hands in his pockets, watching with a certain quiet pleasure the moving lights of the street and the lighted café on the other side through the curtain of drifting rain. There was no sign of the porter that

Renée had engaged and she had omitted to take his number. Sophie asked again and again: "Where is Aunt Thérèse? Why are we waiting here? Where are we going to now?"

The starkly lighted customs-house was swept by draughts which blew the litter of cigarettes and labels along the floor, raising the sawdust to the height of Sophie's nose. The voices of the porters sounded hollow, echoing in the building's vastness, the crowd swept by in eddies, pushing back the little group, jostling it forward, beating against it like waves upon a shifting rock. Renée's porter appeared at last, suddenly and smiling. He had a trunk upon one shoulder, on the other side three cases handle-strung. The rest, he said, were following—he had engaged a second porter. And everything was chalked, here were the keys again.

"A cab?" he asked.

"Yes, if you please."

The name she wanted had come back to her: Hôtel Ajaccio —that was where she and Maman had once spent the night before sailing; it was a modest place, and cheap, if Maman had chosen it.

"Have you got all the things in? The two trunks on top, yes, all right. Here you are." Fifty centimes: he was not much pleased. "Be quiet, Sophie!" The child had grazed her shin climbing in, she sat on the floor wailing. "Hôtel Ajaccio."

But the second porter was still waiting.

She said angrily: "I didn't engage you, I engaged one porter only, you must get your fellow to share."

"In the name of God, Madame, I have carried that trunk not less than three hundred metres, and it weighs as much as a pregnant hippopotamus."

The driver leaned down from his box.

"Where to?" he demanded.

"It's useless to go on," the porter told him, "Madame has no money to pay you with, she was robbed in the customs-house, she has not even fifty centimes."

"Then at least she must pay the minimum charge for engaging."

Renée yielded and gave the porter twenty-five.

"Ajaccio," she said again.

"I've never heard of it," the driver said.

"The driver says he's never heard of it."

In a flash of memory Renée said: "Rue Albert Premier."

"Albert Premier," the porter repeated.

The cab creaked along the rue de la République, the handles rattling, the rain beating on the windows. Sophie sat whimpering on the floor. "Where are we going now?" Armand asked. "To the hotel." "What for?" "Quiet, please, Armand, the driver will be angry if you keep talking, the noise will frighten his horse." "Do you know the horse's name?" "Quiet!" They turned into a darker street, bumping on cobbles; left again, and now uphill, steeply, so that the mare moved at a foot's pace with her shoulders in the collar. At the top of the ascent the cab stopped.

"Albert Premier!" the driver shouted down. "No hotel. Saint-Patrice," he suggested. "Same sort of place."

"All right."

They drove—it seemed—right through the city again. It was close to the Vieux Port that they stopped. A yellow light crossed the pavement from the door of the Saint-Patrice, a porter came out between the café tables with an umbrella and beneath it the children scuttled into the hotel. Expensive, Renée thought. The baroque lounge-vestibule was full of palms and little tables, it smelt of Sumatra cigars. Couples sipping from little glasses looked round as the draggled party came in, and glanced constantly towards it as they went on talking. A big woman in a black décolleté evening dress came in between the curtains, nodded briefly to the cab driver as she passed, and bowed to Madame.

"We are very full, yes, at this season everywhere in Marseille is crowded, but I think I can just fit you in."

"What are your terms?" Renée asked.

The patronne smiled.

"The lowest, nine-fifty."

"You mean—for the three of us?"

"Nine-fifty each. We have no special terms for children, we do not really cater for children."

"But I should have them in the same room with me."

The smile of the patronne widened.

"But you must understand—we charge by the person, not by the room. There are, I dare say, pensions in the sailors' quarter where they charge in that way. . . ."

The porter had already brought in most of the luggage and dumped it in a self-conscious looking pile on the carpet. The driver had gone back for the second trunk.

Renée said, "All right."

The patronne pushed forward the book.

"If Madame will sign. You are, of course, of French nationality?"

"Why, yes."

"But of course, Madame." She took down a key from the rack and called, "Pedro! Number twenty-seven. All that stuff."

The children had been standing patiently. Armand asked:

"Are we going to stay here?"

"Yes."

"Sophie says that she doesn't like this place. She says it's stuffy."

The patronne, who had included the children with the worn luggage in a comprehensive sweep of her yellow eyes, peered forward now to examine Sophie more closely. She beckoned with a middle-finger, smiling. "Here, petite!" Shyly pleased, Sophie looked up at her, turning her face to the light above the reception desk.

"Your little one," the patronne asked gently, "she is quite all right?"

"All right? But yes, only a little tired, it has been a tiring day for them."

"Poor little thing!" The patronne stopped to look at Sophie's face more closely. "Poor little girl!" she said again, smiling. Then, "One moment, Madame."

She crossed quickly and whispered to an elderly man who sat by himself in a corner with the *Paris-Soir*. The man rose and came back with her. He gazed at Sophie, took hold of her chin and turned her face to get the best light. He said something to the patronne.

"I am afraid, Madame," the patronne said softly and rapidly, "it will be necessary for the child to sleep in one of the wing rooms. The rate is a little higher, fourteen francs—there is the extra work in taking *petit déjeuner* so far. I am sorry . . ."

"But I don't understand you."

"M. Lebigre here is a doctor, qualified at Lyon. He considers that your child has some disease, which may be infectious. We have a distinguished clientèle, the best in Marseille, we cannot afford to take risks. The child must occupy a wing room, that is final."

Renée looked from the patronne to Sophie, whose cheeks were now speckled with the rash; to M. Lebigre, who stood apart a little, half-turned away, his hands in his coat pockets. She was aware that everyone was staring.

"I have no wish to question the ability of this gentleman," she said sharply, "but if he bases his rapid diagnosis on the rash which appears on my child's face, then I can assure you that it is of frequent occurrence since birth, and due to digestive trouble. Will you kindly have me taken to my room?"

The patronne had already laid a practised forefinger on the bell-push. A little man with a face the colour of asbestos, feebly moustached, appeared from the door behind as if controlled by a spring-catch. The patronne, her nerves responding to a sense of situation, forgot to control her voice.

"M. Manchon," she said, "I have told Madame that her child

here, whom M. Lebigre considers to be a likely case of smallpox, must sleep in one of the wing rooms. Madame, unfortunately——"

"On the contrary," M. Manchon replied; his voice was very quiet and judicial; "Madame's child will sleep in the children's hospital in the place du Cordier. Under the direction of myself and my late father this hotel has, for a period of almost fifty years, been recognized . . ."

The cab driver, still unpaid, was waiting near the street door. Renée called him:

"Will you help the porter, please, to put the luggage on the cab? I have decided that this hotel is quite unsuitable, it is not the kind of place I am accustomed to."

"I would recommend you," the patronne added, "to drive Madame to some pension in the sailors' quarter, that is more the kind of place to which Madame is accustomed."

One or two of the older women in the hotel were already retreating up the stairs. The bolder, now grouped in unblushing curiosity, were saying loudly to each other, "It is surely unheard-of for a woman to bring a child with smallpox into a respectable hotel." "This hotel was recommended to me as one of the highest class, it is astonishing . . ." "But no doubt the prefecture will take action, if called upon to do so, to prevent the invasion of public hotels by children with smallpox. . . ."

"Hurry, please!" Renée said.

The driver turned upon the patronne.

"And what of our arrangement, will you tell me that? Do you imagine that it's just my grand passion for your tremendous bosom which makes me bring people here off the boats, when I can get twice the fares by going to the other end of the town? Are you going to turn away all the custom I bring you like this? Will you allow me the pleasure of informing you that M. Houlbrecque of the Espagne was only yesterday offering . . ."

The sallow face of M. Manchon became astonishingly coloured.

"What is this drunken fellow doing in my hotel?" he demanded at large. "Pedro, here, will you please summon a constable immediately, tell him that a besotted lunatic . . ."

"Bastard son of the mother of all fools!" the patronne shouted at the driver. "Have you not the wits to see another fare waiting? It's a mile and a half to the fever-hospital——"

"But do I or do I not get my usual on this customer, that's what I'm asking?"

Someone asked: "How long is that child going to stand there spreading germs?"

"Will you," said M. Manchon, "be good enough to remove your child with smallpox from this establishment?"

"Will you," Renée answered, "instruct your man to take my luggage to the cab . . .? Come, Armand, Sophie! . . . and I must repeat, there is nothing whatever wrong with this child."

It was just too late. Sophie, at that instant, had vomited generously upon the carpet and upon the trousers of M. Manchon.

Armand fell asleep directly the driver lifted him into the cab; upright, with his head lolling over, his mouth wide open. Sophie was too scared to cry. She sat holding Renée's hand tightly, her face pallid, staring forward like one who for the first time had seen a mutilated body. Neither she nor Armand appeared to feel the shock when the second trunk was heaved on to the roof.

The driver put his head in at the window.

"Where now?"

Renée had not considered. She had been trying, with her minute handkerchief, to take the worst off Sophie's front, conscious of people staring from the door of the hotel. The money, that was in the back of her mind; Pierre's cheque to be cashed to-morrow. But she had the exchange coupons from the Agence Condé, they would cover the fares. Arriving swiftly at her resolution, she said:

"The station. The station for Dijon."

V

THE rain of the previous evening, blowing north and west, had avoided Baulon, which had lain three days in unhindered sunshine. And now, at dusk, the air in the streets was hot and still. It seemed as you went along the boulevard Maréchal Soult that everybody was there; there was not a table free at any of the cafés, where the men sat with their hats on their knees and their coats open. But the Parc Rousseau was carpeted with people lying beneath the trees, alone or twined in couples, stretched flat, knees humped, or stomach down with the face buried deep in the grass, arms forward, like bodies on a battlefield. There, only the old moved, slowly, along the walks. The few who hurried in the streets were from the shops, just closing. The trams swinging over the Pont des Grecs and along the river side were mostly empty.

The cab they got was an old one, but the springs were good enough; it was almost a pleasant motion after the solid bumping of the train. Coming out of the station yard into the avenue Saint-Roman, where the noises of the street covered the snorting of engines and the couplings clattering, where the smell of trains drifted away, they seemed to have discovered freedom after a whole day's servitude.

And yet, Renée thought, their freedom was illusory. They had been alone in the carriage from Lavalois, the three of them together in a place of their own. That would be over soon. And while, in the long journey, they had mixed with the ebb and flow of travellers, the people they saw now standing at the roadside or walking slowly along the pavement were at home where they were strangers. It was not quite dark: you saw, passing a side-street, the roofs and towers darkly shaped against a fading sky, the converging lines of street-lamps showing palely, discoursing pale lakes of light upon the path and roadway. The fœtid smell of a hot day, of the market-place and stable, was still in the heavy air. It would have been less melancholy to arrive when the town was busy, when you could be lost in the loom of traffic and no one strolling on the footpath would pause to stare curiously into a passing cab; or late at night, when the dark would hide you. At this hour the town was lifeless, crumpled, it had no welcome. She tried to think, "This is Pierre's town, every house that passes is familiar to him, if I shouted Pierre's name people would stop the cab and come to talk to me." But she could not see his tall, lean figure among the crowd at the street corner, she could feel nothing of his presence in the grey provinciality of the façade flowing by. The name of a street caught her eye, rue Jean-Rôdit, and she remembered him saying: "I took my mother to buy a hat once, in the rue Jean-Rôdit . . ." but the picture she had fancied then was so far different that the street she saw would take no place within that memory. They had turned now into a wide boulevard, with the tram tracks in the centre. The horse trotted faster on the downward slope. The houses that she saw between the trees were of the Second Empire, grandiose in aspect; it might be in this quarter that Pierre's people lived. At any rate it would not be much farther. To see Sophie in bed, lying between clean sheets, that was what she wanted most; to stop moving, to be in a quiet room. But the cab creaked on, across the river and up a steep incline, then left into a narrow street of high-porched houses. "Where are we going?" Armand asked. "Where are we going now?" And she answered absently: "I don't know, darling, I don't know."

They came into a wide square of high and sober narrow-windowed houses, its centre decorated with a single plane round which there were a dozen children playing. It was hard for Renée to move, with Sophie sprawling on her lap, but she managed through the small near window to catch the name as it passed: Place Talleyrand. She was conscious only of the simple thought "Then we are there"; but the sudden observation of the name seemed of itself to act upon her stomach, there was a bubble in her throat. Place Talleyrand; she had sworn once, holding a crumpled letter in her hand, that she would never go there. The square was poorly lit, she could not read the numbers on the houses, but the driver seemed to know. He went half-way round, letting his horse drop to a walk. And when he stopped, gently tightening his reins, she saw the faint 17 on the lintel.

The driver, opening the cab-door, smiled. The woman pinioned in her seat by the weight of the podgy child, the small boy sitting on the floor with his back against the valises, looking up with an air of serious inquiry, the torn bag of oranges nestling at the boy's feet, it was enough to make an alderman grin. But Madame was serious. She said in a squeezed voice:

"Will you please ring the bell?"

She did not want to move. She had got into a comfortable position, Sophie was sound asleep, she wanted to stay there in the cab, until Pierre came to take her away. But she roused herself and told Armand to get out. Armand slipped down and stood with his legs straddled on the pavement. He asked sleepily, "Why have we stopped here?" Carrying Sophie gingerly—it was difficult with only one hand free to keep her skirts down—she got down beside him and they stood in a line of two facing the door. The driver, tugging the bell-rope hard, had raised a strident clatter in the basement, but for a time no one came. Renée looked up at the four lines of windows. In the third line there were two lighted.

There were creaking footsteps at last. The door opened far enough for a thin, untidy old woman to look out. She said.:

"Yes?"

For a moment Renée had no words, then:

"I am Madame Pierre Séverin."

"You are Master Pierre's wife?"

"Yes."

The old woman opened the door wide and stood aside.

"They didn't tell me," she said, "that you were coming to-day. I haven't got anything ready."

The entrance hall was lit by gas-lamps. Only one, at the foot of the stairs, was burning now. It was a large hall, uncarpeted except in the centre. There was a sofa on one side, against which an invalid chair was standing; on the other a massive sideboard of figured oak; a chair or two, no other furniture. The air in here was much cooler than in the street; Armand had already begun to shiver. And the smell was the cold, earthy smell of a cellar, flavoured with the scents of old wood and old upholstery, of sandalwood and leather.

Renée went to the sofa and put down Sophie, who woke and began to cry. Armand, clutching Renée's hand, whispered: "I don't like it, let's go. Let's go quickly."

Somewhere above a door opened, and a woman's voice called anxiously:

"Joséphine! Joséphine, who's there?"

VI

THE voice surprised Sophie into silence, and she sat quite still drawing jerky breaths. Armand got up and stood holding his mother's hand. In the silence they heard Madame Eugène Séverin cross the upper landing, come slowly down the stairs, across the next landing, which creaked loudly beneath her feet, down the next flight. It seemed a long time before they saw the skirt of her satin dress. When she reached the turn of the stairs she stood, holding her dress, and peered down into the hall. She said in her slow, tired voice:

"You must light the other gas, Joséphine. Who is it here?"

Ignoring the question, as she had done before, Joséphine turned and went off down the kitchen passage. She said, at the top of the basement stairs:

"I haven't any matches. I must get Barbier's."

Renée let go Armand's hand and went forward to the foot of the stairs. She said: "I'm afraid you were not expecting us." Her voice came watery when she started, but it settled to its normal shape. "I should have sent a telegram, but it was difficult, with the children. . . . I am Pierre's wife. You are Pierre's mother?"

Madame Eugène said, "Yes—Madame Séverin. Yes, I am Pierre's mother." Very upright, with one hand on the banister, the other holding her skirt, she came to the foot of the stairs. "I'm afraid—no, we were not expecting you. We thought you would stay at Marseille, at the Hôtel de Noailles. Pierre told you, surely, that that is our hotel at Marseille? I meant to write to you there. You received Thérèse's telegram?—she was unable to meet you, she had rheumatism very severely."

Renée said: "Yes. Yes, I received the telegram. It was brought on to the ship."

Madame Eugéne put her hands on Renée's shoulders and kissed her cheek. "Such a long time," she said. "Is it seven years? It has been difficult—my husband . . ." She caught sight of Armand then. "And this is little Armand? He is shy, yes?" She pulled him forward by the arm, quite gently, nearer to the light. "Yes, he is certainly, a Séverin. And the little girl—ah, there she is. It is Sophie, is it not? Come here, Sophie."

Renée laid a hand on her arm.

"It would be better, perhaps, to keep away. I'm afraid she has caught something on the boat. I don't know what it is. . . ."

Joséphine had come back.

"Barbier's lost his matches," Joséphine said; "there aren't any in the kitchen."

Madame Eugène sighed. "Can't you find some matches somewhere? No, wait, I want you to get the beds ready. For Madame Pierre in Mademoiselle's old room, for the children in the next one. Ah, no, there are some of M. Raymond's things in the wardrobe there. The one at the end of the passage. You must put something across the window, it doesn't quite fasten." She turned to Renée. "We were not expecting you, or we should have had the rooms ready. The children must be tired, travelling always tires children, I remember how fretful Pierre used to be. The little girl is ill, you say? But surely it is nothing infectious, you would not have let her travel with anything infectious?"

The driver was still at the door, waiting to be paid. "Five francs," he said. Renée opened her bag and felt for her money. She found three-fifty, with a couple of sous.

"I'm afraid, Madame Séverin, I shall have to ask if you can lend me two francs—I was unable to cash Pierre's cheque before leaving Marseille."

Madame Eugène was surprised. To travel from Congerisque, to have no money to pay a cab, it was curious the way people managed.

"I'm afraid—my purse, I don't know where I left it." She called huskily: "Joséphine! Joséphine, go very quietly into the master's room and see if I left my purse there."

From the top of the stairs Joséphine called back: "It is bound to be in the drawing-room, in the usual place. . . . I shall have to use the sheets which M. Raymond had, there aren't any others."

Madame Eugène turned to Armand:

"Armand, will you be a good boy, run down to the kitchen, it's at the end of the passage there, and ask Sergeant Barbier if he will lend me two francs. . . . And now, we had better go to the drawing-room until your beds are ready. But the children must be very quiet. You will understand, my husband is in bed at the present time, he has to be kept very quiet. It would disturb him if he knew there were children in the house."

Sophie had slipped down from the sofa, and stood bemused. "Come, Sophie!" But she would not move, Renée had to pick her up. Looking at the child's eyes, Renée saw reflected her own bewilderment. She felt as if abruptly woken in the early morning hours, she could not collect her thoughts and senses. There was something important that she ought to say at once to Madame

Eugène, who was starting to go upstairs. It came at last, just as Madame Eugène was turning on to the second half-flight.

"Madame Séverin, one minute. I should have told you—I should like to have the children in with me, they will be frightened else in a strange house. And I ought to be with Sophie. . . ."

Madame Eugène stopped and turned.

"Quietly, please. I must beg you to be very quiet, my husband is so easily disturbed. Come, we will talk that over in the drawing-room."

There was something else; the man still waiting to be paid. And at that moment Armand, who had made his way reluctantly as far as the end of the passage, burst into tears. Madame Eugène did not seem to hear him. She had continued upward and reached the landing, where Renée saw the gaslight glinting faintly on her rustling skirt.

★

It was a long time before the room was ready. They sat on the sofa, Renée with one child on either side, Sophie lying back against the prow, Armand upright and staring. Madame Eugène, seated on her little nursing-chair beneath the gas-lamp, talking listlessly as, with the regular, supple action of a 'cellist, she drew the silver thread through her embroidery. It had been very hot in Baulon, she said, it was difficult to keep the milk from going sour. Renée, no doubt, would not feel the heat, being accustomed to Africa. It must be very hot out there, she imagined, though Pierre never told her in his letters. He was a bad writer, he never gave her any news. Renée answered her briefly; her mind was like dry sand, Madame Eugène's sentences made only a shapeless impression upon it. And in the long pauses the Weishardt clock on the medal cabinet clicked the seconds passing with a sound like a coachman's tongue.

Joséphine came at last. The rooms were ready, she said: she had to borrow two blankets from Mademoiselle's room, and one from M. Louis's.

"But I told you, Joséphine, that Madame Pierre wants the children with her. I told you to make two beds ready in the end room."

"The rooms are ready," Joséphine repeated, and went away.

It was Sergeant Barbier, in the end, who rearranged the beds; and he who looked after Sophie while Renée dealt with Armand. Armand was scared, he would hardly allow Renée to move out of his arm's reach. But Sophie, limp and wretched, did not care who handled her. The old man put her over his shoulder and limped to the bedroom, laid her on the big bed, and went to fetch a basin of water. With a piece of flannel from his wife's rag box he sponged her limbs separately as he undressed her, making little soothing noises; and then, having covered her with a blanket, went off to find a nightshirt. It was one which his boy Gaston had had as a little chap, he told Renée when he produced it; it would do for to-night, and would save hunting for Sophie's own. When he had put Sophie into bed he went off again and returned with two apples. The boy would eat his now, he thought, the little girl might like hers in the morning. She was sick, poor little thing, it was a long journey for one so small. One moment—he would fetch some drinking water.

Renée ate most of the second apple herself. Madame Eugène had asked in a whisper, pausing outside the door: "Renée! I forgot to ask you, you had some food on the journey, you were not expecting dinner?" "Oh, yes, we had some food at Lavalois." "Good night!" "Good night, Madame Séverin!" But she herself had had nothing. She was almost too tired to eat now, but fearing faintness she cut the apple with a penknife and ate three-quarters of it. Sophie had fallen restlessly asleep. Armand, in the other large bed, lay wide awake, although she had lowered the gas. He asked for water, but would only take a little sip when she brought it to him. "You are going to stay here?" he asked. "You're not going to another room?" "No, darling, I shall be sleeping here with you." She thought, trying to sort some sense out of her mind's dull confusion, that she would sleep in Armand's bed, for safety and to give him courage. But when she had turned over Sophie's pillow, and rearranged her sheets, and tucked in the blanket at the foot of Armand's bed, she gave way to sudden weakness and lay down for a moment on the upholstered chest which did for wardrobe. There, still fully dressed, she fell into profound sleep.

★

Madame Eugéne, when she left the door of Renée's room, would have gone to bed herself. But Eugéne was often awake till fairly late, and it was wise to let him get to sleep before she retired, for else he would gradually be roused, however quiet her movements, and begin to talk: the endless, whispered, halting talk about the chance of a re-trial this year. So she went back to the drawing-room, changed into the bedroom-slippers that she kept hidden there, too worn for exhibition, and took up her work again. The long, curved orchid leaf, demanding tiny stitches, was nearly covered already; she would just finish this one. And now that she was alone the work gave her more pleasure. As she watched, without the disturbance of conversation, the petal's outline filled precisely by the advancing tide of silver, her thoughts moved easily, she could adjust herself to the awkward turn in her affairs.

She had, of course, been amply warned of what she had to face; a month ago she had allotted rooms for her grandchildren and their mother, had briefly spoken to Thérèse about the money side, but the smaller details of the problem, how to manage the inclusion of a new small family in a routine so well established, these she had half-consciously refused to contemplate, as tumours easier not to lance. Now the trouble could no longer be shelved, it had forced itself upon her unawares. To-morrow morning she would have to deal not with two tired babies, but (she supposed) two boisterous children, and a mother who had shown already unexpected firmness. Still, that was to-morrow. How curious, she thought, that that should be Pierre's wife, so different from what she had expected, with a certain elegance in the smallness of her features, the figure almost of a jeune fille. It was impossible to connect her with Pierre, only that the boy was like his father. Undoubtedly a Séverin: and she could not be sure that she was glad. . . . With a stitch so small that few artists would have troubled to put it in, she finished the petal, ran through and finished off. That would do for to-night. She folded the table-centre carefully and put it away in the bag which Marianne had made for her at school, hung the bag on its hook again. Then, feeling that she had earned her rest, she fetched from the bookcase the *Mémoires* of the Comte de Baillieu.

The page was marked with a tramway ticket, before she had read half a paragraph her mind had fallen into the very shape in which last Sunday's reading had left it. There was a small excitement to goad her on, for the next chapter was that in which her mother was mentioned, "*cette jolie demoiselle du Bellion que j'ai rencontrée chez Monsieur Sauvetache de l'Académie.*" But Madame Eugène read carefully, relishing the savour of a world far closer than the dour provinciality of Baulon: the polished salon of Madame d'Isabeau, the picnic on horseback at St. Germain, the elegant supper which the Comte gave for Elsetti after the opera, the questionable affair (treated with such good taste and yet with humour) of the shoes belonging to Mme Rauquelin. There was still, as she read, an undercurrent of anxiety. The girl's skin, was certainly very dark, deeper you would say than that of a Provençale, enough to make Eugène very curious if not immediately disapproving. And what had she said about the little girl, in a quick, rather offhand way? "It may be a touch of smallpox, I don't know." But how dreadful: and could you have just a touch of a thing like that? She should have sought Thérèse's advice, perhaps it would have been better to have the child taken to a hospital straight away. As it was, there might be night-nurses and fumigation and all the rest of it, the whole house would be in turmoil, Eugène would keep asking what it was all about and would not be satisfied until he knew. Still, nothing could be done till to-morrow, and then perhaps Thérèse would have some good idea, though it would be nicer to manage without her. She drifted back, so easily, to the card-room in the Château d'Espaillon, furnished in the Italian style, where the Comte was talking of a Ruisdael he had lately bought to the Duc de Sèvres and to Madame La Hauchecorne: "If you are not satisfied (I said) with the way I hang it at Espaillon then I will have another château specially built." But the clock of Ste Gudule had already struck the half-hour. She turned over, finished the paragraph, and marked the place with her thumbnail.

She yawned a little, placing three fingers on her upper lip as she had been taught to do in childhood; lit a candle from the gas mantle, turned down the gas, and left the room, pushing up the handle as she closed the door to prevent the squeak that would come half-way. Treading softly, as if she could so diminish the creaking of the boards, she went along the passage and downstairs.

She tried the hall door and found it bolted top and bottom: a relief, to have someone so reliable as Barbier, it was worth while suffering Joséphine for his sake. She went to the end of the kitchen passage and listened at the top of the stairs. Silence, the servants were in bed. Now upstairs again, to the very top, where Madame Nadya's room was. There was no need to go to the door; from the end of the passage whe could hear Madame Nadya's snore, the gurgle of a choked water-tap, sharply broken off, alternating with a strangled whine. To Thérèse's room next on the floor below, where she whispered at the door, "Are you asleep, Thérèse?" and got no answer. And now, a new variant, to the room of Renée and her children. Listening, and hearing nothing, she opened the door a little way and peered across the candle-flame at the darkness within. She could hear, now, Sophie's uneasy breathing. The child was very restless. She whispered: "Renée, are you all right, is there anything you want?" From Renée there was no answer, and Madame Eugène could not see where she was. But from the farther bed Armand's voice came in a terrified whisper: "What's that? Who's there?" Startled and perplexed, Madame Eugène drew back and closed the door.

There was one more call to be made: Marianne. And she reached the door of Marianne's room before she remembered that Marianne was away at St. Gervais. She retraced her steps, and having taken off her slippers for greater caution went slowly down one flight and along to Eugène's dressing-room.

Here the little bed was made up for her, since Eugène when he was ill had to be alone and preferred the larger room, where the sun came generously in the morning and where some of his battle

37

plans were hung across the plaster moulding of the walls. The communicating door was slightly open. Madame Eugène softly closed it, drew up the doormat to prevent any light passing underneath, and then lit the gas.

The candle, still alight, she placed on the dressing-table; and when she had undone the many hooks, taken off her dress, and replaced it with her old silver toilet-gown, she sat before the mirror to see her face. The miniature by Daleuse which showed her in the year of her betrothal was shut away now in one of the drawers; Eugène would notice its absence when he got better and have it out again, but for the time being it need not trouble her. And now, as she worked her long fingers on her forehead, pressing first out, then upwards, pushing the folds away towards the margin of her hair, she could at least be satisfied that her skin was still clear, as white as a Norwegian's; it was quite remarkable, they had always said; and the hair, hardly thinner than when it had been a rich, dark brown. She worked now on her chin, squeezing it between thumb and forefinger, then running the backs of her two first fingers down the throat. She used no kind of cream: that was rather disgusting, for it was made from animal fat, they said; and besides, it would spoil the pleasure that she got from the softness of her skin's texture. It remained a delight to run the palm of her hand downwards from cheek-bone to jaw, just to feel how smooth, how supple her cheek was. It was to the Pichys that her face belonged, *ce vrai visage de Pichy*, old M. de Tordelle had said when he recognized and stopped her in the rue Cambon: a heritage worth all the jade, the little Dresden vases, the Louis XI écritoire. But the eyes, too tired, too grey. She had an impulse to bring out the Daleuse, to see if they had really become deeper-pitted; but that temptation she resisted. The light was bad, it hardened all the shadows, falling too much aslant. And she knew that Daleuse had done the lips too full a rose, it was a fault of his to be admired, no one could mix so exquisite a tint and he would use no other. To-day, he would have painted them that very colour, and "What a likeness!" everyone would have said. Perhaps, in a softer light, the lips would still show redder; at least they had kept their shape, unless the lower drooped a little. She put her fingertips on the lower lip and rubbed it firmly, upwards. But the skin was rough a little there, unwelcome to her touch. She stared again, steadfastly. It was curious, you looked every morning and evening, you could not notice any change. But this evening it had startled her to hear the little boy (how old was he? perhaps ten years she thought) address her in his shy and rather pretty way as "grand'-mère;" and now, as if a fresh light had been thrown upon her face, she saw the reflection with her grandson's eyes. The differences, the lines that would not yield to her manipulation, the poverty of blood, the lack of firmness behind the cherished skin, that was what he had seen. She frowned, and the lines showed deeper. She got up hastily and started to undress.

The pain in her chest had been worrying to-day, aggravated by the little cough which would not loosen. It was perhaps the hot weather, the streets had become so dusty. Putting on the peignoir again she knelt at the prie-dieu, reverently kissed the crucifix, opened her little manual and began to read. Doctor Tischer would perhaps be able to recommend something when he called to-morrow; the mixture the chemist had given her did not seem to do any good. But there was always the risk that the doctor would say something to Eugène, and Eugène would be worried. His anxiety about her always took the form of a certain irritability: "but surely, Madeleine, it can't be anything much, you've always been a strong girl. You mustn't believe everything old Tischer says, he likes to imagine everyone's ill . . . you must look after yourself, of course. It's very worrying, I've always thought of you as a strong woman." No, it would be better to wait till Eugène was well again; if possible till the trial was over. Before Christmas, M. Lecours thought it might be, if the necessary witnesses could be found; he was simply going slow, he said, in order to have the case impregnable before going into action: "We must be sure of our strength, of our reserves. You, M. Séverin, as a soldier, will understand what I mean." In the meantime she would ask Verdier the pharmacist if he could give her something better. He would understand, perhaps, if she explained, the tight feeling in her chest which sometimes seemed to interfere with her breathing. Verdier was always very sympathetic, and his manners were those of the old school of tradesmen. . . . Her devotion concluded, she closed the manual and rose to her feet.

There remained her last duty before retiring. She turned down the light, opened the door into the next room very carefully, an inch at a time, and listened. She thought that Eugène was asleep. She tiptoed to the bed, stepping over the board that always squeaked, felt with her practised hands, straightened the clothes. He was asleep on his side, facing away from her, and he did not stir when she lifted the blanket a little way to bring it farther over his shoulder. Suddenly fearful, because he kept so still, she bent to catch his breathing; and then he spoke, very quietly, but distinctly as if he were awake. "I insist, gentlemen, that you envisage the position as the sketch-plan shows it to you. There, you see where the hill was. Thickly wooded. It was impossible, from where I was at four o'clock, to see General Guéroult's signal. . . . But you must understand, there was a mist that day, there was no

39

visibility. . . ." She waited, quite still, until his voice fell away into husky incoherency, into a gentle snore. Then, having touched his forehead with her lips, she crept back into the next room and very slowly closed the door.

VII

REACHING the centre of the square, Dr. Tischer paused to watch the children playing; and he grinned when one of them called out "Look, there's the old doctor man!" Poor children: everywhere in this quarter the poor children knew him, and there were hardly any others. He called to one of them rolling on the pavement, " 'Allo! Suzette! How's your mother's leg this morning?" "I don't know, Monsieur, you must go to the gaolkeeper and ask him." "Indeed? Then you must give her my kind regards at the end of the week." On the north side he saw that they were starting to break up the tallest of the houses; he could hear the blows of the pick and the débris falling, already you could see clear sky through one of the window-frames. Well, that was a good thing; the whole square, the whole of this quarter, would be better smashed to pieces; but the factory would certainly be ugly, it seemed a pity that the old façade could not be preserved, and people were fond of the places they lived in. M. Séverin wouldn't like it. "A voir, Suzette! Give your mother my kind regards and say I'm sorry she's been indisposed, I'll bandage her leg when she's better."

He was admitted by the boy Gaston. "Good morning, Gaston, how are your parents?" The boy looked at him sharply, screwed his eyes, and tittered; said something unintelligible and flumped away. Tischer shivered. It was extraordinary, how nervous this dark hall always made him; neither the tenements in the rue Eporcine nor the petite-maison at Pellier so quickly enwrapped him. He would have liked to set the door open wide to let in the light and smell of the square. But he put his gloves and silk hat down on the sofa, tightened his face into what he thought the shape of a fashionable practitioner's, plucked the lapels of his frock-coat, started to go upstairs. At the first stage Madame Eugène met him.

He wished her good morning. "It keeps very warm," he said, "warmer than one would expect, I think, at the time of year." She was three inches taller than he, and already he had become conscious, as he was in this house and no other, that his head was too large for his body, his beard too small for his head, his coat, with a shaft of sunlight playing on it from the œil-de-bœuf, insufficiently brushed. He went on, in his mortuary whisper: "I came on foot again to-day, the exercise does me so much good; indeed, I have temporarily lent my carriage to a colleague, whose own is out of order. And our patient, how is he to-day?"

They went up together to M. Séverin's room; where, at the door, she left him.

In a quarter of an hour he rejoined her in the drawing-room, where she sat near the window and he was obliged, taking an upright chair, to face the light.

"Well, Doctor?"

He did not answer at once. Nowhere else was he so cautious, so professional. He gave a twist to his beard, cleared his throat, manœuvred his lips by degrees into the shape required for his opening syllable.

"I think we may say that there is a little improvement to-day. The colour is better. The temperature is normal, as it has been for some time." He paused, seeking for something fresh, something to make his report a little different from what it had been the day before. "There is no loss of strength, of that I can assure you. Indeed, it might be safe to say that some strength has been recovered. I suggested to M. Séverin that he might try getting up for an hour or so this afternoon and sitting in a chair. But naturally, he does not want to take risks, he is nursing his strength, that is understood."

Madame Eugène nodded. On this ground they trod with practised delicacy, no allusion to the affair in both their minds must be too definite.

"I have a feeling," he continued, "that a new interest for our patient, if such could be found, would be very helpful. You will understand, I think, that a mind which has been exerted as his has been in the struggle for health demands some refreshment. If something could be found to occupy his attention, to——"

She cut him short.

"It will be all right when once the date is fixed for the business-affair—I think I mentioned it to you—at Paris. He will find new strength, no matter what his condition, when that is settled. Until then, I'm afraid no other interests are possible."

She spoke with such conviction, with so unusual an air of matured understanding, that he wondered for a moment if in reality she understood the case as well as he did; if the trouble he took in preparing his reports, in serving his half-lies with a sauce of decorous circumlocution, had been needless; if there had always been two play-actors in these interviews instead of only one. But she said immediately, with the helpless gesture he knew so much better:

"He suffers so much. There is always a pain in his side, he says. It is very sad for me."

That signalled the end of the interview.

"Does Madame Nadya want to see me to-day?" he asked.

"No, she will see no one to-day, not even Gaston. She is moving the furniture again, I think, I keep hearing noises."

Tischer smiled. It was permitted him, nowadays, to be a little amused upon this topic.

"The old lady is fond of change in her immediate surroundings."

"When she makes the changes herself. . . . But my sister-in-law will be waiting for you."

He found Mlle Thérèse still in bed. When the rheumatism was bad she stayed in bed till he had made his visit and given her massage; afterwards she would dress and hobble downstairs. Sitting up in bed, Mlle Thérèse had round her shoulders a Persian shawl, caught at the throat with a short length of silver chain From its folds her long arms protruded, the brown hands, strong and large made, set off oddly by the cloud of lace upon the sleeves of her nightgown, into which the high, cobalt veins ran like rivers into a boiling sea. She wore no cap; her brown hair was already dressed and fixed with a silver comb behind, the curls in front swept up and over from the leftward parting like a boy's. You could see now, from the height of her shoulders above the mattress, how tall a woman she must be. She put down her book as he came in and, answering his greeting in her deep voice, pointed to a chair; her hand stretched open, as if purposely to catch the light on the stones of her heavy rings.

He said: "I'm afraid I interrupt your reading."

"It doesn't matter," she replied, "I know it off by heart."

He craned forward to see what the book was. It was *Peer Gynt*, a cheap edition over-bound with Russian leather. From where he sat he could see that one of the parts was underlined in red, the cues in violet.

"And the rheumatism?" he asked.

"A little better. Yesterday I walked as far as the bookshop in the rue Henri-Martin. That was quite a triumph, wasn't it?"

The word "triumph," pronounced with a false grandiloquence, a touch of sarcasm, pricked his imagination. The hush across the dark balcony, the sudden, single claps like the first shots in desert battle, the rising clamour, the curtain plunging like a waterfall. He said:

"You mustn't attempt too much; not yet. It must have given you pain, walking so far."

"I don't mind pain," she said decisively; and presently, when he had begun the massage: "No, it's being a spectacle. Hobbling along, stooping suddenly when it gives you a twist, all the children are quite fascinated, they would cheerfully pay a couple of sous to see it. But, of course, no one knows me here. They say, 'That old crock is the sister of the M. Séverin that one sees sometimes, the handsome old man who owns Number Seventeen. He is an invalid, and is said to be a literary man.'. . . You've seen my brother this morning?"

Working steadily, with a constant, semicircular motion of his thumb-ball, he said, "Yes. Yes, I have made my visit. The condition is perhaps improved a little. You know, there isn't much I can do. Sometimes I feel a quack, I don't like sending in my bill when I do so little."

"But is your bill ever paid?"

Tischer was a little shocked.

"I understand that M. Séverin has had a difficult time this year. Certain investments, I believe——"

She shook her open hand as if waving away a cloud of smoke.

"You should give up coming," she said shortly. "That's the only thing to do. It's quite possible—I don't mean to be impolite —that my brother's health would improve with a little less attention."

He began: "My own view——" and stopped. After all, one had a duty to one's patients, the rôle of a doctor had in some way the obligations of a confessor's. "I was saying to Madame Séverin," he continued, "that if some new interest could be found for her husband, it might prove very helpful."

"And what did my sister-in-law say to that?"

"She feels that nothing can be done until the affair at Paris is settled, at least until the date is fixed. But I understand that we may hope for some developments shortly, before the end of this year."

"Do you believe that?"

"I only know what Madame Séverin tells me."

"And Madame Séverin only knows what M. Lecours tells her. And whereas my sister-in-law is only a fool, M. Lecours is an accomplished liar. He knows perfectly well that he has no intention of proceeding this year. He practically told me so when I pressed him."

He was disconcerted by her frankness. It was easier to play the gentle game of reticence with Mme Séverin, even to deal with Mme Nadya upstairs, than to converse with Mlle Thérèse, who studied no subtleties.

"We can only hope," he said, "that M. Lecours will make more rapid progress than you suppose."

Thérèse nodded, pursing her lips.

"Yes," she said, "it is like falling down the side of a steep hill. Always one hopes that a strong wind will come to drive one up to the top again. . . . You've heard, I suppose, that you have another patient waiting?"

"No?"

"Pierre's child. You remember my nephew Pierre? His wife is here with her children."

"Already? Mme Séverin told me they were coming, but I didn't think——"

"I was to have met them at Marseille. I had to telegraph to say I couldn't go—it was my intention to send Raymond. I thought, of course, that she would put up at Marseille, at the hotel we always use, till someone came. But instead of that she takes the first train and arrives without warning, with an armful of children, and one of them with smallpox. It makes life easier, when people behave like that."

"With smallpox, did you say?"

"I understand so. But I haven't seen them yet. Only Madeleine has seen them. She said nothing to me when they arrived, but put them all together in the same room; in the same bed, perhaps, I'm not sure. This morning she suddenly remembered. 'Oh, Thérèse, Pierre's wife is here, with a number of children, and one of them has smallpox.' Like that. 'It will mean getting two more loaves,' she said."

"But how extraordinary, to travel with a sick child! Did the mother not realize——?"

"According to my sister-in-law, she realized perfectly. I shall be interested to meet that young woman; you never know what a Séverin will marry. The important thing, of course, is to get the child away from here. Eugène would be worried out of his life if he knew there was infection in the house. You'll promise me, won't you, to insist on that? We have quite enough to worry us already, we can't do with any more illness."

He stopped rubbing, quite startled by her earnestness.

"I must deal with the case as I think best," he said; adding, "in the interests of the house and of the child itself."

She said no more, but he was glad when he could get away from her. There was something here which he did not understand. She was, after all, a Séverin, though it seldom showed in her expression; her mouth was her mother's, the lips big and sensual, they would never tighten into wrinkled pods in the Séverin way; but sometimes, when a casual sentence had arrested her, she would turn her eyes upon him and then, it seemed, draw back, to regard him from a distance; dispassionately, as a sportsman watches the boar wriggle to stillness. He remembered, at those times, the

44

remark of Madame Nadya: "My children have always been devoted to each other: they are so much alike." . . . "You will put the compress on again to-night," he said. "It will do more good than anything else. . . ."

She stopped him, just as he was leaving.

"To-morrow I want you be bring your bill—for attendance on me. That is to be separate, you understand? And wait, will you open that drawer over there, the one beneath the cupboard. It's too stiff for me. There's an engraving there by Jean-Baptiste Michelot, that's it, wrapped in newspaper. Yes, Michelot gave it to me. I want you, if you will, to take it to Leguillon in the rue Saint-Vincent, and just ask what he would give for it. Tell him it belongs to me. No, tell him that Michelot gave it to you yourself, when you had attended him after a street accident. You will do that for me?"

He hesitated.

"But in any case," he said, "I would advise you not to part with it. The value will amost certainly go up, taste is the other way at the present time."

"Leguillon will gamble accordingly," she answered. "He can afford to. And there are too many things in this house that one ought not to part with."

He shrugged his shoulders, said good-bye a little awkwardly, and left her.

Going downstairs he took out his watch. Half the morning gone! It was vexing, the amount of time this house took from him, this house where he had no ministry; though it was pleasant, he confessed, to converse with Mlle Thérèse—it still gave him, in some way, a sense of contact with the Paris he had loved as a student, with the larger world he had imagined in his boyhood on the slopes of the Rigi. He stopped on the landing. Madame Eugène was nowhere to be seen, but leftward, in the half-darkness at the end of the passage, he caught sight of Joséphine's black, tight-strapped figure, bent over a scrubbing brush. He called: "Where are Madame Pierre and her children?" and without looking up she answered, jerking her head, "Along there!" To his right the passage was lighter, a door on the street side being open. And he saw, then, a slim boy standing there, stock still, an arrow of sunlight on his curly hair; as if an angel had appeared, he thought. He said, advancing, "Hullo, Pierre!" and then, as he remembered, "No, of course not, I was thinking of another little boy. What's your name?—I don't think anyone has told me."

The boy, on his guard, whispered, "Armand!"

"And it's your sister who's got something wrong with her?"

"Yes, Monsieur."

45

"And what's her name?"

"Sophie."

The door on the right opened and a woman said: "Armand, come here."

Tischer moved forward and bowed. The woman he saw was in a brown overall; her hair had not been done properly, it was pinned in an untidy ball with wisps straying; a small dark creature—Eurasian, his first guess was; perhaps the children's nurse.

"I've come to see Sophie," he said. "Is Madame Pierre in there?"

"I am Madame Pierre."

Tischer bowed again.

"Then your husband is an old friend of mine, I cured him of measles and the whooping-cough in the same year. Doctor Tischer. He may perhaps have spoken of me?"

But he could see, from her expression as she answered, "Why, of course," that Pierre had never done so.

He observed, in a sweeping glance as he went to the bedside, the room's disorder. The second bed not made, trunks open, clothes everywhere. The window was open, but the room still smelt of the night's breathing; and the atmosphere, in this room that he knew so well, was altogether changed, as if it had ceased to belong to the Séverin household. The restraint which the house put upon him was immediately relaxed; he felt as he did among working people. He took hold of Sophie's pillow and moved it so that it should bear evenly the weight of head, neck and shoulders; only a trifling movement; and said over his shoulder, "I'd like the pillow a little higher. Armand, can you get me a book or something?—a glove-box would do." The little girl was drowsy with fever and would hardly look at him. He took her hand and held it, stroking the knuckles with his big thumb. He said: "Poor Sophie!"

His eyes were on Renée, who sat on the other bed. Dead-beat, she looked, the eyes forlorn and tired and a little frightened. But she answered his smile. "A long journey for the little ones," he said, and she nodded. His voice was pitched so quietly that it would not have woken the lightest sleeper. Presently he turned and placed the back of his hand against Sophie's cheek, and began to talk to her—How did she like being in France? Was it not grand to have a Papa who was a soldier?—expecting no answer, until he got a smile from her. Then, still talking, holding her eyes with his, he undid her front, felt with his hand, glanced at the rash on her chest. "Where did you get all these funny spots, Sophie?" She smiled again, coyly. "Next time I come," he said, "I shall bring a great big scrubbing-brush and see if I can scrub them off."

46

Armand, when he had brought a box to put underneath the pillow, drew back into a corner near the window. From the tail of his eye Tischer saw him there, watching; and when he had finished the examination, and washed his hands in the basin, he went and sat near the boy on one of the trunks.

"She looks funny, Sophie, with those spots, don't you think so?"

Armand answered gravely, "Yes, Monsieur."

"Men like you and me, we don't get that sort of thing, not as a rule."

"We ought not to waste your time, Doctor," Renée said.

"Just a minute———"

It was the shape of Armand's forehead which interested him: the two separate bulges, like a pair of breasts, the flatness at the sides resembling the shape of the hats that had just come into fashion. The shaping was not firm yet, the bones must grow before they set into the final cast; but they were there in low relief, the contours that he recognised. The chin had still its childish roundness, but it was small, as he expected, and deep below the lip, which curved out sharply. The boy was looking at him steadfastly, his eyes had become more friendly. But Tischer, as he watched him, had misgivings. "Perhaps I am wrong," he vaguely thought, "the child is in a strange house, it is natural that he should be a little scared."

"You have something here," he said to Renée, "which is far better than a photograph of your husband."

She followed him outside the room, when he had said good-bye to the children, and in the passage he gave his report.

"Whoever in the world talked about smallpox?" he demanded. "It was certainly no doctor, unless perhaps he was a Bordelais. Hare-pox: you could see it from the roof of Notre Dame. No, no, it's nothing to worry about, the temperature will be high for a day or two; you must try and prevent her from scratching. Yes, broth, if she will take it, nothing heavy. You ought, really, to keep the boy away from her. He is the more delicate, it would affect him more severely."

"But if they are kept apart, I cannot be with both. And Armand is nervous in this house, he hasn't settled down yet. If I am to nurse Sophie———"

"I was wondering," he said, "if it would not be better to move Sophie into the hospital of Ste Eunice. It would not be difficult to manage, and the Sisters there are very kind to children."

"No, that is not to be thought of. I understand your making the suggestion———"

"I was thinking chiefly of yourself," he said gently. "As you say, the nursing presents a problem. And naturally there is some

47

nervousness in the household about infection, there are other invalids here——"

"The suggestion came, then, from Madame Séverin?"

Taken off his guard, he answered, "No, from Mlle Thérèse."

Renée nodded.

"I understand. Well, if they do not want Pierre's children here, then I shall find a pension somewhere, for them and for me, as soon as Sophie is better."

Tischer took hold of the end of his nose and stared dejectedly at his watch-chain.

"I'm sorry, Mme Séverin, I didn't mean—I'm sure that Mlle Thérèse was thinking first of your own comfort, of the little girl's welfare. She is really very kind, she has always been kind to me. . . ."

"It doesn't matter," Renée said. "But it's settled; Sophie is not to leave this house unless we all do. I shall make that clear myself when I see Mme Séverin. If they want to avoid infection they must turn all of us out. My husband would agree with that."

With that opening presented to him, Tischer talked for a little of Pierre. But he was shy now, he felt as he always did in this house. He said, as soon as he could, "I will be in again to-morrow, I shall hope to find Sophie better . . . such delightful children . . ." and bowed himself away.

Renée stood in the passage until she heard him go out at the front door; regretting now, that she had not been more friendly. She wanted to find Madame Eugène to arrange about the broth, but did not know where to look for her, and no one was about. The bang of the hall door had left the house in silence, broken only by the spasmodic noise of a workman's pick from the other side of the square. She called "Madame Séverin!" but there was no answer and she dared not call more loudly. She took a few steps down the passage, stopped, and went back to the children.

VIII

UNTIL Sophie grew better, Armand was left much to himself; and would have been content, for he was never bored with loneliness, but for the circumscription of his movements. He had as play-room the one opposite that in which he slept. It was furnished with basket-chairs and an old gate-table, a bedstead pushed into one corner, a sewing machine with the treadle rusted immobile, a shelf of Pourpillon's *Jurisprudence*, a chest of empty drawers. In a single morning he had explored its greatest possibilities; taken out the bedroom things which Joséphine had stacked in the wall-cupboard and crammed them in again; worked the shutters every way and broken the catch. He began to venture afield; first to the extremes of his own passage, and by degrees, with growing temerity, on to other floors.

It was a house of many doors and they were nearly always shut, so that the corridors were dark, and quiet like a ruin. The noises of the square, where children played from morning until after dark, were shuttered by the intervening rooms, the staunch walls, the closely fitting doors; and curiously, the noise which interrupted most the silence of the corridors was the farther sound of work-men's picks on the other side of the square; insistent, boring gradually into your awareness like the click of a woodpecker's beak in a quiet wood; becoming with the sered, stagnant smell which pervaded all the house, the feel of emptiness, an essential part of Armand's new existence. But there were other sounds which broke the stillness sharply. Occasionally, twice perhaps in an afternoon, a door would open on the highest floor, where Armand had not yet ventured, and a voice like that of an old man broken-winded would scream, "Gaston! Gaston!" In time, then, there would be slithering footsteps on the lower stairs, and Armand, crouching in the passage as near the stairhead as he dared, would catch a glimpse of a lanky youth in ragged coat and loose, floppy trousers, who sniffed and tittered as he made his way slowly, slouching from banister to wall, up the four flights of stairs. Then there would be the rumble of heavy furniture being pushed across the floor, and presently Gaston would come down again. Once, when the door on that story opened, someone came out and there were footsteps overhead. Armand stood a moment where he was, panting, and when the voice came—"*Gaston!*"—nearer and louder than he had ever heard it before, he scuttled back to the playroom. After that he made his expeditions in stockinged feet, so that he could retreat more noiselessly. The passages were hard to hide in, and at any time a door might open, someone might catch him. He kept his ears alert as a hind's, he came to know by the creak of any door which one it was, learnt to distinguish footsteps. When a bell sounded in the kitchen he could tell, by the scratch of the wire along the walls or by the note of the bell itself, where it had been rung.

He was chiefly afraid of meeting Grand'mère. Running, one morning, to get away from the stairs when he heard someone coming, he collided with Grand'mère's skirts. She stood, rather startled, and staring down at him asked: "Where were you going, Armand? What do you want?" He had no answer, and she said, looking over his head. "You must try to keep quiet, you ought

49

not to be in this passage. Your grandfather"—she pointed to the door from which she had come out—"is in there, he's very ill, it will make him worse if you make a noise." So that was where Grandpère was, and he was very ill. Maman had told him already that Grandpère was ill, but not in that voice, the voice which Marie-Noire had used when she said that Corporal Trouër was going to die. He said, "Non, non," and crept away. And afterwards he was always afraid of meeting Grand'mère, lest she should ask again, looking away over his head, what he was doing. But he could not altogether avoid that corridor, and when Grand'mère went out, as she did occasionally, he would go down to that floor and creep, a step at a time, as far towards the room where Grandpère was as he dared, listening intently. In that way he suffered his worst experience: when, as he stood one evening nearer to the door than he had ever been before, the handle turned and it opened a few inches. He stood paralysed, the muscles of his neck stiff, his stomach suddenly cold. A great retriever bitch, her fat body sagging between her short, rheumatic legs, came out. With her nose down, and as if she did not see him, she lumbered past him, her tail brushing his ankles. The door closed as if by itself. He heard the flop of her pads as the dog went clumsily down to the kitchen. He ran then, crying, to the room where Sophie was; and would take no food that evening.

The step he welcomed most, when he heard it on the stone stairs which came up from the kitchen, was that of Barbier. It was easy to distinguish by the limp in it; and by its weight, for Joséphine wore thin pantoufles, with the heel trodden down, and Gaston more often than not went in his heelless stockings. Aunt Thérèse, whom he met sometimes, walked with a limp too; but hers was different, and you heard beside it the thump of her rubber-ferruled stick. The sound of Barbier's footstep seemed to make the house safe; and Armand, when he heard it, would run downstairs boldly, even if his shoes were on. Barbier's greeting was always the same; the sudden halt, the jerk back of his chin, the flick of his thumbnails across his ferocious moustaches, the severe "Where do you come from? You'll be in trouble before long," his eyes screwing at the outer corners. Then he would bend and grasp Armand by the shoulder and leaning over smack him heartily across the rump. They had little conversation; it was too awkward a medium for their friendship. But so long as Barbier was above stairs Armand would be with him, and occasionally an apple came suddenly out of Barbier's trouser pocket and passed into Armand's. With Barbier, Armand went into new rooms, rooms that were always locked and where the blinds were always down. There Barbier would strenuously rub the mahogany chairs, whistling with his teeth like an ostler, while Armand watched him. They were richly content with each other's company. Only if Joséphine's steps were heard, the loose heels of her pantoufles scraping along the boards, would Barbier nod meaningly and Armand slide away. Armand had learnt the lesson from the first time that Joséphine had found them together. Looking across him at her husband, she had said: "You have nothing to do all day then, Barbier, but to play with Madame Pierre's children? You think, no doubt, that Gaston and I will do your work between us? He is so useful, Gaston."

Except at such a time Joséphine would hardly speak at all, even to answer his "Good morning." She seemed to be nearly always on her knees, performing a fakir's pilgrimage that never ended along the corridors, scouring with such vigour that he thought the boards would soon be worn away. For so much labour there seemed to be small reward; the floors, as soon as they were dry again, looked just the same; it was performed with an ascetic devotion, the woman's hard eyes fixed steadily upon her work, tirelessly. She was a creature without graces, her chest as flat as a youth's, the shoulder-bones stuck in her thin dress like the stretcher in a hammock. You could see, through the thin grey hair, the outline of her brown skull. Armand would follow her as she progressed, a few feet behind, treading on the wet boards so softly that she could only have sensed his presence. He did not attempt to trespass on her silence, fearing that she might send him away; he was not a little frightened of her. But she, when she saw him, allowed her glance to pass across his body as if it were a piece of furniture. He was awed by her fixity of purpose, which was purified of self-regard and crowned by no apparent satisfaction. He fancied, and the fable grew larger in his ruminations, that she had committed some dreadful sin which she must expiate by hours and years of scrubbing. Sometimes, as he watched the tireless wheel of her thin bare arm, she became in his regard an animal and then a mere machine; so that he was startled when she raised her head and sniffed, or stopped for a moment to scratch the scab upon her ankle. He felt a certain curiosity, whether she objected to his constant presence. But nothing in her expression ever told him; features so set, cut in so hard a metal, crusted in years, could not be governed by the impulse of her secret, deeply coursing mind.

★

When the bell rang from the front door Armand ran down to the last fold in the stairs and watched between the banisters to see who it was. But the front-door visitors were few and regular; he knew by the time of day as well as by the kind of ring which one had come. In the morning it would be Dr. Tischer, and the bell would hardly tinkle with the doctor's gentle pull upon the cord. Almost every afternoon it rang lustily, a shock to the quiet household, by the hand of the Abbé Vignaud, who gave a friendly nod to Gaston opening the door and walked right past him, gathered his skirts and mounted boldly to knock at the salon door, which Madame Eugène immediately opened to admit him. It was safe for Armand to creep near the door—the Abbé's visit lasted never less than twenty minutes, often forty—and he could hear the Abbé's low, amusing voice, with its long vowels and its hissing, spitting consonants, punctuated by Grand'mère's soft laughter. He wondered then what her face was like when she laughed, for he had never seen her laughing; but it was easy to picture the face of the Abbé, whose internal blowing like the noise of cisterns followed and smothered each ripple of Grand'mère's. In Vignaud's oval face, with its immense, square forehead descending to a grey spade-chin, the lower lip was caught as if by thread and needle, tightening the beard-skin into the pattern of clerical severity: yet you could see, perhaps by the brown skin-folds at the corners of his sad eyes, that the lip was a valve, nicely adjusted, to restrain the hot spring of mirthfulness which boiled and bubbled in the Abbé's chest. Armand had not yet spoken to Grand'mère's director; but it was a pleasant part of the day's routine to stand back in a dark corner and see the Abbé swish past, trailing an odour of clothes-shop and rappee; and sometimes Vignaud, catching sight of the child, would aim his straight nose at him, wag his crossed fingers, and say: "Hullo, you, little sheep-snout, peace be with you." It was a nice blessing, Armand considered.

On a Thursday afternoon there was a new visitor, of greater importance. Grand'mère was in Grandpère's bedroom most of the morning; the children's déjeuner was served early; Armand noticed when he passed the open door that there were flowers in the drawing-room, where Joséphine had been dusting and polishing while Barbier did the stairs. At three o'clock there was a carriage at the door, and Barbier in a black jacket went to answer the bell. Armand, commanded to keep to his playroom, had managed nevertheless to slip down to the first floor and take his usual post of observation. And from there presently, when Barbier with many "Sirs" had taken the visitor's hat and gloves, he saw the visitor come up the stairs. There was time enough to watch him, for he mounted very slowly, bringing both feet on to one step before essaying the next, pausing at each as if to examine upon some register the amount of energy he had expended, to calculate his reserves and measure them against the distance still to cover. Yet it was not an old man; Armand could see, at least, that there were no grey patches in the brown hair; a short man, corpulent, with feet so small, in pointed shiny boots, that it seemed a miracle of balance he should stand at all. His face, which he wiped with a little handkerchief as he progressed, was clean-shaven, but had not the semblance of having ever felt a razor; it appeared rather to have been soaked for so long in tepid water that the hairs had floated off, leaving only those above the eyes, hairs which lay sparsely flat, as if adhering by a smear of spirit-gum instead of roots. His tiny eyes were half-covered by the lids, so fleshy that they seemed too great a weight for the muscles to sustain; but the pupils were far from sleepy, they turned, never with idle curiosity, but seriously observing and appraising; not sharply as an auctioneer's, but with a shrewd complacence.

Barbier led the way, limping half a dozen steps ahead; and there was, in their advance, a solemnity which suggested rehearsal. Full of excitement, Armand watched them go along the passage, strained his ears to hear something that would tell him who the visitor was. It might, he thought, be the President of the Republic, perhaps a count or a foreign prince: but presently he heard Barbier announce gruffly, in the voice he had always used for calling roll, "M. Lecours!" The visitor went in, the door closed upon a fountain of little compliments. Armand waited until Barbier had gone downstairs and then edged forward to within a metre of the door. Aunt Thérèse was in there as well as Grand'mère; and Aunt Thérèse was doing all the talking, in her firm, husky contralto. He heard the words "The trial," and again "The trial . . . the trial," and at intervals the low voice of M. Lecours, saying as if he chose the word each time, with meticulous care, from an immense vocabulary: "Yes . . . yes . . . ah, yes . . . I think—yes. . . ." Impelled by a glowing curiosity, Armand moved nearer still. But now M. Lecours had taken up the monologue, joining long, recondite words with a spray of little ones impossible to understand. He was taken by surprise when a hand fell upon the door-knob inside and the door slowly opened. Moving like a squirrel, he fled down the corridor and turned the corner just in time.

As the party came into the passage their voices fell to silence, as if they were entering a church. They moved along the passage, away from him, treading softly. Armand heard a knock and another door opening; he knew it by the squeak, Grandpère's room. Then Grand'mère's voice, almost a whisper: "It's M. Lecours, dear. Do you feel up to seeing him?" Evidently the answer "yes" was given, for the party moved on; he peered out and caught sight of Aunt Thérèse's cherry dress disappearing into the room. The door squeaked and closed. Armand stayed quite still, he was afraid on so gigantic an occasion to go near that room. But he stood and stared up the passage, as a crowd gazes long after the procession has passed, and stretched his ears to catch if possible a word or two of what was said. It was about himself, he somehow thought. Perhaps they suspected that he was not really Armand, that he was a Prussian spy, who had masqueraded as Captain Séverin's son in order to gain access to the house and steal the papers which Grand-père, no doubt, kept locked in his room. If so, what proof had he, when the trial came on? If the witnesses against him could not be refuted, if Maman herself, shaken by the weight of evidence, disowned him, what would he say? Not "I die for France," that was illogical. "I die without dishonour," that was the only phrase. And now, as he waited, he could fancy Grandpère, immensely aged like Elijah, pushing himself by the pillows into a sitting posture, stretching out his hand. "I tell you, it cannot be my grandson." "I die without dishonour," Armand repeated and jumped as he felt Barbier's hand on his shoulder.

"What is it, Barbier? What are they talking about? What does that man want?"

"It's time you went upstairs, Master Armand, you've no right to be loitering on this floor, you know that."

"But tell me, Barbier, what has that man come to talk about?"

"It's about things you'd better not know."

He began to fear that Barbier was against him after all. He went upstairs slowly, wondering if his wits were a match for Aunt Thérèse and M. Lecours in combination.

IX

As soon as Lecours had gone, Madame Eugène went back to her husband's bedside; and supporting him with one arm round his shoulders, took off the old tunic which he used as bed-jacket and slipped away the pillows which had been propped behind his back. She rang for Barbier, who presently brought warm water; and having damped a sponge in it, she bathed Eugène's forehead, squeezed the sponge again and passed it gently over his closed eyes, wiping away the moisture with the silk scarf which she kept in her dressing-table. She asked, bunching the pillow under his head, "Is that all right? Are you comfy?" and then, expecting no reply, tiptoed away.

Thérèse was waiting for her in the drawing-room as she had feared. Thérèse came seldom to that room, preferring to sit by the oil stove in her own apartment; when she came it was on business. She stood now by the window, watching the corner of the Square where Lecours's carriage had disappeared; and, turning as her sister-in-law came in, she said abruptly:

"That man's no use. We shall have to get someone else."

Madame Eugène peered round the room, looking for her work, which in the excitement of Lecours's entrance she had dropped in some unusual place. She said hurriedly, "Won't you sit down, Thérèse, do sit down." She must have the work to occupy her eyes, for Thérèse had always had the advantage of greater assurance when their eyes met. There it was, actually behind the coal-box. She sat on the low nursing-chair and began to sort her threads, one shoulder turned towards the window, where Thérèse had begun to hobble back and forth. (Her nephew Raymond would make her furious by his comment in ironic undertone, "Crosses to prompt side, picks up handkerchief, returns centre, bows.") Thérèse, Madame Eugène knew, would not sit down. In this room she was rarely seated.

"I think you will realize, Madeleine," Thérèse said, "after that visit, that Lecours will never get us anywhere. Obviously he has not the slightest intention of doing anything, except continue to draw fees for his visits here, for our calls on him, for the letters he writes, for wiping his greasy face with a pocket-handkerchief. In the whole of our conversation this afternoon, he never left off being vague. If we——"

"But I don't see what more he can do, before he succeeds in finding this Captain Lenormand. You can hardly be more anxious than I am——"

"What more? He can do more than nothing, surely. Why, my dear Madeleine, it's obvious what a sensible lawyer would do: he would spend a little money wisely, he would consult his Paris connections, he would press for the case to come up as soon as possible. It's always possible to get a case pushed up the list, if you only know the ropes: a good dinner with pretty partners, the suggestion of some shooting, a case of brandy to a secretary or two. The trouble is that Lecours doesn't know the Paris courts, he doesn't know the bar, he hardly knows anyone in Paris at all. He's just a fourth-rate provincial mortgage-monger, with a very wise face and a certain low cunning which gets him a reputation out of paternity cases. It's as plain as a pikestaff. I myself would advise——"

"But, Thérèse, wait, I don't think you've quite understood M. Lecours's point of view. He doesn't think it's wise to hurry on the case, that's how I understood him, I'm sure that's what he said. Without Captain Lenormand there's no new evidence, and you can't——"

"My dear Madeleine, you don't understand legal procedure.

You must forgive me, but remember that I spent hours and days in the courts when Adrienne Mignot's case was on. This thing has to be fought on procedure. This Lenormand is probably dead long since, and we have only Eugène's word that his evidence would really be valuable. . . . Yes, yes, I don't doubt that Eugène's right—at least he's always held to that point—but we're no nearer finding Lenormand than we were five years ago—twenty years ago. This talk of Lecours's about an uncle in Quebec is pure fairy-tale. No, in a case of this sort, you have only to argue that the previous process was all wrong; that political influence was at work (as in some degree it probably was), that the judge was biased, that the defence was not given time to subpœna the proper witnesses. That is the kind of argument which pleases the legal mind, it puts the court in a favourable humour. Then you have only to find a few old gentlemen whose memories are vague, and who will remember much better when counsel has done a little prompting; after all, there were a thousand men or more in a radius of four kilometres when General Guéroult gave his signal, and at this length of time no one can remember very clearly where exactly any one of them was. . . ."

Madeleine worked furiously, her eyes intent, as she had done in former years when little Pierre and Raymond were quarrelling and she had no mind to adjudicate. Having waited for the moment when Thérèse failed for breath, she said, as if slipping sideways into someone else's conversation:

"There is Major Pichereau still living at Bayonne . . . you remember, that Pichereau, the effect his evidence had. Or perhaps you don't feel that sort of thing as I do—a wife has perhaps a better memory for these things. I can see him as clearly as I see you, that Pichereau facing the judge with half one of his green eyes on Eugène. I remember how the judge looked."

"But Pichereau must be in his dotage. He was older than Eugène—of course, I remember . . . I may be without emotions, Madeleine, they are not necessary in my profession, my old profession, only brains are necessary—but you will grant me at least an eye for a scene. Of course I remember Pichereau, with that little smile of his, the way he emphasized himself by tapping his finger on the box. But he must have mellowed now, you forget old quarrels when you're going on to seventy, why, I myself am almost ready . . . but in any case, how unlikely that they would fetch the old man to Paris. They would read his former deposition, it would be quite ineffective in the mincing voice of a barrister, I know just how it would sound, like the epitaphs on very old tombs. What you don't realize, Madeleine, is the way they regard things, down there. They won't give much time to boring business, they've got to get on with things. 'Here is an old gentleman,' they say, 'who is concerned about the loss of his honour, his soldier's honour, an old-fashioned idea. All this business took place a very long time ago, everyone has forgotten about it except the old gentleman himself, and nobody cares. Well, if we can make the old fellow happy by reversing the former judgment, let us do so at once, and postpone the question of public indemnity, and get on as quickly as possible to the very interesting and rather delicious case of Mlle Rosie Delapourpillon of the Auberge des Folies, who is still trying to force the Comte de Noury to pay for her night-attire.' At any rate the attempt is worth making, it's better than doing nothing, paying Lecours to do nothing. One becomes a little impatient, as years go past."

Madeleine, without looking up, saw that Thérèse was standing close by, very tall, looking down at her, waiting for her to say something. There was something she wanted to say, but her throat had become floury. She went on working, hoping that Thérèse would find a new subject or else go away. But Thérèse stood like a brutally patient teacher, both hands on the top of her crutch-stick, waiting. And presently Madeleine's voice came back, words started to trickle like water from an open tap when the main supply is turned on.

"One becomes impatient, yes. It is not only you who become impatient. To me, of course, it means nothing that Eugène has no health, that we have to live in this dismal Baulon instead of Paris. But perhaps if you were to see Eugène in the early morning when he wakes, to hear him at night, see him several hours each day, often lying quite still, his eyes closed, so that he may be awake or asleep . . . but I understand it, the view you describe so well: an old gentleman who is troubed about his military honour, an old-fashioned idea . . . it is, of course, just an affair for the smart lawyers in Paris, to make arrangements, to tell the judge what to say. One pays them enough money and they return to my husband his honour, done up in a smart envelope with the seal of the Republic. That will make Eugène and me so happy, don't you think, when everyone is saying 'Congratulations, Colonel Séverin, it says in the newspapers that you have repurchased your military honour' . . . One requires a little patience, yes, but one requires also a reward for patience."

Thérèse turned her back and went to stare at a coloured aquatint on the other wall; an emblem, she had always thought, of Madeleine's peculiar taste, by which all works before the second republic were sanctified to uniform æsthetic distinction. Poor Madeleine, poor little Mademoiselle Pichy who had shown her one spark of audacity by taking the name of Séverin! Thérèse scraped her under-lip with her sharp, jagged teeth. One would almost pity Madeleine, in that resentful mood of hers, if it were not for the childishness, the whine in her little stifled voice, the suggestion of paraded martyrdom. What, after all, had Madeleine had to sacrifice, apart from her old cronies in Paris, the bewhiskered, lace-capped, bath-chaired denizens of the quartier St. Germain, compared with her own sacrifice? And now she was crying, not aloud, but with moist, oozing eyes.

"I don't think it's any use our arguing about that aspect," Thérèse said shortly. "Our views perhaps differ a little, there are questions of sentiment—it is useless to argue about such things. . . . But we were talking of Lecours, and I was saying that Lecours is doing nothing for us, he is only pretending to be hunting out witnesses. What has he ever done except file applications in Paris and allow the wheels to go round at their own pace? There is no need to talk of what kind of trial we want, it's a question simply of finding a new solicitor. That's what we have to think about."

"But Eugène—I've told you before—he wouldn't hear of it. The Lecours partners have always handled his affairs, he has great faith in Marcel Lecours's shrewdness. Of course, if you care to mention the matter to Eugène—I'm sure I could arrange for him to see you on a good day, not now of course, the interview this afternoon has left him exhausted—if you like to speak to him——"

"It should be taken out of his hands," Thérèse said quickly, "it's ridiculous that Eugène should be pretending to conduct this matter at all. It would be better if he granted you a power of attorney—yes, you must be the one, of course—and then we could get things going. Eugène can't hope, as an invalid, to control his own affairs; obviously he's in no fit position—lying in bed all day—to deal with a man like Lecours."

"But he reads all the letters, all the important ones. He tells me what to reply, he signs the replies himself. His eyes are all right, not as good as they were, but they're all right."

"Yes, his eyes are all right."

"And please, Thérèse, what do you mean by that?"

Thérèse paused. She had been, she felt, a little unguarded; she had caught Madeleine in quite the wrong mood.

"It would be difficult," she said, "for anyone who is not a Séverin to understand."

A curious odour had come into the room. They realized, both at the same time, that the door was open and that Madame Nadya stood there. Madame Nadya said, taking the cigarette from the corner of her mouth, blowing out the smoke and smiling at them superciliously:

"She means, Mlle Pichy, that my son is as daft as a hatter. She is perfectly right."

<h1 style="text-align:center">X</h1>

THERE was still no proper letter from Pierre. A note had come, written on the back of an equipment requisition form, to say that he had lost one of his razors, the one with the very narrow blade— had Renée by any chance packed it with her things? Nothing more. Renée wrote to him, shortly after her arrival at the place Talleyrand, asking with some firmness for information.

"Your mother received me kindly," she wrote, "but so far there has been no opportunity for establishing friendship, your father seems to require a great deal of nursing and I myself have been busy. But I am anxious to know more about your family, for without that I cannot possibly enter their circle—I am sure, Pierre, you will realize that when you think it over. You know that I don't want to pry into anyone's private affairs out of curiosity, and that I am not accusing you of holding things back from me intentionally. We have always been enough for each other, and our families did not matter. But now it is necessary that I should know more, and you must agree that I have a right to this. To make it quite plain, there is a lack of cordiality which may mean that they do not approve of me, but in which I see chiefly an anxiety to keep me out of their secrets. I repeat that I have no wish to pry into their secrets, but I have a right as your wife, as an adopted Séverin if you like, to know just what my position is.

"Oh, Pierre my darling. . . ."

But weeks must pass before she had any reply. In September there were cool winds, neither the stove (for which Joséphine sullenly brought fuel) nor extra clothes would keep her warm, and her malaise increased. In the warmer days her courage had been constant, she had felt a pride in her self-sufficiency. Now it seemed that her spirit was made cooler by her blood's coldness, she shivered constantly, and could not be sure if she was sickening for an illness or if her state was mental, due to loneliness and apprehension. Sophie was well again, only a little pettish in her new surroundings. Armand had colds, one upon the other, he was listless and secretive, reluctant to take his food. The trouble, Renée thought, was that they were too much cramped in the two rooms allotted them, the one where they all slept, the other where they had their meals and where the children played while she did her sewing. In the passage it was draughty, and Madame Eugène did not like the children playing in the passage; she said a dozen times, during the morning visits when she came to ask about the children's meals, "Oh, and Renée, I would rather, if you don't mind, that the children didn't play in the passages. I saw Armand yesterday on the first floor. You see, the noise carries up and down the stairs, it will disturb M. Séverin if he hears it. They can romp as much as they like in their own room, but I would rather they didn't play in the passages. You see what I mean, not in the passages." On sunny days Renée took the children to the Parc Rousseau, where the leaves had already begun to fall, and where the industrious superintendent made continual assault upon the children who would climb upon the public seats. There Armand and Sophie would gaze about them in mild wonder, like urban children in a meadow, and Sophie would sit down in the long grass while Armand wandered by himself, deeply occupied by his own reflections, stumbling constantly against the border of the path and colliding with the push-chairs, answering the screams of nurse-maids with an absent-minded "Pardon!" And presently Sophie would be tired, the walk was such a long one, and they would wander home again, the children dragging behind. Armand, of course, should be at school; but Renée was afraid to send him, there was the risk of his being run over on the way, of his catching things; and besides, he was not yet sufficiently acclimatized; he must feel the new ground firmly beneath his feet before he was exposed to rough contacts. It was not easy to give Armand lessons while Sophie banged a drumstick on the table and Armand's eyes wandered every moment to the window, where he could see the builders working. But until Pierre came back to settle things it was Renée's duty in this foreign land—for so she felt it—to keep his children to herself, never to let them pass the bounds of her protection.

It was in the evening that she felt most lonely, that the hollow-ness of the house oppressed her. The square was quiet at night, no one moved in the house except old Madame Nadya, who could sometimes he heard hammering upon the wooden panels of her room. Occasionally a chair scraped above, as Aunt Thérèse moved to attend to her lamp; downstairs a door would open and Madame Eugène's shoes would squeak as she slipped across the passage to her husband's room. There was no other noise, except a rattle in the wainscots, sometimes a fall of plaster. Renée could sit in the salon if she wished. "If your room is cold at night, Renée, you can of course come down to the drawing-room—or if you want company." But it was too far from the children, and there could be no conversation while Marianne, who taught in the Primaire at Grierçon, sat pale and spectacled at her desk in the corner, running her red pencil in a ribbon of ticks and crosses through a hillock of exercise books. She would rather have sat on the floor above with Aunt Thérèse, who treated her with a chilly politeness, but who had at least taken passing notice of Armand. "He is like his father, the little boy, he is quite good-looking, you must have bred him carefully. I hope he will have more concentration than his father; his father has too much brain for the army, but no concentration. That is the Russian strain, you don't find it in the earlier Séverins; I myself am quite unconscious of it." It was hard that they spoke so little of Pierre—almost as if he were a black sheep of the family. She had hoped there would be early portraits, childish drawings, stories of Pierre's sayings when he was small; so that she could say "This is Pierre's home, I belong here because this is where Pierre belongs." But Madame Eugène would only say, stopping in her talk of bread and milk to glance at Armand, "Yes, Pierre used to be like that, his thoughts were always wandering, he never paid attention to what I told him. Of course my husband—but you were saying that the bread we have is not suitable for children? It is what we always had, for Pierre and Marianne, yes, for Raymond too, but of course if you want it changed. . . ."

Raymond, indeed, had spoken of Pierre, but only casually. Going down towards the kitchen to beg some matches she had met on the stairs a man in the thirties whose mouth was rather like Pierre's, but who was shorter and wider in build, and dark as a raven: in drab, office clothes, with a drooping tie. He had stood aside to let her pass and bowed stiffly, his eyes, she thought, a trifle impertinent, with Pierre's sarcastic little smile. He had gone straight on to the top of the stairs, and then, turning round, had called down to her: "Excuse me, I've just thought of it, you must be my brother's wife? I am Raymond, he may have mentioned me, though I don't know." He had said, leaning against the banisters and surveying her curiously, "My job is the very devil, but at least I escaped the army. Pierre got let in for it, and father let me escape. Pierre, of course, he's a dear fellow, but so terribly absent-minded. I think that's how father got him in; he got the papers all ready and Pierre in one of his day-dreams thought it was some young woman's autograph album, and put his signature before he recovered consciousness." "But my husband takes a pride in his profession," she said a little warmly. "He looks very nice in the uniform," he answered, "he was always a pretty fellow. Cécile— my wife—would like me to wear a uniform; but can you imagine me in it? Fortunately there is no uniform for daily scribblers. . . ."

She had a photograph of Pierre, but it was hardly like him,

done at Congerisque, the print imperfectly fixed, so that it was already fading and she had to keep it in a drawer with her stockings. There was an old pocket-book of his, a torn handkerchief which she had brought away in her mending basket, a shirt which had worn out at the collar and which he had given her for use as cleaning rags. These things she had together in a valise—the locks in her chest of drawers did not work properly—and caressed in her times of greatest loneliness, though they increased the pain of it. Late at night, as she sat sewing, she would close her eyes and try to see Djedoule, the long street of the bazaar, the lighted bungalow as it appeared from the road. But here the air was fresh and moist, there was always a soiled and dusty smell, the smell of crumbling stone and damp plaster, always the distant noise of traffic and of voices in the streets, of boots striking hard paving instead of a carpeting dust. The clock of Ste Gudule chimed the hour, she opened her eyes and saw lighted windows, a sprinkle of lights through the scaffold-poles on the other side of the square. She went downstairs, hoping to meet Marianne, to coax her into talking of Pierre. But there were no lights showing beneath the doors, everyone had gone to bed. Only, at a corner of the stairs, she was startled by Gaston, who came suddenly into the light of her candle and giggled and ran away. She was frightened all at once lest something should have happened to the children, lest she should feel her way to Armand's bed and find it empty. But Armand was there, and to-night he slept peacefully. She took off her shoes and lay on the bed beside him. She asked him in a whisper, "Armand, you remember your father, you haven't forgotten him, have you, surely not?" But he was fast asleep, he only pressed his forehead against her chin and turned over. She had asked him in the daytime, "You're not forgetting father, surely you haven't forgotten him?" He had answered her, "Oh, no, of course," and turned to something else, a basket he was making out of card and string. And Renée doubted if Armand remembered; no one in this house remembered Pierre.

★

A letter came at last. Madame Eugène brought it up herself, when she came for the daily discussion of food, and money matters. "A letter for you Renée—from Pierre." Renée said "Thank you," and put it in the pocket of her overall. "He has been a long time in writing," Madame Eugène said reflectively, "I hope you will find good news of him." "Oh, yes, I expect I will."

When the conversation was done Madame Eugène turned to be agreeable to Sophie, who was in her most placid mood, dumpy and smiling. Renée busied herself with the breakfast bowls, which she always washed herself in a tin bath by the window, until

Madame Eugène, disappointed, went away. Presently she returned. She had forgotten, she had meant to ask, did Renée think the children were getting enough vegetable? There was plenty in the soup of course, but——

"Oh, yes, thank you, quite enough. Their motions are perfect."

Hearing a hand on the door, she had crumpled the letter and envelope back into her pocket.

"I shall be going into the town myself this morning," Madame Eugène said, "is there anything that I can get you?"

"That is very kind, but no, thank you."

"You have good news of Pierre?"

"I haven't opened his letter yet, but I expect he is quite well. He is very strong, Pierre, the climate seems to make no difference to him, although he is pure European."

The letter was not very long. When Madame Eugène had gone downstairs she took it into the bedroom and began again to read. She was hardly through when there was a scream from the next room—Sophie had fallen off the table and banged her head against the bath. There was a small bump where her head had struck. "She has shattered her skull," Armand said, "her balance was imperfect." Holding Sophie on her knee and rubbing the bump with the skin of an onion, Renée wondered if there was anything in the letter she had missed. She had waited for it so long. As soon as she was free she would read it again, more slowly and carefully, to see if there were words or meanings she had overlooked.

XI

SHE had read it twice in the evening; but waking, towards two o'clock, and feeling her loneliness insufferable, she took the letter into the day-room, lit the gas, raked at the stove and started to read it again.

". . . the Colonel, Hédouin, is of the old school, he reminds me somewhat of my father. He is a grey-headed old nincompoop, whose Bible is the drill-book; he believes in order and discipline and regularity and precedents and complicated programmes; he would stop a bayonet charge to tell a man he had his bayonet at the wrong angle; he was probably the most smartly turned-out officer on the field of Austerlitz. Malestroit was a sympathetic personality in comparison. There is no one in the mess that one can talk to—flashy youths with terrible Paris accents, and country dolts, together with a crowd of seedy provincials, billing-clerks in uniform. The army has become a dustbin for the riff-raff of the

Republic, it was bound to happen. I have never believed in democracy as a political possibility. This place stinks to heaven, there is no sanitation at all; if they don't move me soon I shall send in my papers and let my father say what he likes. The one thing that keeps me here is the chance of a minor action against the Bisquorts, who are giving trouble on our south flank. That might be interesting, though Hédouin would conduct it all wrong. I seem to be short of one shirt, I wonder if you took it away, I believe it wanted darning.

"I expect that by this time you have quite settled down. I hope Armand and Sophie are well, I was glad to have news of them in your letter posted at Marseille. You will find my mother rather fussy, perhaps; she worries about father a good deal. The Séverins, as I've often told you, are curious, and they feel themselves cramped in Baulon, where they have been obliged to live since father's early retirement. Don't be worried by their little mannerisms, or think they mean to be unfriendly. You must just stand up to them and everything will be all right.

"You mustn't believe anything they say about me. It's so long since I saw them, they've quite forgotten what I'm like, they know me only as I was when a boy. Everything that's wrong with me now is my father's fault, he made me join the army and I've always detested it. I would have much preferred to be a civil engineer in France; I loathe Africa. This place is driving me mad; I've told Hédouin I can't stand it, but he never listens to anyone's private trouble. Renée dear, don't believe anything you hear about me, I'm not myself in this place. . . ."

She read it, this fifth time, with moistening eyes. It was not the letter she had hoped for, but it breathed of Pierre. There was a burn at the top of the second sheet, made by the ash of his cigarette; she smelt the paper, and thought she could just perceive Pierre's own smell. The violet ink had darkened, but she could see him as he wrote it, his chair turned sideways to a table, his right ankle cocked on his knee, his long, tobacco-stained forefinger stroking his chin. She could remember—it delighted her how clearly—the way he would stop in the middle of a letter and look up at the ceiling, pushing his spread fingertips through his back hair. But her eye caught the date again; the letter was more than a month old, and she could not keep her mind from turning time into distance. And here it was so cold.

Straining out to him, she closed her eyes. Her head was bent right down, her face upon her knuckles; keeping quite still she thought that her spirit could escape to reach him. She saw him now, a blurred figure at the end of a misty tunnel, but his face was turned away. He was bending over, struggling with something, and she knew that she could help him; he was late as usual for parade, she could lace one boot while he did the other. She hurried, but the way was difficult, the cab jolted on the pavé and the driver said he could go no faster. A voice said clearly "Renée!" but it was not Pierre's voice. She looked up, clutching the letter on her knee, and saw Madame Eugène standing by the door.

"Renée, I want you to help me, Eugène is ill."

Renée stared foolishly.

"Ill?"

"He has had a bad turn. He is . . . I think—I think he is dying. I saw your light on, I thought you would be awake, that's why I came to you."

Half-asleep, barefooted, Renée followed her downstairs: a singular figure, Madame Eugène in a flannel night-gown which dragged along the floor, surmounted by a quilted peignoir and topped with a Kashmir shawl, on which her ribboned plaits bobbed and swung as her woollen slippers slithered along the boards, the candle in her hand throwing back her monstrous caricature. At the foot of the stairs she turned to whisper: "I want you to be very quiet; you will be quiet, won't you? I don't want the others woken, I don't want a great disturbance." And at the door of her room, still lower: "I've sent Barbier to get the Abbé and Doctor Tischer. They should be here soon."

The gas in the ante-room was turned very low. The door to the room where M. Séverin lay was shut. "I want you," Madame Eugène whispered, "to heat this milk for me. It should be just warm, not boiling. You'll find a spirit lamp in the cupboard there, and the oil—the oil somewhere. Perhaps you had better bring Joséphine up here. No, don't do that, just stay and heat the milk for me." She went to the door, turned to say something else, and started coughing; for fully half a minute she bent with her face buried in her shawl, and shook, stifling the noise of her cough. Then, she said, gathering the breath for each word, "A glass of water—over there—thank you. Thank you, it's just a cough, it comes on at night. . . . You'll keep very quiet, won't you?"

Renée saw, as Madame Eugéne opened the door, the weak light of a tiny lamp upon a tall baize screen. She caught the sound of heavy breathing, of a faint groan. The door closed.

In bed she had seemed to be wide awake; now she was sleepy, longing for warmth and to lie down; the movements of her hands and feet seemed to lag behind her will, to continue after she had bidden them to stop. She found the lamp and the oil together, filled the lamp with an unsteady hand, spilling oil on the carpet. There were no matches anywhere; she had to feel in the bottom of a drawer for paper, twist a spill and take a light from the gas.

She would have liked to turn the gas high, but dared not do so. She knelt, holding the saucepan over the flame, which gave her a little warmth. There was no sound from the next room.

She thought: "If it were Pierre——" and pictured Madame Eugène's face as she had just seen it; on which there was hardly emotion, only pallor, the candle emphasizing whiteness, marking the little grooves, the twisted corners of her mouth, showing the face old, the eyes tired and frightened. For a moment she felt a warmth of admiration. Had it been Pierre! But she could not picture death, its majesty and terror, as she crouched here, cramped and sleepy, watching through the rising stream the prodigious rococo of the giant wardrobe, the etiolated arras on the wall, the chipped varnish on the panels of the door. She had no image of the face of Eugène Séverin, he was only a name to her, a being who had sired Pierre. She could find no sentiment, hardly an interest, in the thought of his being a few yards from her, dying.

The milk was bubbling and she took it away from the flame. She went to the door and whispered at the keyhole: "Madame Séverin! Madame Séverin! The milk is ready," but there was no answer, only the stifled coughing. She put the saucepan down near the fire, longed to go back to bed, but would not leave her post until Madame dismissed her.

Half an hour had gone when she heard Barbier's limp in the passage. He came in, with a touch of his knuckles on the door instead of his usual double-rap, he looked round and asked, nodding towards the door, "Madame is in there?" She had heard him, the door opened, Renée saw again for just a moment the faint light on the heavy screen.

"Where are they, Barbier?"

"Dr. Tischer was out, he was attending a child with diphtheria in the rue Saint-François quarter——"

"Quietly, Barbier, you must be quieter!"

"I went to him there. He said he could not leave the child at once, he would come as soon as he could. . . . The priest is coming, he will be here almost at once."

"What do you say, Barbier, who is coming?"

"M. l'Abbé."

"But Dr. Tischer, why haven't you brought him?"

"He couldn't come at once, he was attending a child, he will come presently."

"But didn't you tell him that your master is dying?"

"He will come presently."

"I can't understand it. You can't have made him understand. You, Renée, will you go?—no, Barbier, you must go back again, you must make it clear to him he must come at once. Or you must

66

find another doctor, but I would rather have M. Tischer. Quickly, you must be quick. And be quiet, I don't want anyone to wake."

"The milk is ready, Madame Séverin."

"Oh, yes. All right. But I don't want it now, not yet."

She went back into the next room. There was no sound while the door was open.

Barbier, shaking his head, went off again; and presently Renée heard a new step on the stairs. She opened the door to throw a guiding light on to the passage, and standing there called softly, "This way." It was the Abbé Vignaud, with a grey carriage-cloak above his soutane, feeling his way uncertainly along the wall. He came into the ante-room, bowed to her, and set down the chased box he was carrying.

"In there?"

"Yes, Monsieur."

"You don't know—how long he has? Is Tischer there?"

"No, he hasn't come yet."

She opened the door a few inches and whispered, "M. l'Abbé has come." Madame Eugène came to the door. She said "Wait!" and closed it.

Vignaud brought up a chair, sat down, took snuff, and folded his hands! He asked:

"Should we be wrong to have more light? I should like to see that piece of arras more clearly—it might be Dumontier work. Well, perhaps better not, I should not like to upset Madame Séverin." He had the trick of so controlling his voice that, pitched so low as to be inaudible a few feet away, it was yet distinct, flexible in tone. "I myself—you may not agree with me—cannot bear the idea of a man dying in semi-darkness. It's all wrong. Goethe was right—you remember his cry: *More light!* It takes away all the dignity of death, this hole-and-corner business, the closed shutters and the close air reeking of antiseptics. I myself, if I saw any chance of dying, would get someone to carry me to the summit of a high hill. If possible I should wait until the dawn. Think what a splendid death that would be, in the early sunlight, like a picture of the Resurrection. I knew an old Baron once who had the same point of view; he had a villa on the spur of a mountain, it was in the Lausanne district, I think, and whenever he felt ill he used to go there, hoping to look up at the snow as he died. In the end he died in a cell; he was imprisoned for some form of fraud—he was a man who had no sense of other people's property, though in other respects very worthy. I felt sorry for him; of course his punishment was just, but it seemed too bad that he should die so cramped, poor fellow, with so little light and no snow at all. . . . Is that someone coming?"

It was Barbier again, leading Tischer, who was puffing and sweating, who looked dazed and worn out, blinking at the gas.

"I was saying, Doctor," Vignaud continued in his low voice, "that when a man is dying he should have plenty of light, as much light as possible. You, as a medical man, will not agree with me; but then you regard death merely as an interesting physiological phenomenon, the rounding-off of a case. Its dignity and glory are lost on you poor tweezer-pokers."

Already Tischer had taken off his coat and opened his bag. He murmured, with one arm in the sleeve of his white overall, "You have administered already? I couldn't get here before, I had a case I couldn't leave. I ought to get back. I never expected this, I never dreamt of it for a moment. What did you say? Well, perhaps we see a little closer, we understand a little better."

The door of the sick-room had opened a little way, Madame Eugène came in.

"Why are you all talking at the tops of your voices?" she demanded huskily. "I can't bear all this noise. Barbier—is Barbier there? Barbier, you must go for M. Lecours, tell him he must come here at once. Take a cab if you can find one. And M. Raymond, he had better be fetched too."

Tischer, grasping his bag, had passed behind her and was about to go in. She turned and caught his arm.

"No! No, you're not to go in, not yet, he's not ready for you now. It's no good your seeing him, it's too late now, why didn't you come before? What? I can't understand you, I've never heard of such a thing, didn't Barbier tell you that my husband is dying? M. l'Abbé, please! Be very quiet please, the slightest noise will make a disturbance."

Vignaud took up his box, crossed himself, and followed her into the other room. Tischer, still standing and looking down at the saucepan, said as if to himself:

"It's extraordinary, it's incomprehensible. Nowhere am I treated as I am in this house. You must pardon me, Madame Pierre, I have nothing against Madame Séverin. I understand that she is upset, but it's unheard of to treat a doctor like this. I've been dragged away from a serious case, and now I'm not wanted. I'm not allowed to go in. My real duty—I don't know, I had no sleep last night either. I don't know what my duty is."

Renée said: "You'd better lie down, you may get a little sleep. There, on Madame Séverin's bed, it won't matter."

But he would not lie down. He stood near the door, shivering as the sweat dried on him, moving his hands restlessly. "I don't know what I should do," he repeated. He started when a hand knocked at the passage door. "Who's that?"

Renée opened it and admitted Marianne, who stood slipperless in a grey dressing-gown, rubbed her eyes, blinked and yawned.

"What is it? Is there something wrong?"

Renée told her, "Yes, your father, he's had a bad turn."

"He's not—dying?"

"I don't know. I don't really know anything. Your mother says that he's had a bad turn."

"Can I do anything? What are you doing, why didn't Mother wake me? Oh, Dr. Tischer, I didn't see you. You've seen him?"

"No, Mademoiselle, I have been summoned here, and now I am not allowed to see him. And I have a serious case waiting, I ought to go back there. I don't really know what I'm to do."

"Can't we have the gas up?" Marianne asked.

"I think your mother prefers it to be kept low."

"How long have you been here, Renée?"

"I don't know. An hour perhaps. What time is it, do you know?"

Tischer looked at his watch.

"Twenty-past three."

She wanted to go back to bed, but was afraid to seem callous. Some of her drowsiness had left her, and she felt a little pride that it was she who had been summoned. She put the milk over the stove once again to bring it nearer boiling. She and Marianne sat in silence, Marianne with her eyes closed, nodding. Tischer still stood, repeatedly drawing out his watch, murmuring, "I don't know what I ought to do." Ste Gudule chimed the half-hour, the third quarter, four o'clock. Marianne was asleep in her chair when Vignaud came out again.

"Can I go in now?" Tischer asked him. "Indeed, I must go in, I have the right——"

"You must do as you think," Vignaud said. His face was fixed, telling nothing. "But Madame Séverin says not. She has done everything possible, she thinks; she only wants you to stay here."

"But does she realize that I have another case on my hands, a child who may also be dying? What is the use of my being here if I am not admitted? I have never heard of a doctor being treated in this way."

Vignaud, diving into his habiliments for the snuff-box, surveyed him with interest.

"I should go in if I were you."

"But what would Madame Séverin say?"

"I don't know, Doctor, I really can't tell you."

In the passage Barbier's voice said: "In there, Monsieur," and Lecours came in.

Lecours stood just inside the door, slowly surveying the circle like a pegged turtle, nodding to the ladies, his mouth slightly open, his pupils showing like pin-heads in the feeble light. He asked at large, pushing up his stock:

"I am to go straight in, I suppose?"

"He is not well enough to see a doctor," Tischer answered. "But the sight of a lawyer, Monsieur, might perhaps pull him round."

Vignaud said, "You'd better wait, I think. It is M. Lecours, is it not? We have met, I believe, some time ago, at the Secours Mutuels. I should like to have your opinion before I go to bed—if you will be so obliging—on a legal matter which I find of particular interest. An uncle of mine, who has wedded two Persian ladies in accordance with the Mohammedan rite . . ."

The passage door was opened without ceremony and Raymond came in. His clothes had been flung on anyhow, his hair hung over his forehead, but he was wide awake. He turned to Marianne.

"What is all this? Is Barbier out of his senses? Father can't really be . . . Tischer, is that you over there?—why can't we have some light in this room? What's wrong with Father?"

"Raymond! Quiet please!" It was Madame Eugène. "You will be able to come in presently, Raymond, but not just yet. Dr. Tischer, you can come in now. Marianne, you had better take everybody to the drawing-room. M. Lecours, I shall want you presently—I want you . . . No, I can't think, just now, what it is. Come, please, doctor. Quietly, please."

There was complete silence as she opened the door. Then, from within, someone spoke. The voice was gentle, but even, ordinary, firm.

"Are you there, Madeleine? Madeleine. I want to see Thérèse, will you get her, please?"

Tischer had already gone inside. They heard her answer in a whisper, "But I've told you, dear, Thérèse is asleep, she can't be disturbed. Thérèse——" The door closed.

They trooped to the drawing-room, where Vignaud unfastened and folded the shutters. The darkness was beginning to leak from the sky, they could distinguish scaffolding across the square. Marianne turned up the gas, lighting cruelly her own sleep-soiled sallow face, the resentful face of M. Lecours. Renée sat by the fireplace holding her hands instinctively towards the tumbled cinders in the grate; the rest as they found the chairs, facing all ways about the room. Lecours opened his cigar-case, reflected, and closed it. Marianne stifled a yawn.

"I'm going to see him," Raymond said suddenly, and left the room. But he was back immediately. "She's locked both doors, she won't let me in." He started walking between the door and the window, till Marianne stopped him. "Sit down, Raymond, you're getting on my nerves. . . . Why can't mother tell us something? How long has Dr. Tischer been in there now?"

Standing astride, looking at the door, Raymond said, "I don't know. Twenty minutes. . . . You heard what father said—he wanted to see Aunt Thérèse. She ought to know, you might go up and get her down."

Vignaud had fallen asleep on the sofa. Lecours sat quite still, pressing his cuticles, his face grim. He was too well-mannered to look at his watch, but they could see in the fixity of his eyes that his mind registered twenty francs each time the quarter struck. The gas showed feebler as the daylight grew in strength, revealing in greater detail the room's disorder, the wax faces and the motley clothes. "He must be making a fight for it," Raymond said, breaking a long silence. No one replied.

It was a long time before Thérèse came down. She was fully dressed when she appeared, and, leaning on her stick in the doorway of the drawing-room, she looked about her with an air of surprise; as if, making her entrance on the stage, she had found the scenery in the wrong position and the shifters still at work. She bowed to Lecours, who had risen, and turned at once to Raymond.

"You've seen your father?"

"No; no one has seen him except Mother—and the Abbé here—he's fast asleep. Tischer's in there."

"You say he wanted to see me?"

"Yes, I heard him ask."

"I'll go then. You'd better come—and you, Marianne." In the corridor she asked. "What's Lecours doing here?"

"Earning overtime rates."

"Exactly. Who sent for him?"

"Mother."

It was still quite dark in the passage; and Madame Eugène, coming out of the ante-room, could hardly see them. She said, peering forward: "Is that you, Raymond? Oh, where is M. Lecours? He hasn't gone, surely? Will you tell him, Raymond, that he is to communicate with Paris by telegraph. He must get in touch with someone, one of the Ministers, the President if he can, tell him the circumstances, have something done quickly, an order from the Judiciary, M. Lecours will know——"

"Madeleine!"

"Oh, Thérèse, is that you? I didn't think——"

She turned back into the room and they followed her. She crossed to the other door with a quick movement turned the key,

71

which she slipped into the turn-up of her sleeve. They saw, as she turned to face them, that she was trembling, that her face was haggard. She asked:

"Where's Renée? I told her to look after the milk. I don't know if it has boiled; it's no good if it has boiled; I shall have to send for some more. Marianne, go and get her."

Thérèse said: "I understand that my brother is dying, Madeleine. I should like to see him."

"No. No, you can't. Not yet. He can't see anybody yet."

"But I understand that he asked to see me. He had something to say to me."

"That isn't true. He hasn't mentioned your name."

"Mother!"

"Yes, Raymond?"

"Mother, you're forgetting. I heard him."

"You heard what?"

"I heard father ask for Aunt Thérèse."

She stared at him with her lips apart. Her voice came in uncanny falsetto:

"Raymond! Raymond, how dare you tell such lies!"

Thérèse had not shifted feet or arms. She said in her customary voice, husky and without emotion:

"It was a mistake, Madeleine. Raymond is tired, he didn't hear properly. But perhaps you will ask Eugène if he would like to see me."

"I tell you, Thérèse, he can't see anyone. Dr. Tischer is in there, he won't allow him."

"Here is Renée, Mother." Marianne had found her going up to her own bedroom. "She says the milk hasn't boiled, it will only want warming up again. Can I see father now? I think one of us ought to see him."

"Perhaps you would send Dr. Tischer out to us," Thérèse suggested. "I should like——"

"Yes, we have a right to know," Raymond said suddenly. "I don't want to interfere, Mother, but one of us Séverins ought to know exactly——"

She did not seem to hear him. She turned towards the door. As she moved, the key slipped from her sleeve and jumped to Raymond's feet. He picked it up.

She swept round as if he had attacked her. "Raymond!" She struck his cheek with her closed hand. "Give me——" She caught his wrist and twisted his hand round, snatched the key from his open palm, pushed him away and went to the door again.

"Pardon, Madame." Barbier stood at the passage door, his

broken leg pressed against the whole one as if at attention. "There's an old man at the door who won't go away. He asks if M. Tischer can come to his child, who is taken worse."

Madame Eugène looked at him with a puzzled frown.

"But he has gone, Barbier," she said politely. "The old man must have missed him. He went ten minutes ago."

She went back into the sick-room, locking the door behind her. Raymond lit a cigarette and sat down. "I will write an obituary notice for the Paris papers," he said with his teeth closed. "It seems to be the only thing I shall be allowed to do."

★

When she had warmed the milk again, Renée went up to her room and dressed. The children were fast alseep. She lay on her bed, but there was light enough coming between the shutters and through the cracks to make the objects in the room visible in outline; she was restless, her palate dry and her tongue coated; her mind was fully awake. It was no affair of hers, an old man who chanced to be Pierre's father lying in a darkened bedroom, fighting —so she guessed—a losing battle; but the face of Madame Eugène haunted her with its white weariness; she could not stay up here while that was going on. She went down to the ante-room, felt the milk with the tip of her little finger, and replaced the saucepan on the spirit stove, which was burning very low. Putting her head near the bedroom door she could just hear the sound of Madame Eugène moving, her smothered cough. There was nothing she could do, and she went back to the drawing-room.

The drawing-room had grown clearer, and the light from the gas, which no one had thought to turn out, showed only faintly now upon the ceiling. Vignaud was still asleep, with his head hung back over the pommel of the sofa, his mouth wide open, his Adam's-apple sticking up like a tent-pole against the stretched skin of his neck. Lecours had not moved, even his hands were in the same position, but his head had sunk forward so that his chin was smoothly pillowed on the bulging flesh of his neck. His eyes were shut, and there came from his nostrils at every breath a little whine like the sound of a kettle boiling. Thérèse had taken the best chair and appeared to be reading, her head bent down above the book on her lap, her eyes shielded by her long, bony hands; but the head lolled slowly sideways, and her mouth made constantly a gentle, rugged sound, like a murmur of affection or complaint. Marianne, kneeling on the hearthrug with her trunk on the seat of a padded chair, her forehead against her crossed wrists, was frankly asleep. Renée sat down near the window, and presently Raymond placed his chair near hers.

"It is indecent," he whispered, sweeping the room with his

73

eyes, "for the old to sleep in public. Only young and beautiful females should do it. And by that I do not mean Marianne."

He lit a new cigarette from the stump of his old one, held out his case to her, and smiled at her astonishment.

"No? But many do. I would never have thought," he continued, "that my mother had still so much strength in her arm. Look, quite a bruise. It still hurts like sin. Wait a minute, I want you to sit on something lower; here, this stool, it's just as comfortable; and now look up at me as you did when I was on the stairs. Yes, like that. That's good. Could you keep like that, do you think, for an hour or two at a stretch? I wish you hadn't dressed, I don't care for that dress very much, it's too dark; you ought to wear bright colours, it is always a sound rule with an Asiatic skin. No no, I don't mean anything by that, I was talking simply of colour values. Have you ever been painted? No, well perhaps that's a good thing; Pierre would undoubtedly have sold his last pony and got the most fasionable painter in Cairo, or some other mecca of all the banalities, to do you in the figure of Marie Antoinette, with each separate eyelash in exactly the right position, and a nice dash of rouge on each cheek, Ethiopian slaves and palms in background. My God, how horrible! You must let me paint you, just like that but with a better dress—no, you've lost the position now, I must have the throat tight. We will make a beginning next Saturday—oh, no, that will probably be the funeral—but as soon after that as I can get things fixed with Cécile. She may object, she's odd about my models. I had a little gamine from the rue Saint-François to do as Eve. Cécile kept coming in every five minutes with silly little napkins and covering up the parts I wasn't at the moment using. The provincial mind is very difficult to fathom."

"But I didn't know that you were a painter."

"No? What did Pierre tell you I was?"

"Pierre—he never said very much about you. He——"

"No, well that's only what I expected, the Séverins never say anything about themselves, we are ludicrously secretive. Especially since this affair of father's, which everyone must know about and which must never be mentioned. And you take Thérèse over there: the one thing that woman's proud of—the one thing she lives to remember—is her seven brilliant years at the Français. And yet you'd imagine from the dark way in which she alludes to her past that she'd been a notorious procureuse. I'm the only member of my family who's not a poseur, in one way or another. . . . No, I'm not a professional painter, like Lemenils, if that's what you mean. I work on the local paper. It was the least of all the horrors offered me. My father wanted me to be a soldier, I turned that down, and then he had the idea of making me a politician; he thought I would get to a position in which I could wield some influence with the Judiciary—little he knows. But I didn't take to that notion either, since it would have meant sheltering under the coat-tails of father's cronies on the Right. Can you imagine me a politician of the Right? I would rather be a sanitary inspector. So in the end it was the local paper, with the idea that I should ultimately become an André Géraud and hold the opinion of Paris in the hollow of my hand, Well, I have not got quite so far as that, but I am already a man of immense importance. I am sent as representative of my paper to the luncheons of the Comité de Patronage des Écoles Maternelles et de Surveillance de la Crèche Axis-Lepanation. It is a thrilling life. And in the evenings, when there is no light at all. I am sometimes permitted to paint pictures. You must come and see them some time, if Cécile will let you. I belong to the Colombel group, we exhibit at the Sarreméjain galleries in the autumn. But I don't suppose that means anything to you. No, I'd rather you didn't pretend—it's the curse of this country that every little bourgeoise pretends to know something about paintings."

"At least I can learn something——"

"I don't know. You will probably not be thinking. You will say 'Yes . . . yes,' and then all of a sudden, 'How do you like these shoes I'm wearing?' The Colombel group, if you must know, represents a reaction against Matisse and that crowd. Not a classicist reaction, mind you; and we have no use for the sentimentalities of the Barbizons. We believe that beauty attaches to every object —dung-heaps and drain pipes and brick factories—when it is revealed in a particular aspect. This beauty is dependent neither on colour nor on form, but upon what we call the Intention. We argue that no one can create an object—even if it's only a dustbin —without having in his mind some conception of rightness. If, for example, a man paints a fence green it must be because that colour seemed to him the most æsthetically desirable of those that were offered him. Now our aim is to trace the source of that rudimentary æsthetic instinct, to reveal in our own representation of the form and colour of objects the ideality of their original conception. We purify the object by going behind it to its author's unconscious impulse. Now you mustn't confuse this doctrine with that of the Marinetti crowd, which we know to be poppycock . . . but it's no good trying to explain to anyone who has no artistic training. . . ."

He opened a window and threw the end of his cigarette into the Square.

"Why won't she let me see him?" he demanded suddenly and angrily. "He asked for Thérèse, he must want to see one of us;

of course he wants to see someone of his own kind, poor old thing."

But the door, when he went to try it, was still locked. He came back with a fresh cigarette lighted and lay on the floor close to Renée's feet, his hands clasped under his neck, his right knee stuck up and the left ankle perched upon it. The sun had come above the bakehouse at the corner of the Square, and a shaft of yellow light sloped from the window across Renée's knees, across Lecours's pulpous head and upon the abdominal uplands of the Abbé Vignaud. Into the light the smoke of Raymond's cigarette rose straight and blue. The Square was astir now, the creak of axles and the clap of hooves were mixed with strident voices. Thérèse had moved, turned over a leaf of her book and gone to sleep again. "It takes its time," Raymond said. "Death doesn't hurry."

The clock had struck eight when the door opened and Madame Eugène came in. She leant against the side of the door blinking, peering into the corners of the room as if she had lost her way and come into some strange house. "Oh," she said faintly, "you are all asleep. Then I suppose it doesn't matter."

She turned as if to go away. Raymond jumped up. "Mother, is he——?"

Thérèse said: "I am perfectly awake, Madeleine."

Lecours opened his eyes and tried to stand on his feet, which were cramped and bloodless. Vignaud woke with a start.

"Mother, tell us," Raymond repeated, "is he——?"

Staring at the floor, Madame Eugène said with her breath, soundlessly: "It's all over."

In the darker side of the room there was a sound like bucolic laughter. It was Marianne.

"Mother, why didn't you——?"

"What do you mean, Mother?" Raymond asked furiously. "Do you mean he's dead?"

Madame Eugène shook her head. She was struggling for her voice.

"No. . . . No, the crisis . . . over. He's come through. I've got him through."

XII

VIGNAUD had persuaded Madame Eugène to go and rest in a spare room on the third floor, and the house had settled into its routine, when the telegram came. Joséphine, who was washing the floor of the hall, took it, and ascertained from the messenger the name to which it was addressed. She dropped her clout into the bucket, wiped her hands on her skirt, and shuffled up the stairs to Madame's room. "A telegram!" she shouted, knocking the door. She received no answer, the room was empty. There was a child in the passage, that small boy of Master Pierre's who followed her about the house, who was no more right in the head than her own Gaston. She asked him abruptly, "Where is Madame? Oh, I don't suppose you know."

He was startled when she spoke, but he answered quite clearly: "Do you mean Madame my mother or Madame my grandmother?"

"You know who I mean. I mean Madame Séverin. My mistress."

"She is in the little room next to Aunt Thérèse's. I saw her go in there with a pillow and rug."

Joséphine nodded and shuffled away. She had got as far as the next landing when Thérèse met her.

"Where are you going, Joséphine?"

"To Madame. There's a telegram."

"A telegram? Let me see it."

"It's for Madame," Joséphine said, holding it tightly. "I'm not a scholar, but I know this is for Madame."

"Yes, but Madame is resting, she mustn't be disturbed. Let me see it."

Joséphine tried to push past her.

"I have to deliver it to Madame," she said.

"Joséphine, if you are impertinent I will arrange for you to be dismissed."

"And Barbier also?"

"Barbier too."

"Then we will serve in a house where wages are paid, and I shall be able to buy trousers for *le pauvre petit*."

She threw the telegram on the floor and flopped away with a penguin's action down the stairs. Thérèse, holding the stairhead rail and biting her lip, bent painfully to pick up the envelope. She opened it and read:

"Arriving about midday by motor-car with Mme Flandrecauld for short visit trust convenient Louis."

She had already sent Barbier to do the day's shopping, and there was no one with any sense, besides herself, in the house: except that young woman of Pierre's, who romped in the nursery with her children all day long. She could be pressed into service for the occasion. Thérèse hobbled down the stairs, murmuring " 'Trust convenient.' "

The little nursery was in wild disorder; the coffee bowls were still unwashed on the table, neighboured by a sewing-machine, a doll or two and a box of paints. The boy was stretched on the floor, exactly in line with the draught between door and stove, quietly and lugubriously singing a religious hymn as he marked neat parallelograms in the oilcloth with a small gimlet, stopping from time to time to wipe with a dirty rag the mucus which dripped incessantly from his red nose. The other child, clad in drawers and bodice, squatted with her expression of habitual coyness amid a heap of wreckage underneath the table; while the mother, perched on the table edge, was rapidly stitching up the lace of the child's petticoat. Renée smiled a little wearily.

"I'm afraid we're rather behindhand this morning. I meant to do this job last night. Armand, you should get up when your aunt comes in. Go and find yourself a clean handkerchief." She tipped a chair to clear the seat of a pile of little boxes and a pair of scissors. "Do sit down."

Thérèse showed, by a single scouring movement of her eyes, that she had taken in everything. She remained standing.

"Those holes won't improve the oilcloth," she said.

"No, but it's very old. He was starting on the door and I diverted him to the oilcloth. I thought it would be better.'

Thérèse refused to pursue the matter.

"I've had a telegram to say that my brother Louis is coming. He will be here for déjeuner. It's a great nuisance, we always entertain Louis well—he doesn't see us often—but it means doing everything in a rush. I can't disturb Madeleine, she needs a rest, poor creature. So I want you to go out and get some things. Have you a piece of paper? I'll make a list."

"I shall be glad," Renée said, "to do something for the convenience of Madame Séverin."

Her instructions delivered, Thérèse went down to find Joséphine, who would have to be pacified somehow; she must find something or other to give as a present for *le pauvre petit* Gaston, perhaps there would be a pair of shoes belonging to Raymond in the room he used. She called "Joséphine!" The dining-room, the big dining-room on the ground floor which was seldom used now, must be got ready; also the bedroom on the second floor which Louis always had, with the next room for his secretary. "Josèphine!" Arriving at the first-floor landing she was startled to hear someone calling.

"Madeleine!"

Eugène.

She went along the passage and into the ante-room. There she stood and listened. The call was repeated rather crossly.

"Madeleine! Are you there?"

She was in a fix. Tischer should have been back before this; Madeleine had made her promise on no account to go into Eugène's

78

room before he came, and had only agreed to rest on that condition: not that such a promise mattered in itself, but Madeleine would certainly get to hear if she broke it, and there would be a scene, such a scene as Thérèse found so tiresome in real life, such a waste of her talent. She waited till the call came once again; then, opening the door a little way, she said:

"Madeleine's resting upstairs. She'll be down before long."

"Upstairs? Is that you, Thérèse? Thérèse, I heard something about a telegram. Is there a telegram?"

"A telegram? No. Oh, yes, there was a telegram, it was of no importance. Dr. Tischer will be here presently."

"But Tischer didn't send the telegram?"

"No."

"Well, who sent it, what did it say?"

She reflected, but a suitable lie was not forthcoming.

"It was from Louis."

"Oh, he's coming?"

"Yes."

"When?"

"To-day, this morning."

"Oh! . . ." Faintly, "He must have a good luncheon. Tell Madeleine, will you, Louis must have a specially good luncheon, not expensive, but well cooked. Madeleine might do a Russian salad herself, Louis likes that. She must be in the kitchen, it's no good leaving Barbier to do it, he's only fit to cook for Tartars. . . . You'll see that Madi does it properly, won't you, Thérèse? And tell Barbier to decant some of that Meursault; he must do that straight away, and set it to warm. Do see to that, there's a good girl. . . . I wish Madeleine wouldn't run away like this. . . ."

She heard a sigh and the creak of the bed as he turned over. He would go to sleep again, she thought. How weak his voice was!

At the end of the passage she met Tischer. She had never seen him quite so unkempt, so scattered; he looked as if he had been through a bullace-hedge.

"You're very late," she said. "You were expected an hour ago."

'I know. I was busy, The child, Mademoiselle, the little Rosie, is dead."

"Rosie?"

"The child, the child I attended last night. The poor little thing, she is dead."

"But, Doctor, your patients must sometimes die."

He jerked up his head angrily.

"Yes, they must always die when I do not attend them properly. An hour, a full hour, it can't have been less, I was kept here last night just kicking my heels. And Rosie all the time is dying. You people, you, you Séverins, you care about nothing except yourselves. What is the importance of an old man, who is always in bed, beside that of a young child, an only child? You make a farce of my profession, you Séverins——"

Thérèse eyed him wearily. It was exceedingly tiresome that everyone was so out of sorts this morning, and on top of it all the execrable Louis coming.

"You had better see M. Séverin at once," she said. "He is awake now, he should not have been left so long."

★

It was after half-past eleven when Renée got back. Aunt Thérèse would be cross; she had said, "You ought to be back by eleven, you should be able to manage it." It was sunny and warm in the Square, so that she was roused and forgot her headache. But as soon as she opened the door of the house she received the musty smell. The hall still felt damp from Joséphine's ministrations, none of the sunlight came in. She went down to the kitchen to deliver her parcels, and Gaston, to her relief, came out to take them. "You must give these to your father straight away," she said. But he wouldn't move until she had gone; he stood grinning at her, he put down all the parcels and stretched his hands to feel the folds of her dress, he rubbed the stuff with his fingers like a woman buying linen and laughed softly as if she were offering him a poor bargain. "Quickly, Gaston, you must take these to your father," she repeated, and pulled herself away. It was cold down there, where no sun ever came at all. She shivered as she ran up the stone stairs.

She went up to Thérèse's room, pausing at her own stage to hear that the children were all right. Thérèse's room was empty. Meeting Joséphine on the way down, she asked, "Do you know where Mlle Thérèse is?" "No. She's been in my kitchen half the morning, but she's gone now." "Thank you, Joséphine." She went down to the first floor and peeped into the drawing-room. Thérèse was not there, but a man stood in the grate with his feet apart and his coat-tail raised, roasting his trousers by the fire. Evidently Uncle Louis had arrived before his time; it was not yet twelve.

She said, retreating, "Oh, I'm sorry——"

"Come in," he said, "come in."

She was startled by his likeness, doubly remarkable at this first impingement, to Pierre. He was taller than Pierre, his head reaching as he stood on the kerb of the grate almost to the top of the mantel mirror; and lighter in colouring, the tan almost gone, the eyes a brilliant Norwegian blue which showed that the white

80

hair, the beautiful fine hair, had once been golden. They were saintly eyes, she thought, contemplative and a little triste, full of experience and suffering; you expected to find beneath them a priest's face, instead of the hussar's moustache, combed out and up, the scarred chin; a priest's robe instead of the high winged collar and silver stock, the many buttons of the high grey coat, which was sharply angled at the shoulders, loosely waisted; the work, one would say, of a military tailor in Paris. It was an old man. The eyes were heavy-pocketed, the face the pale face of an invalid, the red on the high cheeks mottled and too dull in colour, the head a little stooped, the trunk too plainly corseted. Yet you saw first not his age but his beauty; the magnificence of the combed white brows above the lovely eyes, the boyish smile, a little shy, on his lips, the splendid moulding of his head, the height and dignity of the spare figure. It was an older Pierre, a Pierre made gentler, brought to ripeness as the summers mellow the châteaux of the Saône. Even Pierre's weakness was there, a slight confusion, a drawing-in of the eyebrows as if to hide a harder thought by one which came more easily. He took a step to meet her as she came in, bowing from the shoulders; and because he was so like Pierre she went to him with hardly any shyness, ready to take his hand. She was surprised, when he spoke, how quiet his voice was.

"I'm afraid," he said, "I really haven't the pleasure of knowing who you are."

She said, "I'm Renée."

"——?"

"——Pierre's wife."

His smile widened. "Of course!"

He was a little taken aback; upset, she thought, at his gaucherie over the name. But he took her gently by the arm and put her in a chair. He leant against the back of another and regarded her intently.

"Of course, yes, how absurd that we should have been strangers. But Pierre—he has been away for so long, he writes such poor letters—full of nothing but trivialities—that we don't really know about him, about his—his affairs. They told me that he had a black wife—but that of course was a long time ago, if it was true at all; and you know how it is, young men when they are abroad, if they happen to be in a lax Mess. . . . I was trying to remember . . . but tell me, how is Pierre nowadays, did you leave him well? Yes, Pierre is a good lad. Not really a soldier in the modern sense, he will never be any good on the parade ground, he is not the Saint-Cyr type. Let me see, he is Captain now, yes? That is probably as far as he will get, he has not the concentration required for a senior officer of the modern type. But when it comes to fighting he will be all right. In that sense the Séverins are always good soldiers. Yes, Pierre has more in him than the other boy, than Raymond, more sense of discipline. No one would ever make any sort of soldier of Raymond, he is essentially a Pichy. And you have children, two children, is it not? A boy first and then a girl? You see, I know something, although circumstances keep me so much apart from my family. And your children are with you here, that's splendid. I shall look forward to seeing them, the boy especially, to see if he is really a Séverin. But to-day I shall be engaged, I have a brother coming, my brother Louis."

"But . . . but I thought you were Uncle Louis?"

He drew back his chin in surprise, and then laughed.

"Louis? Why, I am about as like Louis as a carrot is like a potato—neither being any better than the other, you understand. My brother, bless his heart, is a tradesman. A curious thing for a Séverin to be, but we live in democratic times. I'm not conceited, half the people we know here in this place are tradesmen, my wife calls at their houses. Yes, Louis is a carpet-drummer, he bargains for rugs in the bazaars of Isfahan and peddles them to the Paris shopkeepers. '*Très joli, ceci, à très bon marché.*' It's comical, the idea of a Séverin . . . but a good fellow, Louis, poor old chap, a golden-hearted fellow, really a most likeable little man, though I always find it very hard to remember that he's my brother. And you thought I was Louis—how very amusing! No, no. I'm Eugène, I'm Pierre's father."

XIII

THE children, in ecstasy, had stood on chairs by the window all morning. They were rewarded, briefly but sufficiently, by the sight of the motor-car, with its long flat engine-box and its big brass lamps, turning into the Place. It arrived at the door surrounded by excited children; Armand and Sophie heard the clickalick of the ratchet as the driver pulled on the brake. They could see, now, little more than the many-ribbed brown tent which covered the carriage, the grey head of Barbier who had appeared as if by clock-work on the trottoir. The driver had already come round to the side and opened the door; in a moment they caught sight of a giant bouquet of flowers and fruit with a flash of blue satin underneath and the toes of two big black boots; then, nearer the ground than the flowered hat, the black felt hat of a gentleman, and a glimpse of his black cane as the sun flashed on the silver handle. In a few seconds they had disappeared within the house, and the motor-car, still surrounded by its screaming escort of ragged urchins, had been driven away. Armand and Sophie climbed down from their chairs, chuckling with satisfaction. Their day was over, but it had been good.

*

The gong, the great gong from Madame Nadya's old home at Bobroviza, brought out from its long storage and polished for the occasion, had been sounded ten minutes ago. Madame Eugène was still upstairs, fast asleep. Déjeuner for the nursery arrived at last by the hand of Gaston; half the soup had been slopped over from the bowls, the wooden tray was a lake of soup which dripped through a crack in the frame to make a little stream along the passage and across the nursery oilcloth to the table. It was no use complaining. "All right, Gaston," Renée said, "put it down there, I'll mop it up." He seemed anxious to stay. He stood looking at the children, first at one and then at the other, frightening them with his fixed smile. "All right, Gaston," she repeated, "that will do, you can go now."

"A message," he said suddenly, "from the Colonel."

"The Colonel?"

"A message from M. Séverin."

"Yes?" But he had forgotten what it was.

"He sent a message," Gaston repeated, and shook his head and went to the door. There he stopped, ruminating, with his back turned. Presently he remembered. "He says you're to come down. The cover, Madame's cover—for you. Madame is not there, only her cover. Madame's cover for you."

She understood him. "You mean that as Madame is not there I am to have luncheon in the dining-room?"

"No," he said doubtfully, "Madame isn't there. She's upstairs, she's not there."

There seemed, however, to be no doubt about his meaning. She said: "All right, Gaston, I understand," and ran to the bedroom. There was no time to do more than take off her overall, slip on another dress, and fix with a few pins the strands of hair which were falling in every direction. She called, passing the nursery, "You must get on by yourselves, be careful," and ran downstairs.

The stove had been lit in the dining-room, but it burnt poorly and did little to take from the room the chill which had so long reigned there. The mahogany table, the Empire chairs, the heavy sideboards had been furiously polished, the smell of Castile soap and beeswax mingled strongly with the odour of food. There were no flowers: Madeleine would have remembered those. Joséphine, in the dress she had always had for funerals, her dourly patient face

83

bent low above the pile of plates she carried, dragged her flat slippers about the polished floor, while Barbier, holding the decanter as if porting arms for inspection, balanced on his sound leg behind M. Louis Séverin's chair.

"You!" said Joséphine to M. Louis, as Renée opened the door. "Barbier's offering you the wine."

Louis Séverin started violently. He always started a little when he was addressed.

"——no! No, thank you." He turned to Thérèse, who sat on his left. "I have given up wine altogether, on the advice of my doctor. I drink nothing now except Eau de Vichy, and a little Cognac sometimes, after dinner."

Madame Flandrecauld, on the other side of the table, nodded.

"M. Séverin has been forbidden by his doctor," she said at large, "to take any wine. He takes only Eau de Vichy, with sometimes a little Cognac for his stomach."

Eugène nodded to her politely. He always treated Mme Flandre-cauld with the utmost courtesy. Then, turning to Louis, he said:

"You don't want to believe what the doctors tell you, Louis, they're all humbugs. My man, that fellow Tischer, he's a perfect fool. He simply makes me worse. I can't imagine what I pay him for."

Thérèse leaned towards Louis and whispered: "He never does pay him."

"What?"

"M. Séverin did not quite hear," Madame Flandrecauld inter-posed, "he has become a little deaf on the left side lately."

"It's all right, it's all right, Mirabelle, I hear perfectly."

Eugène suddenly looked towards the door. "Ah, there you are!" Joséphine had stuck her thumb between his shoulder-blades, shouting in his ear. "She's come down, Master Pierre's wife." Eugène pushed back his chair and stood up.

"Ah, there you are, Renée. Louis, allow me to introduce you to my daughter-in-law. That rascal Pierre, he has had a pretty wife all these years and told us nothing about her. And this, Renée, is Madame Flandrecauld, my brother's secretary. Barbier—where are you?—get some soup for Madame Pierre."

Louis rose, wiped his mouth cautiously, bowed, and put on his pince-nez.

"Delighted, delighted. I remember your husband, Madame, when he was quite a small boy, quite a little tiny chap."

"He once offered," Eugène added, "to take Pierre into the rug-peddling business. But Pierre hadn't the brains for it. No, no, you want intellect for peddling rugs, you've got to be sharp or the shopkeepers do you down."

"M. Séverin," Mme Flandrecauld explained, "is one of the largest merchants of Oriental carpets and tapestry in France. M. Séverin . . ."

Raymond, who had been summoned to the luncheon and sat with his wife at the end of the table, beckoned to Renée to sit next him, signalling to Barbier to change the places.

"And talking of carpets," Eugène said, "how is business going, Louis? Pretty well, I imagine."

Louis started and put down his fork.

"No. No, at the present time trade is very difficult. The talk of war is having a very bad effect on trade."

"The conditions of trade are made more difficult," Mme Flandrecauld said, "when there is a talk of war."

"But Louis," Thérèse said wearily, "there has been a talk of war ever since I can remember. Surely there isn't any more now?"

"In Paris, yes."

"You must remember, Thérèse," said Eugène crisply, "that Louis belongs to Paris, to the great world. We here in Baulon, how are we poor provincials to know what is going on, what they are saying in Paris?"

Louis took up his fork again and stared at it obstinately. He put a piece of fish into his mouth, swallowed it, and said:

"There is a great deal of war-talk. In Paris and elsewhere."

"But do you mean to say," Eugène pursued, "that it upsets the fellows in Baghdad and places, makes them unwilling to part with their carpets? Of course I don't know anything about trade, it's all a mystery to me, I've never had anything to do with that sort of thing, but I should have thought that the Arabs in the bazaars wouldn't worry themselves to all that extent over a talk of war in Europe. Why, I remember——"

"The difficulty," Louis said patiently, "is not that of purchase. It is the difficulty of sale. People are unwilling to spend money freely when there are alarms. It is always like that." He ate another mouthful and continued, warming to his subject, "There is also the lack of good taste, that contributes to the decline in my business. In Paris, nowadays, the money is owned by people who do not understand the beauty of carpets, who cannot discriminate, who are satisfied with the cheap imitations that they make by machinery in the suburbs of Bordeaux, who can see no difference at all between that and a unique Khorassan. What is the use of my journeys, of my acquiring these priceless works of art, if no one has taste enough to buy them?" He stopped as if a chairman's bell had been rung, hitched his napkin another inch into his collar, and bent over his food.

"The taste in Paris," Mme Flandrecauld echoed, "is at present very bad."

Raymond, who had been moodily discussing a piece of bread, sat up.

"I agree," he said vehemently, "the taste in Paris is execrable. A man has only got to daub in the fashionable style, long white faces and décolleté gowns by Victor Leblondel, and everyone rushes to buy his pictures. If——"

"No one," his wife lisped sympathetically, "will buy Raymond's pictures. I think perhaps he does them too dark."

"At any rate, Louis," Thérèse said with unwonted good humour, "you have a very nice motor-car."

"Yes," Eugène agreed, "I saw it out of the window, it looked to me a very fine motor-car, it must have cost at least sixteen thousand francs."

Louis prodded the sauce Saint-Maurice-de-Robec at the edge of his plate as if hoping to find some more fish beneath it.

"It is worth while buying a good motor-car," he said thoughtfully, "if one uses it for business purposes. The machinery has a longer life, depreciation is less severe."

"The machinery of a good motor-car," Mme Flandrecauld agreed, "lasts a very long time."

"Raymond and I," Cécile said, turning her head so that Uncle Louis should see her green Regnier bonnet, "would very much like to have a motor-car."

Raymond choked and put down his wine.

"Cécile! What ever made you think of that? The motor-car is nothing but an emblem of bourgeois philistinism, an expensive and malodorous article the very sight of which——"

Thérèse had stiffened and coloured, reminding Eugène for a moment of her Chimène.

"Raymond!"

"Raymond!" Eugène thundered. "Are you so lacking in manners as not to realize that you are insulting your uncle? If you can't behave yourself at my table——"

"I understand," said Thérèse, with recovered calm, "that the Comte de St. Aignan has lately purchased a motor-car. . . ."

"Nearly all the aristocracy," Mme Flandrecauld said equably, "have motor-cars."

Renée turned to Louis.

"Do you think," she asked, "that there is any foundation for the war talk you speak of? Do you think there's really any likelihood——?"

Louis looked up sharply as if she had thrown a bread-pellet at his cheek. He wiped his mouth, coughed, and said seriously:

"No. No, I don't think so—for economic reasons. The Germans depend on their bankers, as we depend on ours. The bankers would never allow a war, you can take that as certain."

Mme Flandrecauld flicked with her napkin some pieces of potato that had fallen on to her bosom.

"The bankers," she said, "would never allow it."

"All the same," said Eugène, "the Rhine is not very wide. I, of course, am merely a retired military man, I don't know the ins and outs of things at all. But I should have thought that if a Prussian general wanted to see the scenery on the other side of |the Rhine, and a Jew banker tried to stop him—still, of course, my dear Louis, you know about these things, you go everywhere, you're a man of the world, they tell you things no doubt at the shop-doors in the Porte St. Martin——"

"The trouble," Thérèse said hastily, shooting a glance at her brother, "is that Baulon is too near the Rhine. A great deal too near."

"Yes," Eugène said, "there are not enough Jew bankers between Baulon and the Rhine."

"You would like, then, to go back to Paris?" Louis asked swiftly, glancing up and down again to see if his arrow had struck. Eugène was, after all, being unusually offensive to-day. . . .

"It would be nice if Raymond and I could live in Paris," Cécile said demurely.

"Yes," Raymond said dourly, "Paris would suit you." He looked at her with his painter's eye, at the doll's face, the ribbons on the Regnier bonnet for which the bill was still in his desk, the green embroidery on the gloves dangling from her wrists, the flounces on the organdie frock which would have suited the Bois de Boulogne in mid-July. "Yes, we could live very pleasantly in an attic studio in the Boul' Mich'."

"You know perfectly well, Raymond," she said seriously, "that nothing would persuade me to live in the Boul' Mich'."

"Then I shall have to get Renée to come and live with me."

Conquering her own rage, for fear of an outburst from Eugène, Thérèse said quietly:

"Only there are other places, Louis, besides Paris and Baulon. Of course, when we moved here, this was a good neighbour-hood——"

"Yes," Eugène said, "it was, if one remembers, a good neigh-bourhood. One met other people besides clerks and tradesmen. And now—you have noticed perhaps that one side of the Square has been pulled down, that a factory is going up there? It will be pleasant when the machinery is going, when all the houses round about are turned into tenements for the artisans. Already we are in the midst of a slum, I hear nothing all day but the bawling of children. I don't complain of that, the poor we have always with us, as well as the grocers and sausage-makers. But it will take a little time time to become accustomed to telling one's friends, 'You will find us between the Workers' Benefit Store and the Mechanics' Institute, just opposite the jam-factory.' "

Louis nodded gravely.

"Yes," he said, "the value of the property must already have been lowered. I have the record of what grandfather paid for it, I can't remember the exact figure—Mme Flandrecauld will look it up for me—but it was very considerable, I remember. It is, of course, a very large house. I have been thinking that a smaller one would suit your requirements much better."

"That's quite right," Joséphine said as she pushed his plate for dessert in front of him, "the house is much too big, its size is ridiculous."

"Joséphine!"

"We could do with a smaller one," Thérèse said, "if we had two good young women as servants, instead of a family."

"We could not in any case do with anything smaller," Eugène said decisively. "We constantly have people staying—there are yourself and Mme Flandrecauld, for instance, and now there is Pierre's family, requiring practically a floor to itself. Nonsense, Renée, why shouldn't my son's family be decently treated? You surely don't imagine, Louis—no, no, Thérèse, I'm only trying to put the matter reasonably, as I see it—you surely don't imagine that we could live in one of the new suburban houses which they are running up on the other side of the town? One has, after all, to maintain a certain minimum of dignity. And this house is not really expensive to run. Madeleine's a good housekeeper, she manages very well. I'm only just putting the thing as I see it. Of course I'm no business man, I'm only an old soldier, but I think we both have equally, in our different ways, a respect for the Séverin name. . . ."

"A smaller house," Mme Flandrecauld said didactically, "can be managed at a lower cost."

"And likewise," Raymond whispered to Renée, "a smaller secretary."

Joséphine, pushing the door open with her knee as she carried out a pile of plates, said over her shoulder: "It is a very damp house. Gaston would be much better in a dry one."

Louis covered his face with his napkin and dexterously picked his teeth. He took a phial from his pocket, shook out two minute tablets, put them into his wine-glass and watched the bubbles as they dissolved. Having drunk the solution, he wiped his moustache and beard with a sharp polishing movement of his napkin, dusted both cheeks, sucked his teeth, hiccoughed gently, and said "Ah." The question of the house, it was not convenient to pursue that at this moment. He smiled at Renée.

"And how is Pierre? You have good news of him? He was such a charming boy, and talented, I always saw that he had talent in him. He played the violin, if I remember, he had very good fingers."

"Pierre will never rise in rank," Eugène said sombrely, "he is not sufficiently methodical. He will be a good fighter when the time comes, all the Séverins are fighters—though it is otherwise with the Pichys—but he will never earn distinction as a peace-time soldier. . . . And now, if you will kindly excuse me, Mme Flandrecauld, I will go to my own room. Will you please have my coffee sent up, Thérèse? Thérèse will make you comfortable, Louis, and you, Madame, you must do just what you like, you must treat this as your own home, I want you always to regard this as your own home." He flicked his moustaches, rose stiffly, and made his way to the door, passing his hand from one chair-back to the next. "You must understand, Louis, that I am rather tired, I have been far from well for some time. Last night I had a very bad night, Madeleine was so restless. She kept wandering about my room, I suppose she had lost her spectacles. And that fathead Tischer woke me up at I don't know what hour to take my temperature. . . ."

★

After all, Thérèse thought, it was fortunate that Madeleine was out of the way; it was so much easier to do business without her. Madeleine kept the key of her desk hidden, but Thérèse had always known where it was, and how her papers were kept; Madeleine was so secretive that it was a matter of plain necessity, if only for business reasons, regularly to read her correspondence. She had Louis in Madeleine's little chair—he always liked that one—with his feet in the grate and the fire warming his tidy little trousers, a Sumatra cigar in his stumpy little hand. Madame Flandrecauld was on the sofa, nursing the brief-case which served her as purse and toilet-bag and secretary's-companion. As usual she had refused to make herself scarce. Mme Flandrecauld must be tired after the journey, Thérèse had suggested; no doubt she would like to go to her room for a little rest? Ah, no, not at all, Madame Flandrecauld was accustomed to much longer journeys, she constantly went with M. Séverin to Istanbul and to farther places; the motor-car, besides, went very smoothly on its pneumatic tyres, Madame Flandrecauld was always on duty, even at night M. Séverin sometimes had letters to dictate, she never needed a rest. Very well then,

89

if Louis wouldn't dismiss her, she must stay. Thérèse took the
key from a vase on the mantelpiece—how simple Madeleine Pichy
was!—opened the desk and took out two bundles tied with green
tape.

"I suppose, Louis, you'll want to know how things stand?"

He nodded with resignation, and she handed him the first
bundle.

"That goes back to April."

Louis untied the tape, licked his middle finger and ran through
the bills with great rapidity, Mme Flandrecauld repeating the
figures and jotting them down as he read them out. Thérèse
rummaged in the desk and brought out a black notebook.

"This is Barbier's wage-book. The last signature seems to be
on June the fourth."

Louis took the book. "Eighteen weeks at six eighty-five——"
he said.

"One twenty-three thirty," Mme Flandrecauld said at once.

He wrote in pencil at the bottom of the page, "123.30."

"And this is Tischer's," Thérèse said, passing over another
paper.

Louis dictated: "Eight hundred and forty-five francs . . . that's
a lot, Thérèse."

"Do you think so? About four francs a visit."

Louis shrugged his shoulders.

"That's all?"

"No, there's Lecours. He's getting rather restive."

Louis glanced at the paper. "Account rendered, F.1785.00."

"But, my dear Thérèse, this is preposterous."

Thérèse spread her hands.

"He is a lawyer," she said.

Louis adjusted his pince-nez and stared closely at the bill, as if
his concentrated gaze might shift the decimal point a place to the
left.

"Eugène will have to go into a smaller house," he said decisively.

"A smaller house could be managed at a lower cost," Mme
Flandrecauld said automatically.

Speaking very rapidly, Thérèse said: "It is as you like. I,
personally, do not care a brass farthing where I live, my life is all
over, to me it doesn't matter. Even if Eugène's affair were settled
it would be useless for me to go back to Paris, in Paris my name is
altogether forgotten, and I am too much a cripple to perform again.
'That is an old artist,' they would say, 'who is said once to have
been at the Français, it is the sister of that Colonel Séverin who has
lately had his title restored to him.' Pfui! For me Baulon is better,
I'm quite ready to live in one of the new suburban houses across

the river if that's what you think suitable. I, at least, recognize that we have no claim on you for anything better. But for my own part, I should have thought that the first thing was to get Eugène on to a less expensive lawyer. You can find cheaper lawyers, I imagine, even in Paris."

Louis tapped the nail of his little finger.

"I don't know. I have always thought Lecours a sound man—he and his father have always managed our affairs. His father had the reputation of possessing a very good head for business."

"My dear Louis, I haven't the least doubt that young Lecours is every bit as sound a man of business as his father before him. He has a new suit every time I see him, if that's any indication, and I'm told he drives the most perfectly matched pair of greys in the provinces. I should have thought that we wanted someone who knew less about business and more about law; that's to say, if we want to see Eugène on an officer's pension, which I suppose is the one and only thing we do want to see."

Louis looked at her sharply. He said, with mild indignation: "Pension? I've never thought anything about Eugène's pension. What we all want to see—what I, at least, want to see—is the stain removed from Eugène's honour."

"Oh, well, Louis, you can express it in a sentimental way if you like. Only I thought we were talking of money matters."

"It would certainly be useful," Mme Flandrecauld said, "if M. Eugène Séverin's pension could be restored, especially if the arrears were added."

"Well, what do you think of doing about Lecours?" Thérèse asked briskly.

Louis screwed his eyes and stared into the fire.

"I was thinking about Tischer," he said. "Eugène certainly looks very poorly—it's pitiful, when you think of the magnificent physique he used to have. It doesn't seem to me that Tischer is doing him the slightest good. I'd rather pay for a good doctor than——"

"If you knew Eugène half as well as I do," Thérèse retorted, "you'd realize that the person to do him good is a sound laywer. When that affair's cleared up you'll find that Tischer is at least as good as the rest of the tribe. At any rate he does not prescribe expensive pilules for the stomach. It would be quite a good idea, I think, if you were to call and see Lecours, taking his bill with you. It's so long since you saw him, it would be nice for you both to renew your acquaintance. Then you could run through the charges together, as business men do."

Louis shook his head. "I don't know, I think perhaps Eugène would think I was interfering in his affairs. I don't want to upset

Eugène, poor fellow; I'm afraid I made a remark at luncheon which may have hurt him, I was not really considering. . . ."

★

Slippers in hand, Joséphine crept away from the door. "Talk, talk, talk," she mumbled. It was always the same, they always talked like this, about money, about moving the family into a new house. Perhaps Barbier's wages would be paid, if M. Louis had any money left after paying that sharper Lecours, but that was all. They would never move, they would always be in this damp house, nothing would ever change; and if only they lived in a dry house little Gaston would be quite all right, it was simply the damp which made him funny, she had said that over and over again. In the dark kitchen, the ridiculous kitchen where you had to squeeze past Gaston's bed to get from the cooking stove to the sink, Barbier had just begun on the mountain of plates and dishes which covered the table. Gaston stood with a grey, fluffy cloth, idly rubbing the underside of a dessert plate with a steady circular motion, his long ungainly body bent beneath the low beam of the ceiling. "Hurry, Gaston!" Barbier was shouting. "Pull yourself together, boy, do you think we'll ever get done if you stroke those plates like a girl's shoulders!" Joséphine, coming up behind him, struck her fist in the small of his back. "What are you saying, Barbier, why can't you leave the poor little thing alone? He's doing his best." He looked at her dumbly; she had dropped into the fluid Gascon in which he could never follow her. "You're kind enough to Mme Pierre's children; why can't you show a little kindness to your own? The boy isn't a machine, poor mite, he can't get everything done at once. . . ."

"Gaston!"

That was the serrated voice of Madame Nadya, sounding from the top of the house.

"Quickly, Gaston, go and see what she wants. And don't tell her that M. Louis is here, or she may come down."

XIV

It took some time for Eugène Séverin, on his long legs grown feeble from disuse, to reach his room. He had got downstairs without much difficulty, and during luncheon, with a glass of Meursault inside him, he had felt in excellent case. But the upward journey proved more difficult than he had anticipated; he had to grasp the banisters firmly, to stop and recover at every stage.

Reaching his room, he did not lie down. He was faintly excited

92

by the experience of company, and something Louis had said had made him restless; he could not remember yet what it was, there had been more conversation, he had exerted himself to make a good showing; but Louis's remark was somewhere in his head, he would get hold of it before long. There was a bergère by the window, a presentation from the Mess at Bellegarde after his period as director of the musketry school. He sat down there and lit a cigar. You could see more from that position than from the bed: right into the little street which went down to the river. He could remember that street as he had seen it first, staying here as a boy with his grandparents; it had been a lane then, with chickens scrabbing for food and goats tied by the side, with nothing but the cottage of a peasant farmer on this side of the stone bridge. But the little houses had been built a long time, there were sheds with iron roofs and a polisher's workshop where the stable yard had been, those stables where, on a dreadful night, General Séverin's old mare Chérubine had been burnt to death; and now the little houses were going to come down, so Barbier told him, they were not considered suitable for the factory workers. "It might be better," he thought, "if Louis does force us to move." He remembered then what Louis had said: "You would like, then, to go back to Paris?" That was it, but he couldn't remember just how Louis had said it, or what anyone had replied. It stuck up like a lighthouse now, all the rest of the conversation had faded away, there was just that one remark of Louis's.

He must ask Madeleine—but Madeleine hadn't been there. Where was Madeleine? It was unlike her to leave him so long, surely she couldn't be sulking about something. He went into the next room, but she was not there. He stood for a moment before Hochard's portrait of himself in his colonel's full-dress uniform, the portrait which he would not allow Madeleine to hang anywhere else in the house. Then he went back and rang the bell sharply. Barbier came.

"Barbier, a fire."

"It is laid, sir."

"Yes, yes, light it. And you'd better close the shutters, it's getting cold. Light the gas first. Where is Madame?"

"She's upstairs, sir. She's still resting."

Eugène looked at his watch.

"She's been resting a long time. She isn't unwell, is she?"

"I don't know, sir. Mlle Thérèse said that she was not to be disturbed. Madame is very tired, Mlle Thérèse says."

Eugène clicked his tongue.

"Poor thing!" he said. "We're getting old, Barbier, Madame and I, we're both of us getting old."

Barbier limped to the window and fiddled with the shutters. He didn't know what to say. It came suddenly, as if by itself:

"It'll make you younger, sir, when that business"—he indicated, with a shake of his head, the direction of Paris—"when that affair is all cleared up; the lawyers and all that."

Eugène was surprised.

"You know about that? About what the lawyers are doing?"

"Well, sir, it's what we've always hoped——"

"We?"

"Joséphine and I, sir." He turned away; it was a terrible interview. "Oh, a letter, sir."

He brought it out from the back pocket of his trousers, the pocket where he had formerly kept the Company muster. He put it down on the table and started to go. Eugène glanced at the envelope; it was not a hand he immediately recognized.

"Oh, Barbier! Did you hear M. Louis say anything at luncheon about Paris?"

"About Paris? No, sir."

"Are you sure?"

"Quite sure."

"Oh . . . er—Barbier! Open that top drawer. Is my purse there? Yes, I'm sure it is, look underneath the handkerchiefs. Yes, that's it. Is there any money in it? How much?"

Barbier counted.

"Nineteen francs, sir. And four sous."

"Has Madame given you your wages lately?"

"Not quite lately."

"You ought to remind her, it's difficult for Madame to remember everything. What do we owe you—more than nineteen francs?"

"Rather more, sir. It comes now—I must think—it comes to——"

"Well, if it's more than nineteen I can't do it at once. You must remind me some other time. One minute! That light isn't burning properly, you've got it too high, turn it down a bit. That's better. Listen now. You were talking about Paris—the affairs the lawyers were dealing with. Now listen. I want you to tell me, I just want to be quite sure—you know the day it was all about, you know the day I mean?—yes, yes, Barbier, you needn't be awkward, you read about it in the papers, as all the tramps and beggars in Europe did. Now just think, try and remember clearly. You were there, at Viboire-les-Deux-Auberges, that day; yes, with Major Lancesseur's battalion. Yes, I know I've asked you before; I just want to refresh my memory, I want you to refresh yours. What kind of a day was it? Tell me that. What was the weather like? What? Come, Barbier, your memory can't be as bad as all that, surely it was at

94

Viboire that you got your leg like that! Now think, it was foggy wasn't it?"

"Yes, there was a mist, sir, a light mist."

"Barbier, you're not thinking, you're just answering automatically. Or perhaps you don't recognize a fog, perhaps you'd call any fog a light mist. Now think again. How far would you say that you could have seen on that day? Suppose there was a white flag stuck up in a hedge—or no, supposing someone had been standing on a hill waving a white flag; how far away could you have seen that?"

"I don't really know, sir. I suppose, about a kilometre, or say half, to be safe."

Eugène hammered his knee with impatience.

"I don't mean on an ordinary day, galoot, I mean on a foggy day, a day with a thick fog. Think now, do for God's sake stand still and think what I'm saying. You've just said that there was a fog—or mist, if you prefer that word—that day at Viboire. You remember that. What I'm asking you is: how far away could you have seen a white flag waving on that foggy day at Viboire? Just picture it and think. How far—on that day?"

"I don't know, sir."

"Come, Barbier, think! You'd say, surely, that you couldn't have seen it at more than a hundred metres."

"I expect that's right, sir."

"What do you mean?"

"I mean . . . I mean, sir, I couldn't have seen a flag above a hundred metres off."

"Right! That's all I wanted to know. I just wanted to know how you remembered that day. You'd better write down somewhere what you've just told me: 'I couldn't see anything at more than 100 metres.' Then you'll remember in case I can ask you again. . . . All right, that's all—but I want to-day's newspaper if you can find it. Send the boy up with it."

He examined the letter again; the postmark was Perigueux. Yes, the writing was vaguely familiar, but he could not identify it. He tore the envelope and saw the sprawling signature: Marcel Champenois; of course, yes, dear old Marcel, he should have remembered, the writing was such a picture of the man, hunched and stooping like a mushroom. '. . . in the neighbourhood of Baulon early next month, and it would be a great pleasure to me to visit you, if Madame Séverin will permit me to do so. . . .' That was delightful; Marcel was a dear fellow, so kind and so humorous, the best of all companions, a father to the Mess wherever he was quartered. He went across to his desk, found materials for writing, and began at once to reply: 'My dear Marcel: Thy letter has given me great pleasure. . . .' But his hand was very shaky, he had become unaccustomed to writing; he would leave it till Madeleine came and then dictate to her. He leant back again in the rocking-chair. The cigar had reached its best point; always, an inch or two from the smoking end, the leaf seemed to improve, as if the makers had done it specially to surprise and delight you. How long since he had seen Marcel? It was hard to place, time ran like one of the Marne roads that had scarcely any landmark, where you never knew how far you had got. His eye caught, through the blue smoke, an engraving by Duponchel; he remembered then, Marcel had admired that; it had been a present from Thérèse for his seventieth birthday, and he remembered saying to Marcel: 'Yes, that is quite new, Thérèse got it for me in Paris. I don't know what she paid, but it's good work, Thérèse is always a sound buyer.' That meant that it was over seven years ago; and yet, how clearly he could see Marcel's face, Marcel's weird body like an eagle's claw as he sat in that chair, the chair inlaid with ivory which had come from Bobroviza; how well he remembered the little school-girl chuckle with which Marcel always finished his stories. Yes, Marcel had been on his way to Chaumont, and had broken his journey to spend the night here. Eugéne thought again. No, Marcel had not stayed the night, he had gone on the same evening. Why was that?

Working hard, he gradually arranged the pieces shaken together in his memory. There had been a breeze; no, not a quarrel, no harshness on either side, but something like a misunderstanding. It was clearer now. They had talked quite easily of the old times, of the men they both knew; up to the time of the mobilization—nothing after that had been mentioned. And then Marcel had referred to someone—who was it? Yes, Grouard—and Eugène said, 'Grouard, I don't want to hear about him, he was near me at Viboire, he lied about it.' And what had Marcel said then? Nothing, as far as Eugène could remember. But he had become red and confused, he had shifted in his chair, he had changed the subject in a clumsy way—yes, he had started to speak of horses or something like that. The conversation had got all out of shape, and Marcel had left soon afterwards, saying that his business at Chaumont was urgent.

That, then, was the crowd Marcel belonged to: the sympathetic, tactful crowd, men who came to cheer him up from time to time, who changed the subject hastily if Viboire cropped up, men who were sorry for him because he had got what they thought he deserved. Marcel, with that deceptive friendliness, that social talent that he was so fond of displaying. . . . He took up the pen again and wrote boldly: 'My dear Champenois: Madame Séverin

96

and I are very much obliged by your courtesy in offering us the pleasure of a visit from you; but I regret that at the present time my medical advisers do not allow me to see visitors. I am, my dear Champenois . . .' Stamps? There were none in the drawer. The letter would have to wait, and Madeleine would stamp it when she came.

He thought of going to bed, but it would be a business to get his clothes off without Madeleine to help him. He started to open drawers and turn over the contents. What had Louis meant, was he meaning to be vicious when he said, 'You would like, then, to go back to Paris?' That, surely, was a most offensive remark, a most contemptible thing to say. Just because he had money, Louis thought he could say what he pleased. Fortunately there had been no outsiders present, no one but the family. Was that right? There was Louis himself, and his ridiculous mistress; Thérèse; Raymond and that Bon Marché wife of his; that was all. No, there was that other young woman, Pierre's wife—what was it?—Renée. It was odd that Pierre should have married a mulatto; the girl was certainly an octoroon, but pretty enough, well-spoken; and Pierre had shown something of the true Séverin by the exhibition of a live eccentricity in mating. After all, Pierre's grandfather had picked up, on one of his roving campaigns, a bizarre Ukrainian princess of goodness-knows-what descent. How curious Madeleine was, telling him nothing of the arrival of this Renée. Idly dragging papers from the drawers, he had them all over the desk now and covering his lap; old papers, documents and cuttings, that he looked at once in a while. A letter here from Troismoulins the publishers: Troismoulins could make no kind of offer; such an offer was, indeed, never made in such circumstances; but he would be glad to read, when it was ready, the work which M. Séverin contemplated on MacMahon's engagements; and if M. Séverin proposed also to furnish an account, written from his own standpoint, of the Affaire Séverin, in all its aspects, M. Troismoulins would read that composition with very particular interest. . . . That, of course, was an impudent suggestion, but he had always thought of completing the work on MacMahon, which he, as a soldier and student of tactics, could handle so much better than those retailers of history who never passed outside the gates of the Sorbonne. There might be a little money in it, if he kept a tight hand on this Troismoulins; it would be amusing to say to Louis one day, "If ever you're pinched at all, if ever you want to borrow a thousand francs or something like that at six-and-a-half, don't be frightened to come to me." And the main thing was that the book would be talked about, it would revive memories of the Injustice, it would stir up Paris. The work had made poor progress, his health had never been up to long stretches of industry. Here, in a bundle, were the notes he had made, the sketch-maps copied from those which Vatteblé had lent him. The books of reference were all together on one of the alcove shelves. Really it would not take very long to shake the thing together, and Raymond could do some polishing, he was supposed to be a writer. He felt inclined, being up and dressed, to start straight away, to make a table of chapter-headings. But the light was not very good—the desk was in the wrong position. It would be better to wait till the morning; and then Madeleine could do the actual writing, and help in looking up references, though Madeleine was not very intelligent. None of the Pichys, he reflected, had any intelligence. At present the desk was in a muddle; there were papers strewn everywhere, old letters, newspaper cuttings which drew his unwilling eyes to do the endless penance of reading them again. "Séverin is Cashiered: Verdict of the Court-Martial is Upheld: M. Bettencourt, in a Speech of Three Hours' Duration, proves Séverin's Cowardice: Séverin has left Paris by the Night Train." The night train, oh, God, that train! The cab with its blinds drawn rattling to the station; the long wait in a baggage-shed infected with the stench of the adjacent urinoir; the gendarmes hurrying him through the dense, quiet crowd; the faces, the foolish, gaping faces. . . . He crammed the papers back into the drawers and slammed them shut. Madeleine would have to sort out the desk, it badly wanted sorting.

★

Entering with his usual caution, Tischer was astonished to see M. Séverin dressed, asleep in his chair, with Angèle, his old retriever bitch, lying across his feet. He stood quite still, holding his breath, and for an instant he thought that Madame Séverin's instinct had been sounder than his knowledge. The position was so queer: the head fallen straight forward with the chin upon the manubrium, not lolling over; the arms dropped over the sides of the bergère, and twisted a little outward so that the palms showed, the metacarpus contracted and the fingers bent like claws; the mouth hideously open with a trickle of saliva running from the sagged lip; the eyes—Tischer saw them as he moved a step and caught the gaslight on them—the eyes wide open. It ran through Tischer's mind that once before he had seen a man looking just like that: Dupont the blackmailer, in the back-room of the house over-looking the Quai Vert: Dupont sitting in a chair rather like that one, fastened to it by a quartermaster's poniard through the stomach. But this was Séverin; Séverin who, when he lay in bed pale from inertia and lack of sunlight, yet made you look at him by the beauty of his blue eyes, had yet the gestures, in the slow nod of his head and the liquid movement of his fine hands, of the *noblesse d'épée.* Tischer said softly "M. Séverin!" and the eyes turned slowly upwards. "M. Séverin, are you ill?"

Eugène shook himself, like a dog coming out of the water, and pushed Angèle away with his foot; roughly, making her whimper. He said, quite coolly:

"You're supposed to be a doctor, you should know. What's the time? Oh, I thought it was later. My wife's still resting, I suppose. You've seen her?"

"Yes, she's still asleep."

"Still? Tell me, Tischer, there's nothing wrong with Madeleine, is there? Surely there's nothing wrong."

"She's very tired——"

"I don't mean that. She often seems tired, it's lethargy which belongs to her family. I mean, is there anything wrong?"

"I haven't examined Mme Séverin, not for a long time. I don't like that cough of hers——"

"Neither do I. It disturbs me at night, quite often. But I think it's more habit than anything—Madeleine's always been a strong woman—you can control a thing like a cough if you set your mind to it, it's just a nervous weakness. You've not been putting ideas in her head, have you, Tischer? It was you, I suppose, who made her go to bed?"

"No, M. Séverin, it was Mlle Thérèse who persuaded her. Madame Séverin had no sleep last night. . . . I think it would be well if you, also, got back into bed now. I am told that you went downstairs to-day. You should not have done that without my permission."

Eugène smiled.

"Damn your permission, Tischer. No, I'm not going back to bed yet, I never allow myself to be coddled. My brother Louis is here—did they tell you that? Yes, I had to go down and see him, I couldn't leave him to the womenfolk, a man like that gets irritated if he has nothing to listen to but women's chatter. He's talking, Louis is, about moving me out of this house; that will be whether you consider it advisable or not. You see, he owns this house, in a sense—he did some financial transaction with Lecours which got the title deeds into his hands. I never quite understood what happened—when a lawyer and a tradesman get together they have a witch's broth brewed in no time. Still, there you are, the world is run by financial gentlemen, it's no use an old soldier trying to interfere, one can't complain. A man can do what he likes with his own property, it's rational, I've always said that. It's one of the virtues of our nation, Tischer, that fundamentally we have a respect for property, the poor man's as well as the Jew's, which no one else in the world has. Yes, if Louis wants to turn us into the street he's got a right to, there's nothing to stop him, I shan't say a word against it. But when he talks of my going back to Paris, as he was talking at luncheon, then I say No. That was an impertinent suggestion; the man is too callous to understand a soldier's feelings. . . . Tell me, Tischer, when were you last in Paris? In August, yes, I remember, it was for some international beanfeast of medicos. I was glad to let you go, we all want a change of scene now and then, though we can't all have it. Tell me, Tischer, I ask you this as an old friend and you needn't feel shy of answering, tell me, old man, was there any talk—did you hear anything said, in the cafés, in the music-halls, about—about the Affaire Séverin? Don't be afraid to tell me, I want to know what people are saying now, what opinions are held nowadays in journalistic circles, among the politicians. Tell me frankly, old fellow. . . ."

Tischer took out the thermometer and held it towards the gas, making his customary "Hm-m."

"No, M. Séverin, I didn't hear anything."

"You didn't what? Put that thing away, Tischer, I can't bear seeing you juggle with that toy like a woman threading a needle. You say you didn't hear anything, no allusions, nothing at all about the matter? I should have thought, with this war talk there is in Paris nowadays, public attention concentrating on the army . . . but there, I'm afraid you live in rather a daydream, Tischer old fellow, you look half-asleep now. And I suppose you didn't go anywhere except the Salle de Concours, you didn't mix with anyone except Dutch apothecaries. You have your parts, Tischer, but for a reporter of Paris gossip I must go somewhere else. You didn't, I suppose, hear of this war talk either?"

"Yes, there was a great deal of wild talk in the cafés. But a delegate from Hanover, with whom I became intimate, told me that there was much misrepresentation here of Prussian feeling, and especially of the German Emperor, whom he knows to be a kindly man, though addicted to ostentation, which is a trait of the Hohenzollerns. I was very much interested to have his opinion."

"Yes, yes, opinions are always interesting, especially to the gullible. . . . And if all that comes, Tischer, you may find that France is looking for her old soldiers, for the men who have led troops into battle, not merely parade-ground officers. But look here, listen to me, there is to be no talk of pardon, do you understand? My arm is ready for service, I'm still not a weakling, but I will have no talk of gracious pardons from a corrupt gang of radical politicians. from provincial attorneys who strut about the Quai d'Orsay. The case must be re-tried, it must be acknowledged publicly that the whole previous trial was stage-managed by political tricksters.

That man Bettencourt, do you know who he was? He was the son of a horsedealer at Rennes, he started life serving in a millinery establishment, if someone had let off a rifle a few yards behind him he would have fallen down dead from fright. And he died, that draper's assistant, worth not less than half a million francs. Where did he get the money? Ah, who knows? No one can tell you, they kept very quiet about that in the newspapers. And what about Vaudilhac, the president of the Court? He died at the age of fifty, and worth half as much again as Bettencourt. These things are hard to explain, are they not? They look curious when you put them side by side, very curious indeed. It will be found, I fancy, when the time comes, that there is a very interesting meal for the readers of the newspapers, the people who are not accustomed to probe below the surface of things. No, I'm not going to bed. I may be ill, but a man lives on his courage, not on his physical resources. I'm ready, Tischer, when France asks for me; but France has got to ask, France must be on her knees, she will not find Eugène Séverin on his. Those people in Paris, that flock of sheep, reading their newspapers, believing everything, everything you tell them, they've got to learn, those people, they'll learn all in good time. Sit down, Tischer, for God's sake don't stand wobbling and goggling at me. What do you, you Parisians, care about justice as long as you can hear a noisy speech made by a draper from Rennes? 'It's all right,' you say, 'the soldiers will always be there to look after us when the time comes.' You'll find it different, next time you can't get any food in Paris, when you're watching your children starve, when people are dying in the streets. Yes, you've forgotten about that, you forgot very quickly. Very quickly indeed, my friend. 'It's all over now,' that's what you said, 'let's get some of the soldiers,' you said, 'and have them baited by the shopkeeper-attorneys from Poitiers and from Rennes. That will be a fine spectacle, we can all crowd into the courts and stink together and gape at the prisoner and nudge each other and point to his womenfolk on the floor of the Court.' *Canaille!* But it won't be like that next time, Tischer. It's going to be very different, next time. . . ."

*

Waiting at the end of the passage, Armand saw Dr. Tischer come out of his grandfather's room and go up to Mme Nadya. Dr. Tischer passed quite close, but did not notice him. He was dog-tired, Armand could see that; his hair, usually so tidy, was all over the place; he walked with his eyes half-closed and stumbled on the bottom step of the stairs. When he came down again Armand stood boldly in the middle of the stairs and said "Hullo!" Tischer said "Hullo, Armand!" but he didn't stop.

There was no one else to arrive to-day; the Abbé had come and, finding that Grand'mère was asleep, had gone away again; but Armand stayed in the corridor, because Sophie was sulky and Maman busy sewing; and he was terribly rewarded. It came upon him suddenly, as he stood with his mind floating far from his body to its proper kingdom, where all the streets, the floors and stairs of houses were composed of rollers on which you moved with a wooden tray beneath you, stirring your carriage to a huge momentum by the delicate adjustment of a horizontal rod which only Armand understood: the creak of a loose board, the faint smell of scorched linen, the feel of a presence. Turning slowly, hardly daring to look, he saw what he thought was a man approaching; a little man, not very much taller than himself, with short curls of grey hair stained with light brown, a wide, dark moustache, a beard of separate little tufts, brown-grey. The figure was oddly clad, in riding breeches which went into dirty white stockings and woollen slippers, the upper half in a laced bodice of green crash, a piece of red silk knotted roughly about the neck. It shuffled slowly forward, feeling for the way, not like a blind man but like one playing blind-man's-buff, the arms waving grotesquely. "Who's that? I know there's someone there." It was the cracked voice of an old man, but Armand realized then, from some quality in the voice, from something in the figure's shape and movement, that it was Madame Nadya herself. He crouched against the wall, terrified by the black eyes which looked straight ahead, unseeing. She lurched towards him, but he just escaped her wheeling hand. "Where are you?" she demanded, grasping forward, as if catching a mosquito. "Show me, whoever you are, where the stairs are, I don't want to fall. Gaston! Where is that boy? Blow, someone, call up the hounds, we'll have him." But she found the stairs by herself, and stumbled down, stopping at the turn to spit away the stump of her cigarette and pull out another from the pocket of her breeches. "Where is that besotted boy?" she grumbled, and screamed again: "Gaston!" Presently Armand heard Gaston coming up, not hurrying, and then his silly laugh. "What are you doing, you old fool, you've got no right to be down here, you'll fall down, you know you will." "Stop that, Gaston, or I'll have you whipped, Andryev Fyodorovitch will whip you, or I'll whip you myself. Where are you, you lazy brute, hold my hand, take me to my son's room or I'll tell Andryev Fyodorovitch to whip you this instant, I'll have the flesh taken off your spine. . . ." Armand never moved until Gaston had got the old woman right down to the first floor.

★

Eugène was still sitting by the window, with his eyes shut. He had not realized that Tischer had gone and he was still talking. Hearing the door open he looked up and saw Gaston.

"Oh, Gaston, have you got the newspaper? I told Barbier to send it up. Stop laughing, boy!"

"Why shouldn't he laugh? You're enough to set anyone laughing, sitting here moping all day long——"

"Mother! what are you doing down here? I don't want you down here——Gaston, take her away. Hold her, Gaston, don't let her come near me, I don't want her here."

But Mme Nadya was already in the room and feeling her way towards him, guided by his voice.

"You can go away, Gaston," she said. "Go away at once, I'll call when I want me to take me back. . . . What's all this nonsense, Eugène? That doctor creature says he can't control you, you won't go to bed, he can't stop you talking, he can't do anything with you. What's the matter with you, silly child? Here, light this for me, my hand isn't steady. Careful, Eugène, you're burning my nose, clumsy creature. No, I won't go away, I'm bored. I get no hunting nowadays. Why do we stay in this crazy country where there is no hunting and no dancing and no love-making and nothing but peevish respectability? Gaston, go away, do you hear, or I'll flog you."

"I want Madeleine," Eugène said sulkily. "She's left me alone all day. Why doesn't someone get her for me? I can't look after myself when I'm ill."

"That's no way to talk to me, Eugène, when I come all the way downstairs—a most ridiculous house, nothing but stairs—just to see you. What's the matter with you? You can't still be moping about that affair of Viboire, it's no good whining about that, most men lose their nerve once in a way."

He got up and caught her by the arm.

"What do you mean, you silly old woman? Are you so crazed now that you don't realize all that was a trumped-up affair. Do you mean——"

"Let go my arm, let go!" Like lightning she had the cigarette out of her mouth and was pressing the lighted end into his cheek, missing his right eye by half an inch. "That'll teach you to lay your hands on me, you cub. Where are you, damn you, let me just get where I can hit you." Shaking with fury to find that her fist struck empty air, she collapsed on the floor, kicking. Presently she laughed. "I might have known, they all told me: the Lord knows what sort of creatures you'll bear if you marry a Frenchman. You, Eugène, with your sulking about a crazy lawsuit, the Kuzaks would have had a short way with you, they'd have hunted you down with wolfhounds."

"Yes, and in France they have a short way with Ukrainian ladies who have returned to their native savagery. They lock them up in the Petite Maison and that's the end of the matter. I've never done it before, I've put up with you all these years——"

"Eugène!" she screamed. "What do you mean? Just because I'm an old woman, and gone rather blind, you're going to give me up, me that your father brought away from my lovely Ukraine to this pale and lifeless France where no one ever laughs or sings or cries, I who have borne three children, three French children, three insipid Séverins, I who——"

"It's the only thing to do," he said calmly, "if you go about telling people that the indignities I suffered at Paris were just. When an old woman gets to that stage you can't regard her as your mother, you regard her merely as a wild beast. But they'll be very kind to you in the Petite Maison. On Sundays and Festivals they'll let you out of the strait-jacket and allow you to smash things up in your cell. If you're very well behaved they may let you out in the recreation ground, where people can see you through the palings and get a little quiet pleasure from your antics. . . ."

Mme Nadya, in her perambulations, had come upon the bed; where she lay now on her front, her feet upon Eugène's pillow, her head turned towards her son as if she saw him. She said, with sudden resignation:

"Very well, I shall go to the Petite Maison, if that's what you wish. I should be happier there than where I am now, in this house that is nothing but a pile of staircases, surrounded by my children who bored me almost to infanticide when I suckled them and who have since become more insufferable every year. But I shan't go without a struggle, it would be a pity not to have some fun. That doctor who comes—what's his name? Tischer—he will no doubt be sent to take me away. And I shall go along very quietly till I get to the street, then I'll ask him to set my ribbon right for me, then bang! I'll give him such a bump in the belly with my knee that he'll double up. That ought to make noise enough to get the Square together. Then before anyone can stop me I'll take off all my clothes, every stitch. Then I shall run and climb up the tree in the middle of the Square, oh, yes, I remember where it is, well enough, and make a short speech: 'Ladies and Gentlemen, Bumpkins and Bastards, Frenchmen one and all, at the request of my son, Eugène Séverin, the half-baked young man you see up at the window there, who is famous for having run away from the Prussians at Viboire-les-Deux-Auberges, I propose to retire now to the Petite Maison. Good day, Ladies and Gentlemen!' It will be a most interesting ceremony, of a slightly Ukrainian character."

Eugène went to the door and opened it. "If you think you can find your way to the tree in the middle of the Square, then it can't be difficult for you to find your way to your own room . . . but you'd better not let Thérèse catch you or you'll get a scolding."

She wriggled on to the floor, laughing, steered herself half-way to the door, and stopped.

"I like you when you're like that, Eugène, I know exactly what your face looks like now, very long and very French, stubborn and dignified. I can remember your father looking like that, he was a clothes-prop. 'Nadya, my dear, we do not behave like that in civilized countries, we do not laugh and point our fingers at our hostesses. You must remember, Nadya, my dear, ahem ahem ahem, that you are in Paris now. Paris is quite different from Bobroviza.' You know, Eugène, you're the spit of your father: so genteel, so courtly, so exactly like a waxwork."

She was edging her way, with hands stretched forward, towards the door, which he still held open for her. Just as she reached it her finger touched his sleeve. In an instant she had turned and landed a blow on his face with the knot of her scarf. She went out into the corridor, chuckling, and he slammed the door behind her.

He stood for a moment raging, tempted to go after her. But his legs were groggy, he was tired out and broken. First of all Louis saying that at lunch, then Tischer behaving so badly, and on top of that his mother, whom he had not seen for weeks, coming specially to torment him. No one thought, no one ever realized, what he went through. He started again on the dreary course of reminiscence, right back at Viboire. But that was confused now, he could no longer remember what the field had looked like, what time of day the incident had occurred. He could remember clearly the orderly standing that evening at the door of his quarters in the farmhouse; "General Guéroult is in the village, sir, at the priest's house. He begs you to wait on him at your very early convenience"; nothing of that interview except Guéroult's last words: "Until then, Colonel, I must ask you to consider yourself as if under arrest." Guéroult, a little tiny man, with a Marseillais accent— Eugène could remember his voice but nothing more. Of the court-martial, nothing at all; only the moment, just afterwards, when he had stood in the courtyard of the auberge at Liseuil. That was still as clear as yesterday: his hand wobbling a little as he lit a cigarette, the smell of kindled tobacco breaking into the pleasant country odour from the fumier close by; a fresh morning wind bringing faintly the scent of pasture, reminding him of a holiday at Bobroviza; the crumpled wall of the auberge, a gate standing open, a line of poplars; the feeling, rising from his stomach to his head: *all over, everything finished, dispossessed of all this.* He could feel it now, the pain he had carried since then, like a little hard thing, a walnut or a chip of wood, just below his ribs; a root, from which the memory sprang up fresh like a juggler's oak-tree. He lay down on his face, on the bed where Nadya had been, sobbing.

She had stayed listening outside the door, and presently she came back, opening the door so softly that he did not hear and started when she touched him. But he knew by the scorched smell that it was she.

"Eugène is tired," she said, "Eugène ought to go to bed." She felt for the buttons of his jacket and undid them, took the pin out of his stock. "Eugène is tired," she repeated, her hand on his forehead. "Poor Eugène."

*

Madame Eugène was astonished to find, when a fit of coughing woke her, that it was six o'clock. It was extraordinary that she could have slept so long, and very wrong of Thérèse not to have roused her. She put on her dress and shoes, and without stopping to bathe her face or set her hair she went down to Eugène's room. Eugène was asleep. The gas was on, and there was a smell of tobacco; that meant that someone had been in, and she remembered that in a moment when she had come near consciousness, before turning over and going to sleep again, she had fancied that she heard Louis's voice. It was plain now that Louis had been here; he must have sat some time, talking to Eugène; and no doubt Thérèse had given him permission. She was angry, not only with Thérèse, and Louis, but with herself for yielding to persuasion and leaving Eugène unguarded on this day when he most needed her protection. His face was very white now; probably his temperature had fallen below normal, but she dared not wake him to try it. And where was Dr. Tischer. He should have done something, have seen that Eugène was undisturbed, have kept watch till she returned. He had failed her very badly. She turned down the gas and brought a chair to the bedside, where she sat with her hand resting lightly on Eugène's shoulder; she listened to his breathing, trying to judge if it were regular. His head had slipped down rather low—it had been properly supported when she left him this morning. Presently, when she was sure he slept soundly, she would raise his head and move the pillow so that it rested higher.

XV

MADAME EUGÈNE had hardly believed that Dr. Tischer was serious when, on the second day after the critical attack, he suggested that Eugène should dress and come downstairs for a little while.

But the day was very fine, Eugène himself was acquiescent, even eager. With Dr. Tischer's help she shaved and dressed him: leaning on their arms, Eugène made his way slowly along the corridor. Madeleine had had a fire lighted in one of the rooms which faced back; the sight of the building operations, she thought, would upset Eugène; but he insisted—he was quite gay this morning—that he should sit in the drawing-room, near the window, where he could watch the young women in the Square, where he could see a little life going on. It would do no harm, Tischer said, a change of scene would help to take M. Séverin out of himself; he, speaking with every professional caution, was ready to recommend that M. Séverin be placed in the drawing-room. There, with some misgivings, Madame Eugène left him, propped with many pillows and his knees protected by a rug, when she went to do the day's shopping.

Directly she had gone, Eugène rang for Barbier.

"Tell me, Barbier, where is M. Louis?"

"He is upstairs with Mme Flandrecauld."

"Doing what?"

"When I took him his Eau de Vichy—that was ten minutes ago —he was reading out letters to Mme Flandrecauld. M. Louis had a large post this morning."

"Which room had he got? Which way does it face?"

"The usual room, Monsieur, your old one on the second floor. It faces back."

"Ah, yes, he should be comfortable there, I like M. Louis always to be comfortable. One moment, Barbier: do you happen to know where M. Louis's driver is lodging?"

"I can't be sure, Monsieur, but I recommended him Veuve Tautireau's house in the rue des Suisses. That's just round the corner. She usually has one room at one-fifty."

"Tautireau? Ah, I remember, yes, the little colour shop. That's not very far, that was quite a sensible idea, Barbier. It's convenient for M. Louis to have his driver close by. Now I want you to send a message for me—no, perhaps you had better go yourself —to say that he is to bring round the motor-car. Say that M. Louis wants the motor-car as soon as possible. You understand? But first of all, I have a message for Madame Pierre. Tell her that M. Séverin is going into the town this morning to do a little shopping, and would be delighted to have the pleasure of her company, if she could be ready in about a quarter of an hour. What do you say? That's no business of yours, Barbier. Do what I tell you, hurry!"

In twenty minutes Renée was down. She had, in the interval, set Armand to do sums and Sophie at her wool-work; had finished the washing, made the beds, tidied the bedroom; changed her dress and done her hair again, put on different stockings and shoes. It was a nuisance; she had meant to take the children to the park, this lovely morning; but she did not care to refuse an invitation from Pierre's father, Pierre would not wish it. He was waiting for her standing by the window, holding his watch. "Five minutes late," he said, "that's not right, for a soldier's wife." But he smiled when she started to apologize. "Never mind, never mind, I'm used to it. I've never known a pretty woman yet who didn't keep me waiting, it's the old dodge, you pass it from one generation to the next. Come, I shall have to lean on your shoulder just to get me downstairs—I won't lean heavily. I've not been about for a long time, you know. But I'm giving my wife the slip this morning."

"But won't Mme Séverin be anxious when she finds you gone?"

"Possibly." His weight on her shoulder was considerable. "But she gave me the slip yesterday. And there are dodges known to both sides."

The motor-car was there at the door. Eugène, acknowledging the driver's salute, said: "M. Louis has kindly lent me the motor-car for this morning. Renée, would you like to have the awning down? On a day like this it would be pleasant I think. Yes, driver, Madame would like the awning to be lowered."

He stood very stiffly on the pavement, like a public figure about to lay a foundation-stone, while the driver got out his spanners, unfastened, folded, and strapped the hood. He bowed slightly to a man who stopped to stare at him. Holding the side of the motor-car, he assisted Renée to enter. "And now, driver, will you take us to Peulevey's establishment in the rue de Fontenelle? (My grandmother, Renée, always dealt there.) Yes, yes, it is near the centre of the town." Renée, looking up to her own window, called, "Good-bye, Armand, good-bye, Sophie!" Eugène glanced upwards. "Ah, yes, your children. . . . I myself would always prefer a carriage, these engined vehicles seem to me so noisy and undignified. But my brother Louis, he must always have the most expensive thing he can find. And why not, if it gives him pleasure? For those who have not so much money, good taste has to be the consolation."

Renée was aware, as they drove slowly along the Boulevard Maréchal Soult, that people were staring; not only at the motor-car, of which the grey sides and the brass lamps were magnificently polished, but especially at M. Séverin, who seemed to accept their curiosity with equanimity. He sat very stiffly in his tight corsets, like a footman on the box, his face set as if he were about to encounter some ordeal, the Séverin lips pressed tight together, his head turned a little towards Renée and nodding to her gravely when she spoke; giving occasionally a little smile, in which she could see Pierre. She suffered a sudden pain, returning for an instant to an old experience: the time when she had driven with Pierre, in the ridiculous buggy that dear Major Foursin had lent them, from the consulate at Rabat. 'Your husband,' Georges Pérodeau had said afterwards, 'was wearing his aristocrat-in-tumbril expression; oh, but I assure you, Renée, he had never before looked quite so handsome.' And as if he were determined that the scene should be played, with every detail right, M. Séverin asked; "You are not cold, my dear? If you feel cold I will tell the driver to re-erect the awning."

The figure of M. Séverin, his height, his gravity, the perfection of his grey suit, was sufficient to bring M. Peulevey at once from a far corner when he entered the shop. "I want to buy a gown for this lady," Eugène said seriously, and followed M. Peulevey at a funeral march upstairs. Refusing the low chair that was offered him, he sat on a high one as if on a shooting-stick, his hands and his kid gloves resting on top of his cane. "It is for Madame to choose," he said, "I insist only that it be in the right style for a young lady, the modern style, you understand, and the colour gay."

"Parfaitement, Monsieur. Our Mademoiselle Earôt, who returned from Paris only last week, after examining the styles at the salons of the leading designers. . . . Mademoiselle Earôt!"

Eugène said sombrely, "You can't expect, my dear, to get Paris clothes at a place like Baulon. But you can be sure that anything they give you is in good taste, if you come here with me. My grandmother always bought her clothes here, when she was at Baulon; they wouldn't sell me anything that was not in good taste."

Renée had had no previous chance of interrupting.

"But I didn't realize, M. Séverin, that we were coming to buy anything for me. I really have all the clothes I require. . . ." It was difficult, she could not be quite certain if he meant to pay himself, and until another cheque came from Pierre she was very short. "I really don't think . . ."

But Mlle Earôt was already before them, douching them with her smile.

"Madame requires an evening gown? Or something for afternoon wear? We have some new styles which I have just brought back from the rue de la Paix, very elegant and distinctive for afternoon wear. . . ."

"We will start with an evening gown," Eugène said decisively.

Mlle Earôt said: "Parfaitement, with evening gowns," her voice lingering on 'soir' and softening to a sigh as if she cherished its perfume. She looked searchingly at Renée, like a portraitist making the preliminary survey of his model, her lips pressed together almost fiercely. At last the inspiration: "Ah!" sharply, inside her throat: twenty inspirations. Mlle Earôt was unable to cope with the windfall, she called "Vertue! Céleste!" she almost pushed her satellites towards the wardrobes. From the maze of alleys between the stands Céleste and Vertue tripped back at a canter, each with her right arm outstretched and with half a dozen dresses hanging from the loops beneath her sleeve. Mlle Earôt examined the dresses attentively, but they failed to match her inspiration. She shook her head, "Non, non, non . . . ah!" She took a dress of green velvet from one of Vertue's loops, raised it high, pendant on her little finger; swung it gently to make the skirt flow, twisted it about, took it to the window, brought it back with a dreamy look in her eyes, held it aloft, said reverently: "Daligault."

Renée looked at the dress in silence, Eugène at Renée.

"The sophisticated buttons at the waist," Mlle Earôt whispered, "the mysterious ruché collar." She beckoned for Céleste to light the gas mantle, she turned the dress through thirty degrees. "There, Madame will see the line now, the line from shoulder to hip. That is it, that is what all Paris is talking about, only Daligault could have created that line. . . . One moment! Monsieur must not trouble himself to move. There, you will see now, there, there you have it, the Daligault line, the achievement that crowns Daligault's work. . . ."

"I don't care for that colour," Eugène said. He turned to Renée. "You yourself?"

She said: "Well, no, perhaps . . ."

"But of course!" Mlle Earôt said. "It is not the right colour for Madame. You must see, Vertue, surely, that Madame could not wear this colour, Madame's complexion would be rendered almost —?—almost of no distinction. And the dress is not suitable, besides, to Madame's figure. It is an older woman's dress, it is not-at-all-at-all the dress for Madame. I have shown it you only so that you may see the tendency in taste, the greater economy in the bust that is being chosen to-day. Vertue! Céleste!"

Eugène murmured: "So that is what they talk about in the Paris cafés."

"Perhaps," Renée said diffidently, "something in red. . . ."

Mlle Earôt smiled at her as at a pupil who has arrived promptly at the right answer.

"But of course! Cerise is Madame's colour, directly I saw Madame I thought: 'There, at last, we have the distinction that is necessary for wearing the cerise evening gown which I obtained from Leloutre last week.' You know, perhaps, that we have a special connection with Leloutre, M. Paul always allows me to see his models before the Paris buyers. 'I will give you the first view, Mlle Earôt, the very first,' M. Paul says, 'but I make it a condition that you give my models only to those who have the distinction required for wearing them.' Ah, there you have the real artist! Céleste! The Leloutre in cerise."

They came, at last, to a dress which Eugène liked. Renée must try it on. Reappearing from behind the curtain which Vertue discreetly opened, Renée stood and revolved before Eugène, while Céleste and Vertue manœuvred the giant wheeled mirrors into close formation. The dress was a pretty one, Renée herself was satisfied. "It is pretty, yes," Mlle Earôt agreed, "but it would be a still greater pleasure, if Madame would not mind the trouble, to see Madame in this beautiful gown by Chénot. . . ." For the Chénot a little more light was required. Céleste brought the ladder and lit another mantle. But Madame must see the left side of the dress, and Vertue, struggling to hide her tears and the appalling cold from which she was suffering, once more shifted the mirrors. "Certainly Madame looks well in it," Mlle Earôt said pensively, "it is a lovely gown, I told M. Chénot that it was worthy of him. . . . But, of course, if Madame would like to see herself in a gown of special distinction, one which is really worthy of her figure and colouring—Céleste, the Dufayel!" Eugène, now utterly confused, still nodded and smiled. "Yes yes, it's a pretty dress, that one. I liked the other one too, the red one." In the end it was the Dufayel. Mlle Earôt, standing back a little with her head tilted, had gasped. Never, never before had she seen such loveliness. Before Madame had put it on, the gown had been nothing special, merely a tour-de-force of Dufayel's genius. . . .

"But surely it's very expensive?" Renée said. Her last evening dress, which she had made herself from genoa fabric bought at Congerisque, had cost thirty-four francs.

"For a Dufayel," Mlle Earôt said blandly, with an oblique inquiring glance at Eugène, "not at all expensive."

"To be exact——?" Eugéne inquired. "What? Three hundred and twenty? Good gracious! It's not a very big dress."

At least it was evident to Renée that he intended to pay.

"Oh, that's impossible," she said quickly, "that's absolutely impossible. Some of the other ones were very pretty. . . ."

"Nonsense!" Eugène answered, delighted with his morning. "We don't kill a pig every day. Let's see some afternoon gowns now."

The afternoon gown, reached after four tries, was a slight and becoming frock of Rouillard's in fawn morocain; ninety-five. They went to a higher floor, passing through the pleasant smell of new linen, and chose a hat which would go very becomingly with the afternoon dress. It was a little dearer than the dress; one hundred and four. "But really, M. Séverin, that is too much." "Nonsense, my dear, we don't kill a pig every day." Then to the ground floor, shoes, forty-nine fifty.

"All the parcels are to be put together," Eugène explained to the girl who had sold the shoes. "They can all be sent together; there is a dress to be slightly altered, but the other things can wait for it. Good day, Mademoiselle."

He had almost reached the door before she stopped him.

"Pardon, Monsieur, but I have not the name."

Eugène stared at her curiously.

"You have not . . . but how long, Mademoiselle, have you been in Baulon?"

She stammered: "All my life, Monsieur, I was born in Baulon."

"And you don't know who I am?"

"No, Monsieur."

He stood regarding her intently, taking no notice of her changed colour, which Renée's face reflected.

"To me, Mademoiselle, it seems unwise to spend the whole of one's life in a place—how old are you? nineteen?—to spend nineteen years in the same place without getting to know who people are. Especially in work such as yours. Have the goodness, please, to summon M. Peulevey for me."

Biting her lip, the girl went away; and returned presently with M. Peulevey. M. Peulevey gave his solicitor's smile.

"There is some little difficulty, Monsieur?"

"I have spent most of the morning in your establishment," Eugène said slowly. "I have bought two or three dresses, expensive dresses—hat—shoes. I have told the young lady here that everything is to be collected and delivered together. . . ."

"But of course, Monsieur, that is understood, there is no difficulty, no difficulty whatever, your instructions will be carried out."

Eugène said "Thank you," looked hard at the shoe girl, and went to the door.

"We have the address, of course?" M. Peulevey added.

"It is the same address. I have not removed."

"Of course not. No. The same address. We have it no doubt in our books. You have, of course, an account with us—for the moment the name has escaped me——"

"The name?" Eugène put his hand to his forehead as if he himself had forgotten, as if his head was aching and he could not see quite clearly.

Renée said quietly: "It is M. Séverin."

"Of course!" M. Peulevey said gratefully. "Of course, yes. . . . . It is spelt, I think, with a C . . . . ?"

Eugène banged his cane on the floor.

"May I ask how old you are, Monsieur——?"

"I am sixty-nine, Monsieur."

"And do you ever read a newspaper? Have you read any history? Have you, by any chance, ever heard of Spicheren? Do you ever read anything at all?"

It took M. Peulevey just two seconds to collect himself.

"But—Monsieur, I apologize, indeed I do apologize. It is some time since—since I myself, personally, have had the pleasure of seeing you. I heard—someone told me—I fancied that someone had seen it in the newspaper, that you were abroad for a few weeks, and so naturally I was not expecting to see you, or indeed Madame; whose face, of course, I know as well as my own. You will realize how it is, one is constantly misled by the newspapers, which fill their columns by attaching falsehoods to any name that is well known to the public. . . . I can only repeat my apology, my profound apology. . . . Mlle Godron, since you were too scatter-brained to tell me who it was that wished to see me, it would be wise perhaps for you to write down the address. Madame will perhaps be kind enough to tell you what it is. . . . I must repeat, Monsieur . . ."

But Eugène was moody on the way home, his expression sterner, his eyes directed on the driver's head. He said, as they turned out of the rue de Fontenelle, "I didn't know that Madeleine dealt with Peulevey." Nothing else, until they reached the place Talleyrand.

Handing her down, he said abruptly, interrupting her shy thanks:

"I must see your children, Renée. Not now, I'm too tired. But soon. I want to see the boy—the girl I don't so much mind about —I want to see if the boy's got nerve, got courage. I want to see if he's a proper Séverin."

*

Hearing the rap of a bony knuckle on the door, Louis Séverin stopped dictating and anxiously looked up. He knew the knock.

"Come in. . . . But, Thérèse, it is surely not half-past ten yet?"

"It is twenty-seven minutes past," Mme Flandrecauld informed him.

"And it will be gone half-past by the time you're ready," Thérèse said.

"But I'm not half-way through my letters——"

"M. Séverin has to deal with some very important letters——"

"Nonsense, Louis. You said half-past ten."

Louis gave up the struggle and rang for Barbier.

"Barbier, you know where my driver is lodging. Will you send a message to him, please, that he is to bring the motor-car immediately."

"But he has not come back yet, M. Louis."

"Not come back?"

"No, M. Louis, he has driven off the motor-car with the Colonel and with Madame Pierre."

★

"That is Mlle Séverin?" Lecours asked the clerk. "Is she by herself."

"No, she is with M. Louis Séverin and with a Mme Flandrecauld."

Lecours raised his eyebrows.

"All right, Couette, bring them in. Tell Petin, four glasses."

He opened the double drawer of his desk and took out half a dozen files to spread on the desk; M. Louis Séverin, he reflected, was a business man of the old school, and would like to see a desk well covered. Bowing, he eyed Thérèse as she came in, measuring her battle strength. On the last occasion he could hardly have claimed the victory; but here, surrounded by his own things, the leather padded desk-chair, the filing cabinets, the high-collared clerks, the matured and legal odour of his chamber, he felt like a knight remounted. "Another chair, Petin . . . such a long time, M. Séverin . . . Mme Flandrecauld, it is a pleasure to make your acquaintance. You will take a glass of Madère, Mlle Séverin? . . . We are living in anxious times, are we not? It is hard to remain calm, as all of us should, when there is so much talk of war. Certainly the position, as I understand it, looks far from propitious. For myself, though there are no doubt decent men and women on the other side of the Rhine, I cannot trust them. . . ."

"How late are we, M. Lecours?" Thérèse asked bluntly. "Ten minutes, that's not too bad. We should have been in time but we had to come by the tramway, my brother had mislaid his motor-car."

Lecours smiled.

"I wish that all my clients were equally punctual."

Thérèse nodded.

"I sympathize with you, M. Lecours. It is very difficult to get people to hurry. Sometimes I find it quite impossible to make people do what I want quickly; though I find very often that I get what I want sooner by saying that I may refuse to pay."

Lecours nodded back.

"Yes, yes, I find the same thing myself, the difficulty of making people hurry. Particularly, as it happens, certain people in Paris. It is impossible to make some Parisians hurry. . . . And what do you think, M. Séverin, about the possibility of war in the near future?"

"M. Séverin," said Mme Flandrecauld, "does not regard it as likely."

"I should like to hear, M. Séverin, what you think of your brother's present condition? I was sorry to hear, on my last visit——"

Quickly, but in her quietest voice, Thérèse said: "That reminds me, M. Lecours, I do not think we have yet received a note of your charges for that visit. Can you——"

Lecours was a little surprised. His clients as a rule, and ladies particularly——

"? . . . No, no, of course, Mlle Séverin, our note covering that visit would not be reaching you yet, certainly not before the end of the month. It is customary, it has always been customary with this partnership——"

"Of course, yes, that is quite understood. It was just that I did not remember seeing that visit mentioned in any of the notes that we have with us—it is those that my brother has come to discuss with you."

Louis said hastily: "Incidentally, Thérèse, incidentally. My intention is to discuss things generally with M. Lecours, and one or two of the items in M. Lecours's notes may be touched upon in the course of our conversation."

"M. Séverin," Mme Flandrecauld told Lecours, "wishes to have a general discussion."

Thérèse said rapidly: "You must understand, M. Lecours, that my brother is a business man, and naturally views things from a business standpoint——"

"That I quite appreciate, and if I may say so——"

"By which I mean that before signing a cheque he requires to know, in the most precise detail, just what he is paying for. You will agree, I think, that that is a reasonable approach. I myself, for example, in the old days, never received any salary in advance of performances, even when I dressed on the lower floor——"

"That," Lecours agreed, "is the principle of all business transactions; one does not pay until the goods are delivered or the service rendered. Except in the case of certain payments such as premiums for insurance, and in the case of investment generally, when one pays in respect of advantages expected to accrue later. When, for example, you invest in mining stock, you are given a piece of paper; about so big; you cannot eat it or drink it, you cannot make a dress out of it, except perhaps for one of the young danseuses at the Auberge des Folies, if I may, without indiscretion, allude to a branch of your profession, Mlle Séverin, which you, I have no doubt——"

Mme Flandrecauld could not restrain herself.

"The value of a share certificate," she told Thérèse, "is that it guarantees the right of the holder to draw dividends from the profits of the concern in which he has invested. Without such a certificate——"

Thérèse had drawn her chair closer to Lecours's desk.

"You will agree, I think, M. Lecours, that if there appears to be no likelihood, no likelihood at all, of one's expectations being realized, one is entitled to close the account. That, surely, would be the business view."

For a moment Lecours stared at the cuticle which he had been steadily pressing. Then:

"Let us take the case of a doctor, who undertakes, as far as he is able, to restore his patient's health. He can, of course, make no definite promise——"

"No," Thérèse said, "let us take a short cut, let us take the case of a solicitor. We have no doubt at all, M. Séverin and I, that you have done what you can in the interests of my elder brother. We are not disputing your integrity, that must be understood. We are, however, dissatisfied with the results obtained, we find the charges involved—very high, and we are considering the question of asking another solicitor to handle the business for us. I do not think you can raise any objection. It is rational, if one does not like the bill, to go to another shop. In Paris, when people did not like my performances, when they found the prices of stalls too high, they went to another theatre and sought entertainment from another artist. I had no quarrel, I had always the audiences I required. . . ."

"One minute, Thérèse!" Louis had a respect for lawyers, he had become increasingly uncomfortable. "My sister, M. Lecours, has expressed herself very differently from the way I should have chosen. She has approached the matter entirely according to her own conception. My purpose in making this visit, you must understand, is to have from you a first-hand account of the progress made up to the present time in the prosecution of my brother's unhappy case. I was going to ask you what was the latest news from your Paris correspondents——"

"My dear Louis, I've asked M. Lecours that a hundred times. M. Lecours has no new information for us, he had nothing to say when we discussed the affair at his recent visit."

She took up her wine and drained the glass.

Lecours turned to Louis.

"From Paris, frankly, we have no news at all to our advantage."

Thérèse put down the glass with a clink.

"Exactly."

There were three seconds of silence.

Lecours said deliberately: "I assume, of course, that M. Eugène Séverin and Mme Séverin are agreed that the case should be transferred to the hands of another solicitor?"

"My brother Louis," Thérèse said, "has agreed to pay your account for services rendered up to this date. If further services are rendered, it will be for my brother Eugène to settle the account."

She was looking straight at the bridge of Lecours's nose; instinctively she scraped the pad of her forefinger on his desk as if she were counting out notes. Lecours understood. He glanced inquiringly at Louis. How easy, if only he could have Louis to himself: two men who were versed in affairs, who understood how things were ordered, who could drive bargains and arrive at satisfactory conclusions without a moment's awkwardness, incorporating so much in a nod or a shrug. Louis moistened his lips. Thérèse, aware that the strands of her hawser were snapping, said swiftly:

"I forget the exact total of M. Lecours's present account?"

Mme Flandrecauld spat like a squeezed orange: "Dix-sept-cent-quatrevingt-cinq."

Louis coughed. He never cared for the sound of figures, he would rather see them written down; he liked still better the familiar method that extended from the Sodi Bazaar at Meshidisar to the wholesale houses in the rue Ganterie: two, three figures on the counter, and a questioning glance, the thumb crooked for fifty. Lecours plucked the loose flesh of his neck; to him the mention of figures aloud was practically salacious. Thérèse, without any modesty, repeated:

"Ah yes, seventeen-eighty-five," and added, addressing confidentially a portrait of old Jacob Lecours above his son's head, "a lot of money."

"I was wondering," Louis said slowly, "if perhaps we might arrive at some arrangement with regard to the—financial side of our relationship; a relationship, M. Lecours, which has been a long and happy one; we might, perhaps, make an agreement—merely, of course, a verbal agreement—by which your good offices in connection with this particular affair, the work that still has to be done, is taken all together—over a period, let us say, of twelve or twenty-four months—and tied to a figure which would be equally agreeable to yourself and to me. I am sure it would not be difficult——"

"M. Séverin," Mme Flandrecauld summarized, "would like you to quote a fixed annual charge."

The vulgarity of M. Séverin's proposal tightened all the muscles in Lecours's anatomy. He rang his bell. "Couette, I shall want all the files relating to the case of M. Eugène Séverin, yes, all of them." When the files came he untied the first and bent over the papers, examining each one with attention. He said without looking up:

"You will wish me, no doubt, to communicate direct with my successor when he is appointed? I trust that he will be more successful than I." He was still turning the leaves industriously. "It is not a very easy case. Me. Bellefontaine, in Paris, whenever I write, replies by asking what extra material I have to give him. And I have to reply: none—that M. Séverin does not remember the names of those who would be useful witnesses, that those whose names he does remember are not anywhere to be found, that we have nothing whatever to go on except M. Séverin's own account, which was given when the appeal was heard, and certain suspicions which appear to have no concrete foundation." He was turning the sheets faster and faster. "It is not, I repeat, a very easy case. I was hoping that a letter I received this morning would open the way to considerable progress; but as it is——"

He was too well practised to look up, but he could almost feel the glance that went from Louis to Thérèse. Louis said nothing. It was the affair of Thérèse, all this, it was up to her to decide whether the bait was worth taking. Thérèse decided that it was not; she knew Lecours, as artful as a monkey.

"The letter of which I speak," Lecours pursued gently, like a swan swimming with the current, "is a private one, addressed to me personally. It contains certain confidential matters relating to the writer, and for that reason I am afraid I shall be unable to pass it on to my successor."

"But you could have the operative passages extracted——" Thérèse said.

'How like a woman!' Louis thought, not without satisfaction. 'A moment's curiosity and she betrays herself. That is why the business of the world is conducted by men.'

"Unfortunately—no," Lecours said regretfully. "I think you will understand when I read a part of the letter."

He unlocked a bottom drawer of his desk and pulled out a letter of several sheets. Thérèse, leaning forward, saw with admiration that he flicked out two middle sheets and put back the other two, locking the drawer again and returning the key to his waistcoat.

"Yes, this is the passage: 'You will remember asking me to see if I could trace the whereabouts of a Captain Lenormand, whom you believed to be living in this district and to be in possession of evidence which might be useful in a case you are handling.' (You must understand, Mlle Séverin, that we frequently find it efficacious to make this kind of inquiry through private channels, though it requires a good deal of discretion. Yes, an important part of our work consists in private correspondence of that kind.) 'I am happy to tell you that through a friend in the local branch of the French Veteran Emigrants' Society I have identified as the person you seek a man engaged in the timber trade at Quebec under the name of ——' (in fairness to my correspondent, M. Séverin, I have to conceal the name at present). 'I gather from my friend that Captain Lenormand has certain reasons for concealing his identity, but that if sufficient inducement were offered he might be persuaded to give the evidence you require. There are various difficulties; in the first place, though I am ready to give you further assistance in the matter as far as I can, I am most unwilling owing to my relations with the Bar at Quebec, that my name should be connected with the matter, either here or in France. . . .' You will understand now," Lecours said, "why I have to treat the whole of this letter as strictly confidential."

"Does he give Lenormand's address?" Louis asked brusquely.

Lecours cast his eye to the bottom of the sheet. "Er—no. No, he has not given the address. He was no doubt expecting that I would communicate with him again, sending him instructions; as indeed I intended to do—I was going to ask your advice on the matter, Mlle Séverin. . . . However, it is not perhaps worth regretting ; to instruct solicitors in Quebec would have been a costly matter—Canadian legal fees are very high compared with those in this country—and then, in order to have used Lenormand's evidence effectively, we should have had to bring him over, which would have involved compensation as well as expenses. It is a pity, though, since we have always attached so much importance to finding this Lenormand. . . . Couette, M. Séverin's hat and gloves!"

Thérèse had already risen. "As you say," she remarked, "it would have been very expensive. And is Madame Lecours well?"

"Very well, I thank you, Mlle Séverin."

He held the door for Thérèse and Mme Flandrecauld to go out. Louis lagged behind. He turned at the door and jerked his head towards the clerk, who, at a signal from Lecours, went away. Louis pushed the door shut with his foot and leant against it with his hands in his trouser pockets.

"How much do you want, Lecours, to get Lenormand over here?"

Lecours shrugged his shoulders.

"I've told you—it's impossible to say. There would be legal fees in Canada—expenses—compensation."

"I want a price, Lecours, I want something definite."

For a moment Lecours thought of his dignity. But things were not too good, people were too poor for litigation nowadays. Germaine was complaining about all the carpets.

"Well—say thirty thousand."

Louis shook his head. He said quietly and with finality: "Vingt."

"Twenty-five?" Lecours asked.

"No, twenty."

Lecours nodded. "All right."

"I should like that in writing," Louis said.

Lecours was taken aback.

"But, M. Séverin, I am a solicitor. . . . Between gentlemen ——"

Louis smiled.

"I am not a gentleman, M. Lecours, I am a carpet-merchant."

★

Having limped half a mile from the tramway stop, Thérèse was tired when she got home; but she went to the drawing-room to see Madeleine. Louis had been very guarded on the way—it was absurd how secretive the little man always was, how difficult it seemed to get anything out of him—but she gathered that he had done a deal of some sort with Lecours and that Lecours was going to get hold of Lenormand. Madeleine ought to know; it was, after all, of importance to her. She found Madeleine with red eyes and trembling lips; something had gone wrong. She asked, "What is it, Madeleine, can I do anything?" "No, no, thank you . . . a headache." "Shall I get you an oxyquinotheine tablet?" "No—no, thank you."

Passing Marianne's room on the way to her own, Thérèse noticed that the door was open. She remembered then that it was Marianne's half-day. Marianne was there, sitting at her table without any kind of warmth, her face white and set, her lips tight in the Séverin way. Seldom had Thérèse seen her appearance so Séverin; its hauteur was almost comical behind the pince-nez, above the flat chest and the drab dress of a scraggy school-mistress.

"Do you know what's wrong with your mother?" Thérèse asked. "She seems upset about something."

Marianne tightened her chin and turned out her hands.

"?—Mother enjoys a good cry. . . . I've just written out an advertisement for Raymond's paper. Is this all right? 'To let, furnished, two rooms, ground floor of respectable house, place Talleyrand. Would suit small family.' . . ."

"But what is all this, Marianne? Some joke of yours?"

It was plain, from Marianne's bloodless face, that she was not joking.

She said huskily:

"It's decided, isn't it, that we aren't going to move?"

"Yes, but——"

"Then I presume that we have to let off rooms. There's no other way that I can see of making money to keep a house of this size going."

"But, my dear Marianne, your father would never hear——"

"Father would never hear of anything——"

"But why should you think——? I know we're short of money——"

Marianne's face changed. For a moment Thérèse thought that she was going to cry—it seemed to be a day for crying, altogether a very tiresome day. The tears were there, covering the pupils but not falling; a Séverin never wept in the ordinary way. The lips were apart, but no sob came; instead, suddenly, a torrent of words.

"You can't know as well as I do. Mother talks about money all day long, you talk about it, at meals the conversation is nothing but money. Money, money, money, the money we haven't got and can't get along without. And what does anyone do? Nobody tries to get any money, nobody in this house does any work, nobody does anything about money except talk about it. Except me. I have to work, I have to do a job I loathe and detest, I have to stand up all day long giving the same lessons over and over again to vulgar and dirty children who are incapable of learning anything, and when I get home at night and have got the exercises corrected everyone stands in a circle and talks to me about money. A third of what I do earn goes to mother for my board and lodging just as if I was living in a pension and with what's over I have to buy my own clothes, every single thing I require, everything I've got on. Does anybody ever buy clothes for me? And Raymond and Cécile borrow money from me and don't pay it back. And what does Father do, what has he done all his life? He spends money. He buys clothes. He buys hats and shoes and evening gowns and afternoon gowns for that little half-breed slut that Pierre's married. And next time I see him he will talk to me about money. When you start talking of money . . ."

There must be something funny in the weather, Thérèse thought. It was curious, Marianne going off like this, she was usually so reserved, such a crinkly-pimply sort of female. She opened her bag and took out her little notebook. Marianne had reminded her of something. She wrote: "Raymond owes me 7.50."

XVI

IT was a pleasure to Madeleine when Eugène expressed a wish to see his grandchildren. In the olden days everyone had said how fond the Colonel was of children, that his friendliest smile was always reserved for them; often, when they lived in Paris and drove in the Bois on Sunday afternoons, Eugène had made the driver stop so that he could get down and speak to a group of children playing on the verge; he would bend down in his tight uniform, stroking a little girl's cheek, patting a youngster's shoulder, smiling at the pretty nursemaid. Madeleine herself had never cared very much for children; except those belonging to her old friends, who slipped as quietly as mice into a drawing-room, who sat curled up with a book in a corner, always so tidy, and quite silent until you asked them, "How are you, Lucienne?" when the reply would come in the gentlest, tinkling voice, with so demure a smile and often a little curtsy, "I thank you, very well indeed, Madame." Her own children, who as babies had delighted her with their pretty looks and ways, had grown—it seemed—almost as soon as they had left their cradles into individuals that she did not understand, lean creatures of a pale brown colour with Séverin lips and foreheads, who contradicted and pommelled each other with unheard-of violence, who behaved contemptuously towards all other children, who before they had passed the school age were airing their new-fangled views on topics of which she had scarcely heard. "I have three babies now," she had once written to dear Louise de Guillaumat, "and I shall be able to absorb my life in them. I feel that it is possible, when Nurse brings my little ones to me to say good night, to forget the nightmare of all those dreadful weeks in Paris and to start life over again. . . ." But the babies had vanished, they had turned overnight into haughty Sèverins, and the nightmare of draughty ante-rooms and the stuffy Court, of the day she had fainted, of Eugène's face when he shrugged his shoulders and said, "Fini, ma chérie!" the nightmare had remained.

"I should like to see Pierre's children," Eugène said; and she had rejoiced in that sign of the old life in him. "But not to-day," he added, "I'm too tired to-day."

Her anger, which had cooled since yesterday, returned for a moment. She said:

"You are tired, yes. It is not perhaps very surprising, when as soon as I am out of the way you run off to amuse yourself with a shopping expedition. It's hardly to be expected. . . ."

"You don't understand, Madeleine," he said gently. "It is a

spiritual fatigue. In body I feel well, I feel stronger than for some time past, I believe I could lift up that chair you're sitting on—yes, with you on it—and place it on the table. It did me good, that little drive. But it is not so simple to find spiritual refreshment. You, you have your religion—I respect you for it. But for a man, for one whose reason will not submit to the dictation of his emotions —even of the purest emotions—the way is not so easy." He was lying on the sofa, turned away from her. "It is partly a loneliness of spirit. People forget you, after a time; they see your name, something about you in the newspaper perhaps, and they say, 'Oh, yes, poor old Séverin, I must write to him sometime.' But they don't come to see me, none of my old friends do, I have no company except from that foolish little Tischer. Why, even Thérèse hardly ever sees me, and when she does it is only to talk about money. Thérèse thinks of nothing but money—and that time so long ago that I can hardly remember it when she was an artist. I never can imagine why she didn't stay in Paris, she liked that work, though it wasn't the kind of thing you expect a Séverin to take up, it seems to me that her leaving it was only a gesture. Not a very happy gesture, when you come to think of it: it must have made people think that she held the same opinion that Vaudilhac was paid to hold. Thérèse, of course, would never see that, she is like my mother, she is quite insensitive to other people's mental reactions. . . ."

"But, Eugène, I don't think it's fair to Thérèse to say that. It was, after all, a big sacrifice for her to give up her career. And you know, that evening—well, you know when I mean—she had to go on that night, Günther made her, he threatened her with a lawsuit, and there were people booing in the pit—yes, and in the stalls too. You must admit . . ."

"Thérèse was past her zenith," he said decisively. "She was a good actress, she had dignity, I myself admired her performance very much. But she had no flexibility, her movements were some-what heavy, the public was beginning to tire of her. Perhaps, after all, she showed good sense in retiring when she did. There's nothing more pathetic than an old woman trying to maintain her reputation on the stage——"

"She was twenty-seven——"

"—and in any case it was time she settled to a quieter life; it's a rackety kind of existence, the theatre, it's all right for young girls. I remember that we all wondered how long Thérèse would stand up to it. . . . There's a draught from that door, the screen perhaps could come round a little farther."

Madeleine said, moving the screen: "When you feel well enough to see the children I will get Renée to bring them down."

"No, no, I prefer to see them by myself, they will be more friendly. Young children are always constrained when their parents are present, it will be much better if I see them alone."

★

The chance came when Renée went to see Raymond's pictures. She was reluctant to leave the children alone for a whole afternoon; but Barbier had promised—at some sacrifice—to amuse them, and Raymond had pressed her with a flattery to which she could not be insensitive. "It will be nice," he had said mournfully, "to show my pictures to someone who won't make foolish comments; none of my own family has the ghost of an idea about painting, their idea of critical appreciation is to stand gaping at the most flamboyant Raphaels in the Louvre. In Baulon I've only one or two friends of any sensibility, and they're students, they're very immature, they're of the age when you imagine that Balzac was an artist . . ." Eugène had heard from Barbier of the expedition and he watched from the drawing-room window till Renée disappeared into the rue des Suisses; conscious of envying Raymond, who was going to have the young woman all to himself. Madeleine was down in the kitchen, arguing some matter with Joséphine, and there was no one about. Moving quite briskly he went up to the second floor and discovered the children's room. Barbier was already on duty, seated on the table and solemnly cutting newspaper into the shape of a skull. Stationed on the floor, in opposite corners of the room, Armand and Sophie courteously ignored his eccentricity. Eugène said: "All right, Barbier, you can go now, I will amuse the children."

★

With some hesitation, Barbier went away. Eugène picked up Sophie and set her on the table before him.

"What's your name?"

Sophie only tittered. She did not seem to know.

"Do you know who I am? No? I'm your grandfather—your father's father. Tell me now, what is your name?"

"Sophie."

"Do you like being in France?"

"Yes."

The child was like her mother, Eugène thought, though fair in colouring and plump in the face. It must be the eyes or something you could see it at once. But certainly without the mother's character or intelligence: a pity. Sophie was smiling, sitting quite still, pleased to be inspected; reminding Eugène of that doll of Raymond's.

"Are you fond of your mother?" he asked.

The face broke into dimples. For a moment Sophie was too

much overcome by shyness to speak at all, she pulled at her dress and looked over her shoulder. Then:

"Yes, and I love my daddy too, who's far away across the sea. And my grannie and grand-daddy too."

Eugène turned away sharply. It was incredible that the mother could do nothing about this; or perhaps it was a Pichy strain that had proved ineradicable. The voice, great heavens—it was as if the voice of Raymond's wife had been put through a mincing machine and then let into the child through a twisted conduit. He went across to the corner where Armand knelt over a history book taking no notice of what was going on. Sophie began crying.

"What's wrong with her?" Eugène asked.

Armand answered over his shoulder:

"She can't get off that table unless there's a chair. She's frightfully feeble."

"You'd better put a chair for her," Eugène said shortly.

Armand got up and gave the most convenient chair a push. "There! Stop crying! Baby!" He was going back to his corner but Eugène stopped him.

"Here, have you no manners, young man? You've got to talk to me."

"I apologize," Armand said, and pushed up another chair. "Won't you sit down, grandfather? My mother, I'm afraid, is not at home, but she will be back presently."

Eugène turned the chair a little, caught hold of Armand's shoulders and faced him to the light. "Let's look at you." Armand did not care for that; he looked left and right, avoiding his grandfather's eyes. The grip on his shoulders was very tight, he didn't like the feel of it. It reminded him of something, this old man staring at him like that. "Keep still!" Eugène said. . . . "Yes, you're very like your father. And he used to wriggle too, he never could keep his eyes fixed. Are you going to be a soldier?"

The reply came at once.

"No, a Brother of the Franciscan Order."

"Oh. Why?"

"I desire a life of Contemplation."

"What are you going to contemplate?"

Armand was not sure.

"Is that a history book you've got?" Eugène asked. "Let me see it. What part of history do you like best? Do you read about battles?"

"No, I skip the battles."

"Come here, don't keep wandering away, sit down, yes, you can sit on the floor if you prefer that. I'll tell you what it is, why you don't enjoy reading about battles: it's because the wretched authors of the history books have never seen a battle and don't know how to describe one. They're dull dogs, the old professors who write those books. Now I can tell you what a battle's really like. Give me that book again, let's see what the pedant has to say about Spicheren. . . . 'Spicheren, Prussian Victory.' "

Eugène turned over the page, shut the book to see the name of the writer. "Heaven have mercy! It is not surprising, Armand, that you do not care to read the accounts of battles in this book. The gentleman who writes them is not so very interesting. 'Prussian Victory'—that is all he has to say! And of the Pucelle he says no doubt: 'A young girl born at Domrémy in 1412.' It is better perhaps for our historians to be a little reticent, then they cannot be contradicted. Look here now: you are on the top of a high hill. That is Saarbrücken, down there below you. There's Rotherberg, just over there, and Forbach is in that direction. That's the way Von Kameke is coming. Over there is all woods. Everybody around you is in a tearing hurry, some are digging furiously, some are making a kind of hedge with brambles twisted loosely between upright stakes; there's a smell of soil and sweat, everything's in rather a muddle, there are officers walking up and down shouting orders. . . ."

It was evident that the boy had not beento school yet; he had no idea how to pay attention, his head was half-turned the other way, he showed no sign of interest. But Eugène warmed to his task, surprised to find how good his memory of that day was: the names of the commanders on his wings, the way the ground sloped so as to conceal, from men advancing two hundred metres off, the shepherd's hut in which he had posted Sergeant Bosson, the odd smile of old Dalbécourt as he hurried by, saying in his melancholy voice, 'I've dropped my handkerchief somewhere, I suppose some swine of a fat Prussian will be blowing his dirty snout on it. You might keep a look out. . . .' There were patches that had grown dim, events that could not be arranged in their proper order. What time of day was it that Bosson had shouted to him, in his matter-of-fact way, 'They're in the wood now, sir, shoulder-and-buttock'? He could not be sure whether that was in the morning or the afternoon; there had been no division of time that day, it had been one stretch of excitement sharpened by the fear that Hédouin on his left, who always tended to thrust too wildly upon a moment's advantage, would get out of touch. But he remembered as clearly as if he saw it now the fence which ran down diagonally from the spur where Labonde—no, Amouret—was posted, the first half-dozen uniforms debouching from the wood and scrambling over it, two of them going down, a man in the thicket behind shouting in a silly way, amid all the rattle and cursing and the shudder of guns from Forbach, that his rifle was jammed. Recalling that, the sweat running into his eyes and his hand tingling from the heated bolt of a rifle he had grabbed, he almost forgot his listener, broke from the second person to the first, ran on with a boy's eagerness.

". . . I could see through my left ear—you see things quickly, at times like that—that Amouret had come up, he'd got a lovely position, he had the whole stretch covered to the next part of the wood. I wasn't going to wait then for any more to come out, I shouted to Pionnier to send two sections into the wood, and I went in after them, breaking in along the right-hand edge, see. It was a wild thing to do, you don't want to try that sort of thing, not till your instinct's trained to the point that you can see right through a wood. But I knew if I could get them clear it would give Denoyers a chance, he was just sitting waiting on the lower spur, or so I thought, and I had a shrewd idea that the fellows in the wood would miscalculate our numbers if we made noise enough. It's nasty, fighting in a wood, nothing but rough-and-tumble, but you get to learn the tricks of it. Of course we had the fence to get over then, but they'd made gaps for us. There was one fellow, I remember, had got stuck on the top, with an iron upright in him. He was screaming like a rabbit. I helped him off with the butt of my rifle, and he showed his gratitude by grabbing his gun and crawling after me trying to shoot at my legs, with half his inside hanging out, you never saw anything so droll. . . ."

He noticed then that Armand had turned his face right away. Leaning forward, he caught hold of the boy's front hair and pulled his head round again. The face was dead white.

"What's the matter with you?" Eugène asked. "You're not like a girl, are you?"

He glanced at Sophie. Sophie had been listening intently and she was quietly laughing. She hadn't been able to follow much of the story Grandpère was telling, but she could see the fun of that, a man crawling along the ground with his inside dangling from his tummy, like her old sheep on wheels that Armand had bored a hole in.

"Look at Sophie," Eugène said.

Armand said: "I'm all right."

Eugène continued: "Inside the wood it was like hide and seek, only more exciting, because everybody was hiding and seeking at the same time, and if you got caught you had a knife stuck in you —right through into the tree behind you, and there you were, caught properly."

Armand was paying no attention. He had gone over to the window and was looking out into the Square. Controlling his exasperation, Eugène thought of a way to get him interested.

"Look here, Armand, I'll show you something I got in that wood. Something I'm very proud of, a little present the Prussians gave me. Sophie, you'd better not see this, you go outside for a few minutes, go on. . . . Now look, Armand, see what you think of this. It's the kind of thing every Frenchman wants to have."

He had taken off his coat and waistcoat, and pulled up his shirt. The trophy was not spectacular: a broad groove in the flesh, lined with wrinkled white skin, starting above the hip-bone and running in a lazy zigzag right down the left thigh. "Feel it with your fingers!" Eugène said. "Now I'll tell you just how I got that."

Armand drew back. He said passionately: "No, no, I won't feel it, I won't look at it."

Eugène put his lips together and stared at Armand. He pushed his shirt down again and put on his overclothes. Furiously angry, he kept himself under control. He said gently, smiling just a little:

"Listen, Armand, I want to talk to you. I want to tell you how to be a proper Frenchman, a real Séverin. You must try not to hate the idea of pain, not to let it worry you. In war there's lots of pain, you can't be a good soldier till you've got used to it. The great thing is not to mind feeling pain yourself, then you won't mind seeing others feel it, you won't be frightened of seeing wounds. You ought to practise, practise doing painful things, not making a noise, not minding. Look now, come here just a minute."

Armand came slowly forward, trembling. Eugène suddenly caught his wrists.

"Now look, Armand, this is going to hurt you. It'll make you want to shout. Now I want you to steel yourself. Try and think of something else, get away from yourself, and see how long you can keep enduring it without making any noise." The grip was tightening, the nails were beginning to bite in. "Keep still, Armand, don't struggle, *keep still!*"

But Armand had already stopped struggling, he had made no noise at all. As Sophie came in, unable to bear her curiosity any longer, Eugène was pushing the unconscious body on to the table. A little scared by the white face of her brother sleeping, Sophie watched with interest. Eugène went to the door and shouted gruffly for Barbier.

XVII

When he reached the shoulder of the hill, Duboc pulled up and dismounted. To get to the wood he usually made his way down the gutter which slanted south-west from where he stood and then worked round, leading his horse and following the course of the stream. But he was late to-day, the bog between Lieutenant Trouplin's post and Safe Point had got worse than ever, as the dried slime up to Jojo's chestnuts showed. Le Rochais, who lived always in a fever of impatience for new orders, would be angry. The light had nearly gone, that was something. After a moment's reflection Duboc remounted. The horse started off on the usual track, feeling for his footholds on the loose stones with a cat's delicacy. Duboc pulled his head round sharply and pricked him forward, up a little, where the slope was much flatter. He glanced apprehensively towards the clumps of scrub sprinkled over the hill's crest. "No, no, Jojo, to-day we must hurry. And this part must be done very quickly, see? Very, very quickly, Come on, Jojo, move."

Reaching the wood he slacked the reins, grinned, instinctively running his fingers over the hasp of his dispatch-case. Very little chance of interruption now, and Le Rochais would once more have his customary pleasure of reading the orders: the bolts of all rifles were to be smeared with beeswax and polished with a cambric between the firing of every two cartridges, that sort of thing. A letter, perhaps, from Le Rochais's sweet old mother in Montauban, or still more likely, a scented note from Le Rochais's sweet little half-white lady friend at Njole. Duboc eased up to light the stump of a cigarette which he had kept tucked in his spur. It was against orders, but he deserved that.

*

Le Rochais read Hédouin's message right through again, with increased perplexity. He took to larger ideas slowly. They said of Le Rochais, he was all right on a job of work, give him the necessary men, he'd get on with it. An old hand. He knew just how many Bisquort snipers could hide together in one bramble no bigger than your backside, what sort of water gave you only mild dysentery, what to do with rifle-oil in a high-altitude frost, how far downwind you could hear a clumsy horse moving on loose sandstone. 'The Tradesman,' someone had called him. You sent for him and he arrived with his bag of tools and his mate, usually a young officer perfectly instructed. He gave you a time estimate, the job would take about so long; and back he would come, on the very day, with a report very neatly and concisely written: the fort had been taken, the post established, the troublesome area cleared, just what you required. About larger conceptions he did not worry until they came to worry him.

Hédouin's message worried him terribly. It was full of G.H.Q. stuff, bristling with cautions, impregnated with that judicious stressing of secrecy which Le Rochais could only describe as coy. It was evident that Hédouin was all up on end; they had sent him a long dispatch full of complicated words and he had taken it right on the chin, instead of replying, as La Rochais himself would have done, that at this season the movement of a large body of men between Sigumbe and the coast was physically impossible, and that he awaited further instructions please. Well, there it was, Hédouin had elected to take all this nonsense seriously, and there was nothing to be done about it. But how ridiculous! He read again: ". . . increasing gravity of the situation in Europe. . . ." (Europe? What was Europe to do with Hédouin? Where was this place Europe?) ". . . absolute necessity for the immediate liberation of all superfluous forces overseas" (superfluous!) "even to the point of risk . . . necessity for the observance of the greatest secrecy . . . smallest possible force required for maintenance of the established boundaries . . ." As long as Le Rochais could remember, there had been this talk of the increasing gravity of the situation in Europe, of the greater importance of the European frontier than that of colonial developments—yes, that was the phrase, 'colonial developments.' And now it appeared that, because the chicken-witted electorate had chosen to put in power a set of politicians still more nervy than the last lot, and because some anæmic clerk in a stuffy office in the Boulevard St. Germain fancied himself at writing complicated letters, he, Le Rochais, working on a job of incredible delicacy with just half the number of men he had asked for, in a district where five weeks was the longest time any ordinary man could stand up to the climate, was required to return a third of his exiguous force in a sealed wrapper to march up and down the boulevards of Amiens and give consolation to the chittering inhabitants by waving little flags. ". . . If necessary, the present demonstration must be abandoned, and we must concentrate on strengthening the defences on the February contour . . . at least one officer must be released immediately." Le Rochais laughed. At least one! If *necessary* the present demonstration must be abandoned! Had Hédouin gone out of his senses, writing him a letter in that jargon of the Montargis School of Tactics? He shrugged his shoulders. Well, so, it was off, everything bust up, his work to be thrown in the dustbin, back to the February contour. It crossed his mind for just a moment: Did this mean something? Was there really trouble brewing over that way? There was the farmhouse he had bought at Cartigny; he had a sister living at Chaunes, she was delicate, she had said something in her letters about 'increasing anxiety' which he had had to take no notice of. . . . Well, if he had to let an officer go it would be Séverin. He was a good soldier, Séverin, he was tough, he could work out in the sun all day long, never seemed hungry or thirsty, lived on tobacco. But Le Rochais didn't like him; a moody chap, sensitive, you couldn't make him out at all.

Aubruchet had no brains, nothing but guts, but he was steadier. Le Rochais shouted, "Marsat! Send someone across to Captain Séverin with this letter, and a message that he is to see me as soon as he's done his round. Tell the man you send that he's not to carry a light, and he'd better go round on the bottom track."

★

Aubruchet came into the hut gently swearing; he had taken twenty minutes to find it—there was no moon and he had lost himself in the bush. "You can't see a bloody yard," he said. He unlaced his boots, whistled with the pain of pulling them off his swollen feet. His socks were stuck on tight as wallpaper, some of his skin came off with them as he tugged. Pierre said: "God, Aubruchet, your feet do stink."

Aubruchet took off his cap, pushed the wet black hair off his forehead and foraged for matches.

"I've been thinking," he said, "you're wrong, you're quite definitely wrong, when you say that the proper appreciation of music is purely intellectual. I can prove it. If it's purely intellectual you'd get as much pleasure out of reading the score as out of hearing a concerto played. Wouldn't you now? That's rational. I don't see that you can argue about it. Give me a match, will you?"

"It's no good arguing, with you," Pierre said, throwing him the box. "Are you really such a duffer that you can't appreciate the work of an orchestra as a synthesis of incomplete parts, the simultaneous presentation of a number of ideas which are quite ineffective when separately realized? You might as well say that because you can't get as much fun out of a problem of Euclid by taking each line as a separate entity—angle ABC equals angle XYZ, poring over that—it means that every problem of Euclid is a romantic essay which makes its appeal primarily to the sensory emotions. Well, if it comes to that, I can imagine you saying, 'Great heavens! Have you seen this new little masterpiece of Euclid's? *The sides BF and BW are equal ex hypothesi.* What spirituality! What finesse!' —and going all pink with idealist ecstasy."

"No, but look here, Séverin, I don't think you're being quite rational. The point is this——"

"Oh, for God's sake, Aubruchet, stop talking about what you don't understand. And give me back those matches. Have you seen Le Rochais, did you come back that way?"

"No, I didn't."

"Oh. I'm wondering what he wants to see me for."

"Does he?"

"Yes. After I've done the inspection. Some damn silly thing,

I suppose—am I making sure that the men all sleep with their heads pointing south-east? Absolutely essential in this longitude and latitude and altitude. 'Just a word of advice, Captain Séverin, from an old soldier who's had many years campaigning in the tropics . . .' Did you see your letter?"

"No."

"Over there. Yes, with Le Rochais's mail this evening. The rider says he doubts if he'll be able to get through much longer. Half the country's under flood—so he says."

"Does he?" Aubruchet had opened his letter and found a bill industriously forwarded from a Pont de Flandre outfitter: Two pairs blue socks, f6.85. "Well, it can't be helped."

Pierre was putting on his tunic.

"Look here, Aubruchet, I want to be sure this letter gets off. Le Rochais may be sending a man down to-night if he's got anything important to go, he hates risking anything important by daylight. You might get Giot when he comes in to take it across and find out if there's a messenger going. You won't forget, will you, it's rather important."

"But he won't be sending anyone to-night. You can't see your own hand; the man would never get anywhere."

"I don't know, he might. I want to be sure that letter goes as quickly as possible, anyway."

He looked at his watch and saw that he could spare five minutes: he wanted to see Renée's letter again before he went out. He bent and turned up the wick of the Fleury lamp, squatted with his back to Aubruchet, unfolded the letter.

Aubruchet protested: "You oughtn't to have the lamp as high as that. If Le Rochais saw it, there'd be the deuce to pay."

"Shut up, Aubruchet."

It was worrying and perplexing, he couldn't altogether understand it. The one thing certain was that Renée was in earnest, she was really scared. Of course it might be just nerves, change of climate; the drainage in Baulon, he remembered, was mediæval. "Pierre, you must"—she had written—"you absolutely must make arrangements for me to go somewhere else. I'm quite helpless, I've got no money of my own till your next draft comes through, and it's utterly impossible for us to stay any longer in this house where nobody cares anything about us. The worst thing is that Armand is so frightened, I thought he would get over it but now he's got suddenly worse, I can't get him to tell me what the real reason is, he's become secretive and he mopes all day. Dr. Tischer says he isn't a bit well, but can't tell me what is actually wrong. I'm sure it's this house, not only being so damp, but so large and frightening, and with so many old people. Armand seems particularly scared of your father, who is much older than you probably remember him and has taken to very funny ways. . . ."

"Now look here, Séverin, supposing you'd never seen a musical score in your life, or heard any kind of music at all, and you were taken to a concert and heard Beethoven's Mass in D Major for the first time . . ."

"Oh, for God's sake, Aubruchet, can't you get yourself a book to read or something?"

"Not while you're blocking up the whole of the light."

"Well, find a nail somewhere and pick your teeth with it."

He read on: "You know, Pierre, I wouldn't trouble you like this only I've got desperate. I don't know what to do with Armand at all, he walks about as if he was half-asleep—I know he was always rather dreamy, but it's much, much worse than that now—and he keeps on having those nightmares, and he will hardly let me go out of his sight. I'm certain it will be much better if we can only get out of this house. Oh, Pierre, if only you could come to us. . . ."

He got up and asked: "Where have those biscuits got to, we had a tin of biscuits, hadn't we?"

"Yes, there, you're nearly standing on them."

"Oh, good."

Pierre took out two large handfuls and slipped them into his pocket. "I may be hungry," he said. "I've left you two or three. Is your flask full? You might let me have a drop, mine isn't. Yes, I get a raging thirst, tramping about at night." He had stubbed his cigarette and was pulling on his beetleweb gloves. "Don't forget about that letter, will you?"

*

The way to the A post was easy enough, six hundred metres odd across a flat and open stretch; by day you could see the point. He walked on a compass bearing, feeling the ground with his stick, and came up only a few paces wide, where he was promptly challenged. "All right, Fichet." He asked his routine questions; emptied the sentry's magazine, tested the bolt and trigger; made the man repeat the code of signals; whispered, "All right, Fichet, keep quiet and keep lively," and struck off into the wood. He went slowly here; there was a track to the left which would lead you out at the wrong side; it was easy, besides, to step off the path altogether at any moment, and you might not realize till a stick broke under your foot with a noise like a rifle, enough to tell a practised ear at a hundred metres just where you were. To-night, he was sleepy, after reconnoitring on the eastern slope all day, and shivering with cold, so that it was hard to concentrate on moving carefully. In that state of lethargy he was not much frightened. As a rule this was a job that scared him; at every step you heard a noise, you stopped, listened, and could not be sure if it was repeated; you thought you saw something moving; for a moment you were certain there was something there, right in front of you, not three metres away, a dark shape waiting; again you stopped dead, and you seemed to feel a prick beneath your shoulder-blade, something that had come from behind; you remembered, then, the story they told of Lieutenant Paquier, who had gone out one night on these hills and been found by the patrol next morning, a dozen metres from one of the sentries, flayed. But to-night, with no moon at all, there were no shapes to startle him; he moved in a close, protecting darkness, with only the echoed fear from other journeys, the habitual shudder of a seasoned actor upon each night's first entrance. Chiefly he was sleepy, he wanted to get through with it and go to bed.

Post B. "All right, Osmon." He plunged into the wood again, struck right and upwards.

He had his plan ready, the simple and obvious one. It was old Sergeant Papavoine who had told him, in an expansive moment when they were on reconnaissance together: "You know, sir, if ever you want to be sick for a few days, what you want to do? This leaf, you see, you can't mistake it, that kind of blue colour, shiny, with the fluffy underside. You see how the points go? You'll always find that by the streams in these parts, right at the very edge, growing out of the rock it usually is. That's the one you want to look for—you can't go wrong. Just a little nibble—about a quarter of a leaf this size. That's all you want, don't take any more—why, a couple of those would kill a sergeant-major. Just one nibble and a drink of water if you've got any with you. That's what the old soldiers do. About an hour, it takes, then Ah! the pain, it is terrible, in the stomach, just there, like a red-hot poker twisting round, a-ah, frightful! you think you are going to die. But you don't die, not if you've taken only a little nibble. The doctor comes, he says: 'Yes, poor fellow, a very bad case, very serious indeed, something has poisoned him, send him home at once to his old mother, court-martial the cook and pulverize his breeches. . . .' That's what the old soldiers do, so they tell me." That much was easy, and he would certainly get sent down to Sigumbe (and a damnable journey it would be, on a cacolet or at best a cross-slung litter). But that devil Hédouin, who was sly as a monkey over this kind of thing, who knew perfectly well that Pierre wanted long leave, he was quite capable of defying all the doctors, of having his stomach pumped and the contents sent to the department of tropical medicine for analysis, of raising hell and all the furies before he let him escape. He could see the little smile

134

on Hédouin's face, Hédouin saying in the low purring voice he used for working up unpleasantness, "It appears, Captain, that you have been a little incautious in your choice of diet. It is unfortunate that this should have occurred, making it quite impossible for you to be moved—far, far too risky, the doctor tells me—when you were just about due for leave." Well, if Hédouin—*who's that?*

He had walked clean into the sentry at C.

His heart had leapt, he could hardly speak. He said windily, "All right, all right, Ancel! . . . I just wanted to see if you were awake."

"But I heard you, sir, from ever so far——"

"Good. Give me that. Pouch—how many? All right. Hear anything before I came?"

It was a climb now, on a rocky track which twisted round at every sixty paces so that a compass was precious little good. You slipped now and then, sending a shower of loose stones to rattle down through the undergrowth; you grabbed, and might catch something strong enough to hold you, or else you rolled till the tangled thorn caught your clothes or till you broke a leg or neck, as the case might be, on a jutting slab of sandstone. 'It's just there,' Le Rochais would say, 'that you'll most likely find a Bisquort skirmisher. They like that sort of ground, they know how to use it.' Pierre didn't mind, he was so cold and sleepy, he didn't care if he took a dive right out of everything; only that Renée was waiting for him. *You know, Pierre, I wouldn't trouble you, only I've got desperate.* There was another plan forming as if by itself; it was too reckless, he didn't want to think about it. No, he must square Hédouin somehow, even if it meant showing him a part of Renée's letter and appealing to the swine's better feelings. It would be most un-Séverin, but damn the indignity. *I wouldn't trouble you, Pierre, only I'm desperate.* Hysteria? No. No, that wasn't it. They were bullying her, they were playing the devil somehow with young Armand. He would have to get round Hédouin, unless—yes, he would have to appeal to Hédouin. Damn! He was off the track again.

He swung round and retraced his steps. Now the path went up a little, instead of down as he expected, it was surely thicker laced with branches than it had been before. He turned again, feeling for a gap on the right through which he must have come. but could not find it. And now he was back where he had stopped before, of that he was nearly certain. Ridiculous. He was in a cage and the proper track could not be more than a few metres off, he had been up it twenty times, there was nowhere in this part where you could be lost for long. He returned once more to the other end of the trap and thrust furiously through the thorn, growing warmer with the struggle, wild with his impotence. He had made another seven paces when he felt the rock, almost perpendicular, on his right. Well, the path must be above it, the only thing was to climb up, or he would be here all night. He felt with his hand for a foothold at about chest level. Yes, that would do. There was a branch, he couldn't see where it came from; he tugged, it seemed all right. Farther up? There might or might not. He hoisted himself on to the first footing, felt upwards for a higher branch, yes, one there, but not very steady. Another toe-hold, about where his chin was, he would have to risk his weight on the branch. There, his toe was in, but the branch was giving. He grabbed wildly with his left hand and found a slab jutting. Just soon enough. There was a ledge now, about thigh height, and a crack for his fingers. The top, where the path was, must be an arm's stretch above. The thing was to hurry, you lost strength while you were feeling for holds, you had to risk a bit. Up! His knee caught sharply the slab where his hand had been, it gave him a few seconds of sickening pain. He squirmed and rugged, his fingers were failing. His left knee came on top of the slap, then his right foot. He felt for a higher crack and pulled himself upright. There. He could balance like that, take a rest. The rock face still went up, he stretched as far as he could and failed to feel the top. God alone knew where he had got to. He thought for a moment of going down again, but it was a case of jumping or falling and he could not be sure how high he had come. He must try another bit up. Frightened, he felt again for a foothold and found a poor one. The hand-grip was better, and if he could get his knee where his nose was now it would be all right—provided that his hands found a new hold half a stretch higher. Another struggle left him perched again, secure for a few seconds but with his leg crooked and too much weight on his arms. He wedged his elbow in a fissure, turned sideways and groped with his foot. Another hold, all right —no, it splintered. He pushed out his ankle, bruising it as his leg slipped down. His elbow was coming out, too much weight on it. Ah! The sole of his boot had caught somehow, a crack held it. Half a second's respite. Without any caution he kicked up the other leg and got a sloping rest for it. The muscles of his left hand had been rested just long enough, the fingers found a boss and gripped it. With a tormenting effort he tugged, brought the wrist over, pulling against splinters with the other hand, got his chest above the boss; let go his foothold and scrambled his knees against the rock-face, his toes stabbing for perches. He had his right hand sharing the boss now, the left was done amd must give way for it. Uuu! The left hand went up, all by itself, caught something, tugged at it. Comfortable, fairly. His right hand shot above it and found a ledge, nicely squared, which took the fingers, up to the lower joint. His knee had the boss now, a painful perch, and his hands must explore again, They found a hold which took them both, with comfort enough for a fair tug. His toe sought the boss, missed it, found it, rested cramped. Now wrists up, push, chest coming up, left foot on the good hold. All right now. A full half minute in this perch. And the rock began to slope inwards. He rested till his left arm was giving and then struggled again. Ninety seconds' scrambling brought him to the flat.

He lay full length, trembling, on the rock's crown, content with safety. Then from curiosity he took a piece of paper from his pocket—the envelope of Renée's letter—set it alight, and kicked it over the edge. Kneeling on the lip, he watched the little ball of flame rolling and hopping till, where the face of rock fell away more steeply, it bounced and leapt into space. He counted as it fell: one, two, three. How far? He couldn't be sure, but he reckoned ten to twenty metres. He smiled. Not by daylight!

It occurred to him that he had broken one of Le Rochais's primary laws: no lights in the open. That amused him. But almost at once he realized how damnably foolish his little experiment had been; anyone below could have seen it from half a dozen kilometres. He felt carefully all round him but there was no trace of a path. Ahead the ground still rose steeply, webbed with thicket. He started to scramble upwards, regardless of torn hands and clothes, of the thorn raking his cheeks and forehead; and in twenty minutes, working steadily, he broke out into the open, where the soil, thickly seamed with granite, gave substance only to spare clumps of ragged brush. He was not yet at the summit and he went straight on, south-west by compass, till he reached it. The D and E sentry posts must be roughly over his left shoulder now, perhaps four kilometres off, there was nothing to tell him. He stood as if in a bald patch on the back of a poodle; on all the eastern side, up to eighty paces from his feet, he could distinguish only the blackness of the curling forest. Le Rochais's rule was being well kept, there was nowhere a twinkle of light. He shivered, it was cold again now that he had stopped climbing, and up here he got the wind from north-west. Well, it was no good hanging about; the obvious thing was to go down again to the margin and work along it northward, which should bring him eventually to D. Here, even on such a night, an experienced eye might see his form against the sky line; there would be a noise, hardly audible up here like the chirp of crickets; anything might happen then.

I wouldn't trouble you, Pierre, only I'm desperate.

The second plan, the one he had been trying not to think about, was still making his mind itch. In one way so simple: no painful illness, no awkward interview with Hédouin. He turned to face the wind and moved towards the other valley. On this side the hills were almost naked, granite strewn, descending in a hollow sweep to the valley of the Nsoka. The Kabil range was over there, south by west: seventy kilometres, perhaps, straight. Beyond that the Lsambo. A Jesuit called Pringault had got across that way, with a guide picked up in one of the Nsoka villages; the geologist Couperot, trying the same route, had been caught by Bisquorts before he reached the Nsoka; that was bad luck, they said. It was exhilarating to be alone up here, in the clean wind, possessing an empty world which floated in darkness, right away from the stifling forest, the ticks, Aubruchet's prattle. The wind carried an upland odour, he could fancy he was lifted above and out of Africa. Its lash on his face fortified him, he felt an increase of his stature in this high solitude. You were sufficient by yourself, your weight could drive you as you wanted if once you had stripped off the garments of organization, the binding apparatus of responsibility with all its forms and tickets, routine and courtesies. That was where the difference came, between a Le Rochais and a Séverin.

He sat down and felt for cigarettes, but it was too windy to smoke, besides the risk. He would give himself five minutes and then go back to hunt for Sangnier at D. He looked at his watch. Six, perhaps seven hours more darkness. Six hours, say twenty-five kilometres downhill, allowing for losing your way. The Lsambo had a steamer from the railhead up to Bere, from there it was dug-outs to where the Nsoka joined. The Portuguese bagmen went right up to the Baturo, so Evrand had told him. You could borrow from the Portuguese; there was the gold cigarette-case Renée's father had given him. It was glorious up here right away from the smell of Le Rochais.

*

"You say, Aubruchet, that he started his inspection at the usual time?"

"Yes, sir. I looked at my watch, he may have been five minutes late."

"And you know he inspected the first three posts?"

"Yes, I've seen the men."

"Did any of them hear anything, a shout or anything?"

"No, but the man at D thought he saw a light, somewhere right above him."

"What sort of light?"

"He's not very clear. He says he thought at first it was a shooting star, but he's not sure."

Le Rochais spread his hands.

"How intelligent! It may, of course, have been a firework show on the Lsambo. Or a peripatetic glow-worm. The evidence is very useful. Did Séverin say anything special to you before he went off?"

"No, I don't remember. No, I don't think there was anything particular. He gave me a letter he wanted to get off, he thought a rider might be going down last night—I forgot about it till now."

"You've still got it then?"

"Yes, here."

Le Rochais took the envelope and scrutinized it.

"It will be necessary, I think, to open it. Is that kettle still hot? Light the stove again, will you, get it steaming."

It was a job on which Le Rochais rather prided himself, and Aubruchet watched with some admiration the skill with which he used his stumpy fingers, persuasively clicking his tongue as he coaxed the flap. There! "I dislike doing this, Aubruchet, I dislike it very much indeed."

He spread the paper and read: "Don't worry, darling, I'm going to get back to you—soon. Somehow or other. Courage!"

His eyebrows lifted; he rolled his lips together, sucked a breath through his furred nostrils. "Ah!" With a stub of pencil from his breeches-pocket he copied the note into his diary. He hesitated. "No, no, I don't think it will be necessary to keep the letter, the copy will be sufficient. . . . Are you a married man, Aubruchet? No, of course not. Well, comparatively it is cheap; the cost of a double bed, spread over a number of years—but oh, so terribly permanent, if you are a Catholic. No good for a soldier." He folded the note, tightening the creases with his fist and second finger joints, put it back and smoothed down the flap. "There! You'd never know, would you?" He was not sure what to do next, the affair was so utterly irregular, it was outside his experience altogether. He sat on the trestle bench, balancing the letter by its points between his middle fingers, blowing it round like a windmill.

XVIII

'My dear Madame Séverin: of course I remember you very well indeed, and your delightful children—what pleasure they gave me on the voyage home! It was altogether most kind and charming of you to write to me, and I was delighted to hear from you. So few of the nice people one meets on the boats ever trouble to write afterwards. It would be very nice if we could meet again some-time and improve our very happy acquaintance, and have a long talk about children, to whom, like yourself, I have always been devoted.

'Your suggestion that you should visit us here is one that has afforded the keenest gratification to M. Fleury and to myself, it is a proof of your friendliness which we both value very highly and for which we most warmly thank you. Unfortunately, M. Fleury has to return to Africa at the end of next month, already we are making our preparations, and it does not seem possible to arrange your visit before we go. This, however will only be a short trip, and it is more than likely that we shall be back in France at the end of nine months. We shall certainly not forget to send you an invitation then, and we shall look forward very keenly to the pleasure of meeting you and the dear children again. Please accept my very sincere apologies that I cannot invite you now, as you have suggested,

'M. Fleury thinks that he remembers meeting a Colonel Séverin many years ago. The name, he says, is very familiar to him. I wonder if this might be a relation of Captain Séverin? These connections are always so very interesting. M. Fleury tells me to ask if you will honour him by accepting his very kind regards.

'With every sincere wish to you and to dear Arnould and to little Lotie, believe me, dear Madame Séverin,

'Most devotedly yours,

'Agnès Fleury.'

★

'Madame: I am taking the liberty of writing to you personally to inform you, with deepest regret, that Captain Séverin is missing. He was engaged, on the night of Tuesday last, 19th instant, in the important and hazardous work of inspecting out-post sentries. He failed to return to his quarters, and on the following day a search was made, as thorough and extensive as the exigencies of our present operations permitted. I can give you my personal assurance that no possible steps which might be taken to find Captain Séverin have been omitted; but so far our efforts have been without result.

'I will, of course, arrange for a message to be sent to you by telegraph if any news becomes available. In the meantime I am sending you, with this letter, one which was addressed to you by Captain Séverin just before he started on the performance of the duty which I have described.

'Great as is my own anxiety in the loss of an excellent officer under my command, it can be as nothing to that which you will experience when this letter reaches you. I can but ask that you will accept this expression of the most sincere and profound sympathy of, Madame,

'Your obedient servant,
'Georges F. Le Rochais,
'*Sous-Commandant.*'

XIX

THE door of the nursery was open, and Joséphine saw, pausing outside, that only the little boy was there, with his nose pressed against the window; for once the mother was not with him, and the little girl was probably upstairs with Mlle Marianne, to whom she showed an increasing devotion. Joséphine slipped into the room as quietly as she could; and suddenly, within a few inches of Armand's head, said loudly: "Where is your mother, do you know?"

The child jumped as if she had struck him, jerked up his right hand defensively, stared as at an apparition.

"Do you know where your mother is?" she repeated.

He whispered "Non, non," as if he did not understand her question, and turned slowly back towards the window.

So! Gaston at least was cheerful; his face, if it was always the same, was mirthful in its expression; he was silly, Gaston, but never dour and grumbling. That was the difference; for the rest, what difference was there? Polishing the window with a piece of chamois-leather for excuse, she regarded Armand sidelong: the eyes, how oddly lacking in expression, like the end of a long telescope; he was like her own second child, Barbier's child, that night when she had held him right up till seven in the morning, with his eyes staring at her and moving just a little when she moved, until the doctor and another man had come and the man had held her while the doctor had taken the little boy away. The devilish lie they had told her, to say he was dead, that little one, when his eyes were wide open, when she had seen them moving as she moved the candle. Just like that, this Armand staring out of the window; but the little Barbier child, he had been only three weeks when they took him away; and this Armand, he was tall enough to be twelve or thirteen. So. They said that when a child was got properly, if you looked after him like you should, he came all right, he came to speak clear and straightforward when you asked him a question. Well, Gaston, he didn't speak clear but he knew what you meant, he'd run an errand for you, fetch what you wanted. He looked after that old Russian lady, Gaston did, she wouldn't let anyone wait on her but Gaston. He was slow, he had funny ways, but there was no harm in the boy, even if he didn't take to schooling—and what good was schooling to a boy who'd got to work for his living, anyway? This Armand, with his pale face and Séverin mouth, he didn't do anything, he was frightened of everybody, he was no possible use to anyone alive.

"What are you staring at?" she demanded. "There's nothing to look at there, they've stopped the building, didn't you know that?"

He said slowly, with a certain courtesy, "My mother is in the next room. She told me that she would be back presently."

So that was where he had got to: he was just answering the question she had put to him five minutes ago. And they said, Barbier said, that Gaston was slow.

"Are you going to stand there staring all day?" she asked, and added, with sudden inspiration, "You'll have your grandfather after you."

She saw then, watching his face narrowly, how he shrank back. Yes, he had taken that quick enough, in some ways he was not quite so slow. In her desiccated face the lips squeezed tighter, adding a little grimness; there was the ghost of a smile in her small eyes. It would be amusing to put them side by side, the little Gaston and this Séverin child; to say to Mme Pierre Séverin, "Look, there are our two sons, side by side; the one is, of course, a proper wedlock child, but for the rest . . ."

"It's no good your staring," she said, "they've stopped the building."

* * *

They had stopped building the factory, but no one knew exactly why. Barbier had the news first from one of the workmen, with whom he drank sometimes at the Espérance in the rue des Suisses. ". . . No, I don't know why, none of us know, the foreman doesn't know. The whistle goes, Tuesday, you see, ten o'clock. What's all this? Wages. Wages, Tuesday? Yes, boys, wages to the end of the week. And now you go home, see. And next week? Nothing, no work, no wages. One can't complain, one is a day labourer. I ask, why, but he doesn't know, the foreman doesn't, no one knows, nobody knows anything at all. People down there, they said; someone in Paris, the foreman thinks it is, they fancy now they won't have a factory, not in Baulon; somewhere else perhaps—in Lyon, who knows? They don't want a factory in Baulon, that's clear. Me? I come from Chalons, with my outfit. A year, that was what they told me, a year before all the bricklaying's done—factory, cottages, all that. It's to do with the Germans, that's what someone told me, but you don't know. . . ." Assuredly something, a certain malaise, a certain foreboding, was creeping into Baulon with the November fog. A notice had been posted at the Hôtel de Ville which nobody understood: it spoke in the official jargon of precautionary measures, it called upon the good citizenry of Baulon to exercise its patience, to be circumspect, to behave with prudence, and generally to exhibit the civic virtues, in circumstances which were not clearly specified. The document's slightly paternal tone gained a sympathetic if mystified attention, until an Appeal to Sober and Right-Minded Crossing-Sweepers in the Hour of Crisis was issued, above the initials R. S., from the offices of *Le Petit Baulonnais*. For the generality, the squib was sufficient. The aspect of things was not altered, the rumours were the old rumours which always came from Paris, the trams still clanged over the Pont des Grecs, undoubtedly the volcano might explode at any moment but in the meantime there were vegetables to be bought and money to be earned before you could buy them. The fog, the special fog for which Baulon was renowned, hung in the streets as thick as the dust from a stair-carpet. They cursed it as they cursed it year after year, but they sniffed it, the natives of Baulon, not without a tacit appreciation. The gas lamps in the streets were lighted all day long, giving a yellow twilight which had its charm, an aspect you would remember if you moved to some place where the fog was not so homely, to the banlieue of Paris or to Dijon. The shops blazed their light across the pavements, the windows were full already of the New Year novelties; and if you did not care for the raw air, the yellow odour in the rue des Tambons, you could sit all evening in the Espérance, the De La Paix, the Commerce, the Grand Victor, for the price of a demi-litre of Byrrh; packed close in the warm and smoky fog, discussing with your neighbours endlessly, with passion but without inquietude, the rights of man, the rascality of Martial Venauvière, the obscurities of to-day's Paris Letter in *Le Petit Baulonnais*. It will come in time, they said, herded altogether on the hinder platform of the tram-car; those swine over there, they would be giving trouble before long. But in the meantime, there were the swine in Paris, Jews no doubt, who had turned off the men engaged on the new factory, turned them off at four days' notice, and with children, many of them. And there were the swine of politicians whom the Jewish swine bribed to allow such goings on. "I tell you, Paul Fallouard, I tell you distinctly, there is not a politician in Paris, not one man in the Chamber, Right or Left as may be, who is not bribed by the owners of the Paris businesses. I can tell you that with certainty, I have private information from my nephew who works in the secretariat."

The outward aspect was unchanged, the pace unaltered. They worked, the Baulonnais. From the moment it was light you saw them on the timber wharves, boys from sixteen up, grey-headed gaillards, a folded neckcloth to protect the shoulder against the weight of four six-metre deals, moving with delicacy and firmness across the lighters, along the single bending plank that mounted thirty degrees to the quay-side, straight on to the deal stacks eighty paces off; the chain of men unbroken until half-past twelve. They swarmed, never idle, on the tugs and in the shunting yards; long after darkness, when the swinging arc-lamps splashed yellow pools across the murk of clearing-sheds, they were pushing trolleys, four in line with their heads almost on the ground, up the twisting goods-ramps, climbing like cats to the highest coal stacks, swinging the bales of hemp to shoulder height upon the loading shelf. They were short men, commonly, all bone and gristle, with a sleeveless grey blouse open to the navel, blue linen trousers, sometimes a blue cap to keep the sweat from dropping in the eyes. Lean-faced, the faces shining with a constant sweat, black chinned; a cigarette, burnt up one side, stuck everlastingly to the edge of the lower lip. They called to each other in staccato phrases, they spat, they grunted. There was never hurry, the work moved like the dots on a revolving band, from lighter to warehouse, from warehouse to factory. They had the air, the working Baulonnais, of cool superiority; their hard, quiet eyes, rimmed with sweat and coal-dust, moved slowly across the workshops scornful and faintly derisive, as if an aristocracy were fettered to the galley. They nodded to their orders, always obedient, always with gentle contempt. And their stout women, short-sleeved, heavy-stockinged, reflected their cool independence. Between the river and the avenue Saint-Roman there was no break, no privacy. The sprawl of cottages that reached to the water's edge spread back to the villa gardens, cut every way with lanes; the Baulon laughter, short and thunderous, ran from the open doors across the street to the little cafés, the Tambourin, the Roi des Belges, from the cobbler's shop across the strip of sandy waste where the children shrieked and tumbled. It overflowed, that commonwealth of straitened life, into the broader streets; it kept there for its special use the monts de piété, the little shops where five sous bought a kilo of viand-aux-marins. Baulon's foundation, it merged into the thoroughfares of Baulon, jostled with clerks and students, crowded with Mesdames du Quartier Sacré-Cœur on the tram-car platforms. They were too busy, those of the wharf and factories, to be disturbed by that malaise which gave an odour to the café pavements. The cure for restlessness was sweat and coal dust, children's torn clothes and the squeezing into potage of bones thrice used already, the flavouring of cabbage stalks to feed a man who would carry three tons between shed and lighter before the evening meal.

They set the pace of life, maintained its tempo. The surface might be rippled by the Paris rumours; the undercurrent, lying deep, flowed too strong to be disturbed.

The trams squeaked and rattled along the avenue Saint-Roman, they grazed the pavement swinging round into the rue Jean-Rôdit, they lurched at full speed along the boulevard Maréchal Soult, drew rein as they reached the place des Enfants du Roi and circled solemnly as in a country dance before the Hôtel de Ville. The women lumbered down from the forward platform with their vast string-bags bulging, the conductor rolled a cigarette and lit it from a driver on the other circle, the house-agent's clerk slipped off into the Espagne, his brief-case under arm, for a tonic brandy on his way to the auction office. At midday, for an hour or so, Raymond Séverin held forth to his friend Vasseur, sprawling across the chess-table, on the inner history of the Pont Inférieur election. In the evening he declaimed at the Club des Libérés upon the criminal lethargy of the Foreign Office, upon the scare-mongers who were seeking to strengthen their own position by the manipulation of working-class credulity, upon the fatuous complacency, the sentimental arrogance, of the periwigged bourgeois in the Quartier Sacré-Cœur. But at seven in the morning he was in the tape-room at the office in the place Coupel, laying out with the careless rapidity of long practice the second Paris page of the late edition; at nine-o'clock on the galley-proof desk, at midnight in bed with Cecilé. "No one with an atom of self-respect," he said gloomily to Vasseur, "can remain for more than a month at Baulon." But he remained, while the ridiculous Buchequets, the gross Charlieux and his silly wife, the imbecile daughters of M. Robert Gautrain, were leaving. "The manufacturers and the pawnbrokers, the whole tribe of gutless bourgeois are running away from Baulon as if the devil were after them. You and I, my dear Vasseur, we remain like Horatio to guard the contemptible bridge."

It was partly to rest himself from the confusion of politics, from the touchy air of the clubs and cafés, that he would go to the place Talleyrand on a Sunday afternoon. "At the place Talleyrand," he told Cécile, "they know nothing of what is going on, they are wholly occupied with their own concerns, with the eternal Affaire Séverin which everyone else in the world has forgotten; really it's a relief to be with people who are plainly ignorant instead of those whose ignorance is diluted by epidemic funk into a liquid soup of poisonous garrulity." "Yes, yes, darling Raymond I know just how you feel about that. If we could live in Paris, where people have such sensible ideas, and where you are paid more for writing the newspapers, and where the shops are so much better. . . ." But he knew that they were not wholly ignorant in the place Talleyrand. He had found out—Marianne had told him —that Aunt Thérèse had sold the little property she had at Pontà-Marcq; she had got a poor price for it, Marianne said; that might or might not be so—Thérèse never owned to having done well for herself in a financial transaction; but if it were true that she had taken a low figure, then she at any rate knew how things were shaping. And of course she knew, she spent hours over the Paris newspapers which no one else in the house could ever find, she was sharp as any Jew in watching her little properties. More of them, Raymond thought, than she admitted; Thérèse was always down-at-heel, the clothes she wore had the magnificence of a past generation, she bullied Raymond incessantly for any trifle he might owe her; but she had things up her sleeve, he was sure she had. With him, at least, she never discussed public affairs. They talked always of art, of the rôle of the artist in the theatre. The same argument, again and again: "But I tell you, Aunt, it is utterly inconceivable for any artist to interpret Esther, or even Doña Sol, unless she loses completely her own personality, unless she becomes transformed like the Elements in the Mass, takes inside herself the spiritual conception which the genius of Racine created. From my knowledge, as a painter, of the fundamentals of art . . ." "You have been listening, my dear Raymond, to the romantic chatter of the Quartier Latin, of those young gentlemen who cannot so much as afford to give a supper to a member of the corps de ballet. It was Envermeu—listen to me—it was Envermeu who said to me, when he started my training at the age of twelve years, 'You have first of all to learn, Mlle Séverin, that the theatre offers no pleasure except to the audience, no delicious transports, no bathing naked in warm pools of poetic emotion. The artist, it is she who concentrates all the time, who never forgets herself or her audience, who says all the time, every moment she is on the stage, *I will do this now, I will speak like that, the effect on the mind of the audience will be thus, they will realize exactly the significance of the way my head turns a little to the left, the way my voice drops in the middle of a verse, the little subtleties in the movements of my hands.* It is concentration, Mademoiselle, that is what art means.' And if you, Raymond——" "And from that I understand that the theatre would be greatly improved if only taxcollectors, whose power of application exceeds man's understanding, were allowed to perform. It is easy to understand how you come to possess your financial acumen." "That reminds me, Raymond, that Cécile borrowed fifteen francs last Sunday, which she said you would pay back to me. . . ." If he touched obliquely upon public affairs she would always evade him. "You know, I suppose, that everyone who has any money is leaving Baulon?

Do you think Mother and Father will be packing up?" "That is for your Uncle Louis to decide, he is the owner of everything. But I see no reason——"

Yet Madeleine knew that people were leaving. "If it were not for this house I would be quite desolate," the Abbé Vignaud told her, "all my friends in Baulon are leaving. Why? It is the fog, I fancy, it seems to get worse every winter. Old Mme Delapeyre, she is the latest, she goes at the end of the month to her villa at Argentan. Her house in Baulon is to be sold, if they can find a buyer; but that is doubtful, the house is so close to the river. Poor Mme Delapeyre, her asthma has been getting steadily worse. A move was absolutely necessary, but I shall miss her sadly. You have met Mme Delapeyre, of course? She is among the most charming people of Baulon."

"No, I have not had that pleasure. Mme Delapeyre came here a month after me—my husband's family, of course, has been here a great deal longer than hers—and for some reason she has never called. I am certain, of course, that she intended no lack of courtesy."

"Of that I am quite certain," Vignaud agreed. He knew the reason. "But I am sorry you have not met, she is so very delightful, Mme Delapeyre, and she has memories which would interest you; she moved formerly, as you have always done, in very good society. Yes, I have known her family for a long time. It was a relation of hers, an old cousin long since dead, who gave me at one time a great deal of trouble. She was perfectly certain towards the end of her life of almost tedious virtue that she had committted adultery with the Duc du Montoire, a misogynic old philatelist who lived in the avenue Henri Martin and whom she had never set eyes on. No one could convince her of her innocence, and I found it extremely difficult, as her Director, to prescribe appropriately. She became positively angry that I did not treat her more harshly. . . . The Roquignys have moved to Paris, the Castagnols have gone, old Mme Lossi-Badouin and her daughter, and now Mme Delapeyre. It is very sad for me, the havoc that the fog is wreaking upon Baulon. I hope, dear Mme Séverin, you will stay to comfort me—though I don't like that little cough of yours, I should like you to have more sunshine."

Madeleine shook her head. "No, there has been no talk of our leaving. Eugène would not like it, he is accustomed to this house, he used to stay here when he was a boy, before Baulon had grown up to what it is now. He has to Baulon a kind of melancholy attachment, I do not think he would leave it until the way is free for him to return to Paris. It is to that time that we always look forward."

Vignaud stared at his knuckles.

"Ah, yes, to Paris."

"But you have not yet heard our news," she said. "You must keep this a secret, I am not yet telling Eugène in case he should get too excited. That Lenormand, you have heard me speak of him? Yes, he is the witness so important to us, he is the one man who can prove beyond every doubt that the evidence against Eugène was false completely. M. Lecours has discovered him, has found out where he is living. I don't know how M. Lecours found out, he's very clever, like his father. It appears that Captain Lenormand is living somewhere in America. I don't know what part it is, I suppose he is a settler over there. No, not in New York—some other part, I think."

"And M. Lecours is going to bring him to France?"

"He has promised to do so if he can. The negotiations are proceeding. I have written to Lecours that he must arrange it somehow, no matter what it costs. Of course we have no money, none of us has any money, but if necessary we must borrow from my brother Louis. If this Captain Lenormand cannot be persuaded by letters, then I will go over to America myself to persuade him. No, I am not anxious to do so. I have never been on board ship, and I do not suppose that I should enjoy colonial society. America is no place for a woman. But if necessary I shall certainly go myself to fetch Captain Lenormand. I have made up my mind about that."

Exerting every facial muscle, Vignaud kept back his smile. She was so much in earnest, he would not for the world have hurt the feelings of his poor Mme Séverin.

"I hope it will not be necessary," he said. "It is not the kind of adventure that would suit you. I am sure that if the facts are explained to this Lenormand he will not hesitate to do his duty. And then, as I rejoice in your happiness, I myself have the sadness of losing another dear friend in Baulon."

"But you will arrange things, Father, you will come to Paris too. Nobody can go on living in Baulon. There is no society at all here, no culture. In the summer it is dusty and in winter it's miserable, oh, so dank and cold. And it's dangerous, too, so I've heard people saying in the shops. My servant Joséphine goes round all the doors every night to make sure that Barbier has bolted them; she is afraid, she says, that the Prussians will break in and kill us when we are asleep. They know, those people, they have a kind of instinct."

"There is a lot of foolish talk," Vignaud said firmly. "They will believe anything in Baulon."

"In Baulon they will believe anything," Raymond said to Vasseur. "They believe it is owing to the emperor of Germany that wages have got lower, that they have stopped building the

148

jam-factory. They believe at the same time that the rich tradesmen are moving their families to the other side of Paris because of the severity of the winter, which is just as mild as any winter I can remember. And they are entirely willing to accept the statement of the same rich tradesmen when they dress up in their picturesque sashes and stand on the steps of the Hôtel de Ville and say that everybody is perfectly safe in Baulon so long as they behave like good children. You would think with all the rumours going about that the appetite of the Baulonnais would be satisfied; and yet we journalists have to sweat all day and half the night to keep them supplied with enough new lies from Paris. . . ."

But Raymond himself knew scarcely more than the Baulonnais. He was the channel of news, not the source of it. His business was to sort the appetizing from the ordinary, and with that preoccupation he had hardly time to consider more serious values. He could regard with gratifying detachment the wares in which he dealt and in which the generality took so much interest, but the volume from which he retailed increased his own confusion. His consciousness reflected the inquietude at which he mocked, the sharpened air of café controversy infected him with an excitement that he studiously guarded. He knew, after all, a little more than the others. His friend Louis Davesne on the *Intransigeant* had written that there would be an explosion soon: ". . . within two years, of that you can be quite certain; and you can lay ten to one that we shall be in it, whatever happens, up to the neck." Well, that would be a relief, a solution to many difficulties. Presumably he would have to go soldier. That was an unpleasant prospect, since the taste of three years' service was still bitter in his mouth, and he had no appetite for la gloire. But it would get him away from Baulon, right away from Cécile; more important still, perhaps, away altogether from Pierre's Renée: whose presence quickened his breath whenever he turned from the rue des Suisses into the dour place Talleyrand, and who treated him with nothing more than an amiable civility. Yes, he thought, it would settle many things. He hated everything to do with newspapers, he was a failure as a painter. It would please the old man to have two sons in the army, and it would be fun, perhaps, by the intensive application of a little intelligence, to rise above Pierre. For Cécile, how suitable, to have a gallant husband, and one who was never there.

It was half-past ten, Chivalié would be in before long to take over. He rang for the foreman of the composing-room and gave him the proof-slips for the early edition rolled in a bundle. "Yes, I know I'm late, you'd better for God's sake hurry. Tell M. Chivalié, when you see him, that I had a temperature." He went down the passage d'Oisie, intending to make his usual call at the

Flandres, where he might find Vasseur. But no, he was not up to conversation; too tired; there was something at the back of his head which he wanted to straighten out. Something to do with Renée. He went on without considering direction and found himself by the river. There was only one lamp between the corner where he stood and the Petit Pont, and the mist was so thick here that he could hardly see the water. He made his way slowly along the cobbled towpath, keeping close to the line of granaries for fear of walking over the edge, circumventing cautiously the sacks and tackle lying in his way. A stone that his foot caught shot across the path and plopped into the water. He crept to the edge, looked over and could just discern the ripple. Uuh! It was cold. The weight of fog seemed to deaden sound; he could hear only faintly the noise of wheels on the pavé of the other bank, the gongs of trams in the rue Etanier like the tinkle of goat-bells. The town was drugged, he thought, spread over with soporific vapour which would keep it still until the day of Judgment. The very lamps were sleepy, growing dim. No wonder Renée wanted—yes, that was what she had said, "I want to get away from Baulon." "I will take you to Paris," he had said, "we will have a week there, I can get a week off and Cécile can go to her mother." But she had answered very gravely. "You know, Raymond, that isn't what I want. It's only to get away, to get Armand away from Baulon." "And what would Pierre say?" She had become confused then, and brought up her handkerchief, and presently had left him.

He thought he saw something move, in the deep shadow beneath a lucam, and started, remembering only now that no one in his senses came along here after dark alone. Yes, a figure was emerging. He tried to go wide of it, stepping as near the river edge as he could, but the man came straight towards him, caught him by the arm. "I wouldn't trouble you, Monsieur, only I'm desperate." No, it was a woman. He said sharply, "Leave me alone." "I'm desperate," she repeated. She still had his arm and he could not shake her off.

Approaching the Petit Pont, he saw from the lamp there that it was quite a young girl, whose rags hardly covered her.

"What is it you want?" he demanded.

"Anything. Five francs would help."

"I haven't got as much. I'll give you a drink."

The estaminet below the bridge, lit with a paraffin flare, was empty of customers. Raymond said: "What do you want? A petit armagnac?" "I'd rather have coffee." "A big coffee," he said to the owner, "and a petit armagnac." The owner slopped out the drinks, took the money, and went on reading the *Petit Baulonnais*.

The girl sat on the bench with her back against the vaulting, waiting for the coffee to get cooler. She did not seem to want it. "I've got three children," she said, "one at the breast. You can't go out working when you've got three children. It's all very well to say that François will look after them, but what happens when he's drunk?"

"You'd better drink up your coffee."

"They said it was a year's work, the factory and then the workers' houses. And now they're not building anything, not a chicken-house. There's no building in Baulon. I've got three children, I can't leave them for François to look after."

"I know, I know. But if your coffee gets cold it won't do you any good."

"There's a word here, I can't make out," the stall-owner said, "my eyes aren't very good. *Mesures prophylactiques.* Do you know what that means, Monsieur?"

"Yes, it means that new taxes are going to be imposed which will add to the security of the wealthy."

"Oh. . . . You can't always believe what they tell you in the paper."

"No, but you always do."

"It's not that I didn't manage carefully," the girl said. "I made François give me everything, every penny. I saw it didn't go wrong. I wouldn't let him have more than two-twenty-five every week. I only bought the things the children must have. And the little thing, it's no good his sucking, there's nothing there. He keeps crying."

"Well, there won't be anything there unless you drink that coffee."

"I can't, it won't go down. Everything comes up as soon as I take it. . . . But with five francs—I'll do what you want for five francs, look, it's all right. You've only got to find a place, I can't go where François is."

"I can't quite make it out," the owner said. "*Mesures prophylactiques*, it seems to me a funny word."

"I haven't any more money," Raymond told her. He put his glass down on the counter and climbed up to the roadway. The girl panted after him. "Just five francs," she repeated, "I only want five francs." He left her leaning against the parapet.

He had gone a hundred paces along the road when he heard behind a splash, as if someone had thrown a boulder from the bridge. He stopped and turned round. There was no more noise, no cry, nothing. He ran back to the bridge. The girl was not there. He scrambled down beneath the archway, where the owner of the estaminet was still reading his paper.

"Did you see anything fall in?"

"I don't know. I heard something. Will you tell me again what is the meaning of this curious word *prophylactique*?"

"I don't know, I've no idea what it means. Are you sure you don't know what fell in?"

"No, it's no business of mine. Lots of things fall in, things people can do without. Pro-phy-lac-tique . . .?"

Raymond walked a little way downstream. He thought he could see something floating, but there was no sound. He shivered and went up again on to the road, he increased his pace and hurried towards the place des Enfants. It was better there, more light, people on the pavement, the noise of argument and laughter from the cafés.

He reached the Café de la Bourse and saw through the window that Leprovost was there in his usual corner. Feeling now that he must talk to somebody he went inside, called to the waiter for a vermout justinien, and sat at Leprovost's elbow. Leprovost put down his soiled copy of *Terres Vierges* and smiled sleepily with the spread of his huge sallow face. "I'll have the same thing, tell him to bring two vermouts, thanks, Raymond." He leaned back and yawned like a great cat. He was always like that, always half-asleep, always in the same grey plaid shirt with the collar fixed, no collar-stud, the rag of a yellow tie hanging with the knot five inches below his chin. "You've finished your day's labour, ladling out titbits to the ravenous populace?"

"I have. Do you know, Emile, I've just met a man who didn't know what I meant by *mesures prophylactiques*. He just hadn't heard the phrase. That's the sort I sweat for. You can imagine how keenly they appreciate my subtleties, how rapidly they discern that when I write a leader praising the mayor of Baulon I am just taking down the old gentleman's trousers. Baulon, my God, this place Baulon, why in the world should it have a newspaper at all?"

"My dear Raymond, I have never been able to understand why Baulon should have a newspaper. I've always imagined that it was to provide work for deserving young men who are not quite good enough for the Paris papers. You make a great mistake, my friend, in working at all. No one who works can cultivate philosophy. You should be a student, I myself have been a student for twenty years, I have never yet passed an examination, and I have never regretted reading any one of the several thousand books I have read in that time, whether good or bad. This, for example, is a bad book, it is a thoroughly silly book, and yet it has enabled me to form quite a new theory about that grossly over-rated Tourguenieff, a very interesting theory indeed, and one to which I cannot find any rational objection. Listen, now, I'll explain it to you. Or do you want to talk politics as everybody else in this damned drinkshop is doing?"

"No, I do not want to talk about politics. The political situation, as far as it affects Baulon, amounts to just this. . . ."

"Listen, then, and I'll explain what I've discovered about Tourguenieff. . . ."

But Raymond was not listening. On the topic of Pierre he had never been quite right with Renée, and that might have been the reason for her confusion when he had asked, "What would Pierre say to that?" But it was surely of recent origin, this absolute refusal to talk about Pierre, this embarrassment when his name was mentioned. It was not improbable that she had had a row with Pierre—who, after all, could live on good terms for any length of time with a man so irresponsible, so touchy? If that were so . . . but he must find out the facts if possible. It was quite likely that Aunt Thérèse knew what letters had come from Pierre lately, and she might even have contrived to see them. If not, Joséphine would probably tell him, for the matter of forty sous, when the last letter had arrived. It certainly seemed queer, to pack up your family and send them home like the week's washing, to leave them there for months. And if Pierre had turned nasty, the poor girl would want comfort from somebody. . . .

"So you see," Leprovost continued, "the only possible conclusion was that Tourguenieff was a heroin-addict, and that the whole of his work was in reality the embroidered expression of his unconscious resentment against some unknown Caucasian ancestor who . . ."

"One minute, Emile. Do you know, a queer thing happened just now, down at the Petit Pont. A woman jumped into the river."

"Indeed? The cult of athleticism among women comes, in Europe, from the Germanic races. The type of Brunehaut——"

"No, seriously, she drowned herself. I was there, only fifty paces away."

Leprovost raised his eyebrows with appreciation.

"I always say it's extraordinary the way you journalists manage to be at the right place at the right time. Did you get her story?"

"Yes," Raymond said ferociously, "I had her story. Listen, you lazy overfed bed-louse, I'll tell you what her story was——"

Leprovost waved a benign hand.

"Patience, dear friend, I have not yet finished. I have still to tell you how I make my theory watertight. Let us, for a moment, recapitulate. . . ."

Raymond put two francs on the table and went away. It was getting on his nerves, though he had tried not to think about it: the fringe of black hair on the girl's yellow forehead, the splash, the dark object that he had seen for a moment sticking out of the water. He was a poor swimmer, but he ought perhaps to have got a boat-hook or something, to have called somebody. He would have to get it off his chest by writing a bitter article, which Davesne perhaps would have published for him. He would sit down and write it off when he got home.

But it was late now, going on towards twelve. Cécile would make a fuss about his being so late. "And what should I do if a man got in, with just me and Lili in the house?" "My dear, you would have to spin a coin for him." "It's unkind of you, Raymond, to come home so late, when you know how scared I am. . . ." It was like that every night. Bound down, obliged to be at fixed places at fixed times, the place Coupel at seven, the rue du Parc Jibelot for dinner, always within the shabby streets of Baulon, never away from the sharp provincial accent of the Baulonnais, from the accursed smell of the Baulon sewage. In this street the cafés did late business; there was still some traffic on the pavements, a group beneath the street-lamp continued the discussion that had raged all evening in the Flacon Bleu. A man had the morning paper spread out in the dusty light, "I tell you," he was saying, "this letter from Paris puts quite a new complexion on the rapprochement of the left, this is rationally the most important thing that has happened since the election." 'I could tell them,' Raymond thought, 'just who really wrote it and how much it is worth, that important letter from Paris.' But it was stale to him, that kind of satisfaction, it glowed like a matchstick for just four seconds. 'And those are the savants for whom I sweat in the place Coupel!' His custom was to turn here and get on the tram opposite the Comptoir des Indes; but to-night he walked straight on, and fast, moved by the impulse to include the place Talleyrand in his way home. He wanted, if he could, to see Renée; he had to tell somebody about that affair at the Petit Pont, and she at least would listen quietly to him. But when he reached the square, worn out with walking at that unusual pace, there was only one light showing from 17; the drawing-room, that would be Maman, who indulged herself, long after the rest had gone to bed, in sentimental reading. By this time Renée would most likely be asleep; he should have thought of that. He had a moment's vision of Renée curled up in bed, her face squashed against the pillow, and he wanted to say, "Renée, Renée my dear, won't you tell me what it is about you and Pierre, I'll do anything I can, I'll look after you." But there was Ste Gudule striking. Midnight. He crossed the square again to where the line of naked scaffold-poles reached up into the fog. The light from an open door, where a family of many children and their parents were mealing as if in summer noon, guided him into the rue des Suisses. Someone, a girl, was walking not far ahead, and he thought for an instant that it might be Renée. He quickened his pace to catch up, but she turned off sharply into a passage. He saw her face for a second beneath the street-lamp; a yellow face, with a fringe of black hair falling on the forehead, and he was almost sure that the hair was wet. She had disappeared, he would have followed but his legs wouldn't go that way, they wouldn't budge. He called "Mademoiselle, wait!" but there was no answer. Suddenly he began to run, and arrived in the boulevard breathless. The last tram had gone. The boulevard was empty, beneath its quilt of fog Baulon was asleep. Not sound asleep, he thought, but still, quiescent, waiting for something that she knew was coming. Between the lamps he hurried, fancying that someone followed him. *Just five francs, Monsieur.* But it was Renée's voice. The poplars moved in column past him like a marching army, his feet fell softly on the trodden leaves, the town was sinking farther into the brown darkness, dragging him pinioned in its fall. He heard the voice again and knew he must go back. He turned and walked at the same pace, quickening a little where the road was darkest; to the place des Enfants, past the shuttered cafés, the silent houses in the passage Epicine. In twenty minutes he was at the Petit Pont again, where the owner of the estaminet had gone to sleep, stretched on the bench with his head on the *Petit Baulonnais*. He leaned against the parapet and stared down at the water, where he could just see the swirl against the pile, nothing but that.

XX

IT seemed in December that the fog would never lift. They had forgotten what it was like to look across the Parc Rousseau and see, above the scribble of naked branches, the pasture slopes of Saint-Pierre-les-Fermes. In the new year it was cleared at last by a Flanders wind, frosty and dry. The sky revealed was brilliant, hard; the town seemed oddly clean, the stagnant odour had been swept away; but for the ice in all the gutters, the chill, the rime on lamp-posts, you had said it was an early spring. But the sky's colour dulled, the wind dropped, leaving the chilled air still. The first snow came in the early dusk of January, by morning all the sounds were deadened in the place Talleyrand. The town was under siege again; the roads to the northern villages were said to be impassable already, Paris seemed very far away. The children from the tenements played barefoot in the snow, using the scaffold poles as shield against the snowballs. Their choicest target was the gawky youth who sometimes ventured out from 17 with an empty milkpail; who only grinned when the snowballs broke against his misshapen skull and discharged a handful of broken ice inside his shirt. "He doesn't mind, he's cracked, that Gaston Barbier, pelt him again." But apart from Gaston it was seldom anyone emerged from M. Séverin's house. The children were accustomed to see old Mlle Séverin, that awe-inspiring lady with the high cheekbones and the cold stare, the tremendous hooded cloak and the silver handled walking-stick, come out for her twenty-minutes' round each afternoon. But Thérèse's rheumatism had got bad again; she could only hobble painfully as far as the drawing-room, and most of her time was spent in her own room. In a window of the second floor, the ragged children of the Square could often see a small boy staring out at them; that boy who had formerly passed through the Square on sunny days dressed in a blue coat of many buttons with blue leggings and a woollen cap. He was there for hours at a time, his nose squashed like a ball of suet against the pane, his mouth and chin hidden by the patch of mist which his breath made. Sometimes the little girl would stand there too; but neither was ever seen outside. He kept so still, the little boy at the window, that sometimes the children watching doubted if he were not a statue, like the coloured plaster casts you saw in the rue des Moines. He epitomized for them the inscrutability of that sinister house, familiar to their scene from first consciousness, but never with its mystery and dread. No one knew how long the inhabitants had been there, where they came from, what they did. They called sometimes to Gaston, "What do they do in there?" but he could not tell them. "Is it true they've got an old woman, twice as old as Mlle Séverin, that they pull her flesh with pincers into ribbons?" His head wagged, they thought perhaps he was nodding; but he told them nothing, they had no answer but his giggling laughter.

Madeleine was fearful lest Eugène should not live till the summer. The cold played hard with him, and he kept to his room again. His fire was lighted in the morning and about midday he would sometimes get out of bed to sit at the fireside; with his old tunic buttoned above his night-shirt, his lower half swaddled in a carriage rug, a woollen bonnet-demarin protecting his head and a wolf-skin over his knees. He did nothing. She read his letters to him, the few there were; sometimes a book of memoirs, the campaigns of General Troupenat or Ursin's *Life and Famous Cases*. Occasionally he would interrupt. "That was foolish, an elementary error." "Yes, it was like that in the old days, they had gentlemen at the bar then." But as a rule he was silent, with his eyes closed, so that she could not tell if he were still awake. She went on without thought, her mind receiving not the smallest impression from the words she read; and sometimes she was brought back from far away, from the parties in the place de Strasbourg where Madame de Montiscard had been so witty about poor Empress Eugénie, by a voice demanding plaintively, "Couldn't you skip that chapter, Madi? You know I always find it dull." Their talk was limited to trivialities; that new stuff which Tischer had brought, it was doing no good at all; except when he spoke of the intention which seemed to be gathering substance in his mind.

"I must go to Viboire," he would say abruptly.

"Viboire?"

Patiently, "Viboire-les-Deux-Auberges. Yes, as soon as the weather gets better. It's too cold now, I feel the cold badly, ever since my Algerian service. I don't expect you can quite imagine it, the coldness that one gets in the bones. But when it's warmer I must go to Viboire. I want to see the place again, to get the whole thing fresh in my mind. Of course I have the sketch maps, but they're not good enough, they don't show the detail, and in several places I'm sure they're wrong. I shall take Barbier with me, and someone intelligent who can makes notes on the spot—I might take Pierre's wife, she's a sensible girl. Then I shall have something to give Lecours. That fellow's lazy, he ought to collect his own material, that's what he's paid for. But it will hurry things if I get material for him. I shall be able to get everything much clearer when I see Viboire again."

"When you are strong enough," she said, soothing him, "yes, when the weather is better you will be able to go to Viboire."

But she hoped that the idea would pass from his mind as it had passed before. Twice, since the horror in Paris, he had been to Viboire, measuring distances from road to hedge, making his little maps, giving her figures to write down. It would do no good, another visit; he would only doubt his measurements again, wake in the early hours to puzzle over some confusion in his memory, ask for the gas to be lighted so that he could scrutinize the maps once more. She longed to tell him now of the surprise she was preparing, of how clever M. Lecours had been in tracing Captain Lenormand. But something might still go wrong, and the disappointment would be more than he could bear. For her, the arrival of Lenormand was a dream at once to sustain and frighten. At long last the prospect of a re-trial seemed to have become material, she had something on which her hopes could fasten. But she knew how risky the foundation was upon which she had built a mountain of expectation. She looked every day for a letter from Lecours which would tell her everything was settled, that Lenormand was on his way. But her eagerness was darkened by the dread that when the letter came it would topple over all her hopes:

Lenormand would have disappeared again, Lenormand would be dead. She wrote to Lecours constantly, late at night when Eugène had been settled for sleep. 'You must spare no pains or money. Lenormand must be brought the fastest way, no matter what he asks as compensation. If it is necessary I will go myself to fetch him.' And Lecours's replies were always the same, full of courtesy, entirely vague: the matter was being pressed forward; no effort would be spared; at present there were certain difficulties, certain obstacles unforeseen, but Lecours had every hope that in due course these would be surmounted.

Beneath the dread of failure there lay the larger, instant fear for Eugène's health. When the case came on he would need a vast reserve of strength. He had been young before, and she could recollect—how vividly—his dead fatigue at night, when he had waited all day in the dreary ante-rooms or sat for hours in the little box marking each word in the cross-examinations. Perhaps he had known then, as she had known from the first day intuitively, that it would end in his defeat. But even if victory seemed certain, could he sustain those hours in the polluted air, the formalities, the interminable harangues of counsel? She watched him, day by day, trying to think he had increased in animation, that his eyes were brighter, his cheek a better colour. She asked of Tischer almost pleadingly, "Has he lost strength? Tell me, Doctor, is there any sign of increasing weakness?" But she had ceased to trust his grave assurances, they came too readily or with plainly counterfeited hesitation. "To-day I think he is a little stronger. . . . He seems to be in better case to-day; the condition, I think, shows perceptible improvement." In the spring, perhaps, he would be better. But the winter dragged, there were weeks to go before the warmer weather came.

She began to neglect her own appearance, and grew used to seeing in the mirror the deepening folds about her eyes, the roughening of her skin. She had still, in the huge wardrobe in her linen room, the dresses she had meant to wear again when they got back to Paris, those lovely things of satin and brocade, still giving faintly the odour of Parisian salons de robes, with the silver-embroidered sleeves, the stiffened flounces, the careless profusion of malines. But she had ceased to take them out for airing, to smooth the velvet with her little ebony brush, to iron out the folds. The cupboard was no longer opened, the moths she had campaigned against with so much industry were allowed to have their way. Her own strength would not run to everything; she had dropped one after another the items of her old routine. She had periods of giddiness, after her fits of coughing, and they left her vaguely frightened. Her forces were reduced, she must concentrate now upon a single effort, to have Eugène ready when the time came to go into battle. So very old, he looked now, with the gas light sharpening his wrinkles, and his voice had grown so feeble. But he would rally, perhaps, in the spring.

It was a hopeful sign that he had not lost interest in his grandchildren. "The little boy," he often said, "the little Armand, what is he doing? He's still in the house, surely? But I never hear his voice. I'd like the little boy to be sent to see me. I want to see if he is really a Séverin."

"He wants to see Armand," Madeleine said to Renée, "he is constantly inquiring after him." She was met with a firm refusal. "Armand is not at all well. No, he isn't fit to go." And again, a few days later, "It would give my husband so much pleasure if you would send Armand up to see him." "I am sorry, Mme Séverin, but Armand is not well."

"And Pierre," Madeleine asked, "you have good news of him?"

"Not recently. It's the rainy season where he is, it's impossible at present for him to get his letters through. But no doubt he is all right, Pierre, he has always been very strong."

Eugène was nettled by the resistance to his wishes. "I don't understand," he said. "Is the child in bed? No? Well, he can't be too ill to see me, he can't have got anything that I would catch. Let me see Renée."

She came, and he saw as she stood hesitant just inside the door that she was going to be obstinate: he had seen Pierre with a face just like that, Renée had caught it from him. He reasoned with her: "You can bring him with you, then surely he won't be frightened. He wasn't used to me, the first time, children are always shy with strangers." But she would not yield that much. In the summer, perhaps, when the children could get about, they would be less nervy. At present Armand's health was worrying her; she was sorry, but her mind was made up, at present he should see no one. She spoke quietly, but with a dangerous stress. She was very pale, and he saw how tautly her jaw worked: *Moi, j'y suis résolue!* All right. He himself was no less determined, but he would not argue with a half-breed girl young enough herself to be his grandchild. He dismissed her shortly. "Eh, bien, Madame Renée . . ." He bided his time.

A week had gone when Madeleine heard in sleep a movement in Eugène's room, Eugène's door opening. The impulse was hardly sufficient to arouse her; she came to consciousness slowly and lay still, weighed down with drowsiness, wondering what had made her stir. A full minute passed before she rose, suddenly fearful; opened the intervening door, listened and crept in her night-stockings to Eugène's bedside. The bed was empty.

Lighting the gas, she saw that the passage door was open. She hurried down the corridor and up to the next stage. There, at the end of the passage, she saw a patch of light from an open door.

It was the room where Renée and the children slept.

It occurred to her, as she went towards the light, that he might be walking in his sleep. He had done that once before, and she was frightened now lest he should suffer shock by being woken. Hardly daring to go forward, she crept on with her hand against the wall. Yes, he was in there. He was bending over Armand's bed, scrutinizing the face which lay sideways on the pillow, and he did not see her standing in the doorway. The children were asleep, and she thought that Renée slept.

He had moved back the sheet a little way, uncovering the lower half of Armand's face. With that he seemed to be content. He stood quite still, bent over with one hand grasping the head-post, the candle held in the other close to the boy's face. He was staring with minute attention, frowning a little like a puzzled surgeon. With the cords of sleep not altogether broken, Madeleine regarded the half-lit scene as if it were a group of statuary; the figures were so still, only their breathing moved them. She would have called to him, "Eugène! Eugène, what are you doing?" but her voice was held by fear. Armand might wake and scream.

The child shifted a little, murmured. Madeleine held her breath, sure that his eyes would open. But something else had moved, it was Renée, she was awake.

Eugène, wholly absorbed, did not hear her move up behind him. He had brought his face within an inch of Armand's and Madeleine saw that his expression was becoming grim, the Séverin lips tightening. Transfixed, she turned her gaze to Renée; and thought from the fury in Renée's eyes that she would strike him. It seemed to last for a long time, the moment in which Eugène let go the bed-post and brought his fingers towards Armand's head, while Renée watched him. Then Renée's hand shot out, grasping the candle flame. There was no sound except a slither, as of a mattress tugged across the floor.

The scream that Madeleine would have uttered seemed to go out through the back of her throat, with no more noise than the squeak of a rusty hinge. Someone lurched against her in the darkness and she heard Eugène's voice over her head gasping: "Who's that?"

"It's me, it's Madeleine. Did she——?"

He was panting like a man who has run uphill. "A light," he whispered. "Have you—matches?"

Feeling, she found the box in his tunic pocket. She struck a match with her hand shaking like a spring. The candle was lying on the floor with the candlestick beside it; she stooped and grasped them just before the flame went out. With a second match she lit the candle. The bedroom door had shut, with only the click of the catch. There was no sound from within, Eugène and she were alone.

Eugène's face had lost all its colour and his whole body was trembling. But on his lips there was a little smile, vexed and defiant; like that of a boy caught twisting a puppy's tail and escaped with only the tickle of a riding-crop across his shoulders; a grin of malice. He said nothing. He took the candle from her and led the way to his own room, where he set the candle on the mantelpiece, took off his tunic, and without a word got into bed. Mechanically, Madeleine pulled up the top sheet and turned it down, tucked the blankets under. Already Eugène's eyes were closed. She wanted to speak, but she could think of nothing to say. She blew out the candle, turned down the gas, and moved to the door of her own room. But he called her back:

"Madeleine!"

"Yes."

"I think I'll have the second pillow away. My head's too high. . . . Yes, that's better, that will do."

*

At the moment of waking, Madeline thought that the night's adventure had been a dream; it had that colour, husky and half lit, blended with horror and absurdity. But Angèle, who slept as a rule on the end of Eugène's bed, was curled this morning upon hers. That showed at least that the intervening door had been opened during the night, and now it was shut.

Angèle would have to be destroyed, she thought, listening to the bitch's wheeze; Angèle had become offensive, she often enraged Eugène by slobbering over his feet. And yet, last time Madeleine had suggested getting rid of her Eugène had been terribly upset. "Of course, Madeleine, if you find her offensive she must go. But she means a lot to me, living as I do shut up in one room. It's nice to have a companion who doesn't jabber. Sometimes I think Angèle cares for me and understands me better than anyone in the world. How can she help wheezing, poor thing? She's very old. But still, if she worries you, then of course I have no say in the matter." She pushed Angèle with her feet. The bitch rolled to the edge of the bed and over to the floor, falling on her side with a heavy thump, and whimpered piteously. Madeleine went softly into Eugène's room, when she found him fast asleep. She opened the shutters a little way so as to see his face. It was peaceful. Perhaps the excursion had done him no harm.

She was thinking, while she dressed, of Angèle; perhaps Dr. Tischer could say that the asthma was infectious and persuade

Eugène to have her destroyed; but there was another problem waiting and she could not shelve it for long.

"Renée is very shy," she had told people; "she is accustomed to a small society, and to live in France is quite a new experience for her." For a long time she had clung to that as her own opinion; but now she could no longer blind herself to Renèe's hostility. Hostility? No, that was perhaps too harsh a word. Renèe was unfriendly, she had rather express it thus. A fortnight ago she had made a costly effort, choosing a moment when she had Renèe to herself:

"I'm afraid it is strange for you, living in France; and naturally you miss Pierre. But you must realize that we are all your friends, you must try to feel at home here. I myself, naturally—you will understand that I have an affection for my son's wife."

But Renée had looked hard at the button she was sewing on Armand's trousers, had not even smiled.

"I realize," Renée said, "how very kind it is for you to have us here so long, to give up these rooms to us."

She asked then, as she did so often, "You have heard from Pierre lately?"

"No, not quite recently. . . . I am afraid—there is the question of money. According to our arrangement, I owe you now 223 francs, I think that's right. I'll settle it up, of course, directly Pierre's cheque comes. At present I have no money."

"The money?" Madeleine said. "Oh, that doesn't matter at all. You know about Marianne's plan—I have had to agree to it, though I don't know what my husband would say—we are letting two of the ground-floor rooms to some respectable people. That will bring in a little money, it will be helpful to us. But no, I was not thinking of the money side at all. I only wanted to have some good news of Pierre. Naturally I am a little worried, as you must be."

"But no, Mme Séverin, I see no reason to worry. Pierre can look after himself, he has always been very independent. I have no doubt that he will write presently, and send me some money."

It was like talking to a banker: Renée's face gave nothing away. Had it happened all her life, Madeleine wondered, or was it only now she was getting old that people talked to her like that—Lecours, Tischer and the rest, even the dear Abbé—in that precise, over-courteous way, blatantly withholding their true opinions? It would not have mattered, the obstinacy of this young woman of Pierre's ; only that now she had come into combat with Eugène, and it did Eugène no good to be upset by such warfare. Eugène of course had behaved foolishly; he had put himself in the wrong by this last night's monstrous escapade. But it was Renée who had provoked him by her contumacy, Renée had unsettled him and you must expect a sick man to act in a peculiar way. It was, after all, a curious state of affairs that Eugène was not allowed to see his own grandson. Renée, surely, must realize that if it were put to her in a straightforward way. This morning she would talk to Renée again, would try to get her in a gentler mood and then explain a little how Eugène had suffered a great disappointment, that his military career which had opened so brilliantly had been ruined by the jealousy of his superiors, how for so many years ill-health had increased the bitterness of his failure. Surely Renée would understand that, would try to show him a little affection. But the vision of Renée's face, as Eugène bent over Armand, returned to her. Never had Madeleine seen a face so grey with passion, such animal fury in human eyes. She remembered now an incident long forgotten, that time when she had been in the Parc Rousseau with little Raymond, and an old woman spitting with consumption had bent over him; how, suddenly aware of what was happening, she had caught the beldame by the arms and thrust her back with such force that she collapsed on the flower-bed. There was no comparison of the occasions, but in Renée's face last night she saw the reflection of what hers must have looked like then. She must leave it a little while until Renée had recovered from the shock. In the meantime she must pacify Eugène, try to turn his mind in a new direction. Yes, above all things she must keep Eugène calm.

Reluctantly, in the necessity for someone to share her burden, she went to Thérèse.

"I am worried, Thérèse, about Renée. She keeps herself and the children in her rooms so that I never see them. When I go to talk to her she speaks only of domestic matters, of the food she requires for the children. Of the children themselves she hardly speaks at all. She is never friendly. Eugène wants to see the children and she won't allow him. It's extraordinary, such behaviour, she is like an animal that has run wild into the woods."

Thérèse was still in bed, waiting for Tischer to come and give her massage. Upright, with her bony hands on the counterpane, her flowing sleeves, she reminded Madeleine of Chénot's Bossuet thundering from the high pulpit of the Oratory; so vigorous in colour and demeanour it was hard to believe she had any ailment.

"It is essentially Pierre's affair," Thérèse said dogmatically. "Pierre, it seems to me, has acted very strangely in dumping his family here, practically without a word of explanation, and leaving them as it appears indefinitely. I don't know why the young woman is not happy; she seems to me very foolish, the way she treats those children, keeping them cooped up all the time; but that's not our affair. We are providing her with food and lodging, she can sit in the drawing-room when she likes, we are ready to treat her amiably, what more can we do? I should take no notice of her sulks if I were you. Have you any news from Pierre, do you know when he will be coming home?"

Madeleine shook her head. "I never hear from him now."

"But you write?"

"Lately I have been too busy. I tell Renée to send messages for me in her letters."

"But my dear Madeleine that is no good at all. You must write to him yourself, explain that Renée does not seem to be happy among Europeans, that the children are unwell, and that you think some other arrangement might be made unless Pierre is coming home soon himself. That is the obvious thing."

"But what do you think Pierre would say if he thought we were unwilling to go on providing a home for his wife and children? Surely, Thérèse, you would not have him think——"

"I think that Pierre should at least be asked what his plans are for the future. It's ridiculous not to know that. Unless Renée herself can tell him. She gets letters, I suppose?"

"Not recently. It's some time since she heard from him."

"Indeed? Has there been a quarrel, do you suppose?"

"But how should I know? For myself, I have not the habit of reading other people's letters. In the part of Paris where I used to live it was not the custom."

Thérèse flipped the page of her book and appeared to resume her reading. She said, without lifting her eyes:

"It is not, of course, my affair. But it seems to me that the only thing is for you to talk to Renée, to tell her that she is behaving foolishly, to insist that Eugène be allowed to see Armand when he wishes; I don't suppose he wants to see the other child, who if needful can nearly always be found in Marianne's room—a curious choice of Sappho in my opinion. If you point out to Renée that she is, after all, dependent on you——"

"But, Thérèse, I have talked to her already. It is quite impossible to talk to her."

"Nonsense, Madeleine. If I were in your position——"

"If you were in my position you would find it just as difficult as I do."

Thérèse shut her eyes, trying conscientiously to imagine that she was in Madeleine's position. It was no good. She had never found herself in the positions which were habitual to poor Madeleine Pichy. She said:

"I can assure you that whatever position I was in I should not be afraid of being eaten alive by this young woman of Pierre's who has run like a wild animal into the woods. I am perfectly ready at any time to have a talk with Renée."

The door swung open violently and they heard Joséphine's voice: "Le médecin. Violà!" Tischer stood in the passage, looking four inches shorter than usual, feverishly adjusting his waistcoat, spreading apologies between the ladies like maize in a fowl-run. "Yes, yes, I have already seen M. Séverin, I took the liberty, as you were not to be found, of going straight to his room. M. Séverin tells me that he had a bad night, he was disturbed by something, but I cannot find in his condition any trace of ill-effects. I am really very well satisfied with his condition nowadays, particularly when one considers the harshness of the weather. And you, Mlle Séverin, is the pain any easier to-day?"

Madeleine was about to go away, but Thérèse stopped her.

"One minute, Madeleine, if you can spare the time. I want you to tell us, Dr. Tischer, about the little boy, about Armand. I understand that he is not very well. You're seeing him, I suppose?"

Tischer began to twist the fingers of his gloves. "I have seen him, yes, but not quite lately. Mme Pierre shows herself a little reluctant——"

Thérèse said significantly, "Ah, yes."

Tischer put the gloves in his pocket and straightened his spine. Madeleine's face, those tired, bagged eyes of hers, had just reminded him: that night when Gesmy's grandchild had died. He did not understand the tone of Thérèse's 'Ah, yes,' but he divined that it was unfavourable to the little Mme Pierre.

"It is a question of money," he said quietly. "Mme Pierre has very conscientious ideas about her obligations; she gives me to understand that she is in some temporary difficulty because her bankers have failed to carry out certain instructions—it is, of course, a matter into which I do not inquire; and until the affair is righted she prefers to incur medical fees only when real benefit can be gained, which I have stated to be unlikely at the present time. That, if you wish to have it, is the explanation, Mlle Séverin."

Madeleine was quite aghast. She had never heard poor Dr. Tischer talk in that voice before.

"But surely," she said, "you do not present a separate note to my daughter-in-law? I was under the impression that your services to her were included in M. Séverin's account."

"It was at Mme Pierre's request," he answered. "Mme Pierre particularly desired me to render her a separate account; I had no option in the matter."

"And of course," Thérèse said evenly, "Dr. Tischer may well have preferred to be paid separately by Renée: as a matter of convenience. . . . But you were saying, Doctor, that you can do nothing for the little boy? You mean by that, that the trouble of which we hear need give no anxiety?"

"It gives me as much anxiety," Tischer said gravely, "as any case I have handled. Unfortunately my own services are of very little use. Physically the child is not abnormal, though delicate and nervously sensitive. . . . But I must not waste your time, Mme Séverin, and you, Mlle Séverin, must be impatient for the friction."

Gratefully, Madeleine went away. Thérèse was most provoking this morning; and it was undignified, this discussion of private affairs with a stranger. But at least she would revenge herself by taking up Thérèse's challenge. She found Barbier on the first floor. "Will you take a message please, Barbier, to Mme Pierre: that Mlle Thérèse would like to have a word with her some time this morning, if Mme Pierre can spare the time."

"Now just what is all this about Armand?" Thérèse demanded as soon as the door closed. "My own view is that the child has become morose, being kept shut up as he is. I know he had a bad cold, but that was a month ago. The best thing for him now would be to go to the park and play at snow-balling. That's what he wants, some space. It does not surprise me that the boy is delicate; the mother's notions seem to me extraordinary."

Tischer breathed hard through his nostrils, a nasal rustle marking each rotation of his wrist. It was a work he loved; the steady exertion of his forces calmed him, he had the sense of virtue passing from his body into the sufferer's. He could forget like this the smallness of his person and its silly shape, the fact that his coat was always ridged on the left shoulder, that his trousers were baggy at the knees and frayed at the ankles. He said presently, taking his time:

"Mme Pierre is herself by no means well. For her own sake, I would certainly not recommend her to leave the house at present."

"But the children could go with Barbier, or even Gaston—he knows the way to the park all right."

Tischer sprinkled a fresh supply of powder on his hand. "I think," he said, "that Mme Pierre prefers to keep Armand with her for the time being. He is in an excitable condition, and it is best for him to be kept quietly. I myself have advised that."

Thérèse, with her elbows dug in the mattress, tried to move herself a little way up the bed. Her weight came suddenly on to the swollen joint and she gasped with anguish.

"Careful!" Tischer muttered. "You mustn't try to move like that. I will move you as you require."

"I will move," Thérèse answered, "just—uuh—as I please. There, that's all right. No, leave me alone. That's enough rubbing for to-day; I find the process boring. Listen, Dr. Tischer. Why do you make all this mystery about that child? Surely you can tell me in a straightforward way what, if anything, is wrong with him. Or is it just that you don't know? Bleu! Put that pillow under here, will you? Now tell me, what is wrong with the boy?"

"I have already given my opinion, for what it is worth, to Mme Pierre. And I have told her that it would be best for the child to be taken away as soon as possible from this house, which is damp, and other things besides."

"Yes, yes, I quite understand that a change is desirable, though I do not see how it can be managed at present. But you have not yet answered my question."

"It is not my business, Madame, to answer it."

Thérèse nodded with her eyes half-shut.

"I understand. You resent my curiosity. All right." She waited until he had packed up his things in silence, and had wished her good day, before she said: "By the by, Dr. Tischer, I have decided that I will seek the advice of a new doctor. There is no reflection on your skill, you understand that; but a change perhaps will be good for both of us. Good-bye, Doctor."

"But, Mlle Séverin——"

"It is a theory of mine," she said smoothly, "that the physician and his patient must always be completely in sympathy. It appears now that you and I have not quite that confidence in each other which we had formerly. There is no need, I think, to say any more."

She had taken up her book again, but she saw, with the same oblique vision that had once revealed to her any movement of the stalls, any restlessness in the parterre, that he was wavering.

"It will be a great disappointment to me," he said. "I must own that I have not been able to cure your trouble, but I had imagined, I had at least always hoped. . . ."

"Indeed, Doctor, I am by no means ungrateful for what you have done. And I feel it is a pity, when so much of your work is among paupers, for you to lose a patient who can at least pay something. But unless we have some understanding, in this matter of Madame Pierre——"

The reference to money touched him like a spur. He was splendid with fury. He bowed, more ridiculous than ever with his waistcoat rippled like a sow's underside, and opened the door. In the passage, he saw Renée waiting; and for the first time, burning with offence, he had nothing to say to her. He bowed again and went rapidly downstairs.

Biting her lip, Thérèse painfully shifted her long body into a new position. Then she called, "Is that you, Renée? Do you want to see me?"

Renée came inside.

"I had a message," she said, "that you wished me to visit you."

Thérèse grasped the facts at once. Madeleine. So like Madeleine!

"I sent no message," she said. "But no, wait a minute, I'm glad you've come; come here and sit down, do. Throw those things on the floor. Just ring the bell, will you, and I'll get Barbier to bring some coffee for us. You've no idea how delightful it is to have a visitor—this ridiculous rheumatism, one might just as well be in the vault at Père Lachaise. I am sorry to hear—Dr. Tischer was telling me all about it—that Armand is unwell. With the Séverins, of course, one must expect a little nervous trouble—with the males, I mean. It is a curious thing, the women of the family have always been more or less normal—except my aunt Henriette, who presented herself for admission to the Benedictine convent at Elbeuf in the company of two young officers and a sheep-dog, and who shortly afterwards married a Portuguese admiral. The men, on the other hand, except for that ridiculous Louis, have invariably been as touchy as racehorses. So you must not expect little Armand to be just the same as other children. . . ."

With her friendly smile turned upon Renée, Thérèse watched her attentively. Tischer was right: the young woman was not well. She had become very thin—obviously she was not eating enough —her face was drawn like that of a consumptive, her watery eyes wandered restlessly as those of a child surrounded by strangers. She had not once looked up since she entered the room, and the play of her fingers on the underbar of the chair made Thérèse think of a country girl applying for domestic service. It was plain, Thérèse thought, that Renée had come to her expecting a dressing-down. That, assuredly, was what she required: to be shocked out of her spiritual distemper, to be made to understand that she was hurting herself and the children as well by her unreasonable behaviour. But Thérèse would not pounce suddenly. She was gathering her forces as Paul Envermeu had once taught her. "The mediocre actress"—she remembered how his eyes had wandered round the empty rehearsal room as he pronounced the words with his ox's tongue—"the dainty demoiselle performing in the St. Hubert who imagines that she is a Rachel, she works herself into a bonfire of passionate emotions while the dresser is doing her hair, she makes her entrance sweating all over with tenderness and rage and remorse, she immediately empties her stomach upon the audience, bang! and it is as if a toy balloon had been punctured. The wonderful emotions, the grand passions, what has happened to them all? A magnificent entrance, everyone says. And in six months' time there will be a magnificent exit. Now listen, my little Mademoiselle Séverin, it is unwise to pour a half-cooked omelette on to a cold plate. You must wait, you must be patient, you must look forward. There is a line there, it is in the third or perhaps the fourth Act, that Racine has prepared for the emptying of your stomach. It is for that moment you yourself are preparing, preparing all the time, it is for that that you are holding yourself. And all the time you are making your audience ready, you are gathering their attention, their sympathy, their passionate interest, until when the moment comes they are the horse on which you ride, the ship in which you sail, the army of which you are the supreme commander. It is then, Mademoiselle, that you can exploit the passions you have so carefully nourished. . . ." She was enjoying now the rich tones of her deep voice, talking confidentially, profiting by her listener's silence, watching the little movements of her own hands, the speech of her splendid eyes, in that imaginary mirror which Envermeu had taught her always to hold before herself. ". . . and you find, perhaps, that my sister-in-law is a little difficult, a little fussy. She is elderly, you know, she feels her age perhaps rather more than I do; and she was always a shy woman, I remember so well my first meeting with her, what a pretty, shy girl she was. It is the art of life—you realize that, I am sure, as I do—to see our friends not as they appear to us but as their history makes them, as beings shaped by the stress of circumstance. And Madeleine, I who know her so well can tell you this, she is really a most kindhearted creature, a devoted wife, though one perhaps—you understand, Renée, I am speaking very privately—perhaps she does not altogether understand her husband, perhaps she has not quite—how shall I say?—those identical qualities which would be most useful to a wife of his. It would not be easy, no one understands that better than I, to be a perfect wife for my brother. He has, you see, a certain greatness—he comes, you must remember, of two very ancient stocks, my mother's family were rulers in Asia some centuries before they came to the Ukraine—and it is bottled up, that largeness, that energy of his, in the monastic cell to which he has confined himself since his military failure. It is a character which you will not be able very easily to understand, though your knowledge of Pierre will help you."

At least she had secured Renée's attention; the girl was regarding her now steadfastly, without such expression as Thérèse could identify, but with an almost alarming concentration.

"You have found perhaps," Thérèse continued, feeling her way, "that Pierre is sometimes—how shall I say?—a little difficult to humour. And now that you are so far separated it must be difficult for you—how well I understand how it must be—difficult to maintain by correspondence the easy relations that you enjoyed when you were together. It is of course well known, the strain that separation puts on a married couple."

There was a gentle knock and Madeleine's face appeared. How long, Thérèse wondered with a certain pleasure, had she been listening?

"I am sorry," Madeleine murmured, "I didn't know, Thérèse, that you had Renée with you. I was wondering . . ."

"I have been talking to Renée," Thérèse said, "of some of the peculiarities in the Séverin family. I was saying——"

Renée cut her short. Her voice was curiously impersonal, dry and flavourless like the notes of a player-piano. "Mlle Séverin has been telling me about my husband, what he is like and the allowances I must make for his character. I find that in this house one is not permitted to know anything of one's family—one's husband or one's children, what they are like or how they should be treated. One finds oneself, from time to time, a rather impatient pupil."

Madeleine's face had become red, and now she was silently crying with sparse tears, her mouth working with a clutching movement as if a hand gripped her throat. Thérèse, stiffening, had jerked the swollen joint again; she would have cried out with the thrust of pain but that it was absorbed in the stream of her anger. She had to pause a moment, and then she was able to speak, thinly between tight jaws.

"There are other things that could be said. A domestic animal has to be taught good habits, by kindness, or in some other way. But why waste the time? For a guest, there is always the choice: she can stay or she can seek other hospitality. If it happens that the guest has not been specially invited . . ."

"No!" Madeleine broke out. "No, Thérèse, I will not have that said. My son's wife will be welcome here as long as she pleases, whether she is friendly or not. As I happen to be the mistress of this house, Thérèse . . ."

"If I had only myself to think about," Renée said, her voice unaltered, "nothing would persuade me to stay a moment longer in Baulon. But I have the children to consider, at present I have no money, we must stay here as long as you will keep us. We are entirely at your mercy, I recognize that quite clearly."

"But surely, Renée," Madeleine sobbed, "you could be a little friendly? There is so little we ask of you, only that you should be friendly with us, that Eugène and I should have some pleasure from our little grandchildren."

"For yourself," Renée said, "you may see the children when you like. But M. Séverin, who is so friendly as to visit my bedroom when the children and I are asleep, he will not be allowed to see

Armand. That is fixed, you understand. Pierre can decide for himself when he comes back, but until then Armand will be kept away from his grandfather. If it is necessary I shall take him away to an institution of some kind. My mind is made up about that."

Thérèse turned her head towards Madeleine. She seemed to forget that Renée was within earshot.

"It would perhaps have been better, Madeleine, if you had left the young woman to me. I have had some experience of dealing with this type—it requires a little handling. And now, I'm afraid, the case has become more difficult. I can hardly promise you any further help. . . ."

★

Raymond was not surprised when a note from his aunt Thérèse reached him at the office. It was understood among his friends that anything private should be sent there.

"On the subject of our conversation last Sunday," Thérèse wrote, "I have ascertained that Renée has received no letters from Pierre for some time, though I cannot say exactly how long. I had a talk with Renée this morning, and it appears to me sufficiently evident that she has had a quarrel with Pierre. I did indeed touch on that very subject, and the way she reacted showed that my surmise was correct. Obviously Pierre has treated her badly and she is very much upset, though as I had expected she makes no admission. I should like to do something to give her comfort, but it is difficult for an old woman to help spiritually a young one; a bond between the two ages is not easily established. If it were not that Cécile has the sole claim upon all your attentions, I would suggest that you should see if you can do something.

"Why is it that you never bring your pretty Cécile to see us nowadays? I should like you to give her my love, and to say that in the note I sent her last week she mistook a 'seven' for a 'four.' I am sure she will be anxious to put that right. . . ."

He went, although he hated walking in the snow, to the place Talleyrand that evening. But Renée would not see him; she sent a message that she was unwell. "We do not see Mme Pierre or the little ones very often now," Barbier told him. "They are kept in the two rooms mostly, though sometimes the little girl is with Mlle Marianne. The little boy is not well, I am told. It is sad. It would be nice to see the children running about the house."

He wrote to her: "I hear that you are in some difficulty. Isn't there anything I can do? Do let me see you and have a talk about it." She replied that he was very kind, but no, nothing was wrong, only that Armand was not well and she herself had a touch of influenza. The cold weather did not suit them.

It is her pride, he thought, remembering how oddly Cécile would behave if her amour-propre was touched, how she would not be happy unless he made some positive sacrifice to show himself devoted. "Cécile requires attention," he had said to Renée, "whenever the painting light is good; no woman ever takes a man's work seriously." It was absurd to compare those two, but he thought he could detect the same instinct behind the behaviour of them both: to guard from everyone, from themselves, the secret that the man had cooled. He remained resentful, piqued by curiosity. He wanted to know just what it was that had occurred between her and Pierre. He had told her so much, about his painting, about Cécile's infuriating ways. He expected something in return.

It came at last, but not from Renée. He was on the early evening edition, and hurrying because he had promised to meet Vasseur at the Café de Flandres and look at faïence with him. He rang impatiently and the telegraph desk clerk brought him the Havas 'B' slips in three baskets. It was a part of his routine to select half a dozen, by their value or piquancy, as fill-ups for the lower columns. He turned the basket marked *Colonel* upside down, spread the slips with fingers as nimble as a cashier's, and carelessly glanced them over, appraising the relative values, flicking the best to one side, and automatically counting: three, four, five, six; one more to be on the safe side, since Chivalié had the accursed habit of judging all his column-lengths short. There was one still upside-down, he dabbled with a wet finger and turned it over. *A message from Sigumbe* . . . Sigumbe—nobody had ever heard of it. But as his thumb came to push the slip away to the left his eye caught a word farther on and he read it right through.

A message from Sigumbe states that Captain Pierre Séverin, who has been engaged in an outpost consolidating action against a Bisquort tribe, is missing, and that a military warrant of arrest on a charge of alleged desertion has been issued by eastern divional headquarters at Sigumbe.

He crumpled the slip and put it in his trouser pocket. Pierre! He had never thought that of Pierre. He sat quite still but his eyes and fingers went on working. One more wanted.

It is reported that a baboon which escaped from the zoological park at Bougie last Sunday raided the municipal offices, stole the mayoral insignia, and paraded the streets of the town in these trappings. The animal has been recaptured.

That would do. He pencilled at the foot: "Suggest g-f head —*Mayor of Baulon visits Bougie*" and clipped it with his selections. 'I suppose,' he reflected, 'that Renée has known all this time.'

It was unlikely, he thought, as he listened to Vasseur's raptures over a Moustiers sauce-boat, that the Paris papers would print it. There was just a faint risk of libel—everyone was on tenterhooks since the Lavenu business—and in any case it could have no general interest. He saw when he opened the *Démocrate Français* next morning that he had been too sanguine. There it was, slap in the middle of the first foreign page with a three-line double-pica head. 'The mysterious disappearance of Capt. Séverin,' the *Démocrate* added to its report, "recalls the famous case of Colonel Eugène Séverin, father of the officer now missing, who was convicted by court-martial for cowardly action in a skirmish at Viboire-les-Deux-Auberges, and whose conviction was upheld by the Central Court of Appeal. The case, which lasted several months, focused the attention of all Paris, partly by reason of the brilliance and the distinguished family of the young officer concerned, partly . . .' Raymond skipped; it made him belch, all that stuff, the kind of padding he himself turned out like a silkworm every day. 'It is believed,' he read at the foot of the column, "that M. Eugène Séverin is still alive, and resides somewhere in the provinces." They know their job—he thought—my cherished colleagues in Paris. They don't miss anything, they leave nothing out, they're an ornament to the profession, those clever fellows who write so well that they are employed by the Paris newspapers. Well, he had Renée's secret. He had that all right. And Thérèse, sitting up in bed in her flamboyant Oriental bed-jacket with the *Matin*, she would have it by this time. Everyone in Baulon would have it, Paris would know it, the whole stinking, squealing population of this infernal country would know it now.

XXI

Two or three times a day Sophie climbed up the stairs to Marianne's room, with the intelligent insouciance of a domestic cat obtaining provender from opposing front-line trenches. Her mother and Aunt Marianne met only by chance, on the stairs; they bowed to each other, they never spoke. The third floor was as separate from the second as another country; and it did not seem unnatural to Sophie that the thin, pale woman whom she found on one side of the border and the shorter brown one on the other kept to their respective territories as constantly as the several houses kept to their own side of the Square.

Her first invasion of Marianne's room had been swift and bold. She did not creep along the sides of corridors as Armand did, but walked in the very middle, stumped up the stairs, arrived in Marianne's doorway smiling. Marianne asked what she wanted, but apparently she wanted nothing. She stood quite still, with a pair of fire-tongs that she always carried dangling from one hand, for nearly a quarter of an hour; gazing at Marianne as she worked with benevolent patronage, as if pleased to see her quietly and sensibly employed. The next day she came again at the same time. Marianne put a cushion for her before the oil stove and motioned her to sit down. When that had happened two days running it was recognized by Sophie as unalterable routine. And now whenever in the daytime Marianne was at home, Sophie was with her, either sitting on her cushion and nursing the fire-tongs or wandering about the room among the paraphernalia that Marianne had never bothered to arrange; touching singly each book on a long shelf; picking up a sandalwood box, pressing it against her face and restoring it to its exact position.

Although she detested children, and sighed with relief when the tram bore her away from the din of infant voices at the Primaire, Marianne did nothing to prevent the visits of Renée's child. It would have meant an interview; she could not very well have summoned Renée and to visit her was out of the question. She was, moreover, not insensible to the flattery of the child's liking to be with her. At school they obeyed her: no one had so little trouble as she in keeping order. It was a novelty to find a child who regarded her without fear or caution, and by degrees she became accustomed to Sophie's presence as to the feel of the old woollen coat she wore in the evenings. Sophie was no nuisance. She did not ask for anything to eat, or to be petted. She was silent until Marianne spoke to her, and she went away without demur as soon as Marianne said that it was time for her to go.

"Why are you staring at my dress?" Marianne asked one day.

"I think it's pretty."

It was a dress she had made herself from some old satin that Thérèse had sold her. The colour was rich, with a brilliant sheen when the gaslight caught the folds. Encouraged, Marianne went without an early edition of the *Télémaque* which she had thought of buying and got a new dress in a gaudy rose. It was startlingly unsuited to her own colouring, and vulgarly cut; Thérèse, when she saw it, gave it a look which almost made her weep; but Sophie was delighted with it. She came, for the first time, close to Marianne, murmuring "How beautiful, oh, how beautiful it is!"

and put her face against the skirt. Caught unawares by a novel impulse, Marianne took off her pince-nez, bent forward and kissed Sophie's head.

For a long time Sophie examined Marianne's face, tracing the separate features with her eyes as if she were planning a route upon a field-map. Marianne bore the scrutiny with patience, relieved when Sophie smiled. "Do you like my face?" "Yes, very much, it's beautiful." As soon as the child had gone, she hunted out the hand-mirror from her chest of drawers and regarded her face with the same studious care which Sophie had bestowed on it. It was the colour of camembert; the cheeks were flushed with a brown stain like the remains of a burn, there were pimples below the eyes and a distinct moustache on the upper lip. The bridge of the nose, and the eyes peering concentrically, revealed the habitual spectacles as clearly as if she had not removed them. But the nose itself was good, pure Séverin, a bloodstock feature; and she knew, with her natural taste for sculpture, that the mouth and chin had structural quality; they were Russian, she thought, although the line of fastening between her lips had the Séverin straightness. She could see nothing in the face that a child would like. She tried to smile, but the effect was horrible, as if vermilion lips and azure eyes had been daubed on the Ste Claire of Vivarini. Sophie, she thought, was a common little sycophant, who sought her society from the usual childish desire to be herself admired. But before she slept she rubbed the pimples with a lotion. Next day, arriving just as she had finished dressing, Sophie came in and without hesitation kissed her. It was a soft kiss, given as a matter of course, but not unfeelingly. In the evening Marianne brought home a picture-book and explained to Sophie what the pictures meant. The child admired the pictures but would not take the book away. It was kept for her thenceforward in Marianne's room, where, when Marianne was busy, she indefatigably perused it. It was a foolish little girl, Marianne thought. But on an evening when Sophie had one of her colds and did not appear she was restless, unable to concentrate on the correction of exercises. The stove was burning steadily, but the room was cold.

★

"Where is it you get to when you go upstairs?" Renée asked in the early days of Sophie's disappearances. She went, Sophie said, to visit a lady; a thin, yellow lady. Renée asked no more questions. It was odd, and surely that iceberg Marianne, grown elderly in early middle life, must resent the child's constant intrusion. But Marianne could, if she wished, complain; it would be hard to hurt or frighten Sophie, who was so plump and placid; and in the meantime, it was a relief to get one child off her hands for a little while each day, to have one fewer in the small room, which had always the smell and stain of the last meal, the constant untidiness of too much occupation.

Sophie's absence gave a convenient time for Armand's lessons, which Renée had unflaggingly continued. He seemed to make little progress; his memory had become so bad, and he was desperately slow. It was a triumph if, at the end of an afternoon's intensive coaching, he could follow out correctly the method of long division or haltingly recite the names of the six best authors of France. She persevered, her patience growing callous in the struggle, encouraged because he was never obstinately stupid, never lazy. He was only a little changed, she thought. He had lost his laughter, the little smile she had valued because it was like Pierre's, mature and unexpected. But then, he had always been a serious child; *Il Penseroso* Pierre had dubbed him. You must expect a child to become more serious as he grew older. And if he were no longer demonstrative in his affection for her, he always liked her to be near him. He had lost none of his natural courtesy. He had always been dreamy, and now his dreaminess had become a chronic failing; everything you said had to be twice repeated before he would take it in. His actions were slower, he took twice as long as Sophie to dress himself and to get through his meals. But his appearance was not noticeably changed. He spoke in the same voice, only very slowly and more seldom than before. You would have said that he was only tired, oppressed perhaps by the gloomy house and the cold winter. "But there's nothing wrong?" she said again to Tischer. "Surely there's nothing really wrong with him?" "No, no, my dear Mme Pierre, only that it's strange for a little boy to be in such different surroundings. If you could take him away, to the country perhaps, or to my own dear Switzerland . . ." But he knew as well as Renée that she had not the means to go.

It was plain that Sophie saw no change. She played with him, when the fancy took her to do so, as she had done before, only laughing good-humouredly at his slowness, making up with her own eagerness for his ponderous co-operation. Often she waited on him, picking up a stocking which he did not seem to see by his feet or taking from him the sugar spoon which he held perplexedly and emptying it briskly over his plate. It was done without roughness or ostentation. She seemed to realize that he had become the younger, and to think that it was naturally so.

He did what he was told, helped with the washing up and making beds; but at other times was idle. He had forgotten, it seemed, the purpose of his old playthings, the gimlet and screwdriver which he still held as he stared out of the window but never used. It was hard for Renée to occupy all his time, and she would have taken him out of doors except for her own weakness, a chill in the stomach which seemed in this country to be incurable and which sometimes made her simplest tasks an effort. She was terrified of a serious illness that would end her power of guardianship. There were days when she longed to stay in bed, but it would have meant some woman coming in, probably Mme Séverin, and Armand would have been taken from her at least as far as the next room. She wanted to keep him in her sight, so near that he could reach him instantly if he called for her; until Pierre came back.

Pierre's return: it had become a messianic vision, a thing believed in shadowy conception, a climax the shape of which her mind grew tired and sore in trying to imagine. She was like a passenger carried overseas to an unknown destination, not knowing in what kind or how soon the land would appear; waiting only with tortured patience for liberty from the ship's confinement. Somehow Pierre would get back to her, and until that day the sum of her diminished forces must be bent to keeping Armand for him, to preserving Armand's wholeness, the gentleness of his frail spirit. She would ask him still, "You remember your father, Armand, what he looked like?" and he would say "Oh, yes." She waited till his glance was turned a little from her and tried to see in his eyes some light to show his thoughts. But it seemed as if she saw his face a long way off, as if he were protected from her scrutiny behind a prison window. She was afraid to ask what his thoughts were; such questions puzzled him and made him a little frightened. She could only strive to make him aware of her affection, of her closeness and her infinite power to protect him. "You will wake me, Armand, if anything disturbs you in the night? Just call and I'll wake up." He did not seem to hear at once, but later he answered, "In the night? Oh, yes, yes, thank you."

In these days she put the children to sleep together in the larger bed, with a shielded candle burning close to them on the dressing-table. Until he was fast asleep, she held Armand's hand, sitting in her overcoat at the bedside. Then she put the other mattress down across the door, and slept there. Her sleep was fragile. She was always near enough to consciousness for a little sound to wake her, a footstep in the passage or a cry from Armand. Often she woke imagining that she heard the sound she dreaded: the heavy, slippered feet of M. Séverin. Then she would lie trembling, believing that he had reached the door and was listening there until he should be certain that she slept. And once, as she waited breathless, a finger tapped the door. A voice said: "Renée!"

She did not know if she had really heard it or if to-night her fancies, playing their elfish game, had led her a little farther. She whispered "Who's that?" and heard the voice again distinctly, "It's me, Renée. Will you let me in?"

The voice was husky; familiar, but she could not place it. Shivering, she got up, pushed the mattress to one side and unlocked the door. It was Mme Séverin, standing with a candle in one hand, a folded newspaper in the other; her face as Renée had seen it on the night that M. Séverin had neglected dying, drawn and pale as if at the end of a night-long vigil; though, as they stood there, they heard the clock of Ste Gudule striking eleven.

"Renée, I want to speak to you. Will you come into the other room?"

She would not go. "No, I can't leave Armand sleeping alone."

Madeleine made no protest. "This," she said, giving her the newspaper. "Thérèse has shown it me."

Her finger pointed to the column. Renée only read: 'Desertion of Officer on Colonial Service.' That was enough.

"Yes," she said, "I knew."

Madeleine's lips twisted, she was striving for her voice. It came in a gusty draught, the words squeezed out from a throat tightened by emotion.

"Eugène must not hear of this. Do you understand? You must never, never tell him, do you understand? Eugène must never know."

XXII

THOSE who had lived in the Square long enough to remember the ancient woman who had formerly emerged on fine mornings from Number 17 believed that she was dead. In those short days, when the children were sent before it was light to plod across the snow and get water from the pump at the corner of the rue des Suisses, when the only tolerable time was the huddled, lamp-lit evenings, it was a useful contribution to the dwindling fund of gossip. She had never been aloof, as were the others who came out of that formidable house; she had always been ready with a greeting for the children, "Ho, you little bastards, you keep out of my way or I'll have the hounds on you!" and she had never hesitated, if the fancy took her, to march into their front-rooms, swinging her riding crop and shouting in her queer foreign voice, 'Pyotr! What a stinking hovel! Here, here's something for the brats,' at which she would throw a joint or a bag of flour on the table, laughing at their surprise. Hearing one day that there were rats in the house where four generations of Allards lived, she had driven in her three Flemish poodles and followed them up the staircase on a tarragona pony, screaming encouragement in Little Russian and wreaking havoc in the congested bedrooms until the police were summoned to take her away. They were sorry, those old residents, that she appeared no longer; but now that—if rumour were correct—she was dead, they hoped at least to see an amusing funeral. The wealthy misers who lived in 17 must at least afford ceremonies in keeping with their station; there would be a domed hearse with silver fringes, five plumes, four caparisoned horses, a master of ceremonies, a brace of leaders trapped in silver; the scene in the snow would be magnificent.

It came to Tischer's ears: he had it from Veuve Marcel Lindon as he was lancing a boil on her neck. She would have liked to get further particulars from him, but she knew that he would never retail any news from 17. "The Séverin family are very old friends of mine"—that was all he would ever say. It was Tischer who brought the news to Eugène.

"M. Séverin, I find it very sad, the duty of conveying to you my profound and respectful sympathy in the death of Madame, your mother."

And Eugène said: "Dead? Good God, Tischer, I never imagined—why didn't you tell me she was ill? . . . Fancy, my poor old mother, I thought she would never die. She was a great woman, Tischer, in her way. I should like to give her a funeral of the first class, but of course that's impossible, with the present state of my investments. You will have to arrange it for me, Tischer a very quiet funeral, not at all expensive, but with proper dignity. In the poor places where you work you might perhaps find men who would act as extra mourners at a low rate. . . ."

"It will be necessary," Thérèse said when she heard the news, "to have the funeral celebrated according to the Orthodox rite. I'm afraid we may have to get a priest from Amiens, there is none of that cult in Baulon so far as I know. It is likely that the affair will be costly. . . . You will have to tell Renée, Madeleine, that she must make black dresses for her children. I may have some old stuff which I could let her have cheaply. . . . Poor mother, she would have preferred, I believe, to die at her own Bobroviza, but to get her there would have been impossibly expensive."

Madeleine was troubled not only by the prospect of disturbance to her cherished routine, of the bad effect that the shock might have on Eugène, but also by the thought that Nadya had died without religious consolation. If she had only known! Dear Abbé Vignaud, although he was not of Nadya's persuasion, would at least have found some way to pray with her; he might even, so gentle and persuasive were his methods, have induced her at the last hour to see the error of her church's doctrine, have admitted her to the Catholic communion and fortified her with the Holy Sacrament for her passage into eternity. Thérèse was computing aloud the second-class railway fare from Amiens, but Madeleine, standing tearfully at her bedside, did not hear her. She rang, as she always did in moments of bewilderment, for Barbier.

"It was very wrong, Barbier, for you not to tell us that Madame Nadya was dying. You must have known, Gaston must have told you, I can't think why you didn't let us know."

But Barbier had heard nothing. Gaston was summoned, and Joséphine, suspecting the importance of the occasion, came with him. Barbier addressed him sternly.

"It is you, Gaston, who are responsible for Mme Nadya. And now she is dead and you told us nothing. Why didn't you tell us that she was ill?"

It seemed to Madeleine that his eternal smile actually broadened. He said nothing. It was he who, when the urchins in the Square had pestered him to tell them something about the old woman, had mumbled '*Aveugle comme les morts, cette vieille-là,*' but he had forgotten that. He had no idea of what or whom they were talking.

"Tell me, Gaston," Thérèse said suddenly. "Madame Nadya, is she really dead? Barbier, go up, will you, and see if her door is locked?"

Joséphine took a step towards the bed.

"Gaston is not to be bullied," she said fiercely. "Everybody bullies Gaston—Barbier, like all the rest—because he has funny ways. But if you think Gaston's any different from that boy of Mme Pierre's . . ."

"I was only asking Gaston," Thérèse said with smoking patience, "whether Mme Nadya is dead. He can surely answer a straightforward question."

But Gaston was not in the mood to answer questions. He was excited, and perhaps a little gratified, at being the centre of so large a group. He looked from one to the other with appreciation. "This," he said at last, pointing to a brass ornament pinned on his jersey, "Madame upstairs gave me this."

"Will you," Thérèse said desperately, "take that ninnywit away from me before I go mad?"

"I will no longer allow him," Joséphine answered, "to remain in such company. Come, Gaston."

Barbier had come back.

"I can't get in," he said. "The door is locked; Mme Nadya must have locked it before she died."

*

The idea of dying had occurred to Nadya, for she had always hated the French winter, the urban winter in which even the snow was black, when you saw no trees with branches drooping under the weight of snow or the clear white vistas of the Ukrainian marsh. There was so little flesh left to protect her, and that of a poor quality, that she was only warm in bed; and now that she could not even see the amusing patterns of the frosted windows the cold was not worth enduring. A certain appetite for being alive had made her struggle through former winters, waiting for the pleasure of the sun's warmth on her wrinkled skin. But this time the sun was not worth waiting for; she would lie still, warm beneath the many blankets, until the tiresomeness of her black prison passed away. She had come close enough to Death at last to see that he was friendly, that it was only the middle-aged who were shy of him. She would refrain from food, proving her submission to his power.

She lay then quite still as in a Polar night, unconscious of time passing except as waves of sensuous pleasure, on which there floated visions hazy in their outline but of brilliant colouring: the silver chandeliers hanging from the low, vaulted ceiling of the Swietokrzyska Café, where her brother had fought his duel with Alexis Grigorovitch in the very midst of one of poor Frédéric Chopin's mazurkas, the clink of the rapiers enlivened the music, and the dancers, glorious Asiatic Muscovites with faces like carvings in walnut, never stopping until the viscous gore of silly Alexis Grigorovitch began to make their feet slide and to stain their satin slippers; the hunting sledges breaking from the forest edge and charging full tilt through the festival bazaar on the frozen Beriza, scattering the Zingari fiddlers and overturning the Jewish pedlars' booths, the lanterns crashing with a shower of sparks across the ice; the coloured caps of the serfs pressed round the bear-ring at Jalovka, the glittering uniforms of the Imperial Cavalry at the Saski Easter ball. The flow of time had given to her distant memories a romantic richness, in the darkness where she lay she saw the hues more brilliant, the mansions larger, the men of a uniformly giant stature. It was pleasant to recline among those pictures, to let her spirit pass through its proper region, a thousand miles from the monotones of Baulon, before it fled away to a country unknown. But her body would not suffer itself to be so disregarded. Roused by her stomach's clamour she slowly rose to consciousness, she called faintly, "Andryev Fyodorovitch! Send me Alyosha with some braised pork and pastries, tell her to hurry, I'm sick with the bellyache. And Andryev! Tell Dmitri Iosifov to wait for me, he's not to go without me, I want to see the pups blooded." Then, her voice increasing in strength as her sensations cleared, "Gaston! Where is the brute? Gaston, you son of a mongrel bitch! Are you trying to starve me to death? I'll have you in hell to greet me, you slobbering donkey-boy."

She gorged herself on everything that Gaston brought her, she vomited and gorged again. Her strength returned, so that she could kick the bedclothes off for the pleasure of making Gaston scold her and put them on again; by kicking, wriggling, stretching, striking out at Gaston when he approached to turn her pillow, she kept herself in trim. But she would not get up, as Gaston sometimes begged her. It was deliciously warm in bed, with the two extra carriage-rugs that he had brought, and now that she had made him fasten all the shutters and trim the wick of the stove even her face was warm. He was a useful child, Gaston, he had nailed bits of felt along the sides and bottom of the door so that very few of the household sounds, Thérèse's sheepdog laugh, or the whiny voice of that silly little Marianne, ever reached her. He cut her hair when it began to tickle her neck, he brought her food when she told him. It was seldom the food she asked for, but she knew better than to hope for what she wanted in this country where they were terrified of rich seasoning, this chilly-blooded land of half-flavouring and faint aromas whose cuisine brought nothing to its logical conclusion. And at least there was always a variety of dishes by her. Gaston brought them in the morning and spread them on the dressing-table, which he had pushed up beside her. She stretched, whenever she felt hungry, tasted what her fingers found, and spat it out if she specially disliked it. In the evening Gaston took away the plates that were empty and saw that she had some cold pork spread with savora, which she liked to nibble with her callous gums if she woke in the night, and a litre tumbler of ordinaire laced with cognac and a teaspoonful of vinegar. There were souvenirs she sometimes liked to handle; the hunting knife Dmitri Iosifov had given her for her fifteenth birthday, the lacquered cigarette-box, her spurs and riding-crop, a tangle of brown wool which had been intended as a pilch for Eugène—or was it Louis?—and which was somehow still unfinished although at times she plied the needles furiously: these things Gaston kept within her reach, spread on the bed itself, the commode or the dressing-table; they were sticky, but as her hands were in the same condition it did not matter. Once a week, or as often as she complained, he pushed her over to one side and flapped away those crumbs which had got inside the sheets. With such comforts and in such tranquillity she felt new life coming to her every day.

*

She was asleep when the carpenter came to saw round the lock, and he had worked steadily for three minutes, Madeleine and Gaston watching him in silence, before she woke. They were startled by a furious "Atzka! Thieves! Andryev Fyodorovitch, here, quick, they're going to ravish me! Bring the hounds, Andryev.

Where are you, Cezar, Mirza, on to him, rout him out, rout him out, Cezar, whip 'em up, Andryev, he's away, he's in the wood."

Madeleine called softly, "It's all right, Mother, it's me, Madeleine, I'm coming to see if you're well."

"I won't have you in here," Nadya screamed. "Eugène, take your silly girl away, I don't like her smell. Where's Andryev Fyodorovitch, drat the man! Gaston, come here or I'll flay you."

Obediently, Gaston nudged the carpenter to one side, took the key from his trousers-pocket, unlocked the door and went in. Madeleine stayed listening. "Where have you been?" she heard Nadya ask. "I've been calling you for half an hour. Take this stuff away, hurry, d'you hear! In my country they wouldn't give that stuff to hogs." Madeleine beckoned to the carpenter and stole away.

But Eugène would not be satisfied till Tischer had seen his mother. "To you, Madeleine, it means nothing. It is just an old woman who has passed her span of years long ago, who may as well die now. Yes, I understand that, it's rational, I am always ready to sympathize with the rational view. But for me it's different. I always remember that she's my mother, that she comes of a royal family. I feel her sufferings very closely, her illness affects me far more than my own. . . ."

"I cannot understand," he said when Tischer came, "why you have not been visiting my mother. I took it for granted that you were doing so. What is the use of having a family attendant if one has to tell him every day exactly what he must do?" He seemed far from satisfied when Tischer came back to make his report with a bloody nose. "But, Tischer, you know my mother has wild fits at times, surely with a little care you could dodge her when she strikes, it seems to me a confession of crass incompetence if you can't avoid the fists of a woman who's all but stone blind. What did you do to upset her? Well, if she wanted it, why didn't you bleed her? She seems to have bled you all right. Madeleine, do for goodness' sake get him another handkerchief, there will be a mess all over the house."

He was none the less relieved. Apart from the funeral question —and it would not be unlike Nadya's genius for awkwardness to leave directions for her remains to go to Bobroviza, her heart to be cast into the Caspian Sea—it flattered him to have a mother living, who stood between him and the admission of old age. He had first regarded his residence in Baulon as a temporary banishment, from which, with evidence to prove that his trial had been corrupt, he would one day return to start his life again; and he had lived with that aspiration, his vision always forward, so that he hardly realized how great a part of life the years of impatience swallowed.

It was a sharp reminder, the thought of Nadya dying; it scared him as he realized its significance.

"Tell me, Madeleine," he said, "how old am I now? I never can remember."

But in her irritating way Madeleine ignored the question. She had lapsed into a wool-gathering mood, she regarded him vaguely, murmured something about the preparation of déjeuner and left him to his own reflections. He tried to calculate his age, but was not sure which year they had arrived at. I must hurry, he thought. We reserve ourselves and time catches us out.

He announced next morning that he must go at once to Viboire, there was no reason for waiting. "I have been worried about my mother's health," he said, "but now that Tischer says there's nothing wrong with her I see no reason for further delay. We must take Barbier, who will be useful in various ways, and perhaps Renée to write down the measurements."

Madeleine was sitting by the window, mending a stocking. She said patiently, without looking up, "You know, Eugène, that it is quite impossible for you to be out of doors in this weather. At Viboire the snow would not be cleared at all. You have not been out of this room for weeks now, you know it would be out of the question."

"As far as possible," he said didactically, "I always try to follow your ideas on the question of my health. I realize that it gives you anxiety, I try as far as I can to consider your feelings. But a man who allows himself always to be coddled by his womenfolk will never get anywhere. I am sorry, Madeleine, but on this occasion I must do as I think best. A man with a purpose does not suffer ill effects from a little snow on his boots."

She said nothing. But as soon as the bell jangled she went downstairs and met Tischer in the hall.

"You must come into the dining-room," she said, "I want to talk to you, it is very important. . . ."

To her astonishment Tischer was not violently shocked by the proposal. "There are of course risks," he said in his slow, deliberate way, "and I can understand your anxiety. To nurse M. Séverin during the journey will not be easy; it will be necessary to take very special precautions to keep him warm; but I have often found that a change of scene has an extraordinary effect on a patient who for some time has been convalescent in one room. The very effort required. . . ."

She was not listening, she would not listen to his elaborate treachery. This morning she had had another letter from Lecours: one of the major difficulties had been overcome; he was increasingly hopeful now that Captain Lenormand would be persuaded *in the near future* to make the journey to France. And now Eugène was going to throw away the reserves she had so carefully built up, and Dr. Tischer, who should have run to her support, was calmly proposing to countenance his folly. She cut him short. "I suppose you don't realize," she said wearily, "when you talk about risks, just what those risks mean. It is practically certain that my husband's affairs—the affair in Paris that I have mentioned to you, the event to which we have so long looked forward—it is almost certain to take place in the spring. I know that my husband is only one of your patients, that you are used to losing every patient in the end, that a gamble sometimes makes your work more interesting——"

"But, Madame Séverin, you misunderstand me entirely. If I had not considerable confidence——"

"He is not to go, do you understand? I will not allow it! I will not even allow you to see him unless you promise me that you will advise against it. I have a greater knowledge than you of Eugène's temperament. I know far more how such madness is likely to affect him, and I forbid you, I absolutely forbid you to give your permission."

"Tischer!"

It was Eugène himself at the stairhead of the first floor. Holding her skirts, Madeleine ran upstairs with Tischer panting after her.

"Eugène! What are you——?" But a fit of coughing stopped her.

"You shouldn't rush about," Eugène said irritably as she gasped for breath. "It always starts this. . . . I suppose, Tischer, my wife has been telling you that I am unfit to make the little excursion I have in mind, the trip to Viboire. She has been telling you no doubt that you are to advise against it. . . ."

There was just a chance, Madeleine thought, that Thérèse with her practical outlook would see the folly of his issuing from the sickroom into fields lying under a foot of snow. Thérèse was quite as impatient as herself for the business to be brought to a conclusion, for the return to Paris which would mean that her stage career could be resumed. But Thérèse proved unhelpful. "I agree with you, Madeleine, that it is very foolish for a man of his age to go pottering in the snow. But what can you expect? It's at least two years since he last made the excursion; he seldom goes as long as that without verifying his observations. And no doubt he will be able to get improved results this time. I am told by those who understand such rubbish that measurements are altered in cold weather; it is due to the expansion of metals; that is presumably why the clocks in this house are never right. I would advise you to put on warm underclothes; there is always a good deal of standing about. . . ."

When Madeleine returned to Eugène's room she found that he had already sent Barbier to get the railway tickets. "You can buy them with your own money," he had said, "and Madame will repay you."

★

As soon as it was light next morning she went to the window and saw that more snow had fallen, covering the brown slush in the yard. It was colder. She crept into Eugène's room and saw by the thin light passing from her own that he slept poorly, constantly turning and whispering nonsense. He would find perhaps that he had not the strength to get up; she almost hoped that he would be worse.

But as soon as he woke, Eugène demanded to be dressed. She brought his heaviest things warm from the airing cupboard, and he stood very stiffly as she dressed him, holding the bed-post with only one hand.

"I have decided definitely," he said, "that Renée is to come. It will be helpful for you; you won't have to do any writing. Perhaps you had better tell her at once. I can manage the collar myself, I am feeling very well to-day."

"I have asked her already," Madeleine told him, "but Renée refuses. She is unwell, she says, and she cannot leave the children."

He had expected that.

"I suppose you influenced her? However. . . . It is nonsense for her to say she is unwell. I should have thought that she would be ready to sacrifice a trifle of personal comfort to oblige me; but young people are like that; we have to recognize that filial duty is an idea that has been abandoned completely. . . . But her treatment of those children is ridiculous; she is trying to make them into old women. I shall find an opportunity to correct that."

"——and Eugène, dear, I have decided that I myself am not coming. I do not approve of the excursion, and it would not be rational for me to go. I have made up my mind about that."

He could hardly believe that she was serious. He stared at her face in the glass. The eyes were frightened, but in her mouth there was a line of resolution.

"But what—but who is to look after me, my clothes, that sort of thing?"

"I don't know."

He took the tie from her and fixed it himself. He selected a pair of boots from the cupboard and sat down to put them on. Madeleine got the shoehorn from the dressing-table and knelt at his feet, but he pulled the boots away from her. "No, no, leave me alone, I can manage perfectly myself."

"But those boots are too thin. You must have the ones with the double soles if you are going in the snow."

"I am quite able to choose my own boots," he said quietly. "Before I married you I did everything for myself, I had no one but my batman to help me. . . . You haven't got a cold, have you? You seem very nosy. . . . Tell Barbier, will you please, that I want him up here at once? He will do the packing for me. I should advise you to go to bed, my dear, if you have a cold coming."

It was Joséphine who answered the bell.

"Barbier tells me, that he is to go with the Colonel to Viboire," she said. "I have told him that I will not allow it. He is too old, Barbier, for such an excursion, and I cannot manage the work of the house by myself—there are four floors and more rooms than I have ever counted, and Mlle Thérèse rings for something every ten minutes. It is quite ridiculous; there should be a dozen servants in a house like this, which is damp and not at all good for Gaston. If Barbier is to go, then I myself will go back to Grisolles, where there are dry houses of a reasonable size. It is three flights that the hot water has to be carried up for Mme Pierre's children, and every day there are new boot-marks in the passages."

Eugène sat on the side of the bed with his hands in his pockets.

"You have done very well, Madeleine. I should not have thought that you were sharp enough to arrange so elaborate a conspiracy in a few hours. Where is my purse? Ah, there it is. How much are Barbier's wages for one week? Six eighty-five? I find unfortunately, Joséphine, that I have only four francs in my purse; someone has evidently borrowed all my money. But Madame will give Barbier a week's wages. I shall go to Viboire by myself. No, Joséphine, I am not in the least angry with you. It is impossible, naturally, for you to understand the importance of this excursion. These things are quite above the head of a servant, even a good servant such as you. You cannot be expected to realize how closely the accuracy of details is considered when a case is being tried at law; to you my reconnaissance is mere spell-weaving. I will give you a piece of useful advice, now that you are leaving my service: never wait for the help of other people who do not understand or sympathize with your aspirations. It is the man struggling by himself who ultimately achieves success."

"It is all very well," Joséphine said, "but there's the fire in this room to be done every day, and very often a fire in Mlle Thérèse's room, as well as the one in the drawing-room, and now that Mlle Viguié is dead, and no one else has been engaged to do the washing, and Gaston has to attend Madame Grand'mère upstairs, he can't do everything, poor boy, and there's the ground-floor rooms to be done out on Thursdays. . . ."

Madeleine said: "You can go now, Joséphine. I will have a talk with you later on."

"Tell Barbier," Eugène added, "that he is to order a cab for me, to be here at ten o'clock."

"You'll never be ready by ten . . ."

"You can go now," Madeleine repeated.

Later on, when she could collect herself, she would explain to Joséphine that M. Séverin did not always mean what he said on the spur of the moment; that he was accustomed to the army, where decisions have to be taken in a hurry and where orders are spoken harshly; that in reality M. Séverin held the highest opinion both of Joséphine herself and of Barbier. At present she was altogether too much upset to face such an interview. She dragged in Eugène's trunk, which was kept under the bed in his former dressing-room, and set to work on the packing. The thick pair of boots, she put those in; he would surely have the good sense to wear them when he actually went to make the measurements; his old shooting-suit as spare, since the one he wore would probably get wet; also, on consideration, the dark suit he had worn for Marianne's First Communion, since a second change might be necessary. The underclothes, two complete sets, came straight from the airing-cupboard, but she filled two hot-water bottles and placed them in between, hoping that they would prevent any dampness getting in on the journey. Eight pairs of socks. "You will remember, Eugène, to change your socks whenever you come in? Your feet are sure to get wet in the snow."

"Yes, yes, of course I'll change them when they're wet."

But he had never in his life remembered to do anything like that. Again she was on the point of saying "I have changed my mind, Eugène, I am coming with you after all." But it was still possible, if she remained resolute, that he would abandon the expedition; and her memory, as she wavered, threw back the echo of his voice: *I shall take someone intelligent to make notes. Perhaps Pierre's wife, she's a sensible girl.* So! A person without intelligence would be no use on this excursion. "I have put the oxyquinotheine tablets and the bisurated magnesia underneath the socks, they are on the left hand of the middle tray." "Yes, all right, but really I shall not require any medicines. . . . I shall be glad if you will put in the book of Cicero's orations; I shall want some amusement in the hotel."

He was crouching over the fire, diligently slicing the coal with the point of a poker; his face was very serious, as if he had an important speech to deliver and was making a final choice of alternative phrases.

"I must visit my mother," he said suddenly. "I want to be satisfied that she is quite well before I go."

She had gained the day, Madeleine thought. He had found a loophole, and now he would be able to make a dignified escape from his predicament. But she could not be quite sure. As soon as he had gone she went to her escritoire in the drawing-room and started a letter to the proprietress of the Hôtel Renard at Albecourt where he would be staying: M. Séverin must have a fire of some kind in his room, the bedclothes must be aired each day, there must be no heavy meats in the dietary, M. Séverin would require a tablespoonful of brandy with six parts of hot water and a squeeze of lemon before he went to bed. . . . He was back in his room before the letter was finished and she hastily hid it.

"My mother insists on coming with me," he said. "I have told her that it is not suitable a excursion for an old lady; it will probably kill her, but she won't be dissuaded. At any rate I shall be glad of her companionship. She is bringing Gaston with her."

The cab had already been waiting ten minutes when Eugène arrived in the hall. The Hungarian riding-coat, merino lined, with its high collar and double line of leather buttons, added bulk to his height; a giant of a man he looked, standing motionless, without support, staring at the old sideboard as if it were a vast extent of country which he coolly planned to conquer. "Madame will have the trunk ready by now," he said to Barbier. "You will probably want Joséphine to help you carry it. And there will be Mme Nadya's trunk—I don't suppose Gaston can manage it by himself." He was alone, and still in that attitude, immobile, when a neatly tailored suit containing a little gentleman, accompanied by an urceolate lady, came in at the front door, stamping the snow off their little boots. Catching sight of Eugène they stopped dead. The little gentleman raised his hat. They knew at once who it was; it could be no one but M. Séverin himself, whom they had been so curious to see but whom they had understood to be a chronic invalid. Raising his hat again, the little gentleman said:

"M. Séverin, I believe?" Eugène bowed. "You will perhaps allow me to introduce myself. I am Monsieur Poupoulet."

"It is a great pleasure, M. Poupoulet——"

"And I should like, if you will permit me, to have the privilege of introducing to you also Madame Poupoulet, my wife."

Mme Poupoulet bowed.

Eugène said: "Your servant, Madame."

M. Poupoulet regarded M. Séverin with fixed attention, smiling. He almost nudged Mme Poupoulet in his excitement. Here was something you didn't see every day in Baulon, such a figure of a man, a gentleman of the old school, of the old, the real aristocracy. Mme Poupoulet gazed more shyly but with no less enthusiasm and pleasure: such a kind face, in spite of its gravity, such eyes, you would have said that Greuze had done them. Eugène suffered their regard without impatience; it was the business, the duty of those who were distinguished by their birth or accomplishments to be stared at. At last, feeling a tug on his coat sleeve, M. Poupoulet began to move. But he stopped, bowed again, and said:

"It has been a great pleasure, Monsieur, for Mme Poupoulet, and for myself, to have the honour of making your acquaintance."

"The pleasure is mine entirely," Eugène answered. ". . . but— you have come to see Mme Séverin, no doubt? At present she is upstairs, but she will be down almost immediately."

"Ah, no, no, thank you," Mme Poupoulet said. "We have no wish to trouble Mme Séverin, there is nothing to be discussed this morning."

Eugène was puzzled.

"You have—brought something for her?" he asked. "Or perhaps you wish to see my sister, Mlle Thérèse Séverin?"

"No, no," M. Poupoulet said hastily. "It is very kind of you, but no, there is nothing with which we need trouble Mlle Séverin."

Bowing again, the Poupoulets walked past Eugène and in the direction of the old drawing-room. He called after them:

"Excuse me, I don't think you will find anyone in that room. If you will wait a few moments my servant will attend to you."

"But there is no need for any trouble," the Poupoulets said together; and bowing again, with smiles of politeness and gratitude, they passed into the old drawing-room and closed the door behind them.

Eugène shouted: "Barbier! Come here quickly. There are visitors, I don't know who they are, I don't know what they want."

Barbier was half-way along the corridor with the trunk on his shoulder. He called: "Coming, sir!"

The street door opened again. The cab-driver, muffled up to his moustache, stood flapping his arms for warmth.

"It is no concern of mine," the driver said, "I am quite ready to wait here all day if I am paid accordingly. But I shall be grateful if you will give me, say, half an hour's notice of your intention to start, so that I may work with a chisel round the hooves of my horse Marie Antionette, which at present are stuck fast to the frozen snow."

The Poupoulets had appeared again.

"I think there is some mistake," M. Poupoulet said politely, "I am afraid that we, Mme Poupoulet and I, have given rise to some misunderstanding."

"Barbier!" Eugène shouted again. "Barbier, hurry. This house is full of screaming lunatics."

But Barbier had over-hurried, and the trunk, slipping a little from his shoulder, was wedged in an angle of the stairs.

"One minute!" Madeleine called from behind him. "Barbier is having a little difficulty with the trunk."

Her words were drowned by a raucous voice from a higher flight: "Eugène! What is that you're saying about lunatics? If there are lunatics in this house you're the captain and chief of all of them. I never heard of such a nonsensical expedition, going all that way just to try and prove that you aren't a coward. All the Séverins are cowards. Your father was a coward. He only married me because my father threatened to flog him. . . . Get out of my way, damn your eyes! Who is this buffoon? Kick him, Gaston, for God's sake, I want to get down the stairs, I'll be late for the blooding."

"What are you doing with that trunk?" Eugène thundered. "Get under it, man, get your shoulder to it."

"I wish to explain," M. Poupoulet said at his elbow, "that Mme Poupoulet and I are quite up to date with the rent. We pay regularly on Tuesdays, and we have the receipt for last Tuesday's payment."

"Gaston!" Nadya screamed. "Where are you? What are you doing! If you don't kick that man out of my way I'll tear out your liver with a pair of sheep-shears."

"If any harm is done to Gaston," Joséphine shouted from the third floor, "I will wring the necks of everybody in the house!"

The trunk was clear at last. Barbier stumbled painfully down the remaining stairs and heaved it with a thump on to the floor. Eugène surveyed him dispassionately as he stood biting his lip and ready to weep with the pain in his bad leg. "Not very clever, Barbier!"

"Careful, Monsieur."

Gaston, having found the weight of Nadya's cabin-trunk too great for even his shoulders, was dragging it by one handle down the last flight and leading Nadya with his spare hand. Eugène was only saved by Barbier's tug on his arm from receiving the calvacade on his ankles.

"Gaston! Of all the clumsy louts!"

"I will not have you bullying Gaston!" A third trunk had appeared, with Joséphine bent double beneath it: the Barbier trunk. She came down steadily, scorning to put her free hand on the banisters, straightened herself and let it come to rest between the other two. She looked about her contemptuously, neither red nor short of breath. "What were you saying to Gaston, Barbier?"

"It doesn't matter," Eugène exploded. "Do you realize we have less than twenty minutes to get to the station? Where's that driver? Barbier!"

The Poupoulets were in the very middle of the group. "It appears to me," M. Poupoulet said with a note of severity, "that some kind of explanation is due to Mme Poupoulet and myself."

"Can you, Madeleine, deal with these people? I've no idea what they want."

The driver was back for the second trunk, which he and Gaston lifted between them. "What about that sideboard?" he asked sourly. "Shouldn't that be in one of these boxes?"

"Stop chattering!" Eugène shouted. "Hurry!"

Nadya sat on the bottom stair, slapping her knees and giving little guttural cries of encouragement. "Eugène!" she said suddenly. "Are you warmly dressed? It's cold outside, Andryev Fyodorovitch says. Have you got on your woollen knickers?"

"I have seen to that," Madeleine told her. "Eugène is very warmly dressed. He has his merino trunks and two body-vests."

"Will you ladies have the goodness to stop discussing my underclothes in public? Barbier, I want you——"

"I don't want any of your impertinence, Eugène! I'm surprised, Mlle Pichy, that you allow my son to go on this ridiculous expedition. If I——"

"But, Mother, I have done my best——"

"I told you," Joséphine was screaming at the driver, "that my box was not to go on that cab. I don't want my things mixed up with any of his, I may be only a servant but my property belongs to me, I have as much right to it as M. Séverin has to his, if you don't bring back——"

"All right, all right, Joséphine," Barbier said savagely, "I'll get it down. Gaston, stop grinning and give me a hand."

"If you say another word, Barbier——"

"It's all right," the driver told them, "your box is the one I have put at the bottom, so it only means that I have just to lift down the other two, neither of which weighs more than the Palace of Versailles."

M. Poupoulet had appeared again, bearing triumphantly a small piece of paper. He presented it to Eugène.

"If you will be kind enough to regard this receipt, Monsieur, you will see that the rent is paid up to last Tuesday. Mme Poupoulet and I——"

"Madeleine! Can you do nothing with this infernal lunatic?"

"If he's bothering you for the rent," Nadya roared, "just bump him in the belly. That's what my mother did to rent-snatchers when we lived in Warszawie. At him, boy—you butt the bastard."

"Mme Séverin," said M. Poupoulet tearfully, "I appeal to you——"

But Madeleine was past understanding his appeal. Her eyes were on Eugène, who was looking the other way now as if he had left her far behind. He was tired already, harassed to exhaustion, and in a few minutes he would be out of reach of her care. The childish crossness of his face, the whine of his voice, did not arrive at her perception. She saw only that he was old, and worn as he had been on the last day of the trial, bludgeoned to half-consciousness by the nonsensic clamour; that his grandeur had remained, he stood so straight, so large in that old coat of his, the one he had worn to travel here from Paris. The Poupoulets had gone away at last; and standing alone, waiting with stoic patience for the confusion to sort itself, he had recovered his dignity. His figure was becoming blurred by the moisture in her eyes. She called to him, "Eugène! Here, just a minute," but he did not seem to hear her. He was moving across to the door, he was outside now. Surrendering, she ran after him.

"Eugène, I've changed my mind, I can't let you go alone."

He turned slowly and smiled at her with infinite kindness.

"But, my dear, I could not let you come. You've got a cold, I can see that, you are certainly not fit for this excursion. You must look after yourself, my dear. I would stay and look after you myself, but I have to get the evidence I require, there is no one to help me."

"But, Eugène——"

"Please, Madeleine, no more! I am very late for the train."

★

The growing crowd round the cab had waited with exemplary patience. And so, they said, the Séverins were going away at last, and there would be no more gentry in the Square; presently there would be none in Baulon. It was singular, the fact that so many of the moneyed people were choosing to leave the town all at the same time; the Baulon winter, surely, had always been just as bad. Never had the furniture vans been worked so hard, they were as common in the streets to-day as hearses, of which the business always flourished in February; and no less sinister. There is something wrong, they said, with Baulon; it is owing no doubt, as they say in the *Petit Baulonnais*, to the corruption at the Hôtel de Ville; and now the Séverins are going away to God-knows-where and the great house will be as forlorn and empty as the half-built factory on the other side. It was a pity to lose so fruitful a subject for gossip and speculation; they had given the Square distinction, those Séverins with their imposing figures and their haughty reserve; but at least there was the pleasure of seeing them depart and if all of them intended to get into old Félix Auterbe's cab, including the remains of the old Russian woman which had not yet as far as anyone knew been buried, the spectacle would be one of tolerable interest. Already Félix had brought out larger travelling trunks than had ever been seen before, and the largest of all had slipped when it was half-way up, bang, the whole weight of it on to Félix's bad shoulder, how the children clapped and shouted at the sight of old Félix dancing and cursing. When they were all up the cab looked as if it would fall to bits at any moment. And now Joséphine Barbier was complaining that Félix had done something wrong, he had put the trunks the wrong way round or something, they were arguing so fast and furiously that neither could hear the other, they were at it with their fists now. *Go on, Joséphine, blot his nose out, bite him, Joséphine, courage, Félix, push her in the snow!* But Barbier stopped them, Barbier himself climbed on the roof and got the boxes down, the cab creaking and screaming like a gipsy orchestra. Look! There was M. Séverin himself, there was a figure of a man for you, with a coat that only a military gentleman could wear so handsomely, it must have cost no less than four hundred francs. Look, there he is, look, Antoine, look, Cécile, Petit-Charles, that is the M. Séverin they talk about, he was a great general once but they turned him out for selling secrets to the Prussians. Look, he's smiling, look, Lucille, he's waving his hand to you, there's a fine gentleman for you, how would you like to have a gentleman like that for your papa? That was Mme Séverin behind him with the shawl over her shoulders, and there— great heavens!—there was the old Russian woman herself, walking on her own legs, hanging on to the coat-tails of the idiot-boy Gaston. They gazed in astonishment, wondering not less at the smallness of her stature than at the unusual items in her costume, the tremendous orange feather in her hat, the leopard-skin about her shoulders, the wading-boots up to the knees of her black corduroy trousers. M. Séverin held the door of the cab for her as if she were the greatest lady in all France; it was a treat to see such distinguished courtesy; the boy Gaston had got behind her and was trying to push her up on to the step, which bumped up and down like a rowing boat as Barbier heaved and Félix dragged the trunks to the roof again. But the old lady would not budge, she had decided that she would ride to the station on the back of poor Marie Antoinette. She had broken loose, she had her hands on the shafts and was frantically trying to push herself up. "Shove me behind, Gaston! Andryev Fyodorovitch, where are you, come and hold the stirrup for me, keep still, you brute, hold him, someone, get hold of the snaffle, give me the reins, blast you!" The children pressed closer, they were right under Marie Antoinette's flanks. It was a most interesting old lady; they did hope that Félix Auterbe would allow her to ride to the station; so natural and so gallant a desire deserved fulfilment. But M. Séverin had picked her up bodily: he was inserting her, kicking and screaming, into the cab. Gaston went after her, holding her down on the seat and scolding her like a muleteer, while the cab rocked and groaned with her struggles. M. Séverin jumped into the cab like a schoolboy and banged the door after him: what an agile old gentleman he was, for all his corsets and his dignity! But Mme Séverin had got her dress caught in the door. Apparently she was not going. It looked as if she wanted to go and M. Séverin would not let her; they seemed to be arguing all the time she was disengaging her dress, but the Russian lady and Joséphine Barbier were both making such a din that it was impossible to hear what the Séverins said. It was certainly a peculiar departure, and one that would lend itself to considerable discussion. But now, at the most enjoyable stage, it was all over, Mme Séverin had got her dress free and Barbier had dragged his wife away from the other window, Félix had given poor Marie Antoinette such a cut on the rump that she had started at a canter, the cab slithering crazily behind her. And nothing was left but the two children staring out of an upper window, the Barbiers in violent altercation on the pavement, and Mme Séverin, who for some reason that no one could understand was bitterly crying.

XXIII

He had not expected Viboire to appear as he had first seen it; that aspect it had never recovered, though the shape of it had hardly changed at all. The village itself had never suffered bombardment; there were half a dozen new cottages, but the other buildings had been there since the eighteenth century; the roads and cart-tracks were exactly as his sketch-maps marked them. But he had seen it first in grand confusion, and with a military eye: a position on the map affording so much cover, which could not readily be sighted by artillery in the Surmelin Valley. He could remember Guéroult pointing it out with his square brown thumb, breathing garlic across his face: "You see there, Viboire, Viboire-les-Deux-Auberges, you want to get that position fixed, you'd better slip back and see it if you get the time. Two roads, d'you see, going back to Salaube. This one's the one you want to use if you have to get away in a hurry; it's practically sheltered as far as that point, where I've put a cross—I know it quite well. But you've got the other one if you want it, that may be useful. They're both good enough this time of year; they'll take the guns all right. . . ." He had ridden back that night, losing most of his meagre allowance of sleep; he owed a good deal of his reputation to that kind of thing; *it's uncanny*, they said, *the way Séverin knows the ground, as if he'd helped God make it*; and arriving in the first daylight he had caught sight of the village from the forest-edge on the Cauchois ridge. From that point he could see the two roads, and judge for himself exactly where each of them would be most vulnerable, supposing that a flanking column of the enemy broke through to Vigny-Pistolles. Guéroult was wrong, he thought then: the northern of the two was the one to use; true, it was open for the first six kilometres, but there the range would be sufficient protection; and where it rose into the woods at Esteville it would give a nice position for digging in one's heels, if the circumstance were favourable, and usefully covering the Messelles-Bechelins road on which Duperron might be moving. Descending to the village itself he had found it a larger place than he expected; a transitory metropolis of soldiers, the street blocked with guns and waggons; a battalion, nominally in extended column of fours, filing through like geese in the market; troops bivouacked in the lanes and farmyards, everything covered with white dust, the place stinking of sweaty uniforms and horseflesh. That was his first picture of Viboire, ragged but indelible. He had seen it next after ten years and found no single trace of the flurry of arms which had passed across and temporarily choked it. There was a farm waggon lumbering in the direction of Cauchois, the street was full of poultry with dogs asleep on the cottage steps, the warm, still air smelt of hay. He had met the Curé moving sunnily between the houses. Yes, the Curé told him, the place was crowded with soldiers ten years back, and at one time the Prussians had occupied it; but no, he had never heard of any battle, Monsieur was thinking perhaps of the hills beyond Calaube, where there had been a sharp engagement. And for a moment—so altered was the place's aspect, so much smaller it appeared—he had thought that it was actually the wrong village. But on the lower ridge, which was under barley now, he saw the line of trees grouped just as he had noted them that day: two sets of three, and one standing alone, and the shape of the lone tree reminded him sharply, as it had done before, of a dog begging. Yes, the bridge was there at the end of the street, though narrower than he remembered it; and beyond, the upper road to Salaube went off at a slant, so that standing here by the inn you could not see along it. The priest's house lay back from the road—he would not go near it—and the lane which passed it ran behind the village to the farmhouse where he had spent that night, his last as a free soldier. The line of the farm wall, an angle between two houses, provoked a sudden recollection: just here, he had stood talking to Fauquet, and Fauquet had said: "None of us quite understood why . . ." The corpse of a place, the features of some-one you had known, the reality all gone.

And to-day, as the charrette brought him to the crest of the hill, it was the Viboire of his later visits that he saw lying in a fold of the snow; familiar like a grave often visited, which carries the memory not of the person loved but of a hot Sunday when a wheel came off the carriage, of a fellow mourner's foolish chatter; a quiet, forgotten place. They knew him now, the people in the village: that was the gentleman who came here sometimes to make measure-ments across Turmel's fields, an amiable old man who was a little wrong in the head and who hoped to find buried treasure. They had heard from Jean Turmel—whose buggy had been ordered for him at Albecourt—that he was coming. They saluted him and he acknowledged them graciously, his sad eyes bright with pleasure at their recognition. They would understand one day, he thought, why he came here; when the news that his honour had been restored, spreading like fire through France, came even to this small village. "Why," they would say, "this Colonel Séverin of whom all France is talking, who has just received the Grand Cross of the Légion d'Honneur, it is none other than the tall military man who used sometimes to visit Viboire." The Curé, doubled with age, wading through the slush in rubber boots with his skirts hitched up round his waist, stopped the charrette to speak to him. "It is a pleasure, M. Séverin, to see you in Viboire again. It means, I hope, that you are well." "Fairly, well M. le Curé. I am better than I have been. . . . And have you heard yet that there was once a battle on the hillside there?" "My dear M. Séverin, if it had not been for the incredible and obstinate taciturnity of my parishioners I should have heard of it the moment I arrived here. My own fatal weakness in modern history. . . ."

At Gallier's inn, where Turmel set him down, he rested for half an hour, sipping warm brandy, with the map spread out on the table. He had meant only to glance it over while his feet got warm, but he found himself gazing at it for a long time, sleepily, reluctant to go out into the snow again. It was hard to fix his mind. The lines on the map, he could have drawn them quite accurately from memory, he had pored over it so long and so often; but it no longer made a picture for him, he had lost his old power of trans-lating contours instantly into slopes and ridges. There were little dots in violet ink, marking the positions from which he had made a former survey, with the date against them. There were distances marked in violet, with "checked, '08," against them in red. Formerly he had been able to make his way instantly to the key positions but now he was hazy, he could no longer recollect the reason for those points being chosen. It was comfortable here, there was a melancholy enjoyment in letting his eyes rest on the map to which he had given so much labour, an artist's pleasure in his handiwork. He would stay for a little while longer; perhaps he would order déjeuner and have it before he started.

He found it agreeable to be quite alone. At home they fussed him. Tischer was infuriating with his little sympathetic noises, his paternal flutter, and there was not one hour in the day when Madeleine did not ask if he felt a draught from the door or pull him out of a comfortable position to pummel and bunch his pillow. They meant it kindly, but they did not understand his condition; they made him feel worse by their perpetual sick-room antics, their solicitous demeanour. He should have thought of it before, to take a holiday from his nurses; it would be a lesson to them, how much better he looked when he returned. His eagerness was renewed by that reflection. He left the inn by the back door, went across the yard and into the lane. As if to bless his resolution the sun was out now, and its light on the snow almost dazzled him. Reaching Turmel's gate, he climbed over and, pleased with his agility, struck at a fair pace up the hill.

It was a stiff climb, through the clogging snow, to the copse which he had made his first point. But his mind worked comfortably, reciting again the speech he would make to summarize his defence, that speech which somehow the lawyers had stopped him making. "It is necessary for you to take the military point of view, the point of view of expediency, and to imagine the position as I saw it then. My force, you must recollect, had been considerably reduced by the previous day's fighting, and it was of paramount importance to use it, in its reduced condition, as effectively as my tactical training enabled me. Imagine then the lie of the country, as the map shows it to you. You will see that from the position marked with a line of crosses in yellow, which Major Bouchery vacated shortly before one o'clock, and which by one-thirty was occupied by not fewer than three companies of the second Luckewalde corps, as precisely stated in Werder's published memoir, it was possible for the enemy to advance diagonally upon the southern Viboire-Salaube road without encountering any place at which a small force could make effective resistance. . . ." Yes, but it was just that fact which the map would not show immediately to an untrained eye; indeed, the map made it appear that the wooded knoll on the 140 contour would give the very position which he might have occupied to brilliant advantage. That question, of course, he had examined before; but here his memory was feeble, and there was nothing for it but to ascend to what he had dubbed the Bouchery line and see again just how the ground fell, so that he could describe it with living accuracy. He had reached the copse, and it was another mile to go, or two by the twisted track on which he presently decided. But he reached the place in just under forty minutes, puffed and a little dizzy. He had the whole country in his vision now. He leant on his stick, breathing deeply, aware despite his preoccupation of the land's gentle beauty, the heights and hollows rounded smooth by their flesh of snow, which changed its tint in every further rise until it lay like smoke on the Veraulney upland, the naked tree trunks sloping to the middle distance as if a painter placed them with the easy, steady swing of a narrow brush. He had forgotten, cloistered in a stuffy room in the place Talleyrand, that France was like that, a country of wide slopes bent tenderly, where the trees marched swaggering. And there the knoll was, a little to the south of east, perhaps six kilometres off on an arrow's path; this side thickly shielded with spruce, which straggled northward in a fence that joined the lower ridge. That was just as it was shown on the map, where the line of trees was clearly marked. As he saw the ground now, it looked as if a half-battalion could have been raced there under shelter, from the place marked Four-trees Farm, effectively to cover with oblique fire the troops re-forming on a higher line. He unfolded the map again and spread it on the snow at his feet, doubtful for a moment if he were actually on the Bouchery contour; but according to the map, yes, there was no room for question. He worked along the top of the ridge and descended to the farm. Its identity could not be mistaken: two of the trees had gone but the stumps remained, and he knew the formation of the outhouses as if he lived there. A cart-track ran north-eastward up the slope, and following it he came at three hundred metres to a barrow. It was here—though it had looked so different—standing on the barrow's crest, that he had received the first signal from Pichereau; here, then, with the knoll staring him in the face, with the fall of land as clear as it had been from the summit, he must have given his preliminary order to Lancesseur. But that moment he could not remember: only that Lenormand had been with him, that Lenormand had said in his abominably deferential voice, "That seems sound to me, sir, very sound, if I may say so, sir." But yes, something else: he had felt very sick; something had been wrong with his stomach, or perhaps he had had a touch of summer-fever, for he had been exposed all morning to a blazing sun. His memory would help him no further. The valley with this accursed snow upon it looked altogether different to-day; the trees perhaps were thicker than they had been then. He had stood here on each of his former visits, and surely then he had been amply satisfied. But to-day he could not think, couldn't remember, why he had rejected so obvious a strategy.

Lenormand, it was Lenormand he wanted. Lenormand would have told him why. At twelve-thirty he had seen the first signal—that was noted in the sketch-map's margin. It was shortly after —no, a little before that—that Guéroult's messenger had arrived. That was a vivid glimpse, the man's tired and frightened horse attempting to pull away, the messenger trying ridiculously to hold her and to salute at the same time; then, "What is the time, Lenormand?" and Lenormand's voice like a barber's, "Twelve-fifteen exactly, sir." Yes, he had that very clearly: the messenger struggling with his horse, a white horse—no, a grey horse with white fetlocks —and Lenormand's silky voice, Lenormand staring earnestly at his gigantic Strasbourg timepiece. He had shown Lenormand the message, and Lenormand had said something. What was it? Something like—"It'll be as much as we can manage, all that lot." He had felt very tired, as he felt now, and hollow-stomached. But that was all, all he could remember. He tried again, frantically blowing upon the dying spark in his memory. But it would not kindle, and he found his eyes moistening with the hopeless exertion. He would have to give it up, to give up the whole thing. The fire he had nursed so faithfully had smouldered into ashes; he had waited too long. If only they had found Lenormand!

His feet were frozen almost lifeless, in spite of his heavy stockings. The warmth the climb had given him was gone already; he was exhausted and empty. He would leave it now and come back after luncheon, when his mind would be clearer. He descended very slowly by the track that curved away to the Rosiens road.

It seemed a long way back to the village; it was nearly two o'clock when he reached it, and he found himself unable, after so long an abstinence, to take solid food. But Mme Gallier was sympathetic, she understood at once what his feelings were. It was a pleasure to have a woman like that attending on him, they were so intelligent, these elderly villageoises, their behaviour at once tender and respectful. She brought him mulled grostenquine, and when that was finished, bouillon à la corsicaine, flavoured as Joséphine would not have done it with Auguste Lemarignier himself at her elbow. She tempted him then with quasi-de-veau spitted in the Alsatian fashion, and after that he took cheese of her own making, with a glass of saintonge over which she had scraped a lemon. She stood and talked to him in her soft, deferential voice while he discussed the cheese. Monsieur had heard, perhaps, that there had been other military gentlemen in Viboire making observations? Oh, yes, there had been a number of gentlemen, from the Ministry in Paris so she understood; two of them had been in here, they had sat for a cup of coffee where Monsieur himself was sitting, and one of them had addressed the other as "General"; but Mme Gallier doubted if he were really a General, since he had actually disputed the price of the coffee, and no gentleman of high military rank—Monsieur would surely agree—ever argued about such a triviality, it would not be rational. What had they been doing? ——? How could Mme Gallier, who was nothing but an unlettered countrywoman, know what they had been doing? She had only observed that the young officers in the party had appeared to be measuring distances along the Cauchois road; they had been equipped with telescopes of an extraordinary kind, mounted upon a little scaffolding; they had stood gazing into the little tubes with the lively attention of young gentlemen at the keyholes of ladies' bedrooms, and calling to each other all the time like quoit-throwers at the Easter fête, *Voilà! Quatre-vingt-douze!* and the older gentlemen had written it down in their little books as if the young men had been delivered of delicious epigrams. But what was Mme Gallier to make of all that, since she was nothing but an unlettered countrywoman?

"Tell me, Mme Gallier," Eugène said, "did you happen to hear any of the gentlemen mention the name of Colonel Séverin?"

"No, Monsieur. I should certainly have noticed and remembered it."

"And you say that it was towards Cauchois they moved in making their observations?"

"Yes, Monsieur, they were along the Cauchois road and in the woods on the left side. And I am told that there have since been men working in that direction, digging ditches of some kind on Jules Rivard's land, for which Jules Rivard is claiming heavy compensation. Naturally when a man's land is cut up with ditches and wire fences . . ."

"But one moment, Mme Gallier! Are you sure there were no observations taken up that way, towards the Ferme aux Quatres Arbres, where I was this morning?"

"I can't be certain, Monsieur, but I didn't see the gentlemen there; I heard nothing about it. Certainly Turmel would have complained if they had dug ditches on his land; he would have applied for compensation."

"And you are sure they didn't mention my name, they said nothing of a Colonel Séverin?"

"No, Monsieur, the name was not mentioned. I should certainly have noticed it."

He was puzzled. It was plain that the authorities were frightened. They had got wind of his intention to bring the case for re-trial;

they had failed this time to interrupt the process by political manœuvre; they were trying now to avert the scandal by faking the evidence once again. Was it only to blind the simple villagers that they had demonstrated in the Cauchois region? But he was too sleepy now to reason. Before he began the afternoon excursion he would take a short nap in his chair, his feet on the step of the stove and the carriage-rug over his knees.

When his eyes closed a breeze fluttered the leaves of his mind's album, so that he saw its pictures out of order and in sharp succession; but clear, far clearer now than when he blinked in the harsh reflected sunlight. The pale, expressionless features of prosecuting counsel: "You had with you the officer who cannot be found, Captain Lenormand; and there were also, you say, two runners, though you cannot remember—odd as it may seem—who those runners were. I only want you to tell me this: were all those three men, as well as yourself, standing with their backs in the direction of the signal? And if so, at what were they looking?" "But you do not realize, M. l'Avocat, that I was tired and feverish, I'd had no sleep. . . ." He stood at a street corner, an old gabled house in front of him, the men marching past had the early sun on their faces. Someone spoke—he could see the face and the worn, mud-stained uniform, a man with very broad shoulders, but he couldn't give him a name or rank—everyone was hurrying, but the broad man stopped to speak to him: "In Russia, you know, when the wolves come level with the sledge, they throw something over, the carcass of a deer if they have one handy, or a man they don't much care for. The wolves stop to clean it up; you can sometimes get away like that. That's your little job, old man, as I see things, to stay and be cleaned up by the Prussians. It will make a most heroic story if you do it elegantly; they will get Van Moé to do a nice bust of you and it will be placed in a corner of the rue de Récollets. . . ." He stared at the face intently, trying to remember whose it was, but it was changing to the ferocious snout of an épagneul, straining to get at him, while someone who held him by the arms said, "Keep still, Eugène, you little fool, he won't hurt you!" He struggled and got free; he ran headlong down a dusty street of tall and silent houses; he was losing breath and he stopped to peer into the faces of those who passed him, trying desperately to find Lenormand. The man with the white scarf laughed, his laugh was like Lenormand's, and he would have run away but Eugène caught him. He snatched away the scarf and saw that it was bloody, and the face, grotesquely smiling, was the dead face of Léon Vagniez; Léon Vagniez, the one man he had loved with a religious devotion, lying there in the mud at the bottom of a gully with the yellow leaves stuck to the dry blood on his forehead. He couldn't stop, they were coming over the hill and they would get him if he stopped an instant. He shouted: "Tugny! Go left! Up in the wood," and ran again, buckling his belt as he ran. They were yelling, "Colonel Séverin! He's late, he isn't coming," as he groped his way through the maze of doors and passages, to the front of the crowded Court, calling, "I'm here, I'm ready," and found that Bettencourt's livid face was staring into his, only a hand's stretch away. "Then, why, M. Séverin, did you tell the Court that you believed Major Bouchery had withdrawn his support from your left flank?" "That's a lie, sir," he shouted aloud, "I didn't say that." His voice scared away the ring of fleshy hostile faces, leaving only the faded yellow distemper on the wall, a torn and fly-blown sheet of paper advertising penalties for inebriation. He called, "Madeleine, I feel a slight draught, I think the door must be open," but it was Mme Gallier who answered him, and he remembered then that he was at Viboire. The light was already failing, and he decided, not without relief, that he could do no more that day.

"I shall be very grateful, Mme Gallier, if you will have the goodness to send a message to Turmel, telling him that I want the charrette as soon as possible.

On the way back to Albecourt he sat with his back to the driver, a cocoon of rugs and blankets, watching sleepily the ruffled stream of brown snow flowing beneath the tail-lamp, lonely and dejected.

★

He was more cheerful as he toiled up the slope on the following day. The sun had broken early and the air was warm, the snow damp and slippery. He had brought Gaston, as he needed someone to hold the measuring line, and Nadya, refusing to be left alone either at Albecourt or in the village, was plodding gamely in his wake, with Gaston pulling her on a short length of rope, and Turmel, whose sullen features hid a treasury of patience, pushing her behind. They had as rearguard a sow of Turmel's, with pessimistic but determined eyes, who in spite of all her master's cajolery and threats, his kicks and snowballs, would not relinquish her discipleship. Eugène was cheerful because, waking that morning from long and dreamless sleep, he had hit upon the simple solution: there had been a fog that day, at least a heavy mist; that was why he had failed to see the knoll and the line of advantage which it offered. It was Barbier who had reminded him, in a conversation they had had a few weeks back. "Yes, yes, there was a heavy mist that day." It was odd that he had forgotten.

As he stood to rest on the first ridge he suffered a moment's doubt. In the morning, surely, there had been bright sunshine. But he had known days when the sky was completely changed within an hour, and as Barbier was so certain—an excellent fellow, an N.C.O. of the old type, thoroughly reliable—then that must have been what happened. It would explain at once his failure to put an obvious strategy into effect and the fact that Guéroult's alleged signal, given at 1.50, had not been seen by himself or by his men. He called to Turmel:

"You have fogs in this region, don't you?"

"Down in the village," Turmel told him. "Sometimes. It's mostly clear up here, except in bad winters."

"Yes, but in the summer, you must often get clouds drifting low between the hills. I should think sometimes you can hardly see a dozen paces."

"I don't remember," Turmel said.

But they were all like that, these peasants, they noticed nothing but the dung of their sheep as they walked along.

"Must you bring that sow all up here?" he said irritably.

Nadya, who till this moment had been perfectly docile, said angrily: "Eugène! I won't have you calling me names."

"Pompadour, home. Go home, there's a good girl!" Turmel pleaded.

Eugène turned his back on them and Turmel asked:

"Do you want this bit dug up?"

"Dug up? Why dug up?"

"There will be no difficulty," Turmel assured him. "A couple of my men, with picks and spades, will dig it up for you in no time, as deep as you like to go."

The fellow had got some cracked idea and it was no good arguing with him. Eugène set off by himself, found the path that led up through a coppice of pine, and followed it till he emerged on the 110 contour. Here the ragged remains of a wall guided him along the side of the higher slope, a little upwards, and brought him at least three hundred paces to Barraud's point. The stake was still in position, though badly rotted, close to a gap in the wall. He took off his gloves and unfolded with his icy fingers the copy of Corporal Barraud's memorandum: *My signal was given, in accordance with orders transmitted to me by Lieutenant Vallemont, precisely at 1.15. My position was at a gap in a stone wall shown on the accompanying plan.. by the intersection of the lines marked FF[1] and GG[1]. The position has since been checked by me, under the surveillance of Major Couillard. I estimate that Colonel Séverin, who was clearly visible to me, was not above 500 metres away, at the point approximately indicated by the intersection of HH[1] and JJ[1]. My signal was acknowledged but not checked back.* Eugène set his jaw. There was nothing he remembered so clearly as the way the languid corporal read that statement in the Court, his toneless voice revealing to anyone with an open mind that it had been composed, every word of it, by the officer instructing counsel for the prosecution. "And how was your signal acknowledged, Corporal?" "In the usual way, sir. The letters CR were signalled." "And did you ask for confirmation?" "Yes, sir, I signalled 'PA,' but my correspondent appeared to ignore that signal." Straight out, as pat as you please, and they had all believed him, Vaudilhac had believed him, they had lapped it up like puppies. That was how Guéroult had done it, Guéroult, the little jumped-up whippersnapper from Marseilles, the jealous Protestant to whom a brilliant young Catholic officer was a perpetul reminder of his own inferiority. A word in the mouth of a devoted aide-de-camp, a man of his own mentality; a little present to a Corporal of the Reserves; a whisper among the ragtag of place-seeking politicians who infested Paris; that was all Guéroult had needed to have him thrown to the wolves, a blood-offering for the sins of all the soldiers. And now, what could you do against such people, that yellow-necked Bettencourt, the lisping, sarcastic Pichereau? He'd shake them yet, he'd have them; he'd waited a long time but he would have them in the end, pilloried for the ridicule of Paris. He shouted, beckoning with his extended arm:

"Gaston! Up here!"

Gaston saw his sign at once and began to stumble up the slope, choosing the part where it was steepest: to his considerable annoyance Eugène saw that he still had Nadya on the rope, and that Turmel was in his place behind, with Madame de Pompadour urgently following. He shouted "Don't bring her up, leave her where she is!" but his voice would not carry. In a little over ten minutes the party arrived panting. Turmel respectfully saluted.

"It is here, then," Turmel asked, "that you want a hole dug?"

"A hole? Why in the world should I want a hole dug? I'm not a rabbit, am I? Gaston—take that grin off your face, man, look sharp!—have you got the tape? Don't tell me you've dropped it somewhere—oh, there it is, good, give it me." He took the line and tied one end round the stake. "Now I'm going to stretch the line. When I call to you, untie this end and bring it down to me —not before, you understand!"

It was not easy for an old man to make his way straight down the slope of snow, keeping his eye on the position of the lower stake. But his blood was warmed by determination, he felt at last that he was taking positive action not only in his own cause but in that of justice. Holding the line firmly he went down sideways, half stepping and half sliding, till he reached the end of the fifty metres.

"Now!" he called.

Failing to understand, Gaston followed him down, bringing the party in his rear. They were too much concerned with their own stability in the awkward scramble to heed his furious attempts to stop them, and they reached him in close formation before he had finished shouting. Nadya, shaken by the headlong descent, was becoming petulant.

"I don't understand what all this nonsense is, Eugène. Why do we keep on going up and down?"

Eugène ignored her.

"And now, Gaston," he said with ghastly quietness, "will you please have the goodness to go up again—no, you can leave Madame where she is—and untie the tape as I directed you."

With a grin that reminded Eugène of Angèle's crazy devotion, Gaston went off to do as he was told.

"You will tell me, Monsieur," Turmel said politely, "where it is that you wish me to dig for whatever it is you are looking for?"

"I don't understand all this," Nadya repeated. "I wish you'd tell me, Eugène, what you and this M. Turmel are trying to find. My eyes aren't as good as they were, it's very annoying not to know what's going on."

"I'll explain to you later," he said shortly. But he had no intention of explaining. She wouldn't understand, no one would understand what he was doing, what this meant to him. To-day as yesterday he was utterly lonely.

Gaston came back with the tape-end in his hand and presented it with canine complaisance.

"No," Eugène said, "I want you to hold it. Sit down. Now stay exactly where you are, and hold the tape tight—there, hold it just like that. Turmel, I want you to count the lengths, this will be the second. Now don't move, Gaston, till I tell you."

He started to go down again, and Nadya followed him. "I'm coming with you, Eugène, I want to see what you're up to." Tired of her waywardness, he went on by himself, leaving her to make her own way as best she could. He had brought her on the express condition that she would not interfere with his surveying, and he refused to bother himself when he saw her sliding away at an angle of her own. "Hold it tight!" he called back to Gaston.

"Gaston!"

That was Nadya. She had stumbled and fallen headlong into a trough in the ground. The sight of Nadya's fat, red-stockinged legs sticking up out of the snow, of Madame de Pompadour sniffing suspiciously at her ankles, bereft him of his remaining patience. "Oh, for God's sake! Pull her out, someone, Turmel—no, not you, Gaston, you fathead!" But Gaston had already answered mechanically to her summons, and thirty metres of tape lay in languid coils across the snow. Eugène sat down and spread his hands over his streaming eyes. He was to say then, when he got to the Court, "I know, M. le Président, that Corporal Barraud was a long way off when he gave the signal, but I am unable to state the exact distance as I could find no one competent to help me take the measurements." No! He would start again, he would have that distance measured if it took him till nightfall. He tugged viciously at the tape, which would not yield, and saw when he uncovered his eyes that Madame de Pompadour, fatigued at last, had stretched herself upon it.

"Turmel," he said stoically, "will you kindly remove your accursed sow from the tape? Thank you. And now Gaston, you and I will go back to the stake and begin the measurement again."

He began wearily to climb the slope once more, with Gaston, whose grin would not conceal alarm and exhaustion, scrambling after him. And for seventy minutes they worked bravely, Gaston taking the tape ahead and dutifully marking the end of each length with a peg that Turmel produced for him. Turmel watched them dourly, with detached curiosity; he wasn't going to interfere any more, the old gentleman was best left to himself. At intervals he guided Nadya to a new position from which she could make her comments heard; and she sat in the snow, where he placed her, smoking one cigarette after another, occasionally stretching her hand to stroke the snout of Madame de Pompadour who lay beside her. "You and I, Mirza my pretty one, we cannot follow what that Eugène is doing. We should rather be hunting, you and I, but we are too old to hunt, Mirza, my darling. We must wait until Eugène has finished his games in the snow, or till his father comes to give him a whipping." "How many lengths is that?" Eugene called as each peg went in, and Turmel conscientiously told him, "That was the seventh, Monsieur." "Thank you, Turmel. . . . All right, on you go, Gaston."

It was long past the hour for which they had ordered déjeuner when the lower stake was reached. By Turmel's account they had stretched the tape ten times, and there were just twelve metres over. Tired and cold, Eugène took a little time to calculate the result: 512 metres; allowing for the varied gradients, that would give the direct distance between the stakes as approximately 460 to 480 metres. Obviously Turmel had miscounted, and except for the placing of the pegs his morning's work had been wasted.

"This stake," he asked suddenly, "has someone moved it since I was here a few years ago?"

"No, Monsieur. I know the position well, it has never been moved."

Eugène was doubtful about that. But in any case he meant to come back this afternoon and to do the measuring all over again. 460 metres—it was unthinkable; you could tell by looking that it was not less than 600. Yes, he would do it again, and by himself this time. He was tired now, but after déjeuner he would be strong enough.

He gathered the tape and put it in his pocket.

"All right, Gaston, that will do for this morning. Come, Mother, we are going back to the village now."

But she had fallen asleep across Madame de Pompadour's capacious flank, the cigarette between her lips still smouldering. Thankful that the morning's miseries were over, Gaston put her carelessly over one shoulder and stumbled off down the hill.

XXIV

ALTHOUGH the usual windows were uncovered, the Abbé Vignaud felt as soon as he got inside that it was a house of mourning. The silence was so deep, the face of Barbier opening the door so stretched and gloomy. Against that melancholy his art was too feeble. It was true that Mme Séverin received him with more than her usual eagerness, removed Angèle who was asleep where he liked to put his feet, selected a Ramon Allones cigar for him, took special pains with his Moka coffee; but she was listless while he talked to her, and kept her gaze on her embroidery, in which his quick eye noticed that she was using a wrong colour. Her cough was at its worst to-day, and she hardly tried to stifle it. He had learnt from Barbier on the way upstairs that M. Séverin had gone away, refusing for some unknown reason to take Madame with him. Presently she would tell him about that, and bit by bit he would draw the whole story. But he must give her time, and he chattered industriously, with patient pauses for her fits of coughing, of Paris people whom she had known or whose names would be familiar: of Madame La Fontaine Bernard, of how François Coppée had retorted to Cramoisin's charge of vulgar egotism, of the supper-party at Montlhéry which had been the cause of the Affaire Josselin. He was rewarded only by a sigh: "I have forgotten all that, cher Abbé, I never think of those people now." He tried to amuse her with his own misfortune; on his way across the Square he had passed under the scaffolding and a bucketful of snow had fallen down his neck. It drew her attention, but she was only concerned for his safety. "You must take off your soutane and dry yourself, I will leave you so that you can dry by the fire." He laughed at her. There was nothing so good for the clerical kidney, he said, as a lump of snow carried in the small of the back; he had been told that by the great surgeon Quéveteur, who, it was said, had secured for his laboratory the kidneys of many famous men at their decease, including a cardinal or two, in the face of spirited bidding from half a dozen restaurants in the boulevard Montparnasse.

"No, my dear Mme Séverin, never again will I be persuaded to take off my clothes in other people's houses. It was at the house of Robert de Souprosse that I once arrived in a thunderstorm, drenched to the skin. The servant told me that Souprosse and his wife would not be back for an hour or more; he led me to the drawing-room and begged me to take off my clothes by the fire while he found me a towel and something to put on until he had dried them. I had no sooner acted on his advice, rendering myself an all-but-perfect copy of the Venus in the Uffizi, though a little on the heavy side, for at that time I weighed just over a hundred kilograms, when a junior servant admitted to my presence two elderly maiden ladies, who just before they passed into unconsciousness informed me that they were of English nationality. Poor Souprosse, he never forgave me. The ladies proved to belong to the Court of Windsor, and he was obliged to give up his diplomatic post in London, besides having to pay the fees of a dintinguished alienist who attended them."

But Madeleine, who in her normal mood could be put in good humour by such an artless anecdote, would not surrender her melancholy. "It must have been dreadful for you," she said, "so terribly embarrasing, and dreadful for the poor anglaises."

"It is a good thing that they were Protestants," he said sombrely, "for in Heaven, so our Mother makes us understand, to appear in déshabillé is quite customary."

He was preparing to make his excuses and get away, when she asked suddenly:

"Tell me, Abbé, it was in Paris, before my marriage, that you first knew my husband?"

He was surprised, for she had never spoken of Eugène's early days, the days before his degradation. He shook his head.

"No, the Séverins I never knew, though I was acquainted with the Debreuilles who lived in the same quartier and were intimate with them. I know, of course, of your husband's great military reputation . . . and Mlle Thérèse, I was introduced to her once in the salon of Madame Adrien Giacolette. I remember that very well. I was tired that evening and wanted to go home. I told Joséphine Giacolette that I had to say Compline at Saint-Eustache. 'All right,' she said, 'if you must go and play cards with Charles Enguehard and lose all your money, don't let me stop you. But Thérèse Séverin is coming a little later, after her performance; if you didn't find this company so boring I would ask you to stay and meet her.' Imagine the effect of that on a stage-struck young man, and one who was never without a certain interest in people who were talked about. It was just at that time that Mlle Thérèse was said to have refused the Comte de la Haye-Langres, who had a gigantic Brazilian property, on the frivolous ground that he was quite without intelligence—though of course I never paid any attention to gossip of that sort, or to the story that she had swept into a salon of Mme de Rocheois in front of Sarah, causing a duel of three pistol shots between the ladies in which both the gentlemen acting as seconds were severely wounded—it is merely a vulgar malice that invents these stories, and I am certain that if Mlle Thérèse had had the naughty intention of peppering the divine Sarah she would have succeeded. Still, I was full of excitement at the prospect of seeing so distinguished an artist without her wig and in her own personality, and my humiliation in the eyes of Giacolette was amply rewarded. She came in without being announced, she whispered an apology to Joséphine for disturbing the party and passed behind the chairs to one that was empty in a corner, close to my own. It would have been impossible for anyone to enter a drawing-room more modestly. But the effect was astonishing; everyone stopped talking; there was a kind of breathlessness. You remember, of course, what her hair used to be like, short and curly like a boy's, as it is now, but then of a very rich brown; and she was dressed that evening in a brown robe which made her look many years above her age, so dark as to be almost the colour of mourning, and entirely simple, with no jewellery of any kind, not so much as a ring or a necklace. She was not, as I saw her, beautiful —though of course I have no eyes for that kind of beauty; but the dignity, the self-possession! She whispered to me, without waiting for an introduction, 'Tell me, please, Monsieur, why is there no conversation?' I told her that we had exhausted all the subjects. She said very gravely, and just loud enough for everyone to hear, 'I am afraid you have been talking of things not suitable for the ears of a young lady.' And then she turned to poor old Sainte-Beuve, who was sitting on her other side on the little Russian stool which Giacolette always gave him, so that his feet could touch the ground, and they started to discuss the Parnassiens together, apparently so engrossed as not to realize that everybody was listening to them. I shall always remember what Sainte-Beuve said to me after she had gone. . . ."

She had turned her chair to get a better light, and she was looking away from him at the thawed snow dripping from the houses.

"But why didn't Thérèse continue that life of hers?" she said suddenly. "She was happy like that, always acting one part or another off the stage as well as on it, she could easily have gone on, it was only a gesture, her leaving Paris like that."

He nodded.

"A gesture, perhaps, yes," he said, and leant forward to knock off an inch of ash against the fender. "But in the Séverins, you know, there is always a taste for that kind of ritual. You mustn't misunderstand me——"

"I know," she said, "I know just what you mean, in some ways they are all the same. Eugène—I haven't told you, Eugène has gone off to Viboire to-day. He goes there sometimes, I expect you remember, to take measurements. I tried to stop him, it isn't safe for an old man, this weather, I refused to go with him, I thought he wouldn't go. . . ."

She was crying.

He said slowly, "We have to have pride, we can't live without it. It is not a Christian virtue, perhaps—and yet I sometimes wonder if a guarded pride does not give stability to the Christian virtues. Your husband, he has the pride of a soldier, it must lead him occasionally into rash actions. And you, yours is a wifely pride——"

"I have no pride at all," she said, "I only want to do my duty——"

"But surely, dear Mme Séverin, that is just what wifely pride means. You love your husband, you would go into battle with him if it were allowed you, you are as much his protector as he yours. That is just why you refused to go with him to Viboire— you have said it yourself, you hoped to prevent him from going and thus to protect him. That, it seems to me, was the right action. And I urge you not to go after him, as you think of doing, for in that way you would betray your cause, you would be admitting that he was wiser. No, you must be resolute and wait for him to come back to you. If he realizes the strength of your will to protect him, he will not do anything so foolish again. I am certain that my advice is right. It is no part of a Christian's duty to give way to the whims of those he loves when he knows them positively to be wrong."

"But Father, I can't bear to think of him at Viboire without me, the hotel is primitive, they won't understand what he needs for warmth——"

"It is not given to us, Madeleine, to control everything in the world, to feed with our own hands all the hungry, to clothe every naked child ourselves. We have our duty, prayer makes it certain what our duty is, self-examination takes away the taint of selfishness, and when our duty is clear we can do no more than follow it. Ours is a religion of duty, of large purposes rather than small emotions; it is only by remembering this that we can feel God's sinews strained in our exertion, His constancy reflected in our own. You must be patient, my little Madeleine, you must force your pride to help you. Remember how God's mercy gave him back to you, that night when you sent for me, when you seemed to have lost him. You must be patient, patient and very strong."

★

But soon after the Abbé left the light was failing. She fastened the volets to shut out the dreary spectacle of the Square, with its ragged covering of snow like a soiled and tattered dust-sheet, as the outlines faded in blue shadow; and then there were six hours of evening before she would go to lie in bed, to doze between her fits of coughing and to watch the shutters for the daylight to show through the cracks. She had continued working till there was not light enough to show the tracing, and now, when she had lit the table-lamp which she used when alone to save the gas, she found that her eyes were too tired to go on, her fingers, swollen with the cold, in too much pain. She fetched Baillieu's memoirs and sat with the book open on her knees, but her eyes ran again and again through the same paragraph and her mind stumbled to find its meaning, as if it were written in a foreign language. Angèle was restless, sniffing foolishly along the wainscot, and would not be happy till Madeleine had let her go to Eugène's room, where she lay down to sleep in her usual place, in front of the empty grate. Back in the drawing-room, Madeleine tried again, longing to lose herself in the Fragonardian garden of recollections to which the Comte had so often led her. But she saw this evening that the garden was too pretty, the flowers too trimly planted, the peacocks too neat and small. Seen from the drab solitude of the place Talleyrand, the ensemble had always appeared a gay one, so elegant and lively. But the demoiselle Pichy whom the Comte had met and found so charming, she had never challenged the great Sarah to a duel, never provoked a hush in a literary salon, much less impressed a notable academician with her critical acumen. It was hard for her, to find those memories less magnificent, like a valued picture in which the colours had suddenly grown feeble. Her pride had been that of a royal exile treasuring the memory of splendours to which time may restore him: and now the kingdom she remembered grew small and shabby, a dream not worth the dreaming. Her marriage with Eugène, that was something they could not take away from her. Lucille Duponchez, Jacqueline Labaudouin—she could no longer remember the names of all the girls in her circle who had admired him from a distance, turning at Mass as far as they dared to catch sight of the handsome Major Séverin who was only a little past twenty and yet an officer whose name was known through all France; and the Major, who had hardly seemed to be aware of young ladies except as so many bundles of petticoat to be coolly bowed at, had swooped upon the shy Madeleine Pichy and carried her off

212

before their astonished eyes. "It is very sad that young Séverin picked on the Pichy girl, I can't understand how his parents came to allow it. A pretty piece, of course, and the family is all right, but a young man of that type should surely have a girl with some character, the Séverins are such a forceful family." It was Mme Labaudouin who had said that, and she must have known that Madeleine was too near to miss a word of it. "But of course," Mme Thuillier had answered sadly, "if the young Major expects nothing more than a dainty ornament to show off to the Mess . . ." She had been something different from a dainty ornament when she had sat, white and motionless, for hour after hour in the stuffy law court. And Mme Labaudouin had doubtless told her friends how fortunate it was that her dear Jacqueline, showing an intuition surprising for her years, had firmly resisted the advances of this Séverin who had been so gallant a figure on the parade ground and who had run away from the Prussians at Viboire-les-Deux-Auberges. In part, surely, she had answered the challenge. At the time there had been no children, and she could have gone back to her family at the Château Beaumont-Courtonnier; in time, they said, she could have returned to Paris in the semblance of an honourable widowhood. "Everybody is telling me," Mme Pichy had written, "that that is what any sensible woman would do; you have, after all, been married under what amounts to false pretences." "The time will come," she had replied, "when you will find my decision justified. It is together that Eugène and I will return to Paris."

But the time was long in coming. And now, when she believed it nearer than it had ever been before, she had allowed Eugène to go away from her, to risk on a single throw the store of health she had so patiently guarded. *You must have pride, you cannot live without it.* But the pride of which the Abbé had spoken, that was a transitory thing. Her pride was in and for Eugène, his vindication the object of her only duty. Her love for Eugène was no longer a quick emotion and desire for tenderness. It was a martyr's passion, a faith in him tempered by her own persistent flame.

*

It was a little past eight when she heard the sound of whimpering. She thought at first it was one of Renée's children, though as a rule they were so quiet; and presently she went up to Renée's room. But Armand was sitting quietly by the table, watching his mother at her sewing, and Sophie, Renée said, was upstairs with Marianne.

"Perhaps when the children have gone to bed," Madeleine said, "you would like to sit with me in the drawing-room. Eugène is away, you know—it's lonely for me."

Renée said in English, "Thank you, Mme Séverin; but the son

wakes at night sometimes; I would rather not be so far away from him."

"It is lonely for me," Madeleine repeated as she went away.

The whimper had increased to a dismal howling, like the long, sad cry of tempest wind; and she realized now that it came from Angèle. She had kept away from Eugène's room, where she could not bear to see the bed empty and now she feared to go as if it were haunted. But she squeezed her sac of courage, and with a candle held before her opened the door. Angèle was still lying down; her wail stopped when Madeleine went in, but she would not move, she was shivering.

"What is the matter, Angèle? Why don't you come to the drawing-room? You could lie by the fire there."

But Angèle's eyes made no response, she only whimpered. Madeleine covered her with a blanket; and as soon as she went away the howl started again.

She had borne it for nearly an hour when she remembered that Angèle had got in Eugène's way this morning, that he had lost his temper and kicked her. Angèle might be suffering from some internal injury. She went to the stairhead and called for Barbier.

"Barbier, Angèle is ill, I am afraid. I shall have to send you to fetch Dr. Tischer."

"But, Madame, surely it should be an animal doctor——?"

"No, no, Barbier, I would not allow one of those men to touch her, they are sure to be rough-handed. Dr. Tischer will understand her. He will probably be out; he seems always to make a round of visits in the evening, but you must find out where he is and get hold of him. Don't tell him it is Angèle, tell him just that I want him urgently. Tell him——"

"No, Mme Séverin, Barbier is not to go." Joséphine had followed Barbier up the stairs. She came into the gaslight trembling with fear and anger, her black eyes glistening. "It is madness, the idea of it! If Barbier goes, there will not be a man in the house: what protection have we against the evil thing that is waiting to catch us by the throats? If Barbier goes——"

"But, Joséphine, it is to fetch the doctor. When Angèle has had medical attention she will stop howling."

"No, Madame Séverin, no! It is for Gaston that she howls. I knew it this morning when you tricked her into letting Gaston go. I saw a grey bird which fluttered over Gaston's head as he got into the cab. And now he is dead, out there in the snow, and Angèle howls for his soul in torment. If it were not for the little bag I carry between my breasts, which has the bones of a holy mandarin crushed in powder——"

"I have told you before, Joséphine, they are unchristian, these superstitions. I will not allow you——"

"You will say that to me again to-morrow, when Gaston's little body is carried into this house, wrung like a dish-clout and with the cracked veins spouting——"

"Joséphine! I will not listen to you. Barbier, you are to go at once, at once, please! Joséphine, have you seen my purse anywhere? I can't find it, and it has all the housekeeping money I drew yesterday."

"It is not enough then," Joséphine said, "that you murder my little Gaston and you steal Barbier away from me, but now you accuse me of stealing your purse, which cannot contain more money than you owe to Barbier for wages. If I were a thief, Mme Séverin, it is Mlle Thérèse's purse I would steal, and there would be a chance of finding something——"

"All right, Joséphine, all right, be quiet, stop it, be quiet. I will have another look for the purse myself."

At any rate Barbier had got away.

*

The wail continued remorselessly. Madeleine sat with her eyes closed, praying that Tischer would come soon. At the sound of a gentle knock she got up quickly and eagerly opened the door. But it was only Mme Poupoulet.

Mme Poupoulet stood deferentially just inside the door, "I beg that you will pardon me," she said nervously, "it was wrong, I know, for me to come up to this floor without the conduct of your woman-servant, but she is a little deaf, I think; I cannot make her listen to me. I wanted to explain—I have been very unhappy. There was a misunderstanding this morning between M. Séverin and M. Poupoulet. I am afraid that M. Poupoulet spoke rather rudely. I want to explain. M. Poupoulet is really a most tender gentleman, he is always most courteous, and especially to those who are of good family, but sometimes when he has business worries he is a little hasty. And this morning——"

"I am sure," Madeleine began, "that if there was any fault——"
But Mme Poupoulet would not be interrupted.

"I have come, Madame Séverin, not only to offer my deep apology, but to ask you—for I know you are a religious lady— whether you think God punishes men immediately if they commit the sin of hasty speech. We are Protestants, M. Poupoulet and I, but we always feel a great respect for the Catholic knowledge of sin and punishment, and I should like, if you will be so very kind, to hear what you think."

Again Madeleine tried to speak. But Mme Poupoulet was weeping, and her words seemed to flow with her tears in a swirling flood.

215

"You see, Madame, I am so unhappy. M. Poupoulet has gone out to-night, as he does every Friday, to a meeting of the Féderation Colombophile l'Espérance de Baulon, of which he is a Vice-President, and he has to come back over two bad crossings, and your dog has been howling all the evening. If I were a Catholic I should be crossing myself. It is very difficult for a Protestant to know what to do when her husband is in danger."

Madeleine was touched by the fear and grief of Mme Poupoulet.

"You must stay with me here," she said, "until M. Poupoulet comes in. But as for the dog, I am very sorry that she is being a worry, but it is her illness. My husband stumbled over her this morning; I am afraid he has done her a slight injury."

Mme. Poupoulet was grateful, but she shook her head.

"I am afraid it means that someone is dying, when a dog howls like that, as if he could see the devil bending over him. . . . But yes, I will stay, if you are certain you do not mind, until M. Poupoulet returns. No, no, thank you, Madame, I will not sit down. I have never sat down in the salon of a good family such as this one. I will just stand here, if you are sure you do not mind. . . . It was only last year that M. Poupoulet became a Vice-President of the Fédération Colombophile, and he had looked forward to that honour for so long. . . ."

Madeleine went to the little cabinet in which she kept some items of her jewellery. She had forgotten, till Mme Poupoulet reminded her, that it was also a Friday. Among her trinkets was a cruciform brooch, with the image of St. Michel worked on an ivory medallion in bas-relief; Eugène had bought it for her at Carcassonne and it was said to have been touched by the Holy Shroud. With her back towards Mme Poupoulet, she slipped the brooch inside her dress.

Mme Poupoulet had worn her thin voice threadbare, and during the short gaps in Angèle's lamentation there was no sound except the sharp arrest of tears in Mme Poupoulet's nostrils, when they heard a heavy limp and the thud of a rubber-ferruled stick along the passage. Mme Poupoulet came a little farther into the room, and let go a startled cry when a knuckle struck the door powerfully and a deep voice said "Madeleine!"

"No," she said breathlessly, "don't open it! Wait till M. Poupoulet comes."

Madeleine had opened the door already, and Thérèse stood on the threshold.

"Madeleine," she said plaintively, "can nothing be done about that dog? It's impossible to read with that caterwaul going on; the house is shaking with it."

She caught sight, then, of Mme Poupoulet standing by the sofa.

"Thérèse, I must introduce you," Madeleine said. "This is Mme Poupoulet. This is my sister-in-law, Mlle Séverin."

Thérèse with her rheumatism could not bow, but she nodded to Mme Poupoulet's clumsy curtsy.

"Such terrible weather. One's bowels become quite stiff. . . . Have you, Madeleine, tried the effect of a good flogging on that dog?"

"I think I shall have to go now," Mme Poupoulet said, "I have stayed too long. No, no, certainly I must go. But may I say, Madame, that it has been a great pleasure to meet a sister of M. Séverin, whom M. Poupoulet and I so much admire. I knew, of course, before Mme Séverin introduced us—the resemblance is very remarkable——"

"Yes," Thérèse answered with a bent smile, pushing the door open with her stick. "We were both spanked with the same dog-whip, and the scars as far as I can remember are very similar." She let herself down painfully into a chair. "I would like a cigarette if you have one, Madeleine, it is the only thing which does me any good. Thank you. What do you think's wrong with that wretched animal?"

"I don't know. I've sent Barbier to get Dr. Tischer."

"But, my dear Madeleine, that man Tischer——"

She paused a moment as she lit the cigarette, enjoying the faint disgust in Madeleine's expression; and Madeleine, inspired by a chance remark of Joséphine's which had been wriggling in her head, seized the opportunity.

"I was going to ask you, Thérèse, if you could lend me a little money. I've mislaid my purse, and——"

The word "money" provoked the instinctive caution of Thérèse.

"Who was that daughter-of-joy?" she asked abruptly. "It's a curious hour for visiting."

Madeleine seemed to have forgotten. "Oh, that," she said vaguely, "that was one of the lodgers Marianne engaged. They are very respectable people. . . . If you could lend me just a hundred francs, or even fifty, till the end of next week——"

"I'm not sure—I'm not sure how much I have. Everyone is always borrowing my money, what little I have. Can't you make them wait, whoever it is, till you find your purse? They'll hardly take the bill to court before to-morrow morning."

"No—but, you see—Eugène, I think he must have taken my purse and forgotten to tell me. He would have wanted money for the hotel, and I don't think he had any. And I am going to-morrow to join him at Albecourt. Yes, yes, Thérèse, I know that I refused to go with him, and I still think that I was right, but I can no longer bear the thought of his being without me in a place where they don't understand about his illness. It is my duty to go now, I'm sure of that."

"But my dear Madeleine, apart from the moral aspect—and and you must judge that for yourself, though it strikes me very differently—Eugène will be back the day after to-morrow in any case. A man who likes comfort as much as Eugène won't stay to measure the height of each separate tree. If you want to get him back quickly, then my advice—and I've known Eugène longer than you have—is to stay here and whistle for him."

"But, Thérèse, I can't stand it any longer, Angèle howling like this."

"Well, you've only got to bring Angèle within my reach and I'll make her howl differently. But listen. I really believe that it's much better to let Eugène have his way over this kind of thing. He is an old man, and he still believes that one day his case will be re-tried and his honour vindicated——"

"That is what we all believe."

Thérèse shrugged her shoulders.

"Until recently, yes, I thought there was a chance. But it becomes clear now that this re-trial we have talked about year after year is a mirage. It has served its purpose—a mirage, after all, is an encouraging phenomenon—but now that that young fool Pierre has alienated any public opinion which might have been found sympathetic——"

"I don't understand you, Thérèse, I don't know what you're saying, you seem to be talking in a very queer way. Perhaps you have not seem M. Lecour's last letter, in which he expresses strong hopes that Captain Lenormand will be persuaded——"

"It is a very long time," Thérèse said wearily, "since I had the slightest faith in Lecours's promises. And frankly, I have been growing less and less interested in the matter. For myself, my life is over. It is the special genius of our sex, Madeleine, that we recognize the actual condition of things, we do not stumble after mirages, we do not delude ourselves with abstract notions such as Unflinching Courage and Idealized Art and Perfect Womanhood and Stainless Honour. We attend rather to the making of good soup or to a stage-performance in which each detail is perfectly mastered, according to our capacities. For you, you are a perfect nurse, and no one gives you more credit for it than I do——"

"That is enough, Thérèse; I understand that you do not wish to lend me any money; I do not require any explanation——"

"I am perfectly willing to lend you fifty francs if I have as much in my room; it is only that I would prefer to see it used for some sensible purpose. And if you go to join Eugène at Albecourt I am certain you will only encourage him to repeat that kind of folly."

"And may I ask how Eugène would explain in Court the fact that he cannot give accurate details of the situation which he is describing? Do you imagine that Eugène, who as you say is an old man, would put himself to the suffering which this excursion involves if he were not certain that——"

"I haven't the least doubt that Eugène is serious in his intentions. That does not mean that we are obliged to take him seriously. We must be sympathetic, of course. I myself, as you know, have a very great affection for Eugène. But that does not prevent me from remembering that he is as much a Chubenov as a Séverin. In his boyhood Eugène used to behave strangely; he always imagined that he was Napoleon Bonaparte; he would go up to a perfect stranger and say, 'You, why don't you salute me? Don't you know who I am?' And do you expect me to believe now that a man in his right mind will go measuring the same pieces of ground over and over again? If you had any understanding of the Chubenov mentality——"

Madeleine's body was shaking. When she spoke her voice sounded pale and viscous.

"You will go now, please, Thérèse? I want to be alone. I must ask you to go at once, immediately."

Thérèse said nothing. At the second effort she got to her feet. Madeleine picked up her stick and held the door for her. Without groaning, Thérèse moved her racked body along the corridor. When Madeleine called faintly, "Wait, I'll help you up the stairs," she answered, "No, it is not necessary."

★

It was going on for ten and Barbier had not come back. The wail was no longer continuous; it dropped to a murmur like the voice of the old woman who begged alms on the steps of Ste Gudule, a constant, plaintive whimper; it died away to silence and began again, starting at a low pitch and slowly mounting; ineffably mournful, squeezed out to eerie length as if a heavy weight were pressing the last puff of wind from the dog's belly. And now, in the short silences, the dog's wail was echoed by another. It was Joséphine, standing terrified in the gaslit hall, uttering in pitiful cries her lament for Gaston and for Barbier. Madeleine sat with her head bent down, her fingers pressed into her ears. The brooch lay on her lap now; again and again she pressed her lips against it. But as her rage against Thérèse had quickly cooled her courage dwindled also: she was certain she had lost him.

No longer able to bear the loneliness, she put a shawl about her shoulders, intending to go up and sit with Marianne. "Marianne may be frightened," she thought. At the end of the corridor she found Mme Poupoulet, who had lacked the bravery to return either to the salon or to her own room, and would not be persuaded to move. She would stay there, she said, where she would be in no one's way, until her husband came home. A little impatient with the woman's faint-heartedness, Madeleine left her and went on up to the next floor; where, looking along the corridor, she saw there was still a light in Renée's day-room.

She knew, for it was always the same, how Marianne would receive her: "Yes, yes, Mother, sit down, I should like you to sit with me. But you don't mind if I go on working? I have the papers of the Regional Examination, they have all to be marked by Tuesday." And Renée, Madeleine thought, might be willing to lend back a part of the hundred francs she had borrowed for children's clothes on Wednesday. It took her a few moments to gather resolution; she had always the sensation, when she went to visit Renée, of a beggar standing at a door which might be opened by a brawny footman; but presently she felt her way along the dark passage, knocked gently, and went in.

It was Armand she saw first. He was kneeling on a chair, with his forehead down on the table and his hands covering his ears, quivering as if he had been flogged.

She asked: "What is the matter Renée? What's wrong with Armand?"

Renée started. She was sitting where Madeleine had seen her before, but with her hands idle now, her head bent forward, her eyes staring without expression at an inkstain on the table. She had not heard Madeleine's knock. It was Sophie, squatting on the floor and darning a sock with an air of housewifely competence, who answered coolly:

"Armand is frightened because of the dog crying. He thinks someone's hurting it."

Madeleine was at a loss. It was impossible to mention money, with Armand like that and Renée herself looking so ill and tired. She said in confusion: "I only came up—I only wanted to see if you were frightened. This howling, Angèle won't stop; I have sent for Dr. Tischer, but until he comes I can do nothing."

Renée said: "It doesn't matter. Armand is like this sometimes. Last night he didn't sleep, he's tired to-day."

Armand had heard his name and he looked up, his hands raised as if someone would strike him. Renée must have done something to him, Madeleine thought. It came back to her that when Pierre was very small, and had woken screaming from a night-horror, she had quieted him by stroking his forehead with her knuckles now, without reflection, she treated Armand so, standing behind his back; and presently carried him unresisting to the fireside chair, where she sat and held him on her knees. "It is all right, Armand," she whispered, "it is only that Angèle does not feel well, the doctor is coming soon to make her better." Sophie, provoked to instant jealousy, came to stand beside her and boldly stroked the sleeve of her velvet dress. Without moving, and with the face of a dull schoolchild, Renée watched them.

Madeleine, as she went on stroking Armand's forehead, forgot that he and Sophie were there; she had only the sense of comfort from their being near her after her hours of loneliness, of fortitude sprung from the need to quieten Armand's fear.

"I have wanted to tell you," she said to Renée, "though of course you know already, how much I feel—how much I share your anxiety. It's difficult for me—with Eugène I have so much worry, so much to do—it's difficult for me to be a help to you." She was searching Renée's face for a glance of understanding, for the trace of a friendly smile; she saw nothing there but the look of patience an adult shows while a child describes awkwardly something he has seen. "To-night," she said earnestly, "I have been like you, wondering about my husband. And you have your children. . . ."

There was a long pause in which the dog's howl rose again, before Renée answered. She spoke in the flat voice of a beggar reciting for the thousandth time an imaginary misfortune.

"But to-morrow, or the next day, M. Séverin will be back."

Madeleine shook her head.

"I don't know, I'm not certain."

With her first show of animation Renée asked, "You don't know? What do you mean?"

But Madeleine only repeated, "I'm not certain, I can't be sure he will."

She had waited for a little time, hoping that Renée would find at least a few words to answer her sympathy. But when nothing came she said: "You mustn't worry too much, you mustn't be too frightened about Pierre. It will come right, there will be some explanation. Pierre, you know, has often acted queerly, as a boy he used to do strange things. That's why my anxiety has been less than yours. I used to worry terribly, he would go off by himself for two or three days together. I got accustomed to it in the end and then I didn't worry so much. And besides, he is not an old man like Eugène, he is very strong, he can look after himself, Pierre."

"Who is it," Sophie asked, "who went off by himself for three days?"

"It is only a boy your mother and I know," Madeleine told her.

"But he came back?"

"Yes, he came back."

Renée shook her head like one waking with migraine from a long, drugged sleep. She said to Armand thoughtlessly, "Keep still, keep still, Armand, there's nothing to be frightened of." And then, with an air of reluctance, as if she had been driven to bear damning witness by an arduous cross-examination, "You will not understand, you couldn't understand. It was because I wanted him. I don't think about it any more. There is nothing for me to do, I can write no letters, I can't do anything. . . . And Armand, you see how he is. . . . It was my fault, it was because I wanted him I wrote and said I couldn't wait for him, and now—now there will be no end to waiting." She shook herself again. "But it's boring for you, all that. You must put Armand down, surely he's too heavy. I will make you some coffee."

Grasping at that, Madeleine said, "Yes, please, I should like some coffee." She wanted to say something quickly, to keep the room protected by the sound of voices against the dreadful wailing which invaded every silence. She took the only opening that Renée had provided, she said, "No, no, Renée, it was not your fault, I am certain of that, I have never thought so." Renée, filling the cafetière with her back towards her, said nothing. "We have always known,' she stumbled on, "Eugène and I, that Pierre was peculiar, we are used to his doing rash things, we have always feared that it would spoil his military career. We did our best, we were always strict with him, we punished his escapades even when Eugène admired them. I don't mean there was anything wrong with Pierre. He was good at his lessons, like the other two; he was a clever boy. But it is like that with clever children, the brain grows too fast, their ideas are larger than they understand. I remember when he was very small he climbed to the top of a high tree, no other child of his age would have thought of such a thing, and then he cried because he couldn't get down. He was always more difficult than the other children."

"Who was it who climbed a tree?"

"It was a little boy, Sophie, a long time ago. . . . But we hoped that in the army he would get out of that, that peculiarity. We thought the discipline would cure him. He used to be untruthful, we thought the army life would cure that, and Doctor Leteutre who advised us said that it would remove the abnormality. I don't mean that Pierre was ever a bad boy, he was always affectionate. At the beginning of his foreign service he wrote every month to me, his letters were always charming——"

She realized then that Renée's eyes were levelled upon her with frightening concentration, like a cat's eyes in the quivering moment before it springs. She faltered.

"You mustn't misunderstand me, Renée, I only want——"

Renée's voice had a dreadful quietness:

"You spoke of 'difformité.' That is a word, is it not, which they commonly use for people who are not right in the head? Tell me, please, I should like to know if that's what you meant. Tell me, tell me, please."

"But, Renée, you must remember that Pierre is my own son——"

"I want to know——"

The door had opened. Neither had heard her coming, but Thérèse was there. Thérèse smiled painfully.

"A family group! I have brought you some money, Madeleine. I find that I can spare 47 francs, if that will be enough. . . . Is it that no one has sufficient courage to knock that dog on the head? It is intolerable, even Marianne is going mad with it, she is crying like a child over the copy-books, and the lodger-woman is making more noise than Angèle herself; she says that Angèle has killed one of her chickens, or some such rubbish."

Renée was still staring closely at Madeleine. She seemed to be unaware that Thérèse had come in. "I want you to tell me," she repeated, "if you meant by what you said that my husband is insane."

"Whether he is medically mad is of no interest," Thérèse said abruptly. "We only know that his behaviour has made the Séverin family a byword for cowardice and folly in all France. It doesn't matter, it makes no difference. But I hadn't thought that I should have to go through that again, those arch paragraphs in the newspapers——"

"We don't know yet," Madeleine said angrily, "we haven't any idea what happened. It's wrong of you, Thérèse—and with the children here—to talk of Pierre like that."

Thérèse closed her eyes.

"It is you, Madeleine, after all, who are chiefly interested in the matter of Eugène's case being tried again; it is a subject you have mentioned—if I remember rightly—more than once in the last few years. And if you imagine that the Court will be amiably disposed towards the Séverins on account of Pierre's little escapade——"

"I must tell you," Renée said unevenly, "as I have already told Mme Séverin, that it was on my account Pierre left his post. It was at my particular request."

Madeleine was in tears.

"But, Renée, surely——"

"I tell you yes! Yes, it was at my request. Do you think I don't realize what I'm saying? Are you going to tell me that I'm insane too?"

Sophie, severely frightened, had shrunk into a corner and was quietly sobbing. Armand was by the table, looking about him, bemused. He said "I don't understand. What are they saying?"

"What does the child say?" Thérèse snapped.

"You will leave Armand alone, please. Armand, come here. And I must ask you not to say anything more about my husband. When Pierre returns we will discuss that matter again. I'm tired now, I want you to go away."

Leaning back against the door, Thérèse kept perfectly still. She had got into a bad position, and she would not be able to release herself without a twist of pain which might make her cry out. She waited impatiently for Madeleine to end a bout of coughing.

"It's difficult for me," she said swiftly, "to understand all this. When Marius Authouillet was thrown and killed—he was my lover, everyone knew—I appeared that evening, there was no weakness in my performance. . . . You don't know, perhaps, that at the time of Eugène's affair Cormeilles said I was the greatest artist in the theatre of Paris? No, I agree that it doesn't look like that, this carcass I drag about with me, but you can find it if you like in his *Théâtre Contemporain*. That had to go, the art without which I had no purpose in living, because the citizens of the parterre did not care to see performing the sister of the man who ran away from the Prussians. Perhaps you will not quite realize, it is a peculiar sensation to give up one's art. It is as if one had built a cathedral—perhaps not a very good cathedral, but one took pains and people admired it—and a man driving his carriage carelessly knocked the cathedral down. With just one blow, like that. Perhaps you will agree that there was occasion for wringing the hands and calling Heaven to witness, for a piece of acting in the classical style, a performance in the manner of Medea as she is represented by the École Démadières. But I didn't take that opportunity. I put my things into half a dozen boxes and took a cab to the Gare de l'Est. That was better, it seemed to me. And now I find it hard to understand those women who are in a state of collapse because a few nights pass when they must sleep by themselves. With women such as Joséphine and that lodging-person it is understandable, this mewing and squeaking, these lassitudes and indispositions over the temporary absence of a pair of trousers. But I have never believed that the main business of our sex——"

She was stopped by a spasm of pain, as the door thrust boldly open, jerked her forward. Marianne, driving into the room, said, "I won't stand it another moment, that noise, it's driving me cracked. Mother, can't you——"

"It was lucky for that Authouillet," Renée said, her voice

cutting like a scythe across Marianne's, "that he broke his neck, or else——"

"I expected that," Thérèse answered, gasping with pain. "I expect a remark like that from a vulgar little half-breed——"

"What do you mean, Renée?" Marianne demanded. She had taken her place at the side of Thérèse, her arm supporting Thérèse by the elbow. "What are you——"

"She means," Madeleine said between her sobs, "that it is intolerable to be married to a Séverin. To be the wife of a Séverin it is not enough to care for him, and to love him is thought ridiculous. You are allowed only to bear more Séverins, it is considered a privilege to go through labour for that purpose——"

Sophie in her bewilderment had gone across to Marianne and was holding her arm. Marianne took no notice.

"You mean by that, Mother, that your children themselves are no recompense?"

But Madeleine, in a fit of coughing, could not answer. It was Renée, with her hands on the terrified Armand's shoulders, who shouted, "They are not allowed to be our children, they have to be soldiers, they have to be altogether Séverins. It is the name, you know that, you care for nothing but the name!"

Leaning on Marianne's arm, her mouth twisting to prevent the utterance of her anguish, Thérèse gathered strength once again.

"And the name," she said, "it is that that we, who might have borne children with a little courage, cannot give them."

"Dr. Tischer is here," Barbier announced.

*

Lying with her legs in the air, her monstrous belly spread like a sack of turnips, Angèle seemed unaware of the five women grouped about her, and she bore the pressure of Tischer's gentle fingers patiently, only making little sad noises like the fretful murmur of patients under anæsthetic.

"You should have sent for a vet," Thérèse said in her bored voice. "It's absurd to waste Dr. Tischer's time. What does he know about dogs?"

"Except that I have three of my own——"

"You should have sent for a priest," Joséphine said energetically. "Dr. Tischer may be able to deliver a dog of puppies but not of demons."

Surveying Angèle, Tischer shook his head.

"She is a very old dog," he said hesitantly.

"I am a very old woman," Thérèse remarked, "but I do not make a noise like that."

"For you, Mlle Séverin, I would prefer to see you in bed. I have not the pleasure of knowing who is your present adviser, but I cannot agree with his opinion when he lets you walk about in that condition."

"We are not discussing my aunt's condition," Marianne interposed, "but that of Angèle."

Madeleine said, "Marianne, please!" She watched Tischer anxiously, his tired face reminding her of Eugène's terrible night, as he knelt on the floor with his cheek pressed against Angèle's flaccid skin, trying to hear her heart. The tail of his coat had fallen over and she noticed that his trousers, already patched at the seat, were splitting at the centre seam. His hair had grown too long at the neck and it bristled over his yellow collar. She wondered if he was, after all, a very good doctor.

"You will not forget to make a note of her last sayings?" Thérèse said.

Mme Poupoulet, who stood at the edge of the crowd, said tearfully, "If it were a little boy, instead of a dog, we could give him a solution of ammonium valerate."

"If I could have a few moments' silence——" Tischer protested.

"It is a very old dog," Thérèse said didactically. "the obvious thing is to destroy it."

"Yes," said Marianne, "that is the obvious thing."

"But not here—now?" Mme Poupoulet exclaimed. "I should fall down insensible."

"I will not allow it," Joséphine said fiercely. "If Gaston's soul has passed into that dog and you kill her, where is Gaston's soul to go then?"

"Perhaps into Mme Poupoulet, while she is insensible," Thérèse suggested.

"Angèle belongs to Eugène," Madeleine said quietly, "and without his permission I shall not have her destroyed."

Tischer said: "I think, Mme Séverin, it would be the kindest thing. She is very old and asthmatic, her life can be no pleasure either to the dog itself or to M. Séverin. I would really beg you to let me take her away. I can do it very humanely."

"She is not to be destroyed," Madeleine repeated. "M. Séverin has a very great affection for Angèle, and he would be terribly upset if she were gone when he came back. She is to remain just where she is, and if necessary I will sit up to look after her."

"I think, if I may say so, Madeleine, that you are being rather foolish. Eugène would at least have the sense——"

She stopped short; for no apparent reason, but Tischer knew what it was. He got up and put his arm round her waist: "I am going to help you back to your room," he said. "Have you no sense at all, don't you realize that that pain is getting nearer your heart?"

But she had force enough in one arm to push him away. She whispered, "I thank you, Dr. Tischer, but my heart will stand a good deal. No, I require no assistance."

"What are we going to do," Marianne asked impatiently, "about Angèle?"

Angèle had rolled over on to one side; and as if she had lost interest in the question, closed her eyes. But a moment later she began to howl again.

"I can't stand that!" Marianne said. "Dr. Tischer, for God's sake kill the dog!"

"Marianne!"

"It is Gaston," Joséphine screamed. "He is crying out because you are trying to send him away."

"Joséphine, be quiet! Mme Poupoulet, what is the matter, why are you crying?"

"I'll kill her myself," Marianne shouted, "give me something—— that poker——"

But Joséphine had her by the arms and Madeleine had snatched the poker away.

"Marianne, I forbid——"

They were stiffened to attention by a crack on the street door which sent a tremor through the house. No one moved. It was Mme Poupoulet who spoke first.

"It is my husband," she said. "They have brought back his body."

"What do you——?" Marianne began, but Madeleine stopped her. She said weakly, controlling the vibration in her voice.

"Joséphine, go and see, please, who that is."

Joséphine stood as if she were bound with ropes. "I would rather be slit up from the navel to the chin," she said explicitly, "than open that door for the devil incarnate who stands dripping green blood on the pavement." Then, her voice rising to a shout, "Barbier! Barbier! You're not to open that door, do you hear?"

But the thump had been repeated, and in the moment's silence that followed they heard Barbier limping deliberately across the hall.

"Barbier!"

"Be quiet!" Thérèse gasped.

Angèle seemed to hear the street door opened. She stopped howling and tried to stand up.

"There!" Joséphine said, terrified and triumphant. "She knows, you see, she knows who it is."

Barbier was coming up the stairs very slowly, and his uneven step was joined with another, a double step on every stair; as if two men bore the weight of a coffin between them. They came at the same pace down the passage, the sound of their feet framed in utter silence, Joséphine too horrified to scream.

"Madame is in there, sir," Barbier said.

Lecours bowed in the doorway, quite out of breath with the effort of mounting the stairs. He turned his round, perspiring face slowly from side to side, his little eyes blinking at the gaslight, his moist lips working together in readiness for the moment when he had breath to use them. He was excited, he had hoped to find Mme Séverin alone, the company confused him. They were as still as waxworks, standing in a circle, staring as though he were a ghost: a woman he had never seen before who was quietly sobbing; Mme Séverin herself, tearful and trembling; her daughter, looking scared and angry; the old servant woman, whose features had always been as fixed as an idol's, now gazing at him with her mouth propped open as if by a wish-bone, her pupils melting in the stretched corneas; the terrible Mlle Séverin, her face so sickly pale that its habitual hostility scarcely alarmed him; and in the middle of them all that hideous bitch of Séverin's, lying upside down, with the little doctor who spent all his time in the slums of Ste Estelle bending over her like a mother over her first-born. For a moment he thought he had chanced upon a piece of business in which a lawyer had no proper part; and would have bowed himself away in hot confusion, but Mme Séverin, finding her voice, called him back.

"What is it, M. Lecours?"

He had hardly collected enough wind for speaking. "I must apologize," he panted, "I am afraid—it is very late—very late for making a call. But I have just got back—just got back from Paris."

"From Paris?"

"The capital of France, Mother."

"I received there—some important news. Very important news. That is why—I have come at this hour. I thought you ought to know——"

"About my husband?"

Lecour's stomach went in and out like a pair of bellows. He said, when he had pumped up sufficient breath, "Yes."

"He's not—dead?"

Lecours pumped again.

"——:——:——: No."

Thérèse, profiting by a moment's respite from her pain, said: "For heaven's sake, Lecours——"

He was in going order now, and ready to shout his triumph at them; but he had to wait, rocking with embarrassment, till Mme Séverin had got through a storm of coughing; and even then his natural caution restrained him.

"Perhaps, Mme Séverin, as the matter is of a private nature———"

"Nonsense!" Thérèse snapped. "Everyone in the world knows all about our affairs."

"What is it?" Marianne demanded. "Quickly, M. Lecours, what is it?"

Deliberately, not without a sense of style, Lecours answered:

"Captain Lenormand. He is on his way."

XXV

On the farther side of the compound João took off his sandals so as to tread more quietly, and instead of pulling the mosquito-curtain aside crept under it on all-fours. The cell was nearly dark, and the Frenchman, lying on the bamboo frame with his head turned to the wall, was gently snoring. João felt for the mug and platter, the spoon and fork, the vinegar-bottle, and cautiously piled them together. He was under the curtain again, crawling backwards, when the Frenchman said in full voice, making him jump:

"Is that you, João?"

"It is, Brother."

The Frenchman turned over, stretched his hands for the matches and lit the candle on the table.

"Why do you crawl about like that? It's not dignified. Come here, João, I want to ask you something. The canoes you talked about, the ones that went up last week, are they back yet?"

João hesitated. This was the question he had hoped to avoid. He was prepared for any amount of evasion, but for the last seven months he had been under a vow of truthfulness and he could not tell a lie in positive form. "One doesn't know what to believe," he said. "The boys say they have seen them, but often they talk pure nonsense, those fellows; they always like to have something new to talk about, they are like the citizens of Athens, they are unregenerate, to them———"

"You must talk more slowly, João, I can't follow you at that pace. The boys say the canoes are back, do they? When are they going on?"

"The boys say that they will be going on to-night; the owner is one of those traders who prefer to do the higher stages in darkness, they think it is safer. For myself, I put my trust in St. Benedict, who allows only the oldest crocodiles and the mosquitoes which are very feeble to attack me. If I———"

"To-night, you say? What time?"

"About midnight, so the boys say. But you can never be certain——"

"Tell me, João: this trader, what is his name?"

"I can't pronounce it very well, but it's something like 'Saunier.'"

"Oh! French?"

"No, Belgian, I believe. But for this journey he travels with French papers, issued by the consulate at Kanabir."

"You know all about him then?"

"Yes, I know him fairly well. About once a year, just before the river rises, he comes there. He takes one or two of our goats sometimes, and gives us some wheat-flour. He tells us everything that is going on at Kanabir and in Europe. We learnt from him last year of the burning of an Abbey of our own Order near Estremoz; it was terrible news, we were completely upset for a long time."

"And where could you find him now?"

"I don't know, Brother, I really have no idea. Unless he is with Nkokamabu—he does business sometimes with that ruffian."

The Frenchman sat up.

"Look here, João, I want you to get hold of this man. Send one of the boys, it won't be difficult. Send a message that you have a Belgian explorer who——"

"But listen, Brother, I know just what you have in mind. I have a kind of inner vision which often tells me what other men are thinking. You must realize, I want you to understand once and for all, I am a medical man. I had special training at the University of Coimbra. I say definitely that you are not well enough yet for the journey to Kanabir. In another month, or three weeks perhaps——"

The Frenchman stood up, supporting himself with a hand against the wall.

"There, look!"

"Senhor Pedro! You must be mad."

The Frenchman sat down again, grinned.

"I'm dangerous, João. If you keep me here any longer I may do something terrible. I may get up in the night and cut Bernardin's throat—yours too. I do that kind of thing sometimes, when I'm excited. It wouldn't be lack of gratitude—mere joie-de-vivre. Now listen, João." He lay down again. Already his head was swimming, and he found his voice weak. "You will have to tell Saunier that I am a member of your own Community—yes, I shall want you to fit me out with a habit—who has come to you on a special mission from the Abbey at Bragança, and has reached you by way of Znande. Is that clear? Then——"

"But, Brother, you know I couldn't tell the trader a definite untruth."

"But how do you know, João, that I am not a Benedictine? I might easily have got lost in the hills, and been obliged to borrow clothing from a friendly French officer who rescued me. As for my mission, though I have forgotten for the moment exactly what it was—it would surely be wrong, João, for you to doubt my word if I told you that I was in just that case?"

João shook his flat head as far as it would go on its shallow mounting. "I'm not sure, it's difficult to say. I have somewhere a book of Correia de Marado's Religious Theorems. I shall have to look into the question."

"And then there's the matter of papers—I should like if possible to have something with me when I get to Kanabir. Come closer, João, I can't talk very loudly. Have you had any experience in forging papers? No? Well, perhaps this Saunier will think of something. Now listen. You're sure that none of your boys knows about my being here? You're positive? That's good. Now the important thing is to get me into that canoe of Saunier's without anybody seeing."

"I don't like this," João said sadly. "I've never done anything like it before."

*

On the fourth day, shortly before sunset, the train of four canoes reached Sanalla Dogo. At Sanalla Dogo there was a wooden landing-pier with the tricolour flying on a bamboo pole; an area of about half an acre fenced off with barbed wire; a tiny urinoir of corrugated iron; and an awning of striped canvas, beneath which M. Thiberville sat on his folding-chair before a little table, sipping a petit-verre of Cointreau and composing his monthly report. "*I have the honour,*" he wrote, "*to enclose my monthly barometric chart, which exhibits only a very small variation from the curve recorded in the same month last year. My traffic census shows a slightly lower figure than usual. . . . On Wednesday the 14th ultimo at 15.47 M. Robert Saunier, of Belgian nationality, arrived and spent one night at this Post before proceeding up river. . . .*" And there, by a coincidence which M. Thiberville thought must have some religious significance, were M. Saunier's four canoes again. He got up and smoothed his trousers. He went to the edge of the pier and waved. As soon as M. Saunier saw him, he put his heels together and gave his military salute; for he had once been a lieutenant of the Reserve at Saumur. M. Saunier returned his salute. M. Saunier came on to the pier and all the time they were exchanging greetings they held each other's hands.

It was only when they had sat together for an hour in Thiberville's wood-and-iron bungalow, sipping many little Cointreaus and talking of the difference between the Bruxelles women and those of Paris, that Thiberville put on his spectacles and turned to business. "Perhaps, M. Saunier, you will be kind enough to let me see your papers?" Saunier gave him the wallet of papers which he had already presented on the up-river journey, and which Thiberville had minutely examined. Thiberville minutely examined them again, checking the Portuguese translation against the French text with a scholar's eye. He took his stamp, pushed the right date into position with the toothpick he kept in his breast-pocket, stamped the papers and returned the wallet to Saunier. He smiled. "They are in perfect order, M. Saunier. And now, if I may just have a list of what you are taking down—there are four boats, are there not? The first, personal luggage? You have added nothing to that since we checked over, no clothing, shirts, ties?" "No, M. Thiberville, I have bought nothing for personal wear." "Thank you, M. Saunier. And in the second boat?" He repeated each item as Saunier gave it out, and wrote it down on his quadruplicate form. At the end of each sheet Saunier signed. They came to the fourth canoe.

"In that I have something rather unusual," Saunier said slowly.

Thiberville looked up sharply. It was years since anything unusual had been declared at this Post. Saunier, now that Thiberville regarded him closely, had an odd expression, a certain look of apprehension. All through his service Thiberville had dreamed that one day he would have the glory of detecting some illicit traffic, in drugs perhaps, or Grandu slaves or soël-bark alcohol; but it seemed hardly possible that Saunier, whose face without the stubble would be like a fashionable barrister's, who enjoyed the highest reputation all along the coast . . .

Saunier went on cautiously, picking his words: "You know, of course, of the Portuguese Benedictines up at Sabode? I do a little business with them—it's chiefly for friendship, it hardly pays me, but they are pleasant young men, they live very good lives——"

"Yes, yes, I know of them, of course. There is a Brother João—he is the manciple, I fancy—I see him quite often when he comes to collect their mail and so forth. He was here in October——"

"It was he," Saunier said, "who asked me if I would take as a passenger a member of their community who was sick and who had to be sent as quickly as possible to Kanabir. Unfortunately I was persuaded."

Saunier's eyes were fixed on his glass, which he twiddled round and round between his cracked, squat fingers. Thiberville had him fixed as tightly as if he might plunge his hand for a revolver at any moment. He had never realized before how appallingly Belgian Saunier's accent was, and he noticed for the first time that Saunier's eyebrows straggled in to join each other; a sure sign, old Mme Calbry had once told him, of innate dishonesty. He went to his cabinet and took out a box-file.

"What name?" he asked sharply.

"Bernardin de Macedo."

"De Macedo, Bernardin . . ." Thiberville was disappointed; the record was in order. "Yes, yes, I have him here. He passed here in March '08, registered for permanent residence, Portuguese, bearing papers from Lisbon. Age 27 years, five months—but he would be older now. . . . But why——"

"This is the trouble, M. Thiberville: he's dead."

"Dead?"

"About five hours after I left Sabode. I saw when I took charge of him that he was very weak. Yes, blackwater. It's always the same, they live on quinine, those people up in the forest, they never seem to realize what it must lead to. But João was quite certain this fellow would last to Kanabir—I was to hand him over to the American mission hospital there. Otherwise, I shouldn't have taken him on. It's the devil, M. Thiberville, being landed with a man's body, I've never been in such a case before. And it isn't as if I had all that amount of room. I was hoping to pick up some more stuff lower down, and now—just a third of my storage taken up."

"But, my dear M. Saunier, there will be no difficulty. I have the authority to bury, in a case of necessity; there are quite explicit instructions, we can do it to-morrow morning and you will be released from all further responsibility. You will just have to sign a statement on cause of death, and in return for that I shall give you a receipt for the body and a carbon copy of the burial certificate, which you will hand to the Consul at Kanabir. In case——"

"But I——"

"I have two crepe brassards," Thiberville assured him. "I can lend you one of them and wear the other. It will be necessary——"

"But this is my difficulty, M. Thiberville. The Friar asked me specially—he realized his condition far better than João—that if he died before we reached Kanabir I should arrange for his remains to be shipped to Portugal for burial in the Church of S. Eoric de Pretaza at Alvito, near to those of the blessed Father Gómez Mendeira. Of course if he had been just an ordinary individual— a trader like myself, for instance—I should regard the request as preposterous. But I think you'll see my point of view—a member of a Holy Order, a man of distinguished piety—and I, though I am by no means a religious man, I try to perform my duties as a Catholic so far as my way of life allows me—you can see how hard it's going to be for me to confess that I broke a promise made to a dying saint. You yourself——"

Thiberville clicked his tongue.

"Are you sure," he asked, "that you made your promise verbally? You didn't just nod your head, as one does when a mosquito bites the back of the neck? I fancy that one could establish a difference——"

"I swore with my lips against his crucifix," Saunier said gloomily.

Thiberville sighed. "The conduct of a funeral," he said gently, "would have been quite a new experience for me. But no, M. Saunier, I cannot blame you. I can realize how hard it would be to refuse a dying man. . . . You're sure there's no risk of infection? No, no, I understand, of course not. And you have the body in a coffin."

"No, M. Thiberville, a coffin is not easy to come by in the higher reaches of this river; the body will have to be coffined at Kanabir. But what I should like to have, if you can supply it, is a permit for it to be taken from my boat at Kanabir and placed at once on board the steamer *Villa da Ponte*, which will be due to sail on the 4th. If I have to go through the consular authority at Kanabir there will be delays and I might easily miss the ship. I want, you see, to be rid of the responsibility as soon as I can; already the Friar is just a little bit smelly, it might be awkward to find a suitable depository at Kanabir."

Thiberville was doubtful.

"It's a very special case," he said. "The best I can do, I think, is to give you a note to the Consul at Kanabir, asking him to give the matter prompt attention. With that——"

"I quite realize," Saunier agreed. "It was absurd, of course, for me to imagine that an Agent-de-Rivière would have the authority —speaking with no disrespect, M. Thiberville——"

"Wait a minute, M. Saunier. I must run through the regulations, it is a nice point. . . . I shall, of course, have to examine carefully and identify the body. . . ."

*

It was quite dark when the two men went down to the river. Three of the boats were tied side by side, a single line fastening them to a stake on the bank; the fourth, on a longer line, lay down the stream. The boys squatted all over the landing-stage. A light wind was coming up river, stirring the water. It brought to Thibercille's nostrils a peculiar smell.

"The second and third boats can go on," Saunier ordered.

"Unless you want to check the contents, M. Thiberville? Thank you—yes, they can go, hurry now! Here, Chicha, pull in that one and bring it round to this side of the pier. Yes, right in."

There was no moon, and above the fine-wove darkness the stars showed large and oddly close, so that Thiberville could fancy he hung in the empty sky and looked down upon a widespread twinkling city. He shivered. At night as far as possible he always kept away from the water. By God's mercy it had never been part of his duties as lieutenant of the Reserve at Saumur to examine corpses. And the smell, which became stronger as every coil of the rope fell from Chicha's hands on to the pier, was enough to turn anyone's stomach; it was as if the dung of goats had been stewed in linseed oil. "It's surely extraordinary," he said to Saunier, "when he's only been dead a couple of days. Do bodies always stink like that?"

Saunier was fiddling with the lamp. He had carelessly broken the glass on both sides and the breeze made it flicker pitifully.

"Invariably," he said, "when they are Portuguese."

"The lamp isn't very good. Perhaps I'd better get mine."

"It will be all right when it settles down."

The canoe, a black shape against the rippled darkness of the water, was beside the pier now. Saunier cautiously lowered himself into the stern-thwart. For a moment, as the flame stammered, Thiberville lost sight of him.

"Give me your hand," Saunier said, "I'll help you down!"

"No, no, it's unnecessary. I can see from here."

Thiberville knelt down at the edge of the landing-stage, with one hand across his mouth and nostrils, the other holding the buck-lamp. It was directly below him, a confused pile of linen that looked like a laundry bundle.

"Shall I unwrap him?" Saunier asked.

"Wait a minute."

Thiberville put down the lamp and unfolded a piece of paper. It contained a photograph in faded sepia of a young, smooth, oval face, labelled, "Duplicate photograph of Bernardin de Macedo, of the Order of S. Benedict, taken in the laboratory of the Society at Regoa, November, 1907, authenticated by Fermao Oliviera, Prior of the Order at Regoa." He held it closer to the lamp.

"Now," he said.

With three circles of his hand Saunier unwound a long, yellow scarf. Thiberville lowered the fluttering lamp. What he saw appeared to be not a face but the image of a face done to the life in candle grease: the mouth, cheeks and shin sprouting fair hair, which was clotted with a brown grease below the nostrils; the eyes staring into his own with a fixed defiance. The smell came straight into Thiberville's face as if the dead lips breathed it. He turned away, coughing, and scrutinized the photograph again.

"Give me the lamp," Saunier said sharply, "you'll see better ——"

"It's all right, I——"

Saunier stretched up and took the lamp; which, as he jerked it, went out altogether.

"Bleu! Give me a hand, will you? Thanks, wait a moment, I'll light it again."

"It's all right," Thiberville said. He was on the point of vomiting. "It's all right. It looks quite different, of course. With all that hair. But I can see it's the same. No, I shan't require to see it again."

Saunier had relit the lamp, which burned better now that he had turned up the wick. Leaving it on the pier he got down into the boat again and tossed the scarf over the face.

"You'd like to see the rest of it?" he asked. "Wait, I'll get him unwrapped."

"What? No, no, that won't be necessary."

Thiberville went a little way along the bank and vomited. When he came back Saunier was holding the permit which they had drafted together and which was still unsigned.

"It's all in order, then?" Saunier asked.

"Yes. . . . But there's no need for you to go to-night, is there? You've plenty of time to get to Kanabir by the 4th, I can make you quite comfortable. I would prefer, when I think of it, to go through that permit again before I sign it. I'm not altogether happy about the wording——"

"I am very grateful, M. Thiberville, for the hospitality you offer. But I would rather—at least, I don't quite like the idea of leaving the body unguarded in the canoe all night. Would you mind if I brought it up to your quarters?"

"Well, if you think you really must start to-night. . . . The permit, yes, I'll sign it. If you will be so kind as to hold the lamp. . . . You're cold, M. Saunier, you're shivering. Wait a minute, I'll fetch you an old coat of mine, you can return it when you come up here next time. The pleasure will be mine——."

"But no, thank you, M. Thiberville, I'm as warm as a squirrel. But I don't like to keep you hanging about. If you will be kind enough just to sign——"

"But why are you trembling? Surely——"

Saunier jerked back his elbows.

"I'll tell you frankly, I don't like this job, I can't care for it a bit. Corpses in the ordinary way I don't mind, I've seem them piled in heaps, the time of the Bakatula plague. But a priest's body, it's different, and a monk's, that's worse. And he died without the Office—I did what I could, I said all the prayers I could remember, but I didn't do it right; I know that by the way he stares at me when I uncover him, looking straight up out of Purgatory. Come here and look at his eyes again, I'll show you."

Thiberville crossed himself. "No, no, I know what you mean, I saw."

"I tell you, M. Thiberville, I shan't be happy till I hear he's buried at Alvito as I promised him. . . . Are you sure you don't want to see the rest of the body?"

"Quite sure."

Thiberville signed the paper.

In single file the canoes shot away on the swift current, the boys singing cheerfully. When he could no longer hear their voices Thiberville went back to his bungalow, washed his hands, gargled with a solution of Jeyes' fluid in Sauterne, and sat down to continue his report: "*As requested in your favour of the 2nd ultimo, I am still keeping a sharp lookout for any trace of the missing officer*. . . ." He was not quite happy. He blamed himself for letting the sight of a dead monk turn his stomach over. Still, if it made such a seasoned traveller as Saunier shake like the petal of a poppy. . . .

XXVI

CHERBOURG was flooded with sunshine, and the light wind so warm that Raymond could sit on the balcony of his room in the Hôtel Saint-Pierre-Port to take his coffee. In the quick Atlantic light the people in the street below him seemed to move with a sprightly step, the trams to run faster and the bells to clank more gaily than in Baulon. There were sailors everywhere, and the air had a Scandinavian freshness. The smell, which came to his nostrils crisply, was of bakeries and coffee; but he seemed to feel beneath it the odour of the sea.

His freedom had not been easily earned. Ansellin had made a great fuss: it was all he could do to get along with existing staff, the owners refused to give him the extra sub-editor who was really wanted; at any moment (Ansellin said darkly) there would be stuff coming through from Belgrade which would demand a stream of extra editions; no one had ever asked for a holiday at that time of year, it would be very hard on Chivalié. But Chivalié had been most generous, he would gladly do a week of double-shifts. Maman had renewed her entreaties: it was of paramount importance that Lenormand should be met and conducted to

Paris; if Raymond could not go she would have to do it herself, whatever Tischer said. And Aunt Thérèse had actually supported her with the threat that she would give him no more credit if he failed to manage it. He had seen Ansellin again, been moderately abusive, and obtained his grudging permission. And then Cécile had stepped in with a request to be taken too: she would like to have half a day in Paris, and she hated being alone. "It is the same with all of them," he said to Vasseur with exasperation. "Cécile and I care for each other as much as the opposite sides of a packing-case, and yet the moment I want to go away she falls into a decline. And why? Because it upsets her routine, her tout-ensemble. It is as if I threatened to sell one of the chairs in the drawing-room. Every woman at bottom longs for only one thing: a nice petit-bourgeois husband who comes in for his meal at seven o'clock every evening and taps the barometer and says 'hm-hm.'" Only after a tearful argument, in which he said patiently over and over again, "But, Aunt Thérèse, my sweet, has only given me enough money for my own expenses," had he persuaded her to go to her mother.

But this morning, as he wandered about the streets and up to the Fort de Roule, the struggles seemed to have been worth while. To be outside the range of Cécile's little lisping voice was only a part of his pleasure. He was glad to get away from his friends; from Vasseur, whose company he sought as a man feels his pockets for tobacco, from Chivalié's eternal good-humour, from the gross and garrulous Leprovost. Seen from the distance of a few hours they became small, insignificant and a little absurd. They were a comfortable part of his existence, they made together a medium in which he could say what he liked, be always at his ease; but now they appeared as a bed that has been slept in too long, a narrow form in which he was ashamed to have wasted so much time. He knew that he was different; he could not, for example, imagine Leprovost taking the trouble to climb up this hill, or surveying this view without the trite observation that Pissarro would have done it better. But in Baulon it didn't show, even the pictures in which he laboured to reveal the special moulding of his mind were said by callow critics in the Paris journals to be a virtuose imitation of Dissoubray's early manner. Baulon was a little saucer of aim-less bustle; and for him its centre was not the Enfants du Roi, not the office behind the rue Coupel, but always the place Talleyrand, where they spoke to him as if he were a schoolboy and somehow he found himself behaving with a schoolboy's impertinence. He was taken for granted there, as he was in the Café de Cirque: Maman, if she heard him coming in, would call from the top of the stairs that he was to be sure and wipe his boots; Aunt Thérèse, when he asked how Renée was, said that she was in the sulks at present—it was a woman's affair that he would not understand. "Of course she's gloomy," he would say, "in this tawdry mausoleum. You don't treat her properly, none of you do." "Raymond," she answered, "if you can't learn to talk like a grown-up person I shall forbid you to enter my room; and if you think you know how Renée is to be treated, well, go ahead, there's nothing to stop you." "You see nothing, Aunt Thérèse, except with the eye of a popular young actress who is trying to get a clap from the balcony——" "If your ideas about painting, my dear Raymond, are as crude as your notions of the theatre, then I cannot wonder that your pictures——" But he never accepted the challenge, he never stood on the middle landing and shouted, "Curse the whole lot of you! Give the girl some money and let her go!" He found himself explaining to Thérèse once again how a man of sensibility regards the threatre, while she puffed her cigarette and smiled sardonically. "I am so terribly sorry" he said to Renée, "about Pierre. You must let me know if there's anything I can do." There was nothing he could do. And he rejoiced to think it was Thérèse's money which had brought him to stand here in the spring sunshine, all by himself, with the wind blowing the smell of Baulon out of his clothes. When he got back he would be different. The house would be stripped of the old associations which made it like a castle, he would see it simply as a high building in a rather undistinguished style, he would enter it as a stranger, be more reserved, attract the confidence of Renée and increase her own courage by his contemptuous independence. He was, after all, a Séverin; it was only by breaking free from the preposterous circumscription of the Séverins that he had learnt so.

Thérèse's money: he saw that it was ten o'clock; the *Carolingia* was to dock at half-past ten, and he had to get a ticket from an office in the rue Pecheur, wherever that might be, in order to go aboard. He returned with long strides to his hotel.

The porter sat on his high stool, knitting a baby's binder, with last week's *Chic Amour* spread out before him on the reception desk.

"There is a little story here," he said pleasantly to Raymond, "which may possibly amuse Monsieur. In a room with two double beds——"

"I want to get to the rue Pecheur," Raymond said. "I'm in a hurry. How do I——"

"One moment, Monsieur, I have a plan of the town somewhere, If you'll wait just a few moments, I can show you exactly——"

"Can't you explain——?"

"With the plan it will be much easier——"

"Hurry, then!"

He began irritably to pace the vestibule; and through the doorway of the restaurant he saw a girl's face in the mirror. It appeared only in quarter-profile, but a single glance was enough to tell him that she was not of the type you expected in a hotel like this. She was pretty, with fair hair beautifully managed, and her hat had cost about 80 francs; he would find her copied a dozen times in the Grande or the Casino, but in the Saint-Pierre-Port she was like an Ingres among a pile of Bouchers. He stopped where he could still see the reflection of her feet and ankles. Yes, the shoes were quite good. "I shan't be a moment," the porter called, burrowing into a cupboardful of Bottin, "it's somewhere just here." Raymond went back as far as the restaurant doorway and looked in the mirror again. Yes, a pretty girl of that type; perhaps, if he could dispose of this Lenormand somewhere, they could lunch together. The head turned so that he could see the reflection at full-face. The reflection smiled and the girl came out to meet him. Cécile.

The porter shuffled up behind him.

"Here, Monsieur, I've found it, I can show you now. It you will be kind enough just to hold that end. I'm afraid it's a little bit torn."

Raymond took hold of one side of the map.

"Cécile, what in the world are you doing here?" he demanded.

"I hated to think of you being all alone," she said. "I got 40 francs out of mother—Aunt Thérèse wouldn't give me anything—and 15 from the grocer at the corner, and I came third class."

"——and when you get to that point," the porter said, "you will see the Café de la Manche on your left. There you turn right—you should be careful, it's a dangerous crossing, frequently the tram-car hits you in the small of the back before you have seen it—and go on as far as the policeman——"

"——and I came by the night-train from Paris," Cécile went on pathetically, "and now I feel so tired. There was a woman in the carriage with a baby that cried all the way, the woman told me fifty times that the baby had been dry in the daytime for a whole fortnight, but at night it just couldn't be, you couldn't expect it at that age, she said, and it not only wasn't——"

"——and there, Monsieur, you will find the rue Pecheur on your right. Or there is another way you could go——"

"Yes, yes, yes, thank you, thank you. Yes, it's all perfectly clear. . . . I must rush, Cécile, I'll be back here——"

"But I'm coming with you, Raymond, I want to see what the boat looks like."

"Well, come on then, we'll miss him if we don't——"

"But, Raymond, you can't go like that! Is that the only hat

you've got? At least you must let me mend that hole in your sleeve—there will be smart people on the boat, I can't be seen going about with a tramp——"

"But, my dear Cécile, no one will know us. . . ."

"You must come up to our room—no, wait, I've got a needle and thread in my bag, take off your coat, it won't take a minute. You ought really to be wearing an overcoat, it's not warm enough to go without one. . . ."

He stood miserably in his shirt sleeves, stamping with impatience, while she sat in the middle of the vestibule with the skirts of her green dress falling gracefully about the little chair and the mink tie hanging from one shoulder, to stitch the sleeve.

"It is nice to see Madame using her needle," the porter said sentimentally. "Madame is so rapid, so skilful, and the work is very becoming to an elegant young lady."

Raymond saw that he was right. There was a delicious incongruity in the sight of so dainty a creature furiously stabbing with her needle and biting the thread. He had never hated Cécile so much before.

"There! That's better!" she said.

"You won't forget," the porter repeated, "it is not the first turning after Ste Marguerite, but the second."

Raymond grabbed his coat and put one arm into it. "No, I won't forget. Come on, Cécile." He strode down the street twisting his other arm into the sleeve, with Cécile pursuing him at the trot of a lame puppy and crying "Raymond! wait Raymond! I can't go so fast in these shoes, they hurt me." He called back over his shoulder, "Why did you wear them? Why did you come?" But at the end of the street he remembered that he had not the smallest idea where the rue Pecheur was. He had to stop and ask, and Cécile caught up with him.

"Oh, Raymond, I'm so tired, I didn't sleep a wink and my shoes hurt frightfully. Can't we take a cab?"

"No, we can't. Yes, I suppose we'll have to."

She stood beside him on the edge of the pavement, and the passers-by thought how touchingly pretty she looked with the little tears in her big, childish eyes, as they waited and waited for a cab.

*

They found Captain Lenormand in his cabin. His feet in their rubber-soled boots rested among a litter of papers, glasses and underclothes on the tablecloth, his chair was tilted and his head hung back with the face to the ceiling as if he were being shaved. His eyes were closed, his wide and wooded nostrils gently whistling. Captain Lenormand had not lost altogether the appearance of a soldier. His grey moustache was of a military cut, and Raymond recognized what had once been described to him as the artillery chin. The face looked as if it had been left for a long time in the open, the skin dry and wrinkled, grey with a dirty brown in the forehead's furrows and in the long concentric cracks about the pockets of the eyes, the chin dark with stubble and the neck fluffed with a smoky grey. The mouth, a little open now to show the patchy dun and yellow teeth, was feeble, as if a hem along the lips had broken, allowing the corners of the mouth to spread, the skin which bound the chin and throat to fall and crinkle. It was a short man, wide and heavy in the shoulders, ponderously stomached. His clothes were of a decent country cut, such as a farmer would use on a visit to the city, but too much worn. The tie, of red and yellow in flamboyant alliance, and grotesquely pinned, had been better—Raymond thought—kept away from Europe. The air carried heavily the swirling odours of imprisoned cigar-smoke, of whisky and hair oil. The messenger who had brought them here had gone swiftly away to finish a game of noughts and crosses with a colleague in the deck-stewards' lobby, closing the door behind him. Still in some confusion, Raymond stared with curiosity at the almost mythical personage whose name he had heard whispered from those half-lit days when Maman had frightened him with her mysterious reference to "Father's enemies." Cécile sat down, frowning prettily at the sour, masculine smell, and rubbed a fingernail with the wetted corner of her handkerchief. "I am rather frightened," she whispered to Raymond, "it is the first time I have ever been on the water." He pointed to the lifebelt hanging on the door. "You'd better put that on," he said aloud, "and if we do sink, take a deep breath and hold on to it as long as you can."

At the sound of Raymond's voice the old man stopped snoring and let his eyelids slide back to show the gentle grey eyes. He swung his feet off the table, sat up, winced for a moment at the cramp in the small of his back, and pulled himself on to his feet. He smiled at them, questioning.

"You are Captain Lenormand?" Raymond asked.

Lenormand, with a scared look, shook his head.

"No, no, I've never heard——"

Raymond remembered then that Lenormand was incognito.

"I mean Mr. Bailey. I am M. Raymond Séverin, and this is my wife."

Lenormand shook hands with Raymond and surveyed Cécile with a connoisseur's eye. He was shy and very polite, he smiled with grandfatherly benevolence, pushed the litter recklessly off the table and rang for his steward. "You would like some coffee,

Madame Séverin? And you, M. Séverin, a glass of whisky, or perhaps you would prefer cognac? . . . Yes, steward, coffee for Madame, and a glass of cognac. And perhaps you will just pack up my things, I suppose I have to be off the boat before long. You will have to arrange everything carefully, the customs officers, I'm afraid, have muddled up all my things. . . . Really I think it very courteous of you to have come to meet me, most kind of you, in France I shall be entirely a stranger, I have been abroad so long, it is very agreeable to find friends waiting for me. I look forward, M. Séverin, to meeting your father again; he was, as perhaps you know, a comrade-at-arms of mine. I feel it was so kind of him to remember me, I lost touch with nearly all my old friends when I was sent off to Canada in such a hurry to see after my uncle's affairs. . . . You, Mme Séverin, you will hardly be able to understand the emotion of an old man who sees his dear country after so long an absence. The delay was terrible, last night I could hardly sleep for the excitement of knowing that I should soon see my dear France again."

But he had mastered his impetuosity, and he seemed ready to sit there all day, nodding his kind eyes at Cécile's throat and bosom, talking with modest sentiment in his precise, old-fashioned voice, while Raymond played impatiently with his wine-glass and the steward squeezed himself behind their chairs, grovelling for shoes and handkerchiefs. Cécile yawned behind her gloves, murmuring, "*Parfaitement . . . parfaitement*," growing so pale in the close air that Raymond thought she would be sick and almost hoped so. The ship was alive now with the scratch and scuttle of a regiment of cleaners. Sweating at the catches of Lenormand's cabin trunk, the steward tried to indicate by many little glances, many little flutterings of the laryngeal cords, that Mr. Bailey should be getting ready. In the roadstead a Guernsey packet was sounding her siren with gentle, persistent exasperation, and Cécile was certain that when they got up to the landing-deck they would find themselves in mid-Atlantic. ". . . I myself," Lenormand continued, filling his glass again and talking with increasing confidence, "I myself take a great interest in dreams. I believe that it is scientifically possible, if one only knew the way, to interpret the meaning of everything we dream. Last night, for example, I dreamed that I was back again in my office in Quebec, and that I was reading a letter. Now that was strange, and it must have some meaning. . . ."

It was after twelve when they reached the Georgian portico of the main first-class entrance. There was difficulty at that point about the bar-steward's bill, which came to twenty-nine dollars. Lenormand, it appeared, had made a miscalculation over his expenses and had only twelve dollars in ready money. Rather pathetically he asked Raymond for advice, and between them, under the messenger's wary eye, Raymond and Cécile found a hundred francs. Lenormand thanked them profusely. "Now that," he continued, "is an extraordinary instance of what I was saying just now. I dreamed one night, shortly before I left Canada, that I was in just that situation, having a bill to pay and no ready money. . . ." Raymond, accustomed as he was to giving one sou where five were expected, felt his back scorched by the glare of untipped stewards as he helped Lenormand into a cab. He had two francs seventy in his purse, which would pay for the fare, and he was wondering how he could settle at the hotel. Lenormand sat smiling at Cécile as the cab bumped along the rue Louis Philippe. "How this brings it all back!" he said wistfully.

Raymond left him in a corner of the hotel café, with Cécile and a glass of brandy, while he put his things together and telegraphed to Thérèse for a further two hundred francs. He was away for a long time, but Lenormand was not impatient. He was silent at first, sipping his brandy and bowing to Cécile with a gentle "A vous, Madame!" at each sip. Cécile, glancing at the clock above the counter, saw that the 1.15 for Paris which they had meant to catch had gone already. Presently Lenormand returned to the subject of dreams and told her of one after another that he had experienced, pausing after each with a glance of modest expectation as if he were proud of his skill in dreaming. "But don't you agree with me, Madame Séverin, that there must be some kind of explanation when one has such dreams? I will tell you another dream that I had not long ago: I seemed to be standing in the middle of a road, and a man I'd never seen before came and asked me the way to San Francisco. To San Francisco, fancy! There must surely, don't you think, be some explanation?" Cécile said, "*Parfaitement . . . parfaitement . . .*" A little before three o'clock Raymond returned, but the money had not yet come through. He could do nothing but sit down and order more brandy for Lenormand. "I was telling Madame Séverin," Lenormand said, "of a most peculiar dream I had not very long ago. I dreamed that a man asked me the way to San Francisco. San Francisco—it's a place I've never been to. Now I believe there must be some underlying explanation, and I think, Mme Séverin, that you agree with me?"

"I'm afraid we've missed the best train for Paris," Raymond said, "but there's another good one at a quarter past four."

"To me it makes no difference at all," Lenormand said politely. ". . . I've just remembered another rather curious dream. . . ."

At half-past three Raymond returned to the Post Office and at twenty to four Thérèse's telegraph order came through, with the message, *What nonsense I gave you plenty*. He collected the two hundred-franc notes, arousing the clerk's suspicions by his haste, engaged a cab and drove back to the hotel. Except for a group of sailors playing cinquante-cinq the restaurant was empty; Madame, the porter thought, had gone upstairs, but he had no idea where the other gentleman had got to. He found Cécile lying down in the room which he was supposed to have given up. She could not stand Captain Lenormand's company any longer, Cécile said; he had horrid eyes and a bad smell, and his dreams, she thought, were rather nasty. No, she had no idea where he had gone, she had simply run away from him and now she had a splitting head.

"But, my dear Cécile, what will Aunt Thérèse say if I don't produce the old fool in Paris? I was relying on you not to let him out of sight. What? Yes, yes, I'm sorry about the headache, but you must come down at once, the cab's waiting, we've got to get that 4.15."

"But, Raymond——"

Ignoring her he hurried down and into the street. He had not far to go. The Café du Centre was only two lamp-posts away, and there he found Lenormand exchanging dreams with a shop-girl over glasses of green chartreuse.

"Captain—Mr. Bailey!" he panted. "I am sorry to interrupt, but we have only half an hour to catch the train. Will you, please——"

Lenormand rose, smiling, drank off the rest of his Chartreuse, murmured an excuse to his companion, bowed courteously, and followed Raymond into the street. The waiter came after them. "Pardon, m'sieur, l'addition——" Lenormand clicked his tongue. "If you could possibly oblige me, M. Séverin, with five francs——" Raymond gave the waiter three for two-twenty and took Lenormand's arm. "Come, we must hurry, please." Lenormand, anxious as ever to behave agreeably, broke into a trot to keep pace with Raymond's strides. "That was a very intelligent young woman," he gasped as he ran; "she says she knows of a little book on the interpretation of dreams. . . ."

Cécile had arrived in the vestibule and was receiving in her most gracious way the attentions of the porter; who, engaged with the charms of Madame, had not thought to put any of the luggage on the still-waiting cab.

Lenormand went to sleep on the way to the station, with his head on Cécile's shoulder, and he hardly seemed to wake when, four minutes after the Paris train had gone, they pulled him out on to the platform. Raymond led him silent and docile to the restaurant, where after asking for the loan of fifty francs and a glass of Vermouth he dozed once more, and Raymond thought it safe to leave him while he went for tickets. But he had gone when they came back. They found him in the rue Quatorze. He had bought himself the little book on dreams which the shop-girl had recommended, and an armful of tulips incompetently wrapped in a wisp of tissue for Cécile. The presentation was made ceremoniously in the middle of the street, with the trams furiously clanging behind them. Lenormand had become more than ever friendly, he accepted Raymond's rebuke submissively and was quite willing to be led back to the station. But he would not enter the night-train for Paris, which was waiting now, before they returned to the restaurant for a glass each of crême-de-menthe, which he believed an excellent thing to steady the stomach on a journey. There, towards eight o'clock, they woke him, and before he dozed again they had got him into the train. Worn out and crumpled, Cécile sat in the corner farthest from Lenormand's, with the tulips spread over her lap, complaining in a mousish monotone of Raymond's unkindness. It was an hour before the train was due to start, and already, she said, the odour of Lenormand in the carriage was quite intolerable. Very well, he answered, she could go where she pleased; for himself, he had Lenormand fixed and he was satisfied. He opened his book and went on reading.

The light was poor, the lines ran together and lost their meaning. When Raymond woke he saw Cécile still sitting in the same position, wide awake. Two Sisters of S. Teresa, young and gentle-looking girls, had taken the places opposite Lenormand's. Lenormand had gone.

The train had not yet started. It was five to nine. He caught hold of Cécile's arm.

"Where's he gone? You idiot, why did you let him go?"

She smiled.

"It was so stuffy. I was glad he went away."

He ran to the end of the corridor and jumped down to the platform, burst through the groups and tore to the restaurant. Lenormand was there. In his old corner, with two bunches of tulips and a glass half-filled with Cinzano. His eye were seraphic when he rose and bowed. "You will join me, M. Séverin, in a little glass? . . . I was going to ask if I might borrow just twenty francs. I find myself a little short———" Raymond seized Lenormand's hat, his little book, his tulips, Lenormand himself, and bundled them across the platform. The train was moving when he heaved them in.

When he had presented one of his bouquets to each of the Sisters, who accepted them in grave confusion, Lenormand undid the bottom button of his waistcoat and the top one of his trousers and fell asleep, the Sisters fearfully regarding him from beneath their hoods. He woke at Caen; spat in his handkerchief and sat up. The lamp had been turned down, but there was light enough for him to see the two pale faces opposite. At the other end of the carriage Cécile was asleep and Raymond still pretending to read. Lenormand leant forward and placed one hand on a knee of each of the Sisters. They were too frightened to scream. He addressed them huskily. "I've just had a most extraordinary dream. Listen, I'll tell you. I dreamed that I was walking in a forest without my clothes on. . . ."

Raymond shifted the book so that his face should be quite hidden. His mouth was dry, he couldn't sleep, and he remembered now that he had had no food since petit-déjeuner. The day that had started so well had so soon been clouded, and now he could think of nothing but a continuous irritation. Cécile had put her feet against his knees and he pushed them down angrily. He had done the job all right, he had fetched Lenormand. But he felt that since Cécile's arrival he had muddled everything, he had spent the whole day looking a greater fool than ever he looked at Baulon. . . . The incidents faded as his head bumped and bumped against the window, but in the long and wretched hours of semi-consciousness he had still the vague awareness of his own stupidity. When he drifted farther into sleep the shriek of the engine woke him. The train jerked to a standstill at Lisieux. Evreux passed. In the early light he saw the station-boards of Mantes. Lenormand was still talking to the Sisters, who sat holding hands, stiff with fatigue and terror; about his dreams, his extraordinary dreams and their interpretation; talking, talking.

XXVII

THE windows of the Louis Treize dining-room which Maître Bellefontaine used as his office were always shut, so that the dust and noise of the increasing traffic in the Avenue Mazarine could hardly penetrate; and through the high doors, beautifully hinged, no faintest sound came from the dozen demure clerks who worked from seven to seven in the old coffee room and the butler's pantry beyond. There had been some talk—M. Robert had favoured it—of introducing an American machine on which keys were pressed and correspondence rendered into printed characters; but Me. Bellefontaine, when he heard that the machine made a noise like a kettledrum, would have none of it. When he required to send a letter himself he rapped twice on the door. M. Cottard brought in a blotting-pad, two sheets of paper, a pen and inkwell; asked permission to sit down at the end of the dining-table, wrote out the letter in his handsome long-hand and took it away to make a fair copy. Me. Bellefontaine would have no ink in his room because he thought it made a smell; and for the same reason, no flowers. If the sun started to come in at the window M. Cottard came at once and adjusted the jalousies. Me. Bellefontaine's tastes were severely classical, and he did not care for anything of that sort in his room. Here, as perhaps nowhere else in Paris, the topic which hung this morning in the streets and cafés like a summer mist had found no entrance. Me. Bellefontaine read with his early coffee those pages of the *Temps* which concerned his practice; the rest was reserved till evening, when he took it at home with his after-dinner liqueur. And now the newspaper lay folded on the table, hiding from Me. Bellefontaine's uninquisitive eyes the alarming interview with Von Hotzendorf and the report, which filled the adjacent column, of Vivex's inquiry into German artillery development. Me. Bellefontaine would not in any case have discussed the matter, since it was against his principles to risk the betrayal of any speculative opinion. He stood aloof, he examined the facts, he spoke only, and then with caution, when the facts were sufficient basis for a reasonable deduction. He stood by the window now with his hands behind his back dominating the company with his huge head, his giant eyebrows and scuttle-beard, his tranquil eyes. His height was short of seventy inches, but everyone fancied that he was a big man; and with his thick hair hardly turned from its rich brown he seemed to have ten years fewer than his sixty-nine. He showed no sense of the occasion; it was usual for people to be more or less nervous in his presence, and he would have been surprised to find his visitors at their ease. He had always the air of being wholly indifferent to whether he won a case or lost it: it was perhaps for that reason that he generally won.

Lecours fidgeted uncomfortably. He was still rather out of breath from mounting the two flights of stairs.

"I am sorry," he said, "that we have to keep you waiting, Me. Bellefontaine. It was arranged that M. Raymond Séverin should bring Captain Lenormand here promptly at ten o'clock. I can't understand——"

Thérèse wheeled her chair a little forward and said brusquely, "You can't rely on that boy for anything."

"Raymond, I'm sure, would do his best——" Madeleine began.

"It is of no consequence," Bellefontaine said imperially. "I have no other engagement before half-past eleven. There is a chair just behind you, M. Séverin——"

But Eugène would not sit down. He stood at attention beside Madeleine's chair, erect and motionless, exactly—Thérèse thought —as if his photograph were being taken. In her sidelong glance

Madeleine saw that he was very pale, that his lips were held tightly together and his resolute eyes fixed unmoving on Bellefontaine's forehead. It gave her physical pain, to see him standing like that, as if a pair of bellows blew freezing air against the inner wall of her breast: he kept so still, as he had done on that last day when intuition told her that he had lost; his eyes were proud again, unconscious seemingly of those who watched him. She had fancied she remembered the emotions of that day in all their poignancy; that the darkness of the crowded court, the dreary voice of counsel, the very smell of dust and wood-rot had lived as an eternal present in her mind's close chamber. But the agony she felt now, the cold and sucking pain of long suspense, that was something she had forgotten. She turned her eyes towards Lecours and saw in them the reflection of her disquiet; he was gazing at Eugène, doubtfully, but with something of her own sharp admiration. Thérèse, on her right, was no less impassive than Eugène; she was leaning forward, her chin was resting on her left hand with the flesh thrust upwards by the fingers and her lower lip pushed out as if with sarcasm. Beyond her Louis sat with knees together and folded hands, wearing the measured patience of one who awaits the answer to his offered bargain. At his right hand, her chair a few inches back from his, the insufferable Flandrecauld, canopied by the most baroque hat in Paris, was driving the dirt from her fingernails with little bayonet charges from a pointed paper-knife. It was only five past ten. But already Madeleine feared—and saw how Lecours shared her fear— that somehow Raymond had failed them. The courtesies were over and there had been a period of silence; it lasted, perhaps, for hardly five seconds, but it had been enough to tauten their common sensibility. Even Thérèse had begun to drum her sinewy fingers on the padded arm of her chair, Me. Bellefontaine himself was winding his watch-chair round his thumb. Only Eugène was entirely calm, as he had been during those smoking seconds when the judge was rising to his feet; a giant among pygmies, the pattern of fortitude.

Bellefontaine picked up the sheaf of notes which lay on the table and glanced at the top sheet.

"This Mr. Bailey," he said to Lecours. "I presume that he will be ready to swear to his real identity when that is required?"

Lecours nodded reluctantly.

"There may be a little difficulty; I judge from correspondence that Mr. Bailey is a man of preternatural caution, and he is likely to fear that his disappearance from France at the time to which we are referring might still have unhappy consequences; but there is no doubt, I think, that we shall be able to give him the necessary assurance."

Bellefontaine raised and lowered his head, as if Lecours had given a fairly intelligent answer.

"That is the only difficulty that I have so far foreseen," he said slowly. "And if our assurances are not enough, we may possibly find the material for more"—he sought a word from a corner of the ceiling—"for sterner persuasion. We might remind Mr. Bailey that his papers can hardly be in very precise order . . . However, as you say, M. Lecours, there should be no great difficulty." He closed one nostril with his forefinger and puffed a little volley of breezes through the other. "For the rest, our position as I see it from the minutes of evidence would appear to be very simple. There is, after all, just one point on which Mr. Bailey's evidence should be conclusive: that the signal alleged to have been given by Corporal Barraud at 1.15 was in fact not visible or else not seen from the point which you, M. Séverin, and Mr. Bailey were together occupying at that time. We must, of course, have certain auxiliary facts: for example, that Mr. Bailey was in your company without interval during the operative period. My reading of the minute of the runner Daguin's evidence does not wholly establish that. But no doubt Mr. Bailey's evidence will be entirely clear on that point." He crossed to the door of the coffee-room and rapped. "M. Cottard—the statement for Mr. Bailey's signature! . . . Directly we know that Mr. Bailey will give clear evidence on that crucial question, a word from me to Me. Gustave Ducroquet of the Court of Appeal will suffice, I think, to have the matter pressed forward."

Madeleine looked at him gratefully; his prosaic voice was harsh to her tenderness, but it gave her confidence. Lecours and Louis nodded in unison. Eugène said nothing, and his expression was unchanged. Bellefontaine with the minimum of histrionic effort had fixed their attention on himself, and they were startled by the interruption of Thérèse's phlegmy voice:

"I should have thought, M. Bellefontaine, that for the purpose of pressing Ducroquet you might assume that Lenormand's evidence will be as we require it—so long as we know that Lenormand is ready to give evidence at all. It appears to me rather a waste of time, to conduct a rehearsal."

Bellefontaine wiped his hand from waist to fingertips across his mouth; but he gave no other sign to show that Thérèse's speech was the most outrageous ever made in that room.

"Apart," he said slowly, "from such questions of legal procedure, and legal ethics, as may be involved by the course which Mlle Séverin suggests, would you be satisfied, M. Séverin, to have Mr. Bailey brought into court without our knowing precisely the nature of the evidence which he will be ready to give? I only ask that because——"

"But we can surely assume," Thérèse said, "that he has not come all this way at our expense, and at some inconvenience to himself, to give evidence that's neither unfavourable or useless for our case? Naturally he will require to be primed beforehand, in the usual way, but——"

"I am very ready," Eugène said with dignity, "to be guided by you, Me. Bellefontaine, in this matter. Naturally I cannot guarantee that Captain Lenormand will tell the truth. I have discovered, unfortunately, that men who are normally honest find it difficult to tell the truth in a Court of Law."

"I have little doubt," Lecours said tactfully, "that Captain Lenormand will give entirely truthful evidence, since——"

"Is that what we want?" Thérèse asked.

"——since he has consented—at no small inconvience to himself, as you say, Mlle Séverin—to come over here for that purpose."

Louis nodded agreement.

"Yes, Thérèse, when M. Lecours and I were arranging for Captain Lenormand to come to France it was understood that he should give proper evidence."

"M. Séverin," said Mme Flandrecauld, "has arranged for Captain Lenormand to give satisfactory evidence."

Madeleine was trying to speak, but her cough prevented her. The bout went on for a long time; it was Eugène's exasperated frown that at last stopped it. Her voice came then in an unnatural key, as if it were reproduced by a cheap phonograph:

"I want—I want it to be understood, Me. Bellefontaine, that my husband and I are appealing to the Court for justice. Only for that." She stopped, fighting against her cough. Bellefontaine, without taking his eyes from her face, rapped for Cottard and sent him to get water. Thérèse began, "Yes, Madeleine, but——" but Madeleine had stifled the cough again and overrode her. "We do not ask for any manipulation. You must understand, it is not for a trial of that kind that we have waited so many years, that my husband has come to Paris against the advice of his doctor. It is a question, Me. Bellefontaine, of our honour; and that can not be settled by any dishonourable proceeding. Our only wish is that Captain Lenormand's evidence, which is vital to the case, should be properly heard in court. We do not wish or require, my husband and I, to descend to any legal legerdemain. Our wish——"

She had overrun her tether's length. Bellefontaine gravely regarded old Mme Séverin as she sat bent double with her whole body shaking. He was not unmoved.

"There's some water here, Madeleine," Thérèse said. "You had better drink it."

Eugène took no notice of Madeleine's convulsions.

"My wife," he said quietly to Bellefontaine, "has perfectly expressed my own attitude. I would prefer——"

The door had opened. A servant announced: "M. et Mme Raymond Séverin, with Mr. Bailey and M. Henri Gie."

Bellefontaine nodded.

"You will show them in, please, Léon."

Thérèse tried to catch Raymond's eye as he came in, but he would not look at her. His face was bored and sullen, he was dressed for the Quartier Latin. Cécile—why did the Séverin drag their women wherever they went?—looked in no better temper. But it was Lenormand who held her attention. He was nicely dressed. The noisy tie had given place to a stock of sober grey, his morning suit was new, rather tight at the shoulders but well tailored and of excellent cloth. He held himself with soldierly dignity, he had a grave and pleasant smile, his bow was courtly. He went at once to Mme Flandrecauld and presented to her the bunch of daffodils he had brought with him. Smiling, he turned to Louis.

"Colonel Séverin, I have looked forward for many years to our reunion."

Eugène took a step forward.

"I am Eugène Séverin," he said.

Without haste or embarrassment, Lenormand transferred his daffodils from Mme Flandrecauld's lap to that of Madeleine.

"Colonel Séverin," he said to Eugène, "this is a pleasure to which I have looked forward for many, many years. . . ."

M. Gie, deserted but not at all abashed, stood by himself near the door, his hands in his pockets. He had the appearance of a workman in his Sunday clothes. Louis, signalling an inquiry, could get no reply from Raymond, who had dropped on the nearest convenient chair, leaving Cécile to stand, and calmly lit a cigarette. Lenormand presently put the matter right.

"I have brought M. Gie," he said, "to represent my interests. You will realize that I myself have no head for legal affairs; it will be easier for you, M. Lecours, and for you, M.——?——M. Bellefontaine—to deal with a qualified solicitor." He bowed again, caught sight of a vacant chair and sat down.

M. Gie lost no time in executing his instructions.

"I think it will be convenient," he said to Lecours, "if before we proceed with the matter of my client's evidence we settle the question of expenses. Mr. Bailey has so far received only your advance of ten thousand francs——"

"We can settle that matter," Lecours said hastily, "in my own office. There will be no difficulty at all. You will agree, I am sure, that Me. Bellefontaine's time must not be wasted."

M. Gie was not impressed by the genuflection in Lecours's voice as he mentioned Me. Bellefontaine. Me. Bellefontaine's presence acted only as a stimulus to M. Gie, who lacked as a rule the opportunity to prick the posteriors of celebrated counsel.

"As far as I am concerned," he said, "there is no need for any waste of time. You have agreed honourably to discharge my client's expenses according to a fixed schedule—your letter which I have here expresses the agreement precisely—and all that is necessary is for your cheque to be passed to me. Directly that has——"

He was interrupted by Louis.

"My memory of the correspondence," Louis said in his quiet, dry voice, "is that the balance was to be paid to Captain—to Mr. Bailey immediately after his appearance in court, the allowances being increased according to the number of days that Mr. Bailey is kept waiting."

He glanced at Lecours for confirmation. But Mme. Flandrecauld already had a press-copy of the letter in her hand.

"That is the position," she said decisively. "Mr. Bailey is to receive final payment at the conclusion of the transaction."

"I take it," M. Gie asked Lecours, "that you will be ready to deposit the sum in question with a holder who shall be agreeable to your client and to mine?"

Lecours shuddered. That such vulgarity, in the presence of Me. Bellefontaine himself——

"My dear Louis," Thérèse said sharply, "why don't you pay the man straight away and avoid all this bickering? You know you'll have to pay up in the end."

Her voice brought Raymond to attention.

"If it was your money, Aunt Thérèse——"

"The less said by you about my money the better, I should have thought——"

"I don't understand," Madeleine said miserably. "What is it that this M. Gie wants?"

"He wants twenty-three thousand francs," Mme Flandrecauld said crisply.

"Then, Louis, won't you——?"

Me. Bellefontaine, standing quite still, looked out upon the turmoil as Noah upon the deluge, waiting with stoic patience for the water to subside. He could hardly believe that it was in his own room, with the Décultot panelling, the armoire by Grazzini, that this monstrous talk of francs was being bandied. For some time he had been aware of a peculiar smell, and he noticed now that young M. Séverin was smoking a cigarette. Well, he supposed that before long they would be smoking cigarettes in Notre Dame.

And now the young woman in the green hat—heaven knew who she was or how she had got in—was piping up.

"Don't you think," Cécile asked intelligently at the first pause, "that if we collected all round and all of us gave something Mr. Bailey might be satisfied?"

Madeleine said: "Be quiet, Cécile!"

Bellefontaine gave Lecours a look of mild inquiry.

"I think," Lecours said nervously, "that we may be able to settle the financial detail"—he glanced inquiringly at Louis—"as soon as we are assured that your client, M. Gie, is able to give evidence which relates precisely to the main point of ambiguity. I need hardly say that my clients have no wish to prevaricate in any way, we only want to be certain that Mr. Bailey is ready to give operative evidence."

M. Gie eyed him sharply and then nodded.

"I am able to give you that assurance," he said.

"For example," Lecours continued, "we want to be sure that Mr. Bailey remembers being in the company of Colonel Séverin continuously between the hours of twelve and two o'clock on the day of the Viboire engagement—the 18th August. If we could start by establishing Mr. Bailey's definite memory of that fact——"

"Wait a minute!" M. Gie said pleasantly. "If you were in possession of Mr. Bailey's evidence, and had Me. Bellefontaine to attest your minute of the verbal deposition, then you might be able to dispense with Mr. Bailey's actual presence in court; and since you say that Mr. Bailey is only to be reimbursed after his actual appearance, I can understand, M. Lecours, why you are so anxious——"

To M. Gie's surprise, the old man who had already interrupted him and whose position he had not ascertained, the quiet, dapper little gentleman who looked as if he might be hired to exercise Persian kittens, suddenly jumped to his feet.

"M. Gie!" Louis said, his voice the more impressive because it was so quiet and maiden-ladylike. "I am accustomed to conducting business with some of the most important commercial figures in Paris, in Vienna, and elsewhere. I am not accustomed to having doubt cast on my good faith. I have——"

"M. Séverin," said Mme. Flandrecauld severely, "is unaccustomed——"

"Mirabelle, be quiet! . . . I have made an offer to Mr. Bailey, acting through M. Lecours, in very precise terms. Since you seem to have instructions not to take my offer seriously, the business is closed. I am your servant, M. Gie, and I wish to have nothing more to do with you."

He moved with dignity towards the door. Mme Flandrecauld began: "M. Séverin does not wish——" and stopped. Lecours was trying to say something but was too much overwhelmed to handle his tongue. His intuition, quicker than that of most, showed him that the Séverins were united in their approval of Louis's speech; true, Louis had looked more than ever like a music-master, shaking his solemn little forefinger at the unspeakable M. Gie; but he had shown the Séverin spirit, and even in Eugène's eye there was a sparkle of admiration. Only Madeleine had spoilt the general satisfaction by starting to cry.

With a glance at Lecours, Me. Bellefontaine had gathered up his papers. But before Louis reached the door M. Gie rose and stopped him.

"You misunderstand me altogether, Monsieur," he said quickly. "I had no wish to say anything that might be thought offensive, I only want to be sure that my client's position is properly understood. Mr. Bailey is involved by his absence from Canada in serious business losses. You, as a man of business, will understand what I mean. It would be most unjust if Mr. Bailey were not compensated for a reasonable proportion of his losses, and I should not be doing my duty——"

Louis looked at him with scepticism.

"You are ready, then, to engage that Mr. Bailey will carry out the terms of the agreement made with him by M. Lecours?"

M. Gie nodded:

"Subject to their proper interpretation, yes."

Louis was satisfied. He returned, trailing Mme Flandrecauld, to his chair.

Madeleine, with her face in her hands, did not seem to realize what had happened. Thérèse manœuvred her chair a little closer and touched her arm. She said, with something approaching a ragged gentleness:

"It is all right, Madeleine. They have settled the business."

Madeleine looked up.

"You mean," she asked in an awed whisper, "they have proved that Eugène was right?"

"No, no, of course not. My dear girl, they haven't begun yet. They have merely settled the terms on which Lenormand is to give his evidence."

Madeleine looked at her like a dumb animal; so she had not awoken from the long, dark dream.

Lecours was whispering to Bellefontaine, and presently Bellefontaine cleared his throat.

"Mr. Bailey," he said in his court voice, "I am going to read to you first of all the text of a part of the statement made by Colonel

Séverin in the course of the case which we have under review. I shall be obliged if you will listen attentively, and I think you will readily see then which are the passages which can be corroborated, or contradicted, by you."

It was only a little movement that Eugène made at the words "or contradicted," but Madeleine felt it through her chair. She raised her hand slowly, brought it across her shoulder to the back of the chair and let her fingers rest on Eugène's. But he gently pulled his hand away.

Lenormand remained quite still while Bellefontaine was reading. His eyes were closed. When he had finished, Bellefontaine turned to Eugène.

"The text as I have read it is, as far as you can remember, correct?"

Eugène said steadily, in a low voice:

"It is perfectly correct."

Bellefontaine continued: "And now, Mr. Bailey, I should like you to answer, if you can, a question which I shall first put to you in a general form: does your own recollection of the events of that eighteenth of August, between the hours of noon and two o'clock in the afternoon, in any way conflict with that portion of Colonel Séverin's statement which I have just read to you? I want you to take your time in answering—perhaps, M. Lecours, you will just pass that copy to Mr. Bailey—and consider each detail carefully before you venture to say 'yes' or 'no.' You will realize that this is a matter of the greatest gravity. It concerns nothing less important than the honour of a French officer."

Lenormand took no notice of the paper which Lecours held out to him. When M. Gie touched his arm he started. For some time he had been fast asleep. Finding a piece of paper on his knees, he put on a pair of spectacles and slowly read it through, his lowered eyebrows bunching the flesh above his nose. The room was so quiet that they could hear distinctly an old woman calling a late edition of *L'Intransigeant* in the street below. When he had finished he smiled and nodded. Bellefontaine looked at him inquiringly.

"Well, Mr. Bailey?"

Lenormand did not understand. He smiled.

"It is very interesting," he said.

Eugène addressed him sharply.

"Lenormand, I shall be obliged if you will answer Me. Bellefontaine's question."

But Bellefontaine interrupted:

"Pardon me, M. Séverin, but I do not wish to hurry Mr. Bailey. Perhaps he is not quite clear on some individual point."

M. Gie bent and whispered in Lenormand's ear. Lenormand gravely nodded.

"I am very anxious," he said at last, "to do anything I can for the assistance of my old friend"—he bowed to Eugène—"provided, of course, that my incognito is strictly regarded. It is important, for family reasons, that my original name should not be connected with any scandal. I am very willing to testify in court that Colonel Séverin, under whom I had the honour to serve for a period of nine months or more, was in every respect a pattern of what an officer should be."

He bowed to Bellefontaine, sat back, and closed his eyes again.

"I trust it is clear," M. Gie said combatively, "that Mr. Bailey's original name will not be made known in the course of any court proceedings?"

Bellefontaine narrowed his eyes, snapped them open again.

"I think that that can be arranged," he said guardedly. "In all probability the Court will agree, at my suggestion, that when the minutes are cited the name, Bailey shall be read for the name Lenormand wherever it occurs. Such a procedure is very unusual, but I expect that a precedent can be found. My own knowledge of legal history—modest though it must be in comparison with yours, M. Gie, for example—is fairly rich in convenient precedents. If that arrangement can be made, it should be quite satisfactory to your client?"

"Will it be satisfactory to you, Mr. Bailey," Gie asked, "if the name Bailey is substituted for Lenormand when the minute which you have there is read in court?"

Lenormand opened his eyes and shook himself, showing a mild annoyance at being disturbed again.

"What's that? What did you say?"

Gie repeated the question. Lenormand was slightly confused.

"Yes," he said doubtfully, "yes, that will be all right, provided that nothing is said to implicate me in any way."

Bellefontaine cleared his throat again:

"And now, Mr. Bailey, perhaps you are ready to answer my general question. Do your own recollections of the incidents described in the paper before you correspond with Colonel Severin's description?"

Without answering, Lenormand began to read the minute right through again. He was quite unaware of the shuffling feet, of Cécile's unhidden yawn.

"And now?" Bellefontaine asked when he looked up.

"It is very difficult for me to say," Lenormand answered cautiously. "You must remember that I am an old man now, and the events described here took place almost in my boyhood. I find it very hard——"

"Can you at least confirm," Eugène asked sternly, "that you were with me, as I have stated, between twelve and two o'clock on that day?"

Lenormand closed his eyes, puzzling.

"I remember," he said, "that I was with you in the morning, that day when we retired from—what was the name?—Viboire. Yes, that morning I can remember that I was with you."

"But between twelve and two o'clock," Bellefontaine asked, "where were you then?"

Already Lenormand seemed to be fatigued by so much cross-examination.

"I find it very hard——" he began.

He was roused by a new voice.

"Perhaps you can remember," Thérèse asked, "why it was that shortly after Viboire you found it necessary to make yourself invisible and subsequently to sail for America?"

The lightning led a crackle of thunder.

Eugène turned upon his sister. "Thérèse!"

"Mlle Séverin!" Lecours expostulated. "You have no right to introduce that irrelevance, you know——"

M. Gie was on his feet.

"Me. Bellefontaine, I protest against the introduction of——"

Madeleine was in tears again. "Thérèse, why can't you leave Eugène——"

"Thérèse, there was no reason for that!" Louis said angrily.

Bellefontaine waved a Mosaic hand.

"I am perfectly able, M. Gie, to handle this affair. Mlle Séverin, I must request you to be so kind as not to interrupt Mr. Bailey's evidence."

Thérèse was unshaken.

"My question was relevant and important," she said emphatically. "We are asking Captain Lenormand for certain evidence in regard to my brother's conduct in the field, and he seems to have some trouble in searching his memory. My suggestion is that he may be able to remember more clearly the events which concern his own conduct, and the refreshment to his mental powers may help him to trace his way back to those in which we are interested." She turned to Lenormand himself. "I myself see no reason why the affair I have mentioned should be introduced in court, unless Me. Bellefontaine finds that your memory again requires a stimulant."

She wheeled her chair back a little way and lit a cigarette.

Eugène, red with anger, turned to Lenormand.

"Captain Lenormand, I give you my word that nothing relating to your own conduct during or after the battle will be brought into court."

"As if it mattered to anybody in the world," Raymond said in sudden, cold fury, "what the old fool did."

Lenormand appeared to be asleep again. But he surprised them by saying suddenly, his voice now tinged with alarm:

"Yes. Yes, I remember now, I was with Colonel Séverin throughout the period he has mentioned."

Thérèse took out her cigarette and blew the smoke into Madeleine's neck. "You see, he remembers now."

Bellefontaine gave her the look that he kept for his junior clerks. It was like hurling a javelin at Mount Atlas. He moved a little closer to Lenormand.

"Mr. Bailey," he said deliberately, "there is one point of great importance on which your memory may throw some light if you think carefully. It is alleged that at a quarter past one o'clock in the afternoon—on the day which we are discussing—a signal was sent to Colonel Séverin by General Guéroult, the main import of which was that Colonel Séverin should at all costs hold the position which he then occupied, in order to cover a flanking movement of the cavalry. Will you try to remember now: did you see that signal?"

In the long silence only Raymond was not looking at Lenormand. He watched his father. Eugène was surveying Lenormand as a teacher eyes a pupil struggling to solve a problem for himself; with detachment; his nostrils narrowed as if he were faintly conscious of some peculiar smell. In the moment of intensive observation, when Raymond fixed his eyes that way to save himself from the vulgarity of looking where the crowd looked, he saw how fine a body his father's was, so upright in his old-fashioned suit; how masterly his head was modelled, Dureresque with the quarter-line of cheek and forehead clean pencilled against the off-white of the panelling. His gaze travelled to Eugène's eyes, and he marvelled, feeling his own hand quivering with the infection of suspense, at their quiet bravery.

"Yes."

Lecours started.

"You mean, M. Lenormand, that you did see the signal?"

"Yes," Lenormand repeated. "Yes, I remember that now quite clearly. It is curious how memory works, sometimes I remember a dream that previously——"

Cécile was starting to giggle.

"Be quiet!" Thérèse shouted. "Raymond, take the little fool away."

Cécile burst into tears. But Bellefontaine ignored her.

"I have another question, Mr. Bailey," he said, "one that is equally important: did you report your observation of the signal to Colonel Séverin?"

Lenormand blinked, trembling with the drawn-out abstinence, tortured by the labour of recollection.

"I——"

"Of course you did not!" Madeleine hurled at him. "If you say that you did, you are telling——"

Bellefontaine coughed.

"Madame Séverin, I earnestly request you——"

Eugène said gently: "You must leave Captain Lenormand to answer, my dear; we mustn't interfere with the lawyers."

"Did you report the signal to Colonel Séverin?" Bellefontaine repeated.

Lenormand shook his head.

"I can't remember. I'm sorry, but I can't remember that. It's all quite a blank. I've got a funny memory, I——"

"Your memory is altogether too funny," Thérèse barked. "Perhaps you will be good enough to control its eccentricities."

M. Gie automatically jumped up.

"As Mr. Bailey's legal representative, I refuse to allow any pressure——"

"It is quite all right," Bellefontaine said suavely. "Your client will not be subjected to any improper or discourteous treatment so long as the case is in my hands. Though whether I shall be ready to proceed with it. . . ."

"I am very sorry," Lenormand repeated, "but my memory is not a good one. I can remember nothing at all of what happened after I saw the signal."

He closed his eyes. Raymond, at least, realized that he had once more fallen asleep.

XXVIII

It would have seemed to a less experienced eye than Madeleine's that Eugène was only a little tired that evening, as he sat by himself on a Knole settee in the hotel drawing-room, with the brandy cooling in his glass. The lines on his forehead that you noticed now, they had been there before; the slight unevenness in his breathing, like that of a child who has lately been through a fit of crying, had been evident for the past several weeks. The difference was only in the lateness of his movements; his slow response to speech; the way his eyes, fixed upon some object, held their direction for seconds after it was moved away. The hotel was a quiet one behind the rue de Surène, small and expensive, chosen by Louis because you would not meet travelling clerks or foreign tourists there. The rooms were high, well-panelled, and had the smell of good society. There was not much conversation. The other visitors wondered who he was, the old man of such distinguished appearance with the fine military head; but they refrained from staring. Madeleine had her embroidery and made a pretence of working, while Louis turned the pages of *L'Illustration* and his eyes, without their spectacles, watched the succession of blobs and blurs which passed below them. Thérèse had been carried upstairs in her chair and had gone to bed.

It startled Louis to hear Eugène asking, all of a sudden and in his normal tone, "What is it I keep hearing, all this about the Prussian influence in the Balkans? They say there's something in the newspapers, I haven't seen the newspapers to-day. Thérèse always gets hold of the newspapers and I never see them. . . ."

"It's nothing," Madeleine said, while Louis was still preparing an answer, "there are always these rumours in the newspapers, which have to find something to print every day, and in Paris they must always talk of what is most unlikely."

Louis nodded.

"Yes, yes, you find that kind of thing in the newspapers every day; it is to keep the public attention from more serious things."

An old woman knitting by the stove pushed back her chair and spoke over her shoulder.

"For myself I do not trust the Prussians," she said venomously. "Perhaps my memory is better than other people's. . . ."

She was answered by a young man whose face reminded Madeleine of the Prince Imperial's. He put down a volume of Mallarmé and said: "There is no need to worry, Grand'mère, we know exactly what can happen, we are perfectly prepared."

Eugène looked steadily at the old woman, ignoring her grandson. He was about to speak to her when Madeleine stopped him.

"It is time for us to go to bed," she said wearily. "We have had—it has been a tiring day."

"Certainly you must go to bed, my dear," he answered. "But, for myself, I am not tired in the least. I will follow you later."

He crossed the room and held the door for her. She hesitated, but she was too worn to argue.

"You won't be long?" she said.

"No, no, not very long."

Louis would have liked to retire too, but politeness prevented him. The other visitors had left the room, and finding himself alone with his brother he was most uncomfortable. They were seldom together, and having trodden down the grass of early recollections they had neither topics nor tastes in common. It was upon an impulse, after ten minutes' silence, that he leant forward and spoke.

"I want to tell you, Eugène—I meant to write to you, but I have been so busy, you know how it is, in these days one has to get through twice the work to do the same amount of business, it is only the tourist trade which is prosperous—I have been meaning to write for a long time but I have had no opportunity. I wanted to tell you how sorry I am about Pierre. It must have been a great blow to you and Madeleine, I was terribly upset when I saw the news in the papers, I still think there must have been some mistake."

Eugène was looking at Louis's coat.

"That's surely a very old coat you're wearing," he said reprovingly, "it's all creased at the shoulders. I should have thought a fellow like you, who doesn't have to worry about money, would be more particular about his clothes. . . . What were you saying about Pierre?"

"I wasn't saying anything," Louis faltered. "Only that I was so very sorry when I heard the news—about his desertion from the army. It was a great shock to me, I was very upset, I meant to write to you. . . ."

Eugène's eyes hardly moved. "You could at least get it pressed," he said. "That woman, that old daughter-of-joy you take about with you, surely she could do something. A coat oughtn't to fold like that on the shoulders. . . . Pierre? Were you talking about him? I can't tell anything about Pierre, he never writes to us now. . . . I'm sorry, Louis, but I really must go to bed now. There's no need for you to move, but I'm not used to late hours. I expect there will be some other people coming in soon, they will entertain you."

He looked all round, puzzled, and as soon as he saw the door he left the room, without answering Louis's "good night."

He had forgotten where his bedroom was, but a servant showed him the way. Madeleine was sitting on the side of her bed, wearing her dressing-gown. She had taken out her teeth, and he noticed how very old she looked.

"You should have gone to bed," he said rather vexedly, "it makes that cough of yours worse, hanging about like this. . . . Tell me, Madeleine, what is all this about Pierre? Louis was saying something, I never can understand him, something he saw in the papers about Pierre. He said that Pierre had deserted from the army. What did he mean by that?"

Madeleine turned her back. She said, "I don't know. I don't know what he meant."

Eugène sat down and tried to undo his bootlace.

"Madeleine, are you trying to keep something from me?" he asked suddenly. "Has Pierre done something foolish? It isn't true surely that——"

"Wait!" she said. "I'll undo that for you." She came and knelt at his feet, struggled to untie the knot with her cold fingers. "It's only—it's only Louis, one of Louis's funny ideas. He must have read something—it's quite a common name, he must have made some mistake, Pierre wouldn't do anything foolish."

Eugène breathed deeply through his nose.

"No," he said, "the name isn't at all common, though there's more than one branch of the family. . . . Can't you manage that knot? It can't be very tight, I tied it myself. . . He's an old fool, Louis, he spends all his time talking to tradesmen and he doesn't understand what's going on. Pierre, of course, is a young idiot, he will never make a soldier, but he wouldn't do anything like that . . . . Yes, yes, for goodness' sake cut it! . . . It's funny, Louis getting an idea like that."

He said nothing more while she undressed him.

*

She turned again and again, trying to find a position to relieve the pain in her chest. She was lifted rocking into an uneasy air, where she heard Lenormand's voice repeating, *I'm sorry, but I can't remember. No, I don't remember.* Several times her cough awoke her; once Eugène complained, "Can't you be quiet, Madi, can't you control yourself?" The daylight had begun to show before she really slept.

When she woke again it was nine o'clock. Eugène had disappeared. He had left the hotel quite early, the porter told her when she went downstairs. No one knew where he had gone.

<h1 style="text-align:center">XXIX</h1>

WHEN Eugène reached the Ministry he found it populated by cleaners. At what time, he asked the concierge, would the director of the personnel department arrive? General Caudebec?—the concierge could not say, but he had never noticed the General arriving before ten o'clock: it was understood that he seldom got to bed before seven in the morning, owing to pressure of business at the Palais Pompeien, and he must have some sleep, poor fellow. Very well, Eugène would wait.

But he did not care to be the cynosure of sweeping-women, and presently he went out into the boulevard and wandered across the river to the Tuileries gardens. The clouds were white and high, the cool air in gentle motion, it was pleasant to be out of doors. He sat down to read the newspaper he had bought in the rue de Solferino, but it seemed to be full of names he had never heard of, there was nothing whatever about Pierre. Some children were playing near his seat, he smiled and called to them. "What is your name?" he asked a little boy. "It is Armand, Monsieur." "Armand? I have a grandson called Armand"; and indeed the boy was not unlike him, "but I'm afraid that he's rather a coward. You're not a coward, are you? You will be ready to fight for France when you're old enough?" "Oh, yes, Monsieur." When the children had run away he got up and walked slowly towards the avenue Paul Déroulède. A woman passed him whom he seemed to recognize; it was surely Mlle Longavenne; but she ignored his bow, and he remembered then that Mlle Longavenne would look much older; perhaps there was no one left in Paris who knew him now. Paris had changed, it had lost its elegance. The women's dress seemed to proclaim the boulevard de Clichy, the men were dowdy, the streets screamed with innumerable motor-cars. But here he caught the scent of hyacinths, and looking up at the rearing horses of the Arc du Carrousel, bold on the white sky, he was glad to have come back. It had belonged to him, this city, and in this season there was a tender pleasure in passing through it as spirits pass again. He turned about and made his way towards the Orangerie. He was not, he thought, unrecognized; some of the people passing turned their heads for a second glance at the soldierly old man in the dress of a past decade; and to those who were decent in appearance he raised his hat, and smiled with politeness, and austerely bowed.

He rested twice, and arriving at the quay again found it was already after ten. He hurried back to the Boulevard St. Germain.

An *agent* was on duty now in the vestibule of the Ministry, and inquired his business.

"General Caudebec," Eugène said, "is he in now?"

"I will find out, Monsieur. You have an appointment?"

"No, it will not be necessary."

He took a card from his case, wrote beneath his name "ancien Colonel du 57e," and above, "affaire pressante."

The agent thumbed the card doubtfully.

"I can't say, Monsieur, that———"

"Be good enough to send my card up to General Caudebec at once!" Eugène barked.

"Very well, Monsieur."

*

General Caudebec was in ebullient humour. The delicious Albertine had written to say she thought the night-gown charming and would send him a photograph showing it in use; the further stages in his campaign were a matter of routine which, however familiar, could never bore a simple-hearted and romantic soldier. When Deboust, after a good deal of nervous knocking, crept into the office, Caudebec welcomed him with sunny cordiality.

"Sit down, Deboust, empty your troubles on the desk, I am ready for anything to-day, I should like better than anything in the world to have an artillery engagement with the Supplies Department."

Deboust handed him Eugène's card, by this time creased and covered with finger-marks.

"It's only this. I thought perhaps I ought to bring it to you; Savoureux says that the bearer is making himself a nuisance."

Caudebec held the card at arm's length, wrinkling his eyes. He said, "Séverin . . . Séverin . . . Séverin?" The telephone rang. "See what that is, Deboust." He put the card down on the desk and watched it as if he expected it to jump. Deboust was saying, "No, General Caudebec will not answer private calls, no, he never breaks that rule——" "Here, give me that, you fool," Caudebec broke in. He grabbed the receiver, "Wait, Exchange, wait a minute, find out who that is! It may be someone important. Yes? Mlle Tasserie? Yes, yes, put her through. . . . Deboust, shut off the outside wire, will you? And you'd better see this Séverin, find out what he wants, tell him I've had a heart-attack and died last night, give him a cigar and a lottery-ticket, anything within reason. . . . Albertine? Yes, Madame, we have received your letter . . . yes yes, Deboust, you can go, get along with you. . . . But, my precious. . . ."

Deboust repeated to himself as he went to his own office, "Séverin . . . Séverin?" It came back to him at last. Yes, of course, it was a Captain Pierre Séverin, the man who had disappeared from Sigumbe, who was apparently a deserter; and this, naturally, would be the father. Well, it was a damnable nuisance, when he didn't know which way to turn, with the work of three men to be got through every day. Why hadn't Savoureux dealt with the fellow himself? He waited for a few moments—it would not be dignified to admit a visitor too quickly—before he rang.

"You can bring up Colonel Séverin now. One minute! First of all go across to the Overseas Administration and ask to borrow the file relating to Captain Pierre Séverin."

Eugène, tired and confused by the long corridors, was glad to take the chair which Deboust offered him.

"General Caudebec?" he asked.

"Well, no, Monsieur, General Caudebec is engaged this morning; I am his confidential assistant, I interview all important callers. . . .

You will smoke a cigar, Monsieur? I am very sorry, Colonel Séverin, but I am unable to give you any new information about your son. I made inquiries when your card was brought to me, but I find that so far no new information has come through. You will, of course, be advised by telegraph as soon as any good news comes. I need hardly tell you that we here have been gravely concerned. Naturally we are bound, until we have the means of making a fuller inquiry, to accept officially as our hypothesis the one which has been formed by the officer commanding at Sigumbe. . . ."

Eugène tapped his stick on the floor.

"You mean by that that my son is accused of desertion?"

Deboust was taken aback. Surely the old gentleman must know?

"The word 'accused,' Colonel Séverin, is not the one which I myself would have employed. Indeed, I hardly think——"

Eugène waved his hand. "All right, all right, I have no wish to discuss that matter with you, sir." He turned his chair to face the window. "I shall wait until General Caudebec is ready."

Deboust stood up.

"You must forgive me, Monsieur, but I have already told you that General Caudebec——"

The door swung open and Caudebec, holding a yellow flimsy in one hand and banging it with the other, marched into the room. "Upon my soul, Deboust, for sheer crass imbecility this chit of Madargent's—oh—I didn't realize! . . . You will please report to me, Captain, as soon as you are free."

Eugène had risen.

"General Caudebec?" he asked.

Deboust intervened:

"Colonel Séverin has been inquiring whether we have any news of Captain Pierre Séverin, his son. I have told him——"

"Young Séverin?" Caudebec said heartily. "Doing very well, a capital officer——"

He had reached the door, but Eugène stopped him.

"You will excuse me, Monsieur! I am of course entirely prepared to await your convenience, but it is important that I should have an interview as soon as——"

Caudebec eyed Colonel Séverin sharply. It was his reasonably founded boast that whenever he saw a face for the second time he could give it the name and regiment; he was certain he had not seen this man before. "You will find," he said, "that Captain Deboust, my confidential assistant, will be able——"

Eugène mildly raised his eyebrows. "Formerly," he said, "I was not required to interview subordinates. And as my business is of a private nature . . ."

The last words made Caudebec a little uneasy; old men of this

266

type sometimes turned out to be the fathers of young women, and he would not care for Deboust to witness an undignified debate. Anxious as he was to tell Deboust at length what he thought of Madargent's latest ineptitude, he decided that he must get this business over. "Come along, Colonel," he said briskly, "come along!" As the door was closing behind Eugène he called back, "Deboust! You'll get those papers I asked you for?" Deboust understood: "At once, sir."

★

Sitting in his own office, General Caudebec did not appear to be greatly oppressed with business. His desk, like that of Deboust, was covered by wire baskets crammed with papers; but the General, with his hands locked behind his neck, his shoulders falling as far back as the uncompromising chair allowed, seemed as little aware of the paraphernalia before him as a sated diner of the dessert and glasses. To Eugène he appeared a very young man for his post, and most unsoldierly; but shrewd perhaps, with those eyes which wandered unconcernedly and all at once were brought to focus sharply on his face, not a man to be treated without caution. He was talking, as if to pass the time, with a certain dilettante charm: of the changes in women's dress, of the remarkable way that Fernand Maubec's pastels seemed to catch the feeling of a Paris spring. Trying to show a semblance of polite attention, Eugène struggled to remember what he had come to say. This morning, as he woke, it had been straightforward, and now he was lost in a cloud of confusion.

Suddenly, while Caudebec was still talking, Eugène found his voice.

"I realize," he said gravely, "that for you this is a very anxious time."

Caudebec's eyes swivelled round again. Anxious? Eugène saw the look and thought he understood it.

"I am something of a student of foreign affairs," he continued. "An old soldier must find something to do, and I have been engaged for some years on historical work—which is not yet completed. Naturally I pay close attention to current happenings, and I have, perhaps, the means to interpret the trend of affairs rather more acutely than those without a military training. . . ."

Caudebec had one hand pressed against Deboust's bell; he put the other in front of his mouth. So the old gentleman belonged to that school, to the all-too-numerous body of intelligent citizens who came every day to report that there were spies lurking under all the seats in the métro.

"I think I can tell you truthfully," he said with studied gravity, "that not only in my own Department but throughout the Ministry

267

we are watching the trend of events more closely than we have ever done before; that our work is guided from hour to hour by the reports which reach us of every change in the European situation. I am speaking in strict confidence—you will understand that I should not say this to anyone but an officer of high rank and known discretion—when I tell you that we have in this Department a complete and detailed programme which we are ready at any moment, yes, at an hour's notice, to put into operation. . . ." Deboust was standing at the door. "Deboust, I think Colonel Séverin left his hat and stick in your office?"

Deboust placed a box-file on the desk. "Those are the papers you require, sir. The note on top will give you the information in précis. . . . Yes, sir, I will fetch them at once."

But Eugène had not finished. He took his hat and stick and waited till Deboust had gone. Then, standing by his chair, he began again.

"I shall only take five minutes more of your time, Monsieur." He cleared his throat again. Caudebec saw that he was trembling. "I have come here to offer myself to France. I do not intend to dispute any further the verdict which the Court upheld. All is past now, I have decided to press my cause no further, I shall leave it to history to assess the justice of my degradation. All I ask for now is the opportunity to do my country service. I do not insist on the restoration of my former rank, I am ready, if authority thinks proper, to serve as a junior officer. I do not think that at this time France will refuse to be served by one who formerly did well for her, simply because a verdict was once held against him by a civilian tribunal. I make no conditions Monsieur. At this crisis I offer myself, my experience, my powers, to France."

Caudebec rang furiously for Deboust. He coughed, he rubbed his thumb along the back of his middle finger. He stammered: "I am sure, Colonel Séverin, that I speak for the Chief of Staff as well as for myself when I say that I am much—that we are much moved by your—by your patriotism and generosity. . . ." He raised the lid of the file and glanced at the first paragraph of the summary: *disobedience to definite orders . . . contemptible cowardice. . . .* Good God! "Your generous proposal will be put on record immediately, and will be brought to the notice of the Chief of Staff himself. And if the occasion arises when we are able to take advantage of the services you offer, I shall not fail to advise you immediately."

He rose and shook Eugène's hand. "Once again, Monsieur, speaking with pride as one Frenchman to another, I most warmly thank you."

He nodded to Deboust, who was holding the door open.

Eugène stared through his tears, seeing Caudebec a long way off.

"But I mean——" he began. "My meaning is—I am ready now, at once——"

The telephone rang and Caudebec took hold of it. "You will excuse me, Monsieur. . . . No, Michel, I am very sorry, dinner is impossible, I am snowed under with work. . . ."

Deboust picked up the gloves which Eugène had dropped on the floor and led him with calculated ceremony along the corridor.

★

The boulevard was misted, he didn't know where to go. The *agent* on the steps of the Ministry hailed a motor cab for him.

"The hotel," Eugène said.

"Which hotel, Monsieur?"

"I don't know, I've forgotten. Take me to the station."

"The station?"

He didn't know which station. But he found a ticket in the pocket of his waistcoat and showed it to the driver, who nodded.

"I understand, Monsieur, the Gare de l'Est."

XXX

THE increasing warmth, the lengthening of daylight, had brought to Baulon a measured reassurance. They remembered once again how often the town had trembled with the shock of rumours, that the starting of false scares was by tradition their staple trade. The news from Paris was again alarming, but no worse as far as one remembered than it had been last April. Almost every week the Comité d'Action Artisanale had reminded its members that foreign alarms were the common antidote to the expression of domestic grievance; but much more persuasive was the disappearance of both fog and snow. In a Baulon winter anything might happen; the town's emergence into spring seemed a reminder that security rewarded patience; surely there could be no disturbance of the brisk normality to which they had returned. There were those who watched the sunlit bustle of the streets with derisive eyes. So! the Baulonnais had decided that they were safe again, now that the trees in the Parc Rousseau began to show new leaves; that their fears had been fantastic, the cultured souls across the Rhine would never engage in anything so disorderly, so inhumane as warfare in such charming weather: but they for the most part were the old men, who would rather be deprived of food and drink than of the opportunity for grim prognostication, or sallow-eyed intelligentsia, men like that twisted weed Vasseur, who if the generality chanced to reach their way of thinking would scamper off at once in a new direction. The anxiety had not all gone; but with the spring the Duvauchelle bonnet had come from Paris to enchant all Baulon, and already preparations were in full swing for the Summer Gala of the Ligue de Familles Nombreuses du Quartier Ste Estelle; for a space the familiar, anxious leitmotiv was only faintly audible beneath the arpeggio of reprieve.

That lingering sense of unreality was in the cafés and along the river banks, in the sunless alleys of Saint François and the poplared avenues of Sacré Cœur. To the tenement-dwellers of the place Talleyrand it was an unwelcome portent that the Séverins would not settle down. The Colonel had returned and the old Russian lady with him, but now he had gone off again with Mme Séverin and his sister, to Paris it was understood. "They want him at Paris," Barbier had darkly stated to Louvel the polisher in the rue des Suisses, and it got about before the cafés closed that Colonel Séverin was there in readiness to superintend a sudden mobilization. So half the windows in 17 were shuttered and the house had more than ever the air of having been deserted. The Russian lady had gone back to bed, so Gaston told them; to continue, they supposed, her interrupted course of dying. Young Mlle Séverin they saw as usual every morning, with a shock of books in a strap beneath her arm, hurrying with her ungainly stride to catch her tram in the boulevard Alsace; and sometimes now, when the sun cast deliberate shadows from the scaffolding across the Square, the children they had watched last autumn would appear again, the foreign woman pushing the little girl in a tiny cabrouet, the boy walking solemnly behind. For the little girl the people of the Square had some affection, she would smile to them and lift her skirt like an enfant-de-ballet and wave her hand. But the boy paid no attention when other children called to him, he was a Séverin to the bone; and the sickly woman who looked after them, she was always half asleep. At all events it was a comfort that the Séverins, who must know as well as any what was going on, had thought it safe to leave the children. Perhaps it was true that the troubles which had filled the air all winter had passed away, with the winter fog. Dr. Tischer thought so, he had actually looked more cheerful since the Séverins went away, and had promised at his own expense to take a dozen Talleyrand children to the Fête des Familles Nombreuses. It was pleasant to be reasonably warm; children could be sent out to the pavement so that their elders had more leg-room, clothes no longer required such careful patching. Perhaps the builders would come back soon and get on with the factory. Then they could be sure that things were all right again.

But as yet there was no sign of the builders, and from an upper window you could see right through the scaffolding to the backs of houses in the rue Sablonnière. The snow had thawed and the poles were nude again as they had been in autumn. A bucket was hanging at a tilt from one of the transverse spars; there was still a builder's oiseau on the platform, resting against an upright as the workmen had chanced to leave it; the notice *"samedi à six h."* still swung obliquely on a knotted cord. This was the spectacle, transience made permanent, that Renée saw when she opened the nursery shutters every morning. And now the poles stretched into a clean sky, and the air was gentle in her nostrils, but scented faintly from the tanneries in the faubourg Troisième Pont. That odour, reaching her first on the night she came here, had been carried off by an adverse wind and stifled underneath the fog. Returning, it had the quick familiarity of time long past and in the interval forgotten, and now she felt as if each month had been a year's endurance. Nothing had changed: the children of the Square had hardly grown older, the same carts sauntered through each morning, old Papa Verrou with his matted whiskers and searching, philosophic eyes still sat outside on his little stool with his crutches propped against the wall. She woke in the morning slowly, her mind rising with reluctance to a higher layer of consciousness, and her waking seemed to be incomplete, as if she had not yet broken free from the realm of illusion. The objects coming by degrees into her sentience were round and solid, Sophie's voice was plain to her hearing, the square, the scaffolding appeared in bold perspective; yet by their very closeness the things she saw and felt possessed an unreality, like the formidable images in a night's first dream. She stretched her hand to touch the bedpost and was surprised to feel it. Crossing the Square she closed her eyes and shivered, fancying she could wrestle free from the pinioning deception. But the little shops in the rue des Suisses had still the same appearance; she turned the corner, the tramcars rattled in the boulevard; the dream was whole and concrete, there was no way out.

No letter, nothing in the papers, no news. "You needn't worry," Raymond had said, "I know Pierre. He knows how to do things, Pierre does, he'll get through somehow." She had answered slowly: "Get through? . . . And what will happen then?" But she had almost ceased believing in the chance of his getting through. She heard his voice sometimes, when she sat alone in the evening, faintly, as if it came from the waking world from which her dream withheld her. She would open the door, trembling, and once she saw him in the shadowed corridor, standing with his back against the wall; but his face eluded her and he would not answer when she called to him, "Pierre, Pierre, where are you?" She realized then how Baulon had ceased to be strange to her; they had grown familiar, normal—the smell, the scaffolding, the noises in the Square; normal, hardening, to permanence, a concrete loneliness. Into this narrow, twilight world he would never find his way, her Pierre of fibrous flesh on knotted muscle, with eyes that were always cynical except when they smiled at her. Pierre in his faded uniform, with his sinewy, hirsute wrists, smelling of baked flannel and the smoke of a cartridge lately fired.

★

In the evenings Angèle cried again, lonely for her master. It was frightening to have the house so empty. Marianne stayed in her own room, where Sophie was often with her. If Barbier came upstairs to talk to Renée and the children, Joséphine would follow and shout for him; and except for Angèle's howling there was nothing to break the silence of the house but Gaston's staggering footsteps as he made his periodic journey to Mme Nadya's room. Despite her fears, Renée was glad to be by herself. Her ears listened for Pierre's voice, and she seemed a little closer to him when she was quite alone.

But on the second evening Mme Poupoulet made some excuse to visit her, and profiting by Renée's bare politeness became established in the wicker chair. Her husband was busy with the Colombophiles; it was sad, she said, to have no company but her own, Mme Séverin must forgive her but it got upon her nerves, the dog howling. Yes, she would be grateful for a cup of coffee if it were made very weak. She had put on her hat to come upstairs and she sat in polite discomfort on the edge of her chair, churning her coffee with the little spoon, her eyes shining with tears. Renée, watching her sad face with impatient pity, saw that she was much older than the style of her dress would show; it was a child's face with the skin grown old and mottled, its shape unaltered, the eyes expressing still a childish innocence. She was surprised when Mme Poupoulet began to talk.

"We have been wanting to tell you, M. Poupoulet and I, how we sympathize with you in your great trouble. We read about it in the newspaper, we both wept when we heard that it was your husband who was the deserter. 'It is not at all impossible,' I said to M. Poupoulet, 'that in spite of the disgrace Mme Pierre Séverin still loves her husband.' If that is so it must be very hard for you. I wanted to tell you how tenderly I feel for you, it is as if a daughter of my own had been disgraced. You will understand . . . but perhaps I should not have spoken, I am too much a stranger, you may think, to have spoken on such a matter. It is only that my sympathy is so great. . . ."

Renée's sudden anger had already turned to a kind of pity.

"It has been anxiety for me, yes," she said. "But no, I do not think about it very much, it seems to have happened a long time ago. I have my children, they occupy my time and thoughts."

"But you have heard nothing?" Mme Poupoulet pursued. "Perhaps I ought not to ask, but I feel for you so much, I can picture what it would be like if M. Poupoulet disappeared from the bank in a disgraceful way; I want so much to know if you have any news of your husband, if anything——"

Renée said: "No. No, at present there isn't any news, I hardly expect it. It is fairly evident that my husband fell into the hands of hostile tribesmen and it is very unlikely that they would preserve his life."

"But how——?"

"Of the charge of desertion I know nothing. It seems to me to be slenderly founded, but it is useless to argue such matters. In military circles there can never be any argument—I fancy that my father-in-law will tell you that. And my husband, as I say, has probably perished now, so there will be no one to contradict what the military authorities say. . . . Is your coffee finished? I have plenty here in the jug."

Mme Poupoulet had been shocked out of all her shyness.

"But, Mme Séverin—no, no, thank you, no more coffee—but, Mme Sevérin, what are you going to do? You have your children to bring up, to be educated, you will want to have a house of your own. Unless your husband's death is proved you cannot marry again, and I suppose that as he was a deserter there will be no pension and there will be money difficulties. I understand that M. Séverin is by no means wealthy. It will be hard for you, with the two children to bring up all by yourself; children are much more difficult when there is no father. It's terrible, it is a tragedy. . . ."

Renée took away Mme Poupoulet's cup and poured the coffee she had left back into the jug. With her back to Mme Poupoulet she said, "Yes, one is involved by the loss of a husband in many inconveniences. And now, it you will excuse me, Madame Poupoulet, I must go and see if Armand is asleep."

*

Armand had his arms round the pillow and his lips were smiling. He often smiled when he slept. She put the candle where it would not shine against his face and sat to watch him. When he was awake she did not care to watch him often or too closely, fearing he would be puzzled by her curiosity; but at night she would sometimes sit here for an hour. If he chanced to wake he was only glad to see her, and when she kissed him he would shut his eyes again and fall asleep. That was a sign, she thought, that he was getting better.

He was more than ever like Pierre. He had become less sluggish in his movements, and Renée could see Pierre in him when he turned his head to answer a question, Pierre's impatience in the way he tugged the laces, his thin wrists very strong, to do up his boots. But he had increasingly a quality that was not Pierre's, a feminine grace in his endearments. Pierre, when he was most affectionate, was always stiff and solemn; he would light a cigarette, striking the match against his boot in the manner of the poilus, he would pull at his beard-skin, jerk back his elbows to spread his chest, and then betray himself by grasping her shoulder and giving it a little shake, by the sudden lighting of his queer, deep smile. In the days of his early passion, when they had courted flagrantly in the alcoves of Mme Einzel's café at Cherchel, he had often been seized by a passing embarrassment and sat for a while with his eyes away from her, nodding to answer her questions as he would in giving some permission to a corporal. Armand could never be like that. He was sometimes dreamy, he had not recovered altogether from his chronic lethargy. But now that he was so much better, he always pulled his chair close up to hers to stretch and stroke her arm; often he followed her about the room, and would wait with a touching patience if she were too preoccupied to suffer his embraces. He had begun to be attentive to her needs, he frequently surprised her by his quickness in seeing what she wanted, a spoon for her coffee or a footstool. He spoke very little, content to let Sophie chatter; but every day, it seemed, he smiled more often. For three weeks now he had been without a cold; his appearance was wan and sickly beside that of children in the Square, but Dr. Tischer said that that would alter now she could take him out of doors.

Already he was rewarding her enduring patience; she had fanned the life in him with the steady breath of her devotion. And now, while she dreaded to release him from her constant grasp, she was afraid of being so important in his scene. Her own physique had not yet answered to returning summer, again and again she had a struggle to get out of bed and begin the day. Added to her work of teaching and caring for the children there was the commission for babaresque embroidery she had undertaken when she sold her dresses back to Peulevey; that meant an average of four hours every day; and the thought continually hung over her, "I can last perhaps for two, three weeks, perhaps another month." Before she had added, "until Pierre comes," and now it was no use to count on his ever coming. If she should be ill, unable to get out of bed?—and it was no rare thing for those accustomed to hotter latitudes to die from a European winter. She wanted Armand to love her as he did and yet to be self-sufficient, to command himself, to be another Pierre. Not rash and headstrong as Pierre was, but having all Pierre's assurance, Pierre's unconscious valour. When Pierre came back—no use, no use, she could not banish that delusion—when Pierre came back she wanted Armand to be as he would have him.

Armand's arm was stretched out over the side of the bed. She gently held his wrist and kissed his hand. He did not wake, but she thought his smile grew wider. It was so small, that hand of Armand's. She would not have strength to go with him much farther, and he had so far to go.

★

It was Armand, next afternoon, who saw the cab arriving. Sophie had complained of headache and been put to bed. "Someone is coming, Mother," Armand said. And then, while she sat with her heart furiously beating, faintly: "It's Grandfather." They heard the hall door opening and Eugène's voice: "Barbier! I want you to pay this cab." Then Angèle's excited, asthmatic barking as he came up slowly to the first floor. Already Armand was frightened, and Renée had to hold his hand. "It's all right, Armand, he won't be coming up here." But very shortly they heard his steps again.

Eugène stopped when he reached the second stage and seemed to hesitate. Then he came uncertainly along the corridor. He called roughly: "Madeleine! Are you up here?" Armand drew back into a corner; he was trembling with fear. "It's all right, Armand," Renée said again. "Grandfather won't do anything to hurt you, I shall be here." Eugène had reached the door now. She opened it and let him in.

He stood by the table and looked all round the room. Renée stood opposite so that he should not see Armand; but Eugène was not looking for him.

"Where is Madeleine?" he asked. "Do you know where my wife is? She's not in the drawing-room."

Renée was frightened by his eyes; they were moving all the time, and he hardly seemed to see her.

"But has she come back from Paris?"

He was startled into concentration. He stared at Renée, puzzling. "From Paris?" Then, "Of course, yes, she is still in Paris. No doubt she wished to do some shopping, she knows that I am quite able to travel alone. . . ."

But he was still confused, like one who has lost his way in a country where he cannot speak the language. He had grown much older, she thought, in the few days that he had been away; he was holding the table and breathing shortly as if he had climbed a steep hill.

She said: "Won't you sit down, Grandpère? Would you like me to get you something to eat?"

He sat down. He nodded. "Yes, I would like something. What? I don't mind. No, I haven't had anything—some coffee this morning, perhaps, I don't remember. Some soup, yes, that will do."

She had some stock in her cupboard with a few vegetables. She brought them to the table with a knife and chopping board. He did not speak while she was getting the soup ready, but when she had put it on the stove he asked if there had been a telegram from Paris. "I am expecting a telegram," he said, "from the War Office. It is very important, it may come at any time. I shall want to see it directly it comes, I have to be ready to return to Paris at a moment's notice. You're quite sure that no telegram has come?"

"No, I'm certain."

She helped him to take off his overcoat and moved his chair nearer to the stove. He was quite submissive, like a sleepy child. "After luncheon," he said, "I shall want some paper. I have to get plans all ready for the mobilization of a hundred thousand men. In Paris they do not realize the gravity of the situation; it's very important that I should have detailed plans to put into operation directly they call on me."

She tasted the soup with her own spoon; perhaps a little too much paprika, but it was quite good. Eugène would only take half what she had made. He asked for cheese and coffee, and drummed his fingers impatiently while she was getting them ready. "I must lose no time," he said again. When he had drunk the coffee he closed his eyes and dozed for twenty minutes. Waking, he asked: "Is Madeleine back yet? What am I to do? I can't do everything for myself." She sent Armand to get his slippers and took off his boots for him. "It's kind of you," he said then.

Armand had gone back to his corner and crouched there with his eyes turning fearfully towards his grandfather and back again to Renée. Perhaps Eugène would like to go to bed, Renée suggested; she could ring for Barbier to come and help him. No, he would wait till Madeleine came, he didn't care to be by himself. She moved him into the wicker chair and brought a quilt to put over his knees. He seemed quite helpless and content for her to move him as she wished. "The journey has been tiring?" she asked. "Yes," he said, "yes, it's tiring, that kind of thing."

It was only for Armand's sake that she wished to be rid of Eugène. She could hardly believe now that she had ever been scared of him. He seemed to be comfortable there, with the stove warming him, though still bewildered; a very old man who only wanted to be peaceful, to be cared for. She had brought the pen and paper that he wanted, but he couldn't see well enough to write, he said, and his hand was shaky after the journey. She offered to write for him but he preferred to wait till Madeleine came. "My wife," he said, "always helps me with that kind of thing." He asked twice again, like a child expecting a present. "You're sure there's been no telegram?" His mouth, which as a rule he kept tightly shut, was open, and he was gently dribbling. He did not seem to mind when she brought a handkerchief and wiped his chin. "I'm tired out," he said, "I had such a busy time in Paris. The people there are stupid, it's very hard to make them understand you." He shivered. "It's cold," he said, "I shall go to bed as soon as Madeleine comes."

She brought up a footstool and arranged the cushion behind his shoulders in the way that Pierre liked to have it. Presently he noticed Armand.

He called to him very softly, "Armand, won't you come and talk to me?"

Armand shrank back and lowered his head. Renée said: "Won't you talk to your grandfather, Armand?" but he was deaf to her as to Eugène.

"He is shy, the little one," Eugène said kindly. "Don't let us bother him. He is like Pierre, Pierre was always a shy boy. He gave us a lot of trouble, Pierre did. He was a difficult boy, it was useless to thrash him." Something seemed to cross his mind then. He screwed his eyes and joggled his head as if it were a dice-box. But the memory he wanted would not turn up. "You have met Pierre, my elder son?" he asked her. "He is a soldier, my elder boy. He has been for a long time with the Colonial Infantry, it suits him, that rough-and-tumble soldiering. We never hear much about him now."

He was still worried because the thought that had brushed his mind would come no closer. And before long he told her to ring for Barbier; he was tired and would go to bed.

★

Half an hour after Eugène had gone, Barbier came back to her.

"The Colonel wants you to go and see him," he said. He was grave and worried. "The Colonel's in a bad state," he told her, "I've not often seen him so bad, I cannot understand how Madame came to let him travel alone."

Renée did not want to leave the children or to see Eugène. "*It was useless to thrash Pierre*"—that had been sufficient to quench her passing tenderness.

"Do you think, Barbier, that I must go to him?"

He nodded. "He would be upset if you didn't go. We can't let anything upset him, when Madame isn't here and he's so poorly. I wanted to get Dr. Tischer but he wouldn't hear of it. 'I don't want that old goat, you're not to bring him'—that's what he said."

Renée was angry. "That's nonsense, Barbier, If M. Séverin is really ill we must get the doctor, whatever he says. Yes, I'll see him myself."

Eugène lay on his back, very still. Barbier had turned down the gas and Renée, standing a few feet from the bed, saw his face in heavy shadow. The exertion of getting to bed had made his breathing worse and he spoke haltingly.

"Is that Renée?" he said. "Your name is Renée, that's right, isn't it? Of course, I remember; I'm an old man but my memory isn't as bad as that. Come here, Renée, come close to the bed, I want to hold your hand. Ah! It's nice and warm. I want you to stay with me for a little while. I can't go to sleep as early as this, it's lonely being all by myself. I can't think why Madeleine doesn't come, I thought she would come on a later train. It's the shops, you can't get a woman away from the shops in Paris. You're sure she hasn't come? And there's no telegram? I'm expecting a telegram from the War Office, it may come at any moment. Bring up a chair, I want you to sit down, I want you to sit close to me so that I can hold your hand, then I won't be so lonely."

He was gathering breath while she brought a chair, and for several minutes he was silent, with his eyes closed, so that she thought he had gone off to sleep. But his grip on her hand suddenly tightened; she was astonished that he had so much strength.

"I want to know," he said urgently, "tell me, how long is it since you heard anything of Pierre?"

She would not be troubled to prevaricate.

"A long time," she told him, "a very long time. The fact——"

He turned over on to his side so that he could look at her face.

"It's true, then, what they told me at Paris? Pierre is missing, he—he deserted?"

She nodded. "Yes, that is true. Pierre wanted to come back to me, he knew I needed him, he decided that that was the easiest way. It was rash of him. . . ."

"Why didn't you tell me?" he asked pathetically. "Why haven't I been told before?"

"It was my affair," she said.

He did not seem to hear that answer. She felt his hand trembling.

"I don't understand," he said feebly, "I can't make it out, Pierre doing that. He isn't a coward, Pierre, he was a troublesome boy but he wasn't a coward. With Raymond I would not be

278

surprised, he's nothing but a Pichy. I have always thought of Pierre as a Séverin. And I tell you"—his voice was rising—"a Séverin can't do anything like that, there is no grain of cowardice in the Séverin———"

"I have told you already," Renée said calmly, "that Pierre acted as he thought best in my interest. I wrote to him———"

"You mean, you put him up to it———?"

She hesitated. She wanted above all things to maintain her dignity, to avoid the cheaper sort of lie; but it was useless to explain things to one in Eugene's condition. She said:

"Practically."

He nodded. "I see." He was smiling, as a marionette smiles when it is operated clumsily, the corners of the mouth held too tightly and revealing too much of the gums. "You persuaded Pierre to act as a coward, and now you are trying to make the little boy—that Armand of yours into a coward too? That is why I am never allowed to see him, hein? Ah, yes, my little Renée, my pretty moricaude, we are coming to the truth now."

She stood up and tried to draw away. "There is no advantage in discussing the matter. . . ." But his grip was stronger than she supposed, he pulled her lower, hurting her hand.

"No, no, don't go away," he whispered. "I'm not going to hurt you, I only want you to stay here so that I shan't be lonely. You can lie on the bed, then you'll be quite comfortable. Listen, my dear. Have you ever thought how it feels to me, I who regard the soldier's as the highest of all virtues, to be told that my son is a coward, a deserter; to find that my grandson is too timid even to speak to me? Listen, keep still! I was at Paris—you may not know—to negotiate an affair of honour. There was a slander— it was a long time ago, but it has not been put right yet—a slander upon my virtue, my courage. I went to Paris to uphold my good name, the good name of the Séverins. And what did they say, the attorneys in Paris? Here, they said, is the father of a deserter, of a coward; here is a man whose son ran away from some piffling gang of negroes, and he comes to us to try and vindicate his own courage. That was nice for me, wasn't it? Everywhere I went, in the hotel, in the streets, people were nudging each other and pointing at me. 'That is the father of Pierre Séverin, the deserter.' Yes, and now I am left all by myself to recover the good name of my family, I have to make my own courage do for my son's which you have destroyed and for my grandson's which you are sapping from the roots. You, who have made me the laughing-stock of Paris———"

"That's enough," she said, "I won't listen to that kind of talk. As for Pierre———"

But he kept his hold on her wrist. "You," he said, "you

little half-caste bitch, I'll show you who's going to get the better——"

She lost her nerve. She shouted: "Barbier?"

He let her go at once. "It's all right," he said, "it's all right, Renée, it's all right, my dear, I shan't hurt you. I'm a lonely old man, I haven't anyone who really cares for me and understands me. But I'm not beaten, oh, no, they haven't beaten Eugène Séverin. No, you're not quite as clever as you think, you won't have it all your own way with my son and with Armand. Don't go away. Renée! Renée, come here, don't leave me all alone."

XXXI

THÉRÈSE had a letter from Louis at the beginning of May. She noticed that it was postmarked Vienna. She despised that place. She had played there once at the Wittelsbach-theater, in Calderon's *Médecin*; the train had arrived two hours late after a long delay in the suburbs for which there was no explanation; her dressing-room had been draughty and badly lighted, the house had applauded her reputation, missing every subtlety, and been still more enthusiastic about De Franceschi, who was petite and souriante. They were a superficial people, the Viennese, with an invincible frivolity; they liked to see nice dresses and to hear pretty tunes; they admired and doted upon artists simply because artists entertained them; in the hotel she had occupied, where the stucco walls were larded with bad copies of Nurillo and none of the doors exactly fitted, a spotty girl had asked if she were acquainted with the acrobatic dancer, Jean d'Auvray. . . . Thérèse smelt the envelope; yes, she thought she recognized the characteristic odour of Vienna: vegetables and varnish. She wheeled her chair back a little to get nearer the light; not easily, for of late the neuritis in her left arm had become more serious; and opening the letter read: "Titi chérie, . . ." How absurd of poor Louis! He had never changed that opening, and the petit-nom had been dead for fifty years. She put aside the first page, which was sure to be concerned with her own legs and Louis's stomach, and went on at the top of the second.

". . . no little anxiety. Here I find that everyone is discussing the possibility of some military enterprise in the Balkans, which in general seems to be contemplated with the keenest appetite. That by itself would not be worth much attention, for the Austrians are always talkative and always enthusiastic about something, and this kind of chatter has been going on for a long time. But Herr

Josef Weingartner, who is a highly respected member of the business community and with whom I have certain stock-exchange dealings, has informed me confidentially that acting on political information he is selling out the whole of his interest in a tobacco concern at Rysbroeck at a loss of 34 per cent on the purchase price in November last. Weingartner is not a man to drop 34 per cent on a large holding without substantial reason, and the significance of his action seems to me too serious to be ignored. . . . It has always been recognized that in the event of an European crisis the position of Baulon will be extremely grave; and I should be very much happier if Eugène could be persuaded to remove his household to some less vulnerable part of the country. . . . I am, of course, ready to give Eugène free choice of locality, my only stipulation being that the house must be reasonably small and one that can be inhabited without extravagance. Business is increasingly difficult, and it will be impossible—so M. Lecours informs me—to sell the present house at anything but a nominal price; I understand, moreover, that t.c. insurance rates on all estate in the Baulon district are likely to be advanced by as much as 28 per cent in the near future. You will realize, then, that it is quite impossible for me to maintain Eugène in an extravagant style. . . . I am writing this to you because I think that you will be able to put the matter before Eugène and Madeleine in a way that is reasonable and will not cause them undue alarm. . . ."

So! It was not often that Thérèse got anything so useful from Louis. She held a block of preference shares in a printing house at Brussels; it was only a matter of twenty thousand Belgian francs, but she had always been careful about her smaller investments. She worked across to her desk and wrote to Braquehais: "I want to take up securities to the value of $5,000 in Union Pacific Second Debentures if available not higher than 114½. Please advise me by return if you can realize the necessary amount by disposing of my holding in the S.A. des Imprimeries Eckendorff. I suggest offering separately in five groups, and I believe that the extra commissions will be outweighed by the advantage in price. I shall expect you to use some discretion and intelligence in handling this business." She rang for Barbier. "Barbier, I want you to catch the Paris mail with this; you had better send Gaston with it to the Enfants du Roi —tell him not to loiter, he must be there by half-past ten. And then will you go to Madame and say that I shall be greatly obliged if she will spare me a few minutes this morning, as early as she can."

*

But Eugène would not leave Baulon. "Not yet," he said, "it is not time yet for me to go to Paris." There were other places, Madeleine suggested; they might live in the country, Eugène had onec been fond of the country scene; or perhaps on the Mediterranean coast, where the climate was so gentle—Dr. Tischer had agreed that that would be good for all of them. "I don't know those places," Eugène said, "and at my time of life you want to live in some place that you know. Baulon is much pleasanter now that we are through the winter, it is really a healthy place, it is for that reason that my grandfather came to live here." But chiefly he wanted to be ready for the telegram which might come at any moment from Paris; from Baulon he could get to Paris quickly, and when the telegram came there must be no delay. His trunk was kept ready packed, with his old uniform and equipment, with a month's necessities. And he had his work to do, which allowed, he said, no time for the business of moving. He worked every morning; Madeleine would prop him up with extra pillows and spread the map of the eastern frontier on a table beside the bed; on this he pondered, and at intervals Madeleine put figures where he directed, with little strokes and arrows in red, violet or green. Each day he made some alteration to his dispositions; Madeleine cut tiny slips of paper to be gummed over the previous symbols and wrote his new figures on top. She did her part skilfully, she had always been nimble-fingered; and with patience that cost her more than she would ever have admitted, for sometimes when she had made one entry he would ponder for a quarter of an hour with his eyes closed before he dictated the next instruction, and if she gave way to her cough it worried him. "I know, my dear, that you can't help that cough, it's a little nervous weakness, we all suffer from some little trouble like that. But if you could try to check it while I'm working—you see, it upsets my train of thought, I have to go right back to the beginning. What was the last figure I gave you? Two battalions? But, my dear, that makes nonsense, you must have misunderstood me. You'll have to gum that over, and then write *Three battalions*. . . . No, no, in green, surely you must realize that that figure has to be in green. . . ."

"It is no good," she said to Thérèse at the end of another week; "Eugène is determined to stay at Baulon. Nothing I can say makes any difference, he is anxious about the telegram from Paris that he is expecting."

"Very well then, I will see him myself. You must arrange a time. That telegram, surely he doesn't really—never mind, I will see him."

Eugène was by no means anxious to see his sister. "I know, she will talk to me about money, she and Louis are exactly the same, money is the only thing that matters to them." But he consented when he heard that she wished to discuss a letter from Lecours. "All right, I will give Thérèse ten minutes, but it mustn't be longer. I have my work to do, and Tischer would not approve of my undergoing the strain of a long interview."

Thérèse was brought downstairs by Barbier and Gaston. Barbier had recommended Joséphine, who was just as strong as Gaston and more reliable, but Thérèse would not have her; she was vindictive, Joséphine, she might do anything. Gaston was made to hold the footboard and went down backwards, giggling all the way, leaving go with one hand when he wanted to wipe his nose; the chair pitched and swayed; Joséphine screamed up the stairs that it was cruelty to make a young boy lift a weight like that. "You look very white, Thérèse," Eugène said as she was wheeled into his room. "Perhaps you don't get enough air in your apartment. I wonder if you ever have a window open?"

"I have had a letter from Louis," Thérèse began; "Madeleine may have told you——"

"From Louis? But I understood it was a letter from Lecours that you wanted to discuss with me."

Thérèse turned her chair so as to get Eugène's face in a better light.

"You needn't go," she said to Madeleine, "unless you wish—— Yes, Eugène, I have had a letter from Lecours. It is chiefly about that farmhouse at Bapaume which belonged to Cousin Alexandre— the matter is quite unimportant. But Lecours just mentions— I thought you would like to know—that he is engaged in new plans for the prosecution of your affair."

Eugène sat up.

"What does he say? Have you got the letter? What does——?"

"No, I haven't got the letter with me. But he gives no particulars, he only mentions the subject in his last paragraph. Naturally he will write to you when he has really begun to do something. For my part I have no great faith in Lecour's manipulations, as you know. The way he handled the Lenormand business was ludicrous; no one but a dunce would have brought that man to Bellefontaine before he had been properly coached."

Madeleine was aghast. There had been no single mention of Lenormand between her and Eugène since her return from Paris. She looked to see how Eugène would suffer Thérèse's bald impertinence, and was relieved when he answered with only moderate acerbity:

"Lecours acted precisely according to my instructions. It happens that by Lenormand's cowardly fear of implicating himself the whole of our cause was betrayed; but I should not have countenanced any other procedure. To you, Thérèse, it may seem peculiar, a soldier's notion of honour; in the Paris green-rooms no doubt they have other ideas——"

"We do not wish to discuss that matter," Madeleine said. "Eugène and I are satisfied that the affair was honourably conducted; that is all we desired."

Thérèse smiled. "So that is what we have been waiting for all these years, for a little affair to be honourably conducted? It is a pity there were no reviews in the newspapers, '*Throughout the scene the performers conducted themselves in a strictly honourable manner.*' For my part——"

"It is my affair, all that," Eugène said sharply, "it concerns no one but me. And if you have come here merely to animadvert——"

"Thérèse, I must remind you," Madeleine said, "that Doctor Tischer will not allow Eugène to have an interview lasting more than ten minutes. It is about some letter from Louis——"

Thérèse smiled again. Dr. Tischer! "I was coming to that," she said, "only Eugène seemed to want to talk about our good friend Lecours. Well, Louis insists on our moving into a smaller house. I really can't blame him, this has always been a most extravagant place to keep up, it is only common sense——"

Eugène nodded to Madeleine. "You see, I told you, whenever Thérèse comes to see me it is about money."

"Yes, but, Eugène, Thérèse has not expressed Louis's meaning properly. He is chiefly anxious——"

Eugène raised his eyebrows.

"Oh, then you know all about it, you've read Louis's letter? I see how it is, there is a little conspiracy among my womenfolk, now that I can't get about. I understood from what you told me that the idea was yours and Tischer's, this plan of moving me out of my old home into some villa at Poitiers or God-knows-where. Now it appears that the scheme comes from Louis and is to save him some money."

"No, Eugène, it is not just to save Louis money. Louis's first concern is for our safety——"

"Safety?"

Thérèse said dryly: "Louis has private intelligence which shows the international situation to be extremely serious. That means that Baulon——"

"So Louis has heard that the international situation is serious! He has indeed! He's a sharp fellow, Louis, he ought to be a diplomat. Of course, to a poor soldier who knows nothing of politics it never occurred that there was any trouble in the wind, it simply never entered my head for a moment——"

Thérèse began to show her exasperation. "The point is, Eugène, that Baulon is no longer a safe place to live in—nearly everyone else in the town has realized that already, nearly everyone has gone —and Louis is offering to bear the expense of our removal to a healthier neighbourhood. To refuse such an offer would be pure folly, you must surely see that."

"Thérèse means," said Madeleine, "that in the interests of us all, especially for you, with the important work you have to do——"

"I agree with you, Thérèse," Eugène said simply. "The offer is too good for you to turn down. It is very thoughtful of Louis, I appreciate his kindness very much. Of course he can afford it, he won't notice the amount involved, it's a bagatelle to a man of his means, but it was very thoughtful of a busy man like Louis to consider our situation. For myself, unfortunately, I am obliged to remain in Baulon. I have promised General Caudebec faithfully to stay at Baulon until I am summoned to the War Office. That may occur any day now. I shall stay in this house for the time being, and if Louis decides that he has to sell it over my head in order to pay for a new motor-car—and of course he has every right to do so, I quite recognize that—then I shall have to find other accommodation. There's a place in the rue des Suisses where Louis lodges his driver when he's here, that would probably do me very well, since I have no false ideas about an officer's dignity. But as for you ladies, why, I think it would be absurd for you not to move elsewhere while the way is open. Oh, yes, my dear, so long as I have Barbier to do one or two things for me I can get along perfectly. Yes, the more I think of it the more I agree with Louis. Baulon is no place for civilians any longer, I should really be very much happier if you were somewhere safe. You too, Thérèse, why shouldn't you go back to Paris and resume your stage-work? —there is nearly always the part of an old woman to be acted in every play; you would have to give up that chair of yours, but no doubt that could be managed with a little scientific massage; in Paris there are very good masseurs. No, no, you could hardly be wheeled about on the stage, that would be just a little too comical! Yes, I would be much easier in my mind if all of you were moved to somewhere perfectly safe. For me it is impossible. General Caudebec insisted that I should not leave Baulon, and a soldier's first business is to obey orders. Yes, my dear, I know they are just over there, the Prussians. But it would not be the first time that I have had a good view of Prussian soldiers. The Prussians can come if they will. Until I receive new orders I remain in Baulon."

*

After all, it did not so much matter. Her life, Thérèse thought, had ended a long time ago, and now that her pleasure was to read the newspaper, to observe from a distance the paraded ironies of event and custom, she was as well off at Baulon as elsewhere. The sustaining hope of Eugène's vindication had died so slowly that she had hardly been aware of its passing. A few years ago—ten years, or more than that?—André Coubronne had written begging her to come back to Paris. "Perhaps you do not realize," he had said, "that when the great days of the Français are discussed—and what else is there to discuss nowadays?—it is always your name, *l'incomparable Séverin*, which is on everybody's lips. Among the younger artists I find many who do not seem to realize that you are still alive. Think of the pleasure, the excitement, if I were to lead you into one of these soirées-de-foyer! It would be like the incarnation of Pallas Athene!" She had replied to him frigidly: "Yes, it would be amusing for you to trundle in the plaster cast of a Greek goddess, rather weighty in the bosom and a trifle mildewed after long storage, and to make it do antics, as if you were Pygmalion or an Italian marionettist. Unfortunately, my dear André, your Parisians decided many years ago that a woman whose brother had run away from the Prussians could hardly be human, much less an artist. I accepted their decision, and until the verdict on my brother's conduct is reversed, as some time I still hope it may be, you will not find me in Paris, in the foyers or elsewhere." And now she had been to Paris and found it vulgarized; there was nothing but the small-talk of politics, at the Richelieu of all places they had been doing a comedy of trivial adulteries by that charlatan Raoul Salvatierra, the most admired actress in the capital was a puppy-faced gamine from Montauban. Yes, it was just as well to have had that glimpse of sober reality. Her portrait in the rôle of Esther was hung already in the Salle de Molière at the Odéon; one must learn to be content with immortality.

And yet she found it growing stronger, her desire to get away from Baulon. Her new doctor, ignoramus as he was, had probably been right in saying that Baulon was as bad a place as you would find in France for her complaint; and as June approached she felt returning with an unexpected warmth the hunger to visit once again, perhaps to remain there, the cottage on the Morbihan coast where once she had spent three summer weeks with Marius and which was still in her possession. Despite the fog and the raw airs she found Baulon more tolerable in winter. As the weather grew warmer the noise seemed to increase, one became more conscious of the town's closeness and provinciality. Her window looked north over ugly roofs and crude advertisements towards the chimneys of the Lombardeau factory, she could only see the tops of the intervening trees. The Baulon smell grew riper under sunshine; the urchins' voices sharper and more fretful against their obbligato, the everlasting groan and jingle of the trams. Formerly she had claimed a few friends in other parts of the town: Marionneau the 'cellist and his daughter, the Tranchepain, who shared her memories of Adolphe Taine and the salon of Mme Falliès: they were dead or else they had gone away, no one came to see her now. It taxed her fortitude to have so close a hedge of pain about her movements. She could not read for a long time without discomfort, she had to shift from one cramped position to another, the book would fall and then it was agony to stoop so far as to pick it up again. Her room, which formerly she had kept in order by herself, had become untidy; Joséphine, supposed to clean it every day, would furiously sweep the carpet and roll it up, would push Thérèse and her furniture into one corner and flood the floor with soapy water, scour the panels of the door against all protest, until in her fury Thérèse would send her away with the books and shelves undusted, the windows thick with grime. This time last year she had enjoyed her morning walk, when almost without exception she had made her way along the boulevard MacMahon and sat for a while beneath the poplars in the old wool market; there was no traffic there and seldom any children, only the pigeons to disturb her agreeably with the clap of feathers as they worked their overweighted bodies into flight, to swing above a line of river barges, circle the twin towers of Ste Gudule and flutter to her feet again. But now she remembered only the streets of the centre, where, as the saying was, you had to choose in walking on the pavement whether to have the left eye struck by a glass of beer or the right by a passing tramcar; the Musée des Arts et Antiquités with its dreadful Persian vases, its one faked Rembrandt and its cheesy Pharaoh; the dog-stunk, ash-strewn, pandemoniac office of the Crédit Meuse-et-Marne. It had forced itself into the place Talleyrand, that tastelessness of Baulon, and now it seemed with the dirt and disorder to invade the very room where she lay prisoner. She was a little frightened; not of the German soldiers, who could come if they pleased and were welcome to make a rubbish heap of the town; but of her mind's and senses' narrowing horizon.

*

She was pleased when Raymond paid her a visit, even if he came in his habitual mood of truculence demanding sympathy. She told him to get himself a glass of bénédictine if he wanted it ('I can't serve you myself, Raymond; look—like a stuffed raven!') to stop fiddling with his brief-bag and sit down. "It must be a month since I've seen you," she said indifferently. "Is it that you are engaged all the time in intellectual conversation with dear Cécile, or have you been unable lately to think out a new system of the theatre to discuss with me?"

Raymond filled his glass, perched himself on the edge of the bed and put his feet on the wheel of her chair. He said explosively:

"Does anyone in this mansion of imbeciles realize that there's going to be a war? Has it occurred to any of you that it would be a good deal safer to live on top of a powder-magazine than in this place, with things as they are at the moment?"

Thérèse surveyed him patiently.

"I wish, Raymond, you would take your feet off my chair. . . . No, no, of course I know nothing of what's going on. You, working all day in the place Coupel, which for all intents and purposes, is the centre of the universe, you have your finger constantly on the pulse of Europe. I, an old woman in her dotage with nothing but the Paris newspapers——"

"But then why, if you know what's going to happen——"

"In the first place one cannot be quite certain that it will happen. I can remember just this sort of talk going on when you were dribbling down the front of your jersey. No event is certain until——"

"But, Aunt, seriously, you're not going to stay on here, are you? You don't love Baulon as much as all that? I've never been able to understand why you came to live in Baulon at all. I should have thought——"

"Paris was impossible," she said, "you know that. I had to live somewhere, my savings were very small. And although it may seem quite laughable to you, I used once to be fond of your father. Fond? Well, I don't know, but I was proud of him. He was a good-looking man—he's handsome now, though you of course wouldn't notice it—he had an air, one picked him out in a crowded drawing-room. And as a soldier he had a phenomenal reputation. When he was in Paris we often went about together; we were proud of each other, like a betrothed couple. Then there was the Viboire affair, the *affaire Séverin*, the news of the court-martial first of all, then the notice—I needn't go into all that, you must know what happened. I told my friends to wait: we should see what happened in a civil court: the truth, I said, would come out then. I had a quarrel with Yvonne Moimeau: she considered herself my rival, she came and said how sorry she was that my brother had got into disgrace; I struck her across the forehead, only with the back of my hand, but she couldn't go on for a fortnight, she threatened to bring an action and it was all over the town. Well then, you see—or perhaps you won't, you aren't very perceptive in these matters—but it must be plain enough what my position was when the verdict was published. At any rate the canaille made it plain enough in the theatre. Are you listening, or are you just not interested? My friends—Envermeu amongst them—wanted me to make a gesture. The *affaire Séverin*, it was nothing to do with me or my art, I should wash my hands of the matter. In twelve months, they said, Paris will have forgotten that you were anything to do with the officer who has disgraced himself. Well, that was not the gesture which I preferred. I said that I believed my brother's word rather than his enemies', that the trial had been dishonest, that if Paris could do without Eugène it could do without me too. I joined him in exile. It all sounds very foolish to you, no doubt; but then you do not understand what anger is, you have never been hissed by a mob. . . . If you're not going to drink any more you'd better put back the stopper."

Raymond put his glass down on the bed and returned the bénédictine unstoppered to the cupboard. He was interested; Aunt Thérèse was seldom so expansive.

"I don't know," he said slowly, "it's difficult to say how a normal and rational person would have reacted. I myself would not stop painting just because Cécile produced a half-black baby in the boulevard Maréchal Soult. I didn't even sweep out of Baulon when the news came through about Pierre. They asked me in the cafés what I knew, I said that my brother seemed to have been rather rash, that was the end of the matter. I didn't fight a duel or slap anyone in the face even. Perhaps, after all, I lack the artistic temperament. . . . But in any case I don't see why you have to stay here now."

"No?" She pressed against the arms of the chair to turn her body into a new position. Watching her speculatively, Raymond saw how she winced, as if an electric charge had passed right through her. "Your father," she said, "suggested that I should go. 'Baulon is no place for civilians,' that's what he said. And I only ask you to imagine his remarks if I did go. Or perhaps you can't even imagine that? 'Thérèse lost her nerve. She is, of course, an old woman, it's natural that she should have been frightened. She was alarmed by the reports in the newspapers and went away as fast as she could.' As if I cared, in this state, whether the Germans come or not!"

"Father knows, then, that there may be trouble?"

"We all know that."

"And he's not going to move?"

"No. At least, not yet. He is expecting a telegram from the War Office, he thinks they may make him commander-in-chief at any moment. . . . Yes, yes, I know, but what is one to do?"

"And mother?"

"Well, what do you suppose?"

"That cough," he said reflectively, "have you noticed it?"

"Noticed it? I can hear it up here. Of course that man Tischer——"

"It's not Tischer's fault, she won't let him even look at her. I spoke to Tischer about it and he says she won't admit there's anything wrong. And it's worse since she got back from Paris. Don't you think if we put it to father that for the sake of mother's health they ought to move——?"

"You can try. You have my blessing."

"And what about Renée and the children? Are they to stop here too?"

"Presumably."

"You mean—because they can't do anything else."

"If you must be so precise."

He began to walk up and down the room.

"Those children ought to be moved," he said; "we owe at least that to Pierre. I don't see why——"

"I personally," Thérèse broke in, "am not aware that I owe anything to Pierre except to thank him for treating us to a scandal we could well have done without. If you think——"

"But, Thérèse, we don't know, we don't know what happened. And anyhow, I don't see why his children have to suffer for Pierre's follies. Surely——"

"Very well, Raymond, if you feel sentimental about the children, why don't you talk to your father about them? I personally feel that they're the victims not so much of an unsatisfactory father as of a stupid and obstinate mother. She lets the girl spend all her time cuddling up with Marianne—a most unsuitable person, as all teachers are, to have anything to do with children—and the boy she keeps tied to her bodice-buttons, she won't let anyone see him, she won't send him to school or let him play with other children, she's systematically rude whenever we try to take an interest in the children or do anything for her. If Renée——"

"Yes, yes," he said angrily, "I know, I know, I know." She had reached the point at which it was useless to talk to her. It always surprised him that Thérèse, who seemed to have a masculine intelligence, was no less prone than other women to swerve into her own toboggan-run of primitive emotions; but he knew that once she had started on that headlong plunge it was no use appealing to her reason. "Sahamarana!" he said bleakly. "You want to make a grand gala of it. . . . Thank you for the bénédictine." He went half-way to the stairs and came back again. "I wish you'd go somewhere else. It upsets me, seeing you here in that state. You ought to be at some thermal establishment. Tischer told me that was the only thing now."

She turned her head far enough to look at him sideways. "It's kind of you, Raymond, to be so concerned about me. A thermal establishment, good God! If you're nervous, there's no reason why you shouldn't go away, you could surely get newspaper work somewhere else. I myself find it a little invertebrate, this shivering and whimpering over rumours. Perhaps before you go you would just open one of the windows, those cigarettes you smoke. . . ."

★

Very well, they didn't want him, they didn't believe him, they could stew in their own juice! At the corner of the rue des Suisses he turned to look back through the scaffolding across the Square and thought how grotesque the house appeared in the ruthless June sunlight; like a ballroom dress, already a little shabby, hung ghoulishly in the beggars' carnival, the Marché aux Jupons at Saint-Antoine. You could see now that in every other house some of the windows were broken and few curtained; the Square was no longer properly swept, the gutters were getting choked with rubbish the rusty frame of a bicycle and a shattered bidet were propped against the central plane. The Séverins could stay in the place Talleyrand if they chose; Raymond would not go there again. "I've done my best," he said to Vasseur; "a man should be loyal to his family, don't you think?—but they seem determined to stay on, they won't listen to anything I say. I shall keep away from the place, it gives me the shudders, it's like the dismantled scenery of last year's play."

He realized, now that the frame in which he lived was trembling, that he had always found pleasure in this time of year, when the heat had not yet become unbearable and the town's life had already come into the open air. It was a sign which oddly awakened recollections that Cognard, the foreman of the casting-room, arrived at work now with a loose-necked sporting-shirt beneath his navy waistcoat. Within a week Mlle Cuillerdier had responded by discarding her Gandois stays and entrusting her contours, as far as one could see, to bands of silk and yellow safety-pins. The day of judgment might be approaching, as the bald and bearded proclaimed in the cafés; there seemed to be more of those women, triste, thick-stockinged, soberly clad, who found their way to Ste Gudule and knelt there for a few minutes every morning, perhaps a greater number of votive candles on the multipointed sconce before la Vierge Protectrice; but the shops in Jean-Rôdit did no less than their usual business in flowered cretonnes, men of agreed respectability went bareheaded or in the infectious chapeau Manhattan, at twelve o'clock it was hardly possible to get a table for a family of five in the boulevard Maréchal Soult. The news was none too good; but you read it with a tranquil courage on the seats of the Petit Parc or the sooty steamer that took you in the evening for three sous to Voie Chappelle, with the sun on the back of your neck and shoulders. As Raymond sat in the doorway of Les Beaux

Alliés an old man with three left fingers missing threw a *Paris-Poste* on his table and struck it with his palm, making the glasses jingle. "They are hiding the truth, those people of the press," he said vehemently. "It's the government, they don't want us to know. But I know—those swine, Monsieur, across the river there. Look! My hand. One, two, three fingers. In battle? No, no, don't you believe it! Prisoner of war. First one, then the next, with a blunt bayonet, snick, snick! snick!—like that. . . ." Raymond nodded. "Indeed, yes, but how terrible, yes, I agree, Monsieur, the men who write the newspapers are lying scoundrels." Across the busy traffic, the little carts bouncing on the pavé, the triple-jointed trams, he could see the upper deck of the steamer bearing a load of laughing children in pink cotton uniforms with their Sister stuck up like a black snowman in the middle. To-day was the Fête des Familles Nombreuses and he thought he would go to the park and see the fun before signing in at the office; the evening was going to be lovely, there would be a picturesque religious ceremony and the progeny of the poor would dance very rhythmically without the least suspicion of æsthetic emotion. "Yes, yes, Monsieur, that is most interesting, and now I'm afraid I must say good-bye." He ought, of course, to be painting, but he had no concentration. It was better to enjoy the sunshine.

For this summer they were perhaps reprieved. The June issue of *L'Europe Philosophe* had an impressive contribution from Jean-Ferdinand Dubreuil. "Those who speak so glibly," Dubreuil wrote, "of the European structure crumbling at any moment beneath the insistent pressure of national irritations have overlooked that powerful element of high moral sensibility in the general will of the European peoples which must be reckoned with in every scientific survey. Even in Berlin, which our population has imaginatively filled with bellicose sub-humans. . . ." That might be so: Dubreuil's lectures at the Sorbonne were at present under students' boycott, and that would indicate that he was not without intelligence. It was pleasant reading on a sunny morning, and for the moment he was ready to share a popular delusion. The Baulon programme did not seem to be altered by political uncertainties. Next month the pious would make their annual pilgrimage, f7.50 first class and f3.50 third, to the Church of the Sacred Girdle at Châtel-Secours. At ten o'clock each morning, invariably on time, the 14 tram arrived at the Petits Enfants, circumambulated the châlet de nécessité and the statue of Le Roi Soleil, and grumbled off again to Saint-Antoine. On any day you would see the familiar figures at the boulevard tables: chubby Mougnet, the town clerk, with his little bag, always on the very point of hurrying back to the Hôtel de Ville; the painter Sieurez expressing with his pock-strewn Andalusian features an eternal, mild surprise; Funeuve, the long and sprawling, dirty and tobacco-scented owner of the Parfumerie aux Jeunes Vierges de France. Cécile was talking, as she always did at this time of year, about a September holiday at Dinard. He listened quite patiently. As a rule he would be eloquent on the monstrosities of Dinard, the shoddy grandeur of the salle à baccara, the cultivated harlots of the plage, and would end by saying crisply, "In any case, we have no money, voilà!" But now he welcomed every suggestion of permanence, even the prettiness of the Baulon scene: the friends who paraded their unbarbered originality and were not after all so very distinguished; the gradual softening of street-sounds in the long evenings; the smell of a cheap supper through an open cottage doorway, where a working family would loll with a sliced gherkin between them until they could no longer see each other's chairs, drugged with the peaceful rumble of their own tireless voices. Only when he went home late at night, with a clear moon leaving odd blue shadows beneath the trees and in the little alleys, was he frightened. The town was so empty now, and utterly without protection. He ought, like the Hebrew prophets, to shout a warning to the sleeping houses. At such an hour the enemy might come.

XXXII

Towards the end of the month the weather broke, he became depressed and lonely. Instinctively he wanted to go "home"—for so he called it—to the place Talleyrand. But no, there was no one there he could get on with, they despised him, he had decided once and for all not to go.

He was on his way to the place Coupel, standing on the crowded platform of a tram, when he caught the odour of rappee and found that the Abbé Vignaud was pressed against him. "It is terrible," the Abbé whispered, "the way they crowd these cars. I've been told that advantage is sometimes taken of the crush for immoral practices." He sighed. "But I hardly believe that—one would have to be so very quick. . . . If you could lend me ten centimes I should be extremely grateful, it's simply impossible for me to get at my purse." In the folding of the crowd at the next stop they were wedged apart, but Vignaud, holding his umbrella so that it drained on to Raymond's neck, continued talking over a woman's shoulder.

"You've seen your mother lately? You know, Raymond, I'm worried about her, she ought to get away. No, no, I don't mean so much because of all these scares, they're always going on; but I don't like that cough, I'm sure she'd be better at a higher altitude, some place where she would get more sunshine." The tram stopped with violence, jerking the outside passengers against the taffrail; Vignaud saved himself by curling his free arm round the woman's neck. "Listen," he went on (everyone was listening), "I think your mother ought to be just a little more self-assured. Of course it's not my business, it certainly isn't my rôle to discourage conjugal fidelity; but not long ago, when your father went off on a turnip-shooting excursion to Viboire—you remember?—I strongly urged your mother not to go after him, and my advice proved quite successful. . . . Do you get down here? So will I, my bowels are already shaken right out of position. . . . Ah, what a relief! The scent of that woman—where do they buy such stuff . . . ? Well, I can't help thinking that your mother might very advantageously take the same line again. If she were to pack her bag and go off to Dax, for example: do you imagine your father would take very long to follow her? Yes, I know about the telegram he's expecting, but a telegram, after all, can be forwarded, or someone might even inform the Ministry of his new address. Of course it's not for me to suggest such a thing to your mother, I can only—as it were—slip the idea into an outer fold of her mind. And you know how greatly I admire your mother for her constancy. She is a good woman, Raymond, a very noble woman. Unfortunately I seem to have been designed by almighty providence to deal with sinners, who bore me terribly and with whom I am always successful. I much prefer the virtuous, and I can never make any headway with them at all. . . ."

His mother was the last person whom Raymond wished to see at place Talleyrand; but the Abbé with his customary insinuation had laid the duty upon him, and at any rate it was an excuse to surrender his resolution. He waited only till Saturday. In the day between he had bought Galissard's *Life of Yvonne Moimeau*, and he sent it up with his compliments to Aunt Thérèse to indicate that he had been to the house without paying her his usual call. Was Maman at home? he asked Barbier. Yes, but she was with the Colonel, and Dr. Tischer was also there, perhaps M. Raymond would wait for a few minutes? All right, yes, he would go and wait in the salon.

Barbier stopped him at the foot of the stairs.

"You won't mind my asking you, Monsieur Raymond, but seeing that you know things, with your newspaper work, I mean, I was wondering, if you could tell me whether there's any truth in this talk, you know what I mean? It's hard to make it out, one day they say one thing, and different the next——"

"I'm sorry, Barbier, I can't tell you a thing. I know just as much as you do, nothing more. If I knew——"

"You see," the old man whispered, "it's Joséphine, she keeps on at me, she's frightened for Gaston. 'If the Prussians come here,' she says, 'Gaston will be made into a soldier, him that wouldn't know a bayonet from a billhook.' Of course they let him off his Service, the doctors did that, but you can't be certain it would be the same with a war on."

"But surely, Barbier, it's just as likely to happen anywhere else? It won't make any difference where you are, if a war starts."

Barbier was doubtful. "I suppose so," he said, "I suppose that's right. . . . But you know how it is with Joséphine, when she gets an idea in her head. She keeps on all day, it's terrible. I have to keep my old chassepot primed and loaded to please her, I'm terrified of that young Gaston getting hold of it. And she keeps on: Why won't the Colonel go somewhere else? She won't stay in this house, she says. But Monsieur Raymond, what can I do? You couldn't try to persuade the Colonel——?"

"If I see him I'll try," Raymond said, retreating up the stairs. "And look here, Barbier, if I get news of any trouble coming I'll let you know, that's honest, I promise you. And tell Joséphine she'd better leave that chassepot alone, she's more likely than not to kill a policeman."

He met Tischer on the landing and was instantly pulled into a corner.

"One minute, Monsieur Raymond—if I may—just a word with you." He was hoarse and conspiratorial. "I am wondering if you can persuade Monsieur Séverin—I have tried myself but it's quite useless—can you not persuade him to move away from Baulon? You must know yourself how things are, it's no longer safe, Baulon, I feel quite certain it isn't. And Madame Séverin, I don't at all like that cough of hers, she is in a very poor state of health, she gives me a great deal of anxiety. There's nothing I can do, you see, she won't even allow me to examine her properly, and she ought to be receiving special treatment. It would be better for her to be taken right away from your father, but I suppose that's out of the question. At least they could move somewhere else, it would be a great relief to me. It's not that I want to give up the case—your father and mother are old friends of mine, you know that, I have, if I may say so, a strong affection for them, it is just for that reason that I find myself so anxious. And Mlle Thérèse too—of course it's not for me to make any comment on her case, since she has places herself in the hands of another physician, but I confess to feeling a good deal worried; that species of arthritis cannot be fought without skilful massage, and it is not everyone who has the natural ability; and if it comes near the heart—but the case is no longer mine, I can make no comment without impropriety. But, M. Raymond, I cannot tell you what a relief it would be if your family could be persuaded to leave Baulon."

Raymond spread his hands. "But, Doctor, who am I in this house? I have just one outstanding merit: I have never deserted from the army. But everyone knows that's only because they couldn't make me go into it. I tell you I'm of no reputation here, I'm nothing more than a newspaper man and a failed painter, they wipe their boots on me. Oh, yes, of course, if I can. . . ."

*

He found his mother in the drawing-room. He understood, when he saw her, why Tischer was anxious. Her face had been like that once before, the night they had waited for Eugène to die; the lips drained of colour, the eyes moistly reflecting the light from the window. But now its very structure seemed to have gone, as if the flesh were of modeller's clay and had softened in a warm room. She stood with her hand on a chair, she seemed to have grown smaller. She was trembling and breathless after a fit of coughing.

Embarrassed, he went to the other side of the room. A sketch in pastel was pinned, a little crooked, on the wall there; one of his own earliest drawings, utterly commonplace. For years Madeleine had pointed out that puerile sketch to callers, often in his own presence: "You see? Raymond did that, already he is quite an artist." Perhaps she did so still—except that there were no callers. In his mature work she had never shown the faintest interest. He stood still, facing the wall, until she had stopped coughing.

It was Madeleine who spoke first.

"You don't come here very often now, Raymond."

She had her handkerchief to her mouth, and he could hardly have told from her voice whether she reproved him for coming so seldom or for coming at all. He was ashamed and nervous. He said rather harshly: "Sit down, Maman, why don't you sit down!" and to his surprise she obeyed him. "I want to see Father," he said, "it's very important, I want to see him at once if I can."

She shook her head.

"No, not to-day. Certainly not to-day. . . . This morning your father was working for nearly two hours at his maps—it is the dispositions he is making, no, you wouldn't understand, but it's very urgent—it has left him exhausted." She put up her handkerchief again and turned her head away. Then: "He was quite

296

exhausted this afternoon, I had to send for Doctor Tischer. Doctor Tischer says that he must rest for the remainder of to-day, he is not to be excited. It has reduced your father's strength, that visit to Paris—that wicked Lenormand. . . ."

"But I met Tischer on my way up," he answered gently, "he said that it would do Father good to see me."

His opposition at once made her firm. Her voice grew stronger, it sounded for a moment as he remembered it from first childhood.

"No, Raymond, you are not to go. Doctor Tischer does not really understand your father's health as I do; he is a good doctor, very patient, but he doesn't really understand the case. . . . Cécile, she is well?"

"Yes," he said, "yes, I think so, yes she is all right. . . . I've been thinking, Maman, you ought to get away from Baulon, it would do you good. That cough of yours——"

"It is much better," she said quickly. "In the winter the fog gets into my throat, my throat has always been rather delicate. In the warm weather it gets all right."

"But, Maman, I don't like the idea of your being in Baulon if —well, if there should be trouble of any sort. Of course it may be all nonsense, one shouldn't be alarmed by the newspapers. I don't want to alarm you, but you know, surely, that Baulon would be the first place in danger if the country were invaded. It may not mean anything, all this talk, but I'd be much happier——"

"You must leave that to your father, Raymond," Her voice had grown tired again. "Your father will know if it isn't safe——"

"But Father doesn't realize——"

"——Your father is in close touch with the situation, he had special intelligence from the Ministry when he was in Paris. And the maps he is working on, everything is shown on them. You must leave that to your father."

Raymond took out a cigarette and put it back again. He was losing patience, but he collected himself to try one more approach.

"It would do you both good to have a bit of a change. I am sure Father wants a change of scene, it's wretched for him, always to look out on the same view. Just think, if he could see mountains from his window——!"

"What you do not understand," she said with a tired dignity, "is your father's sense of duty, his national duty. No, no, of course, you haven't heard about it, about the telegram he is expecting. I'm not sure if I ought to tell you, it's a secret matter. You will promise me, Raymond, that you won't put it in your newspaper?

Your father is waiting here for a telegram from the Ministry. It may come at any time. It is our duty to wait here, your father's and mine. . . . You will give my love to Cécile? I have meant to call on her, but I've been so busy, your father likes me to help with his work as far as I can. . . ."

He got up and buttoned his jacket. "Yes, Maman, I'll give your message." He kissed her cheek mechanically. "Good-bye, Maman. You will give my regards to Father?" He slipped away, a little awkwardly, while she shook with another fit of coughing.

He had reached the top of the stairs when he heard her coming after him. He turned and she caught him by the arms. She was crying now: there was a runnel of tears on the brown, wriggling skin beneath her eyes and on the little hairs which crowned her cheeks, her mouth was twisting feebly. She held him close, making him feel through her thin hands the fearful palpitation of her body, until she had breath enough to speak.

"You'll be careful, Raymond, my little Raymond, you must be careful, promise me, Raymond! Pierre is gone, and Father—so ill, so terribly ill. I have only you, Raymond, Marianne doesn't love me, I've only you."

★

He wanted to get away from the house quickly, before anyone saw him, to get away and never to come back again. But at the fold of the stairs Gaston, coming up to answer a screaming summons from Mme Nadya, stood to block his way and stared at him with idiot curiosity. Raymond pushed past him and hurried on, determined at least to avoid another meeting with Barbier. He was not yet free. Barbier was in the kitchen, he could hear him wrangling with Joséphine; but a woman he had never seen before appeared from the old dining-room and accosted him by name. "M. Séverin!—I know you're M. Raymond Séverin, I can see the likeness to your mother and father—I wonder if you can tell me, M. Séverin—I know you are the editor of a great newspaper—I wonder if you can tell me whether it is true, what they tell us about the danger from Germany. It is not for myself, you understand, I am anxious only for M. Poupoulet. Perhaps it's wrong of me to ask you for special information—it's not that I'm unwilling to pay for the newspaper. . . ."

"I don't know," he said curtly, "I'm sorry, Madame, but I can tell you nothing, I'm just as abysmally ignorant as you are." He pulled the door shut behind him and never looked back until he had crossed the river. It was raining again.

★

He slept badly that night and dreamed fantastically about Pierre. They stood together high and dangerously upon the scaffolding and looked across the place Talleyrand. On the other side a party of workmen was about to demolish the houses, starting at the bottom. "I suppose you realize," he said to Pierre, "that Mother and Father are in there?" Pierre did not hear him, it was Madame Poupoulet who spoke. She was walking unsteadily towards him on a transverse spar, she called to him, fearfully: "Do you think, M. Séverin, it's dangerous, those people taking off the bottom of the house?"

"No," he answered, "no, I don't suppose so." They had hacked away the bottom courses now, the house stood balanced on a single pile, and the workmen laboured patiently, swinging their picks against the brittle façade. "You've got no right——" he called, but his voice was tearful and might fail to reach them; one of the workmen turned his head for a moment and answered in a quiet voice: "We have to do it, Monsieur, we have to earn our money." Pierre, he thought, was going to sleep; he stretched his hand to shake him but Pierre was too far off and he was terrified of losing balance, He shouted, "Pierre, you must do something, something!" "Quiet!" Pierre said. "Quiet! I find it very interesting." The men were whispering together and he could hear their voices clearly. "It will save a lot of time," they said, "if we set the place on fire." He struggled then to clamber down, to rush across the Square and stop them, but his mother called from the window of the salon, "Keep still, Raymond, keep still, I'm afraid of your falling." He couldn't speak but he waved his arm, he pointed down to the man who was already setting light to a piece of paper. She seemed to see but she took no notice. "We've got to wait," she said, "we're waiting for a telegram." The flame was creeping up the wall like a serpent, he could see the flicker through the smoking windows as the wall began to bend and shrivel. "You're wanted at the place Coupel," Lenormand said behind him. "They want the news about the fire, they're going to bring out an extra edition." "I can't go yet," he said, "not yet, leave me alone!" The house had disappeared, it was hidden behind the smoky curtain. Lenormand tugged his arm but he dragged away; for a moment the smoke had cleared and he saw Renée's face at the window. She was screaming, "Pierre! Rescue! Raymond!" He struggled, but Pierre had got his other arm. "It's all right," Pierre said, "you're not to interfere, she's used to that sort of thing." He wrenched his body free and his elbow struck against the bed-head. He lit the bedside candle and Cécile opened her eyes. "Oh, Raymond, how unkind of you, you've woken me from a beautiful dream."

★

Nothing remained of it except Renée's terrified face, her voice calling to him. That was with him all morning, like a piece of flint lodged in his forehead. He left the office at one o'clock, having completed the feuilleton pages for next morning and done the second leader. "I'll be back at three," he told Chivalié, "to make up six and eight. You might run through the Havas alpha slips—there won't be anything centre-page, but just in case——" He made his déjeuner of a Courpière salad and gateaux-brie with a half-bottle of Donjeuse; he had no appetite for anything more. By half-past one he was in the place Talleyrand once again.

He crossed the Square quickly, anxious to avoid his mother's eyes if she should be looking out of the window. The house was silent as he made his way upstairs. He knocked at the nursery door and heard a chair scraping; then Renée's voice, faint and rather frightened: "Who's there? No, you can't come in!"

"It's Raymond," he called. "Can't I?"

She came to the door then and he heard the key turning.

"Why do you lock the door?" he asked as she let him in.

She answered in a low voice, she didn't want the children to hear: "Your father: twice he's tried to get in here."

He couldn't understand.

"Why?"

She nodded over her shoulder. "Armand. You know. Your father wants to get hold of him."

"That's foolish," he said, sitting down. "You've got persecution mania. Besides, why shouldn't he see Armand?"

"I won't let him," she answered. "He's not to see him."

The point was not worth arguing, and he hadn't come for that. "All right," he said, "you must do as you think best." He tilted his chair back and caught hold of Armand by the ear. "Come here, you brat!" Armand came cheerfully. There was nothing wrong with him, Raymond thought; the boy had grown used to his surroundings and he was quite all right again.

But Renée: he didn't like the look of her, no, he didn't like it. Her face was not as he had seen it in his dream, wild with terror; but dull, tired to vacuity. The expression reminded him—yes, of the forger François Rouez. It was in his reporting days, they had caught Rouez after a four days' hunt across the Landes and he had witnessed the police examination. It had stayed vivid in his memory, that lamplit scene: Rouez sitting quite still with his head a little on one side, saying, "I suppose so, I suppose so"; the gendarme stabbing his cheek with a penholder to keep him awake; the man's look of utter indifference, through which occasionally there showed a sullen contumacy. And Rouez had moved much as

Renée moved now, uncertainly, as if the motor of his limbs were running down. Raymond was sorry already that he had come. This at one time had been the naughty-room; long confinements had given him a distaste for it; and he liked it no better now that its old smell of naphthalene was ousted by that of meals and drying linen. He had broken, he felt, into a close and curious but settled life. Sophie, ironing a doll's chemise with the tray of a match-box, was stolidly contented; Armand had gone back to his corner and resumed his book; while Renée, it seemed, so far from being grateful for his visit, was only impatient for him to be gone. Yes, the dream had sprung from his too sympathetic imagination; the girl was a soldier's wife, accustomed to narrow quarters, essentially a little stupid; there was nothing for him to do.

"Oughtn't you to get out a bit?" he asked vaguely. "It's a terribly stuffy room."

She seemed surprised at his question.

"But yes, we go to the park almost every day now."

"Yes, but not only that," he said. "You ought to see people."

"But I haven't any friends in Baulon. And I'm too busy."

"Too busy?"

"Yes. I do work for Peulevey."

"For Peulevey? That old pimp? Why?"

"Well, they pay me."

"You ought to get about more," he said solemnly. "There's a theatre in Baulon, it's the worst in Europe but you ought to go."

"But I couldn't leave the children."

"Oh, damn the children! Yes, Armand, you you're a nuisance. Never mind, you'll grow out of it." He was suddenly inspired. "Look here, Cécile and I will take over the children. I expect Cécile knows what one has to do, changing the nappies and so on. It would do her good, occupy her mind for a while. Then you could go about and do things. Wouldn't you like that, Sophie—to stay with your Aunt Cécile? Of course you would! And you, Armand?"

Armand shook his head.

"No," Renée said, "Armand must stay with me."

"You ought all to go away," he said gloomily. "I don't see why you have to stay here just because mother and father do."

She shrugged her shoulders.

"Money."

He spread his fingers up the back of his head, as Pierre would have done.

"I'll get a hundred francs off Aunt Thérèse," he said doubtfully, "and buy a blue ticket in the Luxembourg lottery. A prize in the second ring is seven thousand. I could take the whole lot of you to Florence with that."

She took his words quite gravely; Cécile, he thought bitterly, would have been just the same.

"No," she said, "I must stay in Baulon."

He threw away the measure-tape which he had been plaiting between his fingers.

"Oh, my God!" he groaned. "Are you waiting for a telegram too?"

Like most of his jokes, it fell without making a splash or ripple. She said: "A telegram? Perhaps."

"But who from?"

She was puzzled by his obtuseness.

"But—from Pierre."

"Oh."

So that was it, she hadn't resigned herself, she wouldn't admit that Pierre was gone. He lived again through a moment of his nightmare, when she had called for Pierre to rescue her. She was looking out of the window now and he was able to observe her face without embarrassment. Yes, she hardly realized that he was with her. She was just waiting, with time hardly moving past her stalactic patience, waiting for Pierre.

"Perhaps, after all, I shan't win anything," he said; and went away.

*

Chivalié was all behind as usual and Raymond found the alpha slips unsorted on his desk. His thoughts were still of Renée, his mind still clouded by the effluvium of his dream, while he turned the slips face upwards and fingered them into subject-groups as his eyes disposed. He should have done better, he thought; but they had hardened her, the Séverins, that house—it was like a fever-barrack. . . . *Renewal of turbulence in Bengal . . . 800 Hindus reported massacred in Rajshahi territory.* . . . No interest: basket E. . . . But why should he be concerned with Renée? Surely it was pure sentimentality, and now that she had become so stubborn . . . *empty coffin mystery: the "corpse" which escaped from its coffin at Lisbon is still untraced but is rumoured to have crossed the Sierra de la Culebra into Spain. Information from the port of shipment now suggests that the adventurer may be of French nationality.* . . . He tossed that one to Bréhier. "Something more about that Portuguese coffin business. You might do something with it—it's a bit unusual." It was curious, about Renée. Cautiously analysing his feeling for her, he was certain that his interest was quite unphysical. Perhaps it was purely sentimental based on the abominable neglect she had suffered from the Séverins; or perhaps it was merely that she had been

Pierre's property, and he had always envied what belonged to Pierre. No. No, it went deeper than that, it was more interesting. He felt about her, he thought, as he would have felt about an unfaithful lover, one whom he had loved first and who had given herself to someone else, sacrificing first his happiness and then her own. A bitter tenderness . . . *that the assassination was deliberately and carefully planned. The Archduke and Princess were accompanied by General Potiorek, the military governor.* . . . He took the slip across to Chivalié. "What do you think of that?" Chivalié took it rather impatiently, knocked his spectacles back on to the crown of his nose and read it with his head on one side.

"Saraïevo? Oh, of course, Bosnia. . . . Does that matter?"

XXXIII

THEY were all in groups at the doors of their houses as Tischer went along the rue du Manège à Vapeur, men and women together; from the confusion of their talk the same word still emerged, but pronounced more glibly now it had become a familiar, almost cherished token of evil: *la mobilisation*. ". . . you've heard, Clémont has told you, that Petit-Charles has gone already . . .? Si! La mobilisation. . . ." The older children had stopped playing and were oddly silent, as if they inhaled an unfamiliar air. They nodded and smiled to Tischer, the men who saw him, and some of those with their back to him turned round. The child who had trotted after him all the way from the Pas Alcibiade repeated incessantly: "My father says, monsieur, will you be kind enough to call on your way home and see his groin?" "I've told you," he said for the fifth time, "I will if I can." From one of the groups a woman with an infant at the breast came towards him. "Have you heard anything, Doctor? Have you any news?" "No, no, Marie-Christine, how should I? I'm too busy to hear anything." "You're not going to go away, are you, Monsieur?" "Go away? Of course not." Opposite douzebis he was stopped again. "François is better," a scrofulous ragpicker told him, "but it will relieve me and Rachel if you can spare the time to come again."

"But you won't forget," the child Simon said once more, "that father is most anxious you should see his groin?" "Yes, yes," Tischer said, "I will look in and see François if I can find the time. No, Joseph, I haven't heard any news, nothing since this morning. Yes, things look bad, but who can say . . .?"

He pushed through the gossips to the open door of douzebis and went into the shop-room. Félix Dumont and his eldest son were standing at the counter, sharing their evening meal with a scraggy cat which picked its way between the glasses nosing for crumbs; behind, the youngest children were being undressed for bed. "Have you any news, Doctor?" Mme Dumont called. "No," he said gruffly, "none at all." He went out at the other door and climbed the outside stairs.

He was short of temper. He was getting older now and his work was never reduced. To the heat of July, which always taxed him, there had been added a slow anxiety. They looked to him, these people of the Ste Estelle, for reassurance; he belonged, they thought, to the grand world, he would know what was going on and from him bad news would come less harshly; they seemed almost to believe that he could influence the course of happenings in their favour, repair the world's injustice just as he stitched a cut above the eyebrow. It had seemed to go so slowly, that warm July, and to have taken from him too much virtue. He was always a little busier than he cared to be, a little short of breath. He was a man who sweated copiously. "I can't imagine," M. Séverin said, "why you wear those black clothes all the summer. They look so dreadfully hot. At least you could take off the waistcoat." He had answered, smiling, that the waistcoat hid a tear in his shirt; he had not had time to repair it. "But doesn't your wife do that sort of thing? You have a wife, haven't you?" "Yes, M. Séverin, but she has been blind for some years now." And besides, he had his dignity. The suit might be old, and the big wings of his collar might droop like sodden sails when he sweated, but he owed it to his profession to maintain that vesture of gentility. He paused now on the stage outside the bedroom to wipe all round his neck. But Camille was calling fretfully, "Who's that? Is that you, Doctor?" and he went inside.

The room was right under the roof; the single window had been papered over so that the sun came only through the skylight, making the air dry and fiery. There were two double-beds, ingeniously set cornerwise so that you could just squeeze between their ends. On the one that was now in shadow Camille lay naked, his knees drawn up and his arms spread.

Tischer stood blinking in the dusty light.

"What have you done with the bandage?" he asked.

"I couldn't help it," the boy said, "it was itching like a swarm of ants."

Tischer bent down and saw the gangrened bandage snaked across a sprawl of clothing.

"Who took it off?" he demanded.

"Lucienne. I asked her."

"Little fool!" Tischer picked up the bandage. "Do you realize it can infect anything it touches?"

"It itched so frightfully," Camille repeated.

Tischer felt the boy's head. Yes, of course, he was feverish again. What could you expect in this place?

"Where's the water?" he asked, looking round.

"There's none here. I finished what there was. I'd like some more."

"All right."

Tischer took the ewer, went down and through to the street, and filled it at the pump. The expedition gave time for his temper to cool, and when he got back he spoke with his habitual gentleness.

"I've got some new stuff. It's better, it'll keep it cooler." He sat on the end of the bed to spread the ointment, with the lint on his knees; the room was choc-a-bloc with clothes and packing-cases, there was no space to do anything. "But you mustn't take the bandage off again. Don't you understand?—bugs, this bed's covered with them, they'll walk into that sore place the moment you let them."

Camille did not seem to listen. He lay still for half a minute, gasping, and then started to wriggle his back again.

"Tell me, Doctor," he said, "has the war started?"

"The war? Who said there was going to be one? No. There's too much silly talk in this quarter."

He began to clean the septic area. Camille bore it with the utmost patience.

"I don't want it to come yet," he said, close-mouthed. "Not till I'm better."

"You mean you want to fight? Still, old man, quite still, I won't be long."

"Yes," Camille said.

"But you're a good tradesman, aren't you? Don't you like your job?"

"At twelve francs a week?"

The door had opened. It was the slatternly Lucienne.

"Pardon!" she said. "There are two gendarmes. For you, Monsieur."

"What do you mean?"

"They want to see you. They've been looking for you, some-one told them you were here."

"Present my compliments," Tischer said. "And say that I am no longer attached to the prison staff, and I have no time for suicides. Dr. Geniève or Dr. Lepesqueur, they both know perfectly well what to do, they are on the list for suicide duty. And Lucienne, when did you last change the sheets for Camille?"

"This morning, Doctor."

"But you don't mean to say these were clean this morning?"

"No. You didn't say clean ones. You just said change them. There aren't any clean ones."

He shrugged his shoulders, perfectly accustomed to such behaviour.

"Well, go now and send away the gendarmes. Wait. Take this with you and empty it, it should have been done this morning."

"I'm sorry, Monsieur, if——"

"Go on!" he said patiently.

But she was back again in a few moments.

"They say, Monsieur, that it isn't for a suicide. It is very important, they say, they have to see you."

He was in the middle of the bandaging.

"I can't possibly——" he said. "Wait. Tell them if they must see me they must either wait or come up here."

They came up. They stood awkwardly behind him as he went on with the bandaging, a little surprised by the boy's nakedness. Tischer asked over his shoulder:

"Well?"

"We are sorry to trouble you, Monsieur," the stouter said, "but you have failed to comply with the new order. There is a new order—you were notified at the beginning of last month—that aliens must appear in person to register afresh. There were fifteen days given——"

"I'm not an alien," he said. "I am international, I belong to a profession that knows no tribal borders. Or if you must be precise, I am an honest Swiss from the canton of Grisons, and I have been in this country nearly all my life. And if you think I have unlimited time at my disposal, as you appear to have, you are singularly mistaken."

"I am very sorry, Monsieur," the constable said, "but there is a new order, it applies to all aliens. Strictly speaking you are liable to immediate arrest, but if you will be good enough to give me the full particulars, enabling me to lay a statement before the commissioner, and be kind enough to promise that you will attend without fail to-morrow morning, we may be able to adjust the matter."

For a moment Tischer said nothing. So it was like that! He would let them arrest him, he thought angrily, and see how they set about to prove him an undesirable alien. But Camille, lying on his front and twitching slightly with the pain as the bandage was fastened, was asking wearily: "Who are all these people?" "Suppose that I couldn't see Camille to-morrow!" he thought.

He said: "But the superintendent, M. Froumenton, he knows all about me."

"It is a question of complying with the regulation," the constable said firmly.

"All right. Name, Karl August Tischer. Nationality, Swiss. Religion, Lutheran. Occupation, attending invalids and attending at the police-station. . . . And if you want a testimony to my character," he concluded with mild irony, "I would refer you to M. Eugène Séverin."

"Séverin . . .?" the man said politely.

Lucienne had stayed in the room throughout the interview. When it was done she squeezed into a corner to let the men pass out.

"I want some warm water," Tischer told her. "If your mother hasn't got any go along to the café-bar, will you, and ask Louis Lemarchand if he can spare you a kettleful. Do hurry, there's a good girl. " He was thinking, as he held up the glass and measured out the antipyrin with scrupulous accuracy, "In a week's time, when Camille will probably have died, the police will say that I wanted to keep him out of the war."

Lucienne came back with a little boiling water in a saucepan. "All right," he said, "that'll do."

"Is there anything else, Monsieur?"

"No, thank you, Lucienne. Unless you can kill some of these flies."

He opened his second bag, where he carried sponges and a napkin or two for these occasions, poured the hot water into an empty chamber-pot and cooled it. It was no good leaving Lucienne to do this kind of thing.

"How long do you think it will be," Camille asked as Tischer sponged him, "before my arm's all right?"

"I don't know. It depends whether you keep on taking off the bandage."

He dried Camille's body carefully, using the towel as if it were a feather duster, and carried him on to the other bed. Very quickly he smoothed the crumpled sheet and swept away the crumbs. The flies would not be driven from a big gravy stain on the pillow, but it was useless to worry about that.

"Do you feel cooler now?"

"Yes. But it's difficult to breathe."

He lifted Camille back and covered him with the top sheet. "You must keep something over you," he said. "It'll keep the flies off at any rate. I want you to keep the arm that way—yes, like that—as long as you can. Is that fairly comfortable?"

"Yes, Monsieur, very comfortable indeed."

"Do you think you could go to sleep?"

"If you could stay for a bit———"

Tischer looked at his watch. He had promised Mme Séverin to be in again this evening—M. Séverin was in a nervous state and had been complaining of a headache. Then there was François Einlich, the pleurodynia in the rue Pigerre, the groin of Simon's father. . . . But Camille, such a quiet fellow, so pathetically patient.

"All right," he said, "just a little while."

He set the door ajar to get a little more air and turned over a washing-basket to sit on. Stretching his arm, he rested his knuckles below the boy's clavicle and began to stroke him with a slightly twisting action, murmuring *hmmm-mmm, hmmm-mmm*. He was hotter than ever and very unhappy. That arm, it should not be there at all; it was like allowing a naked fire in a storehouse of petroleum; but what sort of life would a cabinet-maker enjoy without a right arm? At the infirmary they would have had it off as a matter of course. Yes, but how much did Loison know about traumatic necrosis? And how did one differ from a fishmonger if one had never the pluck for a gamble? . . . *Hmm-mmm, hmm-mmm*. Camille had closed his eyes, and was lying quite still. Tischer felt himself growing drowsy from the heat and the slightly mesmeric action of his own arm.

At the end of the street a woman was crying the *Petit Soir*. Her voice grew louder as she came along the avenue d'Orléans, carrying a word that he could not quite catch. It died in the wider clamour of many voices, everyone in the street was shouting.

Camille opened his eyes. He asked sleepily: "What's that? What's all that noise?"

"It's all right," Tischer said, "it's only the bicycle race from Amiens which has just finished. Bertrand has won."

Camille nodded. "Good. I'm glad it was Bertrand." He shut his eyes again.

The shouts broke down to a flickering chatter, the noise came to the bedroom as to a horseman riding through a hostile crowd. Tischer was no longer in doubt. He could work as hard as he liked now, patching, strapping together, spending a year to make a new man: they would break up bodies faster than he could bind them, they would always overtake him. Camille, miraculously, was fast asleep. The shouting began again, far off. Presently he heard, as if through a swinging door, the staggering melody of the *Marseillaise*.

XXXIV

LAME and turgid, the melody still leaked through the rumble of the Chambon presses and the chirp of typewriters to the bureau de rédaction in the place Coupel. It was going on for one o'clock in the morning. Raymond had taken off his tie and collar, a glass of Armagnac stood near his inkwell, he wrote steadily and mechanically, leaving empty the bottom half of every sheet where his pen slid on the grease from his wrist. Every few minutes the editor's door opened and Ansellin, happy as a shopwalker on holiday, came out to rally his men. The country issue was already on stone, the town edition had to be held till two, in the meantime the mid-morning and lunch editions could be devised in frame; possibly, Ansellin thought, they could get out an hourly edition right through the day—they'd buy them. "Where's Letellier? How many's he doing now? Ring for him, someone!" Letellier, streaked with sweat and oil, was glumly satisfied: three-seventy, he'd worked the Houlfort up to three-seventy, yes, my God, he had, and he couldn't make it do one copy more, or, my God, there'd be not one spot of white on the pages. The wires came faster than the men could decode them, either repeating previous news or irresponsible and contradictory: the Germans were advancing on Antwerp, the Germans were retreating from Liége, the English viewed the affair with pious detachment, the English were coming in, in Paris all was bravery and confidence, Paris was in a turmoil of suspicion and alarm. At one o'clock a message fell on Raymond's desk like a nosegay into the morgue: Clothilde, the loulou of Mlle Nugent-Pruvôt, which was beloved by all Paris, was reported to be making a good recovery from the distemper. Excellent. They might perhaps have one more extra edition to honour the recovery of Clothilde. His pen was going very nicely now, it didn't matter what you put as long as you filled up the columns—Ansellin was right, they'd buy them. He picked up the topmost of the Bosquet slips: "A report forwarded from Amsterdam states that the supply of rations to German troops moving westward from Cologne has been interrupted by an error in organization." That was just the sort of thing. He wrote, without one erasure: "Already the much vaunted Prussian machine is proving under pressure to contain rusty cogs and ill-fitting pistons. At Cologne the supply of munitions and other necessities to troops moving westward has completely broken down, and it is feared by the German General Staff that the men, whose initial ardour has already been cooled by privation, may at any moment mutiny against their officers. . . ."

He turned over the next slip and wrote without a pause: "A power-ful Russian force consisting of five divisions is concentrating a few miles east of Posen. The men, hardy fighters of Caucasian and Tartar stock, are well disciplined, in high spirits, and eager for the offensive to begin. . . ." He stopped to push a lock of hair out of his right eye; looked across to Chivalié's desk and saw Chivalié sitting sideways with one hand in his pocket and his head on his shoulder, writing and writing. Coignard was round again for copy. "There you are, that lot, you'll have to check it over." The accustomed vibration seemed to have increased, the note of the machines was loud and higher. Europe was in arms, and the loulou of Mlle Nugent-Pruvôt was getting better. They were moving, thank God, after July's dreary question-mark, they had something to do, something to do, something to do. The noise in the street grew louder, the clap of running feet, the clank of the basement grating, the distant shouts. It came again, in bucolic cadences, the disease of song, the weary half-tuned epidemic melody of the *Marseillaise*.

When he left the office it was growing light. Cécile had tele-phoned twice to say she was frightened; the Germans, she seemed to think, might arrive at any moment. "You must tell them to wait," he told her. "Where are you off to?" Chivalié asked: "Home," he said. "There's enough copy to last a month, unless Ansellin wants to wake people up and sell them papers all through the night." But he didn't want to go home, he wanted his share of the fun. His limbs were tired and his vision awkward, but in the cool, free air he was no longer sleepy. He started off towards the Enfants di Rou.

The streets, littered with newspapers, were almost deserted now. In the rue Porcelaine a knot of stragglers passed him, lugubriously singing, but they were all alone, ludicrous and forlorn. A man lay asleep in the doorway of the Verrerie Bovin, with his head in a puddle of vomit. On the other side of the street Mme Huys-mann's delicatessen shop had been wrecked and some of the contents were still strewn over the pavement, trodden flat and brown. The untidiness was general, but the streets were quiet now. The air was warm from yesterday but not yet stifling; a little wind blew up from the river; the sun, still friendly, stood just above the houses in a naked sky.

It appeared, then, that the Baulonnais had grown tired of celebrating their war. Or perhaps the shadow of a doubt had cooled them. They had talked of it so long, the war that was coming, yet no one seemed quite to know what kind of thing it was or who was its sponsor. There were people in Paris who arranged these things, who knew—one supposed—what a war was like and how to manage it; but hitherto their warfare had been internecine, even in Baulon one knew that a government laboured only for the continued right to govern. It was a pity that the fête was so soon over. The noise of the crowds, the tramp and singing, perhaps they had signalled nothing but relief from tension, welcoming change to overrule the unbearable ennui of a working day. Already the face of wartime appeared a little dowdy. For himself, escaped from the airless racket of the place Coupel and enjoying the gentle sunshine, he would gladly have rubbed it out.

In the place des Enfants du Roi the war had been welcomed with some extravagance; the roadway was carpeted with rubbish, which the birds and scavengers were trying to clear away. A trio of workmen, stokers from the gas-plant, stood on the steps of the Hôtel de Ville facing the wall, and Raymond guessed what they were looking at. He went slowly across the square, conscious of the quickened perception attending danger, his mind recording like a dry-plate an oblong stain upon the pavement, the tilted roof of the Crédit Foncier, the plop of his left shoe where the sole was torn. He was drowsy, not much frightened. It was what he thought, a new order for mobilization. ". . . The following classes at the stations undermentioned." His glance went down quickly. "At 10.30 at the Ecole de Commerce: . . . 1901 class, division supérieure. . . ." Somebody had got it in hand, this war.

One of the stokers asked him with a wry smile, "You, Monsieur?"
"Yes."

*

The lecture-room at the Ecole de Commerce had assumed what Raymond recognized as a military flavour. A score of men besides himself sat about the benches undressed to socks and drawers, the door into the next room kept opening and a man in uniform who perspired with superficial competence barked out a name. One of the men he recognized, Flamant, a clerk in the Affréteurs Baulonnais. "I'm all right," Flamant said nervously. "V.D.—I'm covered with it." "You're wrong." another man told him, "they don't mind V.D." "But aren't you burning to serve your country?" Raymond asked him. Flamant shook his head. "In this weather, no." At twelve o'clock the sergeant came to say that the rest of them could go away, they would not be wanted till the afternoon.

"At one-thirty prompt," the sergeant said.

Raymond returned to the place Coupel. "I am not quite sure what's happening," he told Ansellin, "they seem to be in no hurry to equip me with weapons. Either they are postponing the war, or else I shall probably miss it altogether." Ansellin was not much interested. "We shall be sorry to see you go," he said, "it is always useful to have an odd man about who has been trained in the routine. But La Patrie must come first. In the meantime you might give a hand to M. Chivalié, he has got himself in a mess trying to fit nineteen half-columns into a seven-column sheet." "He's lazy, M. Chivalié," Raymond said. He was back at the school shortly before two. Flamant had been done and was dressing. "They've passed me," Flamant said gloomily. Raymond began to undress. "The Germans, one pities them," he said. "The French are merciless." "Séverin!" the sergeant called.

The doctor had a black beard which swept to his nipples and the rest of his head was covered only with a grey fluff like a baby's. His actions were mechanical, like those of a plucker in a foie-gras factory, his speech as clipped and querulous as an old woman's. "Yes, take off that, come over here. Bleu, what a chest! Positively concave. Spit in this, make water in that, lie down, raise your knees, get up, cough. . . . Now put that in your mouth, blow. Hard, harder than that, you're not trying. Look at the tube. Try and get the liquid up to my finger. Go on, you're not trying." Raymond pushed the column another centimetre up the tube and released it, panting. "What's wrong with you?" the doctor said. "You don't take drugs, do you? Absinthe? You're tired?—so am I tired, we shall all be a great deal more tired before we're through with those swine. Now blow again. Go on, up to where my finger is now. Now hold it there. Hold it. Hold it, man, hold it, steady —till I count thirty. One—two——" Raymond held it. He tried to get his tongue wedged in the mouthpiece but he had lost the trick of it. There was a pain in his chest, but he would hold it somehow just to show the damned corpse-raker. He watched the column dancing, he heard through the drumming in his ears the doctor's voice, "Steady, steady, try to keep it steady? Eleven— twelve——" The orderly sitting at the table, the weighing machine behind, had dissolved into mist. The tube itself was leaning back and fading. A yellow curtain came down over his eyes and he pitched into humming darkness.

He shook his face to get the water out of his eyes. The orderly had thrown half a jugful over his head. He heard the doctor ask: "When was this man last examined? What grade then? Bleu! I shouldn't have thought it possible. Where's the sputum? What? Yes, you're probably right. Turn over, you."

The clerk had his pencil hovering.

"Gamma, sir?" he asked.

"Wait!" the doctor said. He pulled the stethoscope away from his ears, scoured them with his fingers and put it back. "Say 'brun!' . . . All right, that'll do." He turned to the lieutenant-commissioner. "If you think this man's going to be the slightest use, you can have him. In ordinary circumstances he might live another ten years, you never know. But if you care to try the experiment of firing a cartridge just behind his head you'll probably find—pouf! like that."

The lieutenant nodded and turned to the clerk.

"SS," he said.

The sergeant opened the door and shouted, "L'Hernault!"

"What does that mean?" Raymond asked.

The clerk was writing a ticket in triplicate.

"Service spécial, Monsieur," he said, handing him the flimsy. "To report at the Commissariat Central, to-morrow at eight o'clock."

Raymond dressed and went out into the street. He was puzzled. The doctor thought he might fall down dead at any moment, that was evident; though, God knew, he didn't feel like that. And the lieutenant—Debehaigne, he had known him before, a man not without some rudimentary intelligence—had decided that he was not to be used in the war. So! If a man was flourishing, if he had another forty years ahead of him, they sent him off to be knocked down by the Germans; and if nothing in the world could keep a man alive for more than a year or two the important thing was to keep him out of the Germans' way. He was not, then, to be a hero. But he felt no relief.

He wanted to tell somebody, to see if there was some other interpretation of what the doctor had said about ten years. But along the tables in the Maréchal Soult he saw none of his friends. He ought, perhaps, to tell Cécile what had happened; but he was not in the mood for Cécile. From habit rather than duty he went back to the place Coupel.

★

They did not seem to be enthusiastic about Raymond at the Commissariat Central. They were busy, they kept him waiting with half a dozen weedy nondescripts in an office containing one bench and a map of Baulon. Here, as at the Ecole de Commerce, they were taking the war quite leisurely, he thought; and he longed to shout out, "Allow me to inform you, gentlemen, I have just ten years at the very outside to live." At nine o'clock he was summoned to the desk of a double-chinned secretary.

"Your name is Séverin," the secretary informed him.

"True."

"And you are normally employed, I believe, in the drapery business of Peulevey?"

"Yes. I stand in the window as a model for matrons' corsets."

The secretary eyed him without appreciation and examined his papers again. "Ah, yes, I see, journalist; reporter, I suppose. (In passing, M. Séverin—I am empowered to bring you before a military tribunal if any disciplinary measure is required. Stand straight, please, feet together.) Unfortunately the duty which is vacant at the moment requires some intelligence; I was hoping I would find one good man in the batch they've sent me. However, it can't be helped. You will proceed immediately to the East railway station, where you will find Constable Méré on duty at the level-crossing or in the yard. He will instruct you and you will then relieve him. You will yourself be relieved some time this afternoon if I can arrange it. Till then you will be held responsible for good order in the station area, which Méré will define for you. To-morrow you will resume duty at the same post at 4 a.m. No, I don't want any questions, Méré will tell you anything you want to know. Right, dismiss! Wait. Bauchard. An armlet for Acting-constable Séverin. And a flag."

The armlet was roughly made of white cotton with the letters A-S in blue.

"Have I to put it on now?" Raymond asked.

"Of course."

"I can't wait till I get to the station?"

"No. Why?"

"But any of my friends might see me as I go along."

"That's enough!" the secretary said. "Don't forget your flag."

★

For an hour after Méré had left him Raymond paced disconsolately between the barriers of the crossing and the station house, the flag stuck up his sleeve. In this quarter they suffered the war calmly. The station itself was almost deserted, in the street there was little traffic, the pavé grew painful to the soles of his feet as the sun climbed. At intervals a train came, a line of sixty trucks closely tarpaulined; the barriers went up, the barriers went down again, the little queue which had formed of carts and motor drays went jolting on: on to where the houses stopped and the road, inclining a little northward, mounted between its escort of poplars to the sun-soaked tableland of Poëlviennes. The three poplar-shaded tables outside the Café de la Gare were still vacant; occasionally a decrepit waiter came out to flap them with his napkin, stood for a few moments gazing at the station and went inside again. "There should be some troop trains?" Raymond asked a porter who was lying on his barrow in the yard. "Troop trains?" the old man said sleepily. "No, I don't think so, they're going the other way. Through Echaupère, so they tell me." A little scorched breeze came, puffing up chaff and sand into the quivering air.

It carried a dust cloud to the second cable-pole towards the town and weakening dropped it there. The flag in the window of a station cottage drooped again. From a long way off, somewhere eastward, a rumble came, more like the constant fall of heavy cases than the roll of thunder.

At eleven o'clock Cécile arrived in her organdie frock. She had discovered his whereabouts from the Commissariat, and she brought him some hot soup in a vacuum flask.

"But my dear Cécile," he protested, "how on earth can I feed here? Don't you realize that I'm on duty—look at this flatulent armlet—I'm responsible for good order at this station; if anything goes wrong I get hauled before a military tribunal. And in any case I couldn't touch soup."

"But you must have something to sustain you," she said pathetically.

"I'm perfectly all right," he told her. "So far I haven't had to arrest anyone, there have been no runaway horses, no trouble of any kind. I do wish you'd go away, you're making me look more of a fool than this damned armlet does. Yes, yes, my dear, I quite understand that you want to be a vivandière, the intention is most patriotic——"

"But can't I stay and see you do something, hit someone with your baton or something like that?"

"By all means," he said irritably. "If you stay long enough you'll probably see me telling the time to two urchins or performing some service of that kind. But I should rather you stood a little farther away. . . ."

She had hardly gone when Vasseur came and surveyed him from the other side of the street.

"Go away!" Raymond shouted. "You can't loiter here."

"I only wanted to have a look," Vasseur said, crossing over. "Engrand told me it would be worth the walk. I like it, that armlet, it makes you look rather pastoral. What does A-S mean?"

"I haven't the remotest idea. Go away. What are you doing? Why haven't you joined the colours?"

"I am fifty-two, I'm too old even to be an operatic policeman, and my life is regarded as very valuable to the Republic."

"Now that's curious," Raymond said. They were wandering instinctively towards the Café de la Gare, the aged garçon was already flapping the chairs for them. "That's very interesting indeed. . . . Yes, two petits armagnacs. . . . They told me that I mustn't go to the war because I've only ten years to live—less, the man thought. 'My God!' the doctor said. 'You look a miserable creature, bleu, I never saw such a wreck. Your life must be preserved at all costs.' Well, if that's how they look at it——"

"What doctor was it?" Vasseur asked with interest. "(A toi, chéri, à la victoire!)"

"(A toi, cher petit!) It was that man from the hospital, Brayelle. You know the man I mean? Is he supposed to be a good doctor, do you know?"

"Oh, yes, an excellent doctor; except that he knows nothing about anatomy or medicine."

Raymond had his back to the street and the inspector of patrols had propped his bicycle against one of the poplars before he noticed him. Seeing the uniform, he got up and raised his hat.

"It is absolutely forbidden," the inspector said, "to take refreshment when on duty."

"This man was a little affected by the heat," Raymond told him. "He fell unconscious in the station yard, I brought him across here for a cordial."

The supervisor nodded judiciously.

"If I might have the pleasure, M. le Commissaire——?" Vasseur said. "Garçon, one more."

"You are to be relieved," the inspector told Raymond, "at four o'clock, and you will then be off duty till four o'clock to-morrow morning. (A vous, Monsieur!) Have you anything to report?"

"Nothing," Raymond said. "I find it a little dull here. You may have heard from the Secretary that I have only ten years to live—I suppose you couldn't find me anything a bit more interesting?"

The supervisor put down his glass and stared up the empty street.

"Dull?" he said. He wriggled his shoulders, smiled faintly, brought his lower lip up to his moustache and blew sharply as if he were trying to spit into his nostrils. They heard the rumble again and it seemed to be louder, as if heavy furniture were being shifted clumsily across the eastern sky. "Dull?" the supervisor said. "Well, we shall see."

★

The clouds came up overnight, at four it was drizzling, no one any longer sang the *Marseillaise*. Raymond crossed the river by the Pont d'Autriche and reached the station through the alleys of Ste Estelle. The crossing was closed and a train was rumbling through. Against the barrier a file of waggons was drawn up; there was no light anywhere and he could not see how far the file extended, but it seemed to go back a long way.

The agent-suppléant on duty did not appear to be in the street and he went to look for him in the station. None of the lamps was lighted there, and the floor of the baggage-hall seemed to be carpeted with bodies. He picked his way to the platform and there

316

a man came to him out of the shadow. The man said, shouting against the train's uproar:

"You've come to relieve me, I suppose? You're ten bloody minutes late."

"I didn't know where you were. What are all those people doing in the baggage-hall?"

"Sleeping."

"But—have they the right to?"

The man laughed. He was very small, with an untidy moustache, a wharfinger's clerk perhaps. He laughed thinly, exuding bloater.

"Try and move them," he said.

"Where do they come from?" Raymond asked.

The man jerked his head. "Over there."

Raymond looked that way, and between the railway trucks saw the sky shot with flashes, for a moment luminous, then dark and cracked with lightning. The train had jerked to a stop, and in the deep, near silence the boom of yesterday came with a new vigour, seeming to vibrate within his neck and forehead.

"Well, I'm off," the man said.

Raymond returned to the street and stood there shivering. There was nothing for him to do. It was chilly, and the rain had set a nerve in his tooth pulsing. He wanted to go back to bed.

An express screamed through on the other line, throwing a fountain of sparks against the sky. The wagons of the freight train jerked clangorously into movement, the tail light glowed and the barriers ramped as if by intuition. The men talking in twos and threes beside the camions jumped back into their places, the cavalcade set on. It was longer still than Raymond had imagined. He watched with a dull fascination the passage of odd shapes moistly outlined against the dark houses: the towering bulk of the lorries, forty in a chain, the haughty snouts of 155s, the restless, tossing heads of trace-mules, a convoy of field kitchens, guns, camions, more guns, infantry marching; with scarcely the sound of human voices, no word of command, rarely a man's short laugh or a phlegmy curse flung at the driver too close behind; only the shudder of wheels on the pavé, the whine of limber-joints and axles, the chatter of hooves and cough of engines against the recurring undertone, the intermittent thunder from the eastward, light-splashed sky. Presently a whistle was blown, the barriers fell again. The train, like a high crenated wall of blackness, hobbled into the station and stood there panting with its after-end across the roadway. When the jostling of the rearmost trucks had ceased it left a curious quietude, in which the distant rumble seemed louder than the men and horses stamping, the creak and jingle of harness. The light rain continued, blurring ghostly the contours of guns and camions; the smell of mobiloil and horses was faint in the damp air. On the nearest lorries the men were very still, lolling together and half-asleep. It was a patient army. The barrier rose, the foremost driver flicked his cigarette-butt into the road and let his clutch in with a jerk, the line was moving again; a field-gun battery, an ambulance, lorries, a troop of horse, more lorries; a ribbon with no ending.

There was traffic beginning to flow in the other direction; he became aware of it as the day grew lighter, the flashes paling in the brightening sky; market traffic, he thought at first, but it was not the market day. Sleepy still, and wretched with the throbbing tooth, he watched the shadowy pageant in the feeble light, confused by the grey shapes intersecting. The sweep of cloud was moving westward, and where the sun first showed was torn away from the horizon. The light came yellow then through the streaking rain, and he could see the carts more clearly as they passed him at walking-pace, with the drivers hunched beneath a coat or piece of sacking, the loads towering behind their shoulders. At first they came singly, a minute or more between; but soon the wagonettes, tired horses plodding with the drivers at their heads, a pram and a donkey drawn behind. Soon, where the carts were open and the covering had slipped, he could see the loads they carried; a mangle and a children's pen, garden forks and a blackboard, tin trunks with clothes oozing from the lids, a three-colour Madonna with a sad grin leaning against a cooking-stove, a child lying on a crate of fowls fast asleep. Where the road narrowed at the crossing there was a danger of collision; and feeling the need to justify himself in a scene so active he nervously took his stand between the files, unrolling his flag. From there, with the wheels all but touching him on either side, he could see the faces better: faces of men and women worn out, dogged, perplexed, but aloof and rather contemptuous. A man leaned dwon from a haywain and asked him in a sleepy voice, "Is this Baulon?" "Where can we go?" another demanded, a toothless crone pushing a wheelbarrow in which a boy sat hugging a little dog. Raymond didn't know. "You must go on," he said vaguely. "Go on, you must keep moving." The rain had stopped and the sun grew warmer, but he was still sleepy and irritable, consciously dirty; his tooth was still aching. He shouted angrily to a man whose sheep had run amok and were holding up the wagons. "You, you fathead, why can't you keep your cursed beasts together? Go on, hurry, get them off the road!" The wagon driver ahead was waiting with stolid patience; he called, "That's right, Uncle Henry, you look sweet in the armlet, it's nice to have you in charge." But he had no temper for raillery. He hurried on a woman leading a goat hung with saucepans, a lame girl bent beneath a feather bed. The incongruousness of the caravan was lost for him in its monotony. He waved his little flag mechanically, goading the pilgrims as if they were one herd with their cattle. A girl of some sixteen years, who marched stoutly with a heavy child on her back, stopped to ask some questions. Her dirty face was marked with tears and he would have paid attention, but the engines chugging just behind his back confused him; he heard, "Mélanie—pardon, Monsieur, but I've lost Mélanie, can you tell me where I could find her?" "Farther on," he said briefly, "go on, you'll find her farther on."

The railway line was clear for nearly an hour, and then train after train cut the street; trains on the down line, moving slowly, as if they heard the sky's reverberation and had no mind for the eastward journey; open trucks, piled high and grey with standing soldiers. The last train stopped with its tender just past the crossing, holding in deadlock the whole vast traffic of the road. From the foremost trucks a dozen men, stiff with cramp, climbed painfully down and stood unconcernedly to relieve themselves along the line. A corporal came and leant against the barrier. "Where's this?" he asked, "Baulon? Good, we're getting on. It's possible we shall still be in time for the war. We left Auxerre at eight o'clock last night."

"Any news?" a poilu called from the second truck.

"The loulou of Mlle Nugent-Pruvôt is considerably better," Raymond answered.

He was standing idly with the flag stuck into his pocket. A hand pounced on his shoulder. "You," a man said, a lieutenant of artillery, "why don't you do something? We can't be here all day."

"But what?" he asked. "I can't move the train."

"No, you couldn't move a go-cart. But you can make the engine-driver. Go on."

Raymond climbed over the barrier and went to the engine-driver's cabin.

"You," he said to the driver, "can't you move this train?"

"Yes, M. Albert Caucisson, if you can move the signal."

He went back to the officer.

"The man says the signal's against him."

"Do you realize," the officer said, "that you're holding up three batteries?"

As he pondered for an answer to the youth's impertinence, Raymond was seized by the arm. A short man with a lawyer's bag stood there trembling with anger and impatience.

"Are you in charge of this crossing?" the lawyer shouted in a foreign accent. "I've got to get to Poigny-Selègue, I can't wait, I'm in a hurry."

Raymond turned to the lieutenant. "Perhaps you could bring up one of your firing-pieces," he said, "and blow away the barriers and all this mess. This gentleman is in a hurry to get to Poigny-Selègue, the war is getting in his way."

"I won't stand for any back-chat," the foreigner said.

Raymond struck him on the mouth.

"That's right," the lieutenant said.

The foreigner turned round and moved away. "You'll hear about that," he said over his shoulder.

The train had started to move, the engine sneezing a shower of smuts. It got under way slowly, the men who had jumped down sauntered back to the moving trucks and were hauled over the sides by their companions. The corporal, with one leg over, turned, bowed, and blew a kiss to Raymond. "A Berlin!" he called, grinning. But they were less ebullient in the trucks that slowly followed: a heterogeneous jumble of artisans and peasants in uniform, a man with a hollow face and a student's perching eyebrows, a pale schoolboy biting a dead cigarette, men with silicon faces from the blast-furnaces of St. Denis, a youth like Baudelaire, a fat Donnemarie butcher with a tattered, humorous moustache; united, not so much by their grey cloth as their unmoving, sleep-starved, slightly contemptuous eyes. Raymond was automatically counting the trucks: nineteen, twenty, twenty-one: the last one was still out of sight round the bend. The sun had not yet reached its full power, the night's rain had cooled the air and the day was lovely, a day for a holiday excursion. But the men were unshaven and dirty, Raymond got the stink of their clothes as the trucks crawled past. His sight became blurred by the unbroken passage of uniform and sleepy faces, he blinked, turned his knuckles in his eye-pits, looked again. They were still passing, truck after truck of smut-soiled men, scarecrow warriors packed upright in their boxes, too weary to brush away the phlegm from their moustaches or the dribble of nicotine from their chins. And now they seemed to be all the same, narrow and hungry faces, hollow-eyed, passive and slightly scornful, always marked with a quiet superiority of understanding, dignified by immovable contempt. He realized suddenly, as the trucks were gathering speed, what it meant to be a Frenchman. The attribute he had never observed, never suspected, was blazoned there in the sunlit brick-wagons, the pride of them, their minds' cool greatness, the tired men who travelled so contemptuously into battle. There was no one else, no one in the world like that. His forehead had gone ice-cold, a choking draught came up to his tautened nostrils and spilt over moistly into his eyes. He struggled to cry out, he got his voice free only as the hindmost truck passed him. He shouted, frantically, waving his arms, the warm tears flowing down his cheeks, *Vive! Vive! Vive—la—France!*

XXXV

SHE saw that Armand was getting out of bed, but she did not move. Her body was in a position of perfect rest, and her mind, under the opiate of weariness, had the sense of vast power chained by reluctance. She had dreamed that Armand was grown up, a tall man very like Pierre, that he was waiting to take her away from Baulon. She thought that if she kept quite still the grown-up Armand would come back to her again.

Her eyes stayed open, held by Armand's figure against the window. The free, delicious world of her dream, the power to shake the universe with a finger's movement, receded before the steady tide of material sensation. Armand was out of bed, she realized now; he had strayed a little way from her protection. And still she did not move, her will hesitant to batter through the wall of glass which kept her separate from him. She tried to call out; her voice was slow to obey, and even when it came he did not seem to hear her. But the sound quickened her own consciousness, the force of custom overcame the dead weight of resistance, her limbs moved and carried her out of bed.

She approached him carefully, fearing to frighten him; and whispered, standing beside him at the window, "What are you looking at, Armand, what do you see?"

He was neither startled nor ashamed.

"It was Father," he said, "I saw him down there."

She opened the window to see better, letting a cool breeze into the room. The Square, lit grey from the open sky, was empty.

"Where?" she asked him.

He pointed across to the scaffolding.

"Over there."

She carried him back to bed, where he lay contentedly. She put on her winter coat, her outdoor shoes, and locking the bedroom door behind her went downstairs. The big hall door was bolted at the top, but standing on a chair she worked and got the bolt undone. She ran across the Square and into the shadows beneath the scaffolding, climbed over the builder's barricade and picked her way among the débris of deals and stone. It was very quiet here; no noise came from the town, there was only the distant rumble as of heavy traffic rolling over the eastward arch of sky, so constant now that her tuned ear hardly perceived it. She called "Pierre! Pierre!" but there was no answer.

She knew she was awake now by the coldness of the shoes on her unstockinged feet. But perhaps she had only dreamed of Armand saying that he saw his father.

Hurrying back, she thought that someone watched her from the salon window; a man's head, it could only be M. Séverin. She left the door unbolted and ran up the stairs, frightened as she passed the first landing. But no one stopped her, the house was silent. She found Armand still wide awake.

"Yes," Armand said, with a child's calm certainty, "yes, he was there, I saw him."

XXXVI

Fouché, deputy divisional superintendent of police at Laruns, had hardly rolled himself into bed when his telephone rang again. He turned the receiver over. "Allo! Allo! Allo! what's that? what is it? speak up, I can't hear you! Eaux Chaudes? The constable at Eaux Chaudes? But why does he want me, why can't you deal with him? What? Oh, all right, all right, you'd better put him through. . . . Allo! Allo! Allo! Yes, yes, superintendent . . . a spy? what do you mean, a spy? how do you know? . . . Well, it doesn't matter, you must lock him up. Why in the name—What's that? Allo! Allo! what do you say? . . . Violent? I can't help that . . . no, no, certainly not, no. I'll send an escort in the morning. . . . Yes, yes, of course, good night, good night, good night."

"That man Bérard at Eaux Chaudes," he answered his wife, "a perfect imbecile, too old for his job, I've told Mouly that a hundred times. Yes, he's arrested some half-wit peasant who can't account for himself. Why in the world he had to babble to me about it—Yes, poor old Bérard, the man went for him, gave him a black eye or something. And apparently the lock on Bérard's cellar is not quite what it should be, and Mme Bérard is so frightened she has gone to sleep with her uncle. Dear, dear! What a thing to bother me about!"

When he went into the office next morning the formal report which Pantin had taken over the telephone was on his table. "Gives name of Jean-Baptiste Picard. . . . Age apparently between thirty and forty, above the normal height, thin face, fair hair." Tt-tt-tt— why was it that a garde champêtre could never introduce the smallest touch of originality into his descriptions? ". . . but his voice did not seem to me like that of a labourer." That was better, though probably quite untrue—what did Bérard know about voices? "The man admits that he has crossed the frontier, but states that his motive was patriotic. He has been employed at the irrigation works at Monterrubio . . . when I attempted to arrest prisoner he struck me a cowardly blow on the left eye, which will require medical treatment. I overpowered prisoner after a prolonged struggle, in which I received some slight assistance from MM. Dupin, postmaster, Lepauvre, wineseller, Ursin, Tranchot, and Pinon, quarrymen. . . ." So! In Fouché's experience spies were a little more dainty, and they came into France more frequently by the wagon-lit coaches of the rapide-supplément.

"Pantin! Get me Pau—Commissariat Central." He took the pipette from his ephedrine bottle, flung back his head, douched both nostrils, and sneezed wetly and luxuriously. "And Pantin! I want that Place-Beauvau memorandum—what was it! Yes, 4396, I'm almost sure—it came in May, about that officer, you know the one I mean. Nntzz! Blast my nose, where are those salts?"

Pantin gave him the salts and the telephone.

"You're through to the Commissariat, sir."

"Ah, good. Allo! Allo! Allo! Fouché, Laruns . . . Francoual? Ah, M. Francoual, I shall be grateful for a small service. If you would get through to Monterrubio—yes, yes, Burgos—and find out if a man called Picard—Jean-Baptiste Picard—has been recently employed at the irrigation works there . . . twenty thousand thanks."

"That's the memorandum, sir."

"Good. What time do you expect Bérard's prisoner?"

"Any time now, sir."

Fouche glanced through the memorandum. ". . . be correct, there is good reason to suppose that he intends to make his way back into France. The need for special vigilance on the Spanish frontier. . . ." Yes, yes, he remembered it all by heart. "Pantin. Where's the photograph?" "Under your elbow, sir." "Good, good. Ring up Mme Fouché, will you, and tell her that she is not to give me anything with so much as a pinch of spice for dinner. And give me the newspaper. . . . Swine, Pantin, that's what they are, pigs of swine!"

Bérard came in ten minutes later.

"Well, Bérard, you look a fine sight, yes, they've done you up very prettily. Never mind, never mind, you are wounded for the defence of your country, your wounds are glorious, Bérard, you should be proud of them. Think, you are one of the first heroes of the war. What have you done with your poacher? Oh, he's in the charge-room. Wait, let's have a look at him." He went to the other side of the room and glanced through the one unfrosted pane in the intervening window. "Yes, Bérard, a veritable monster, you are much to be congratulated, no doubt he was armed to the teeth. No don't bring him in, I don't want him just yet, ask the sergeant tp put him in the cells. Nntzz! Damn my nose! Pantin! I don't like the look of our friend Berard's prisoner, he is altogether too hirsute. Will you arrange, please, for the immediate removal of his beard and whiskers? Then he will look much better."

The telephone rang again. Pantin answered.

"It's Pau again, sir."

"Good. Give it me. . . . Allo! Allo! Allo! What, already? You're very quick, M. Francoual, really remarkable. He was? For how long? Only four days! And he was discharged? Oh, he just made off! Perhaps he didn't like the smell of the foreman or something. . . . No, no, quite a trivial matter, we can deal with it here quite perfectly . . . sixty million thanks. . . . Pantin! I shall want two— no, better say three—men here in plain clothes to meet M. Picard, to make a little party for him. M. Galampoix across the road would perhaps oblige us with the loan of three of his clerks, as he has done before. You might go across and ask him. The same ones as last time, if possible, the ones that look like perfect imbeciles. In a quarter of an hour. And in the meantime I shall just go along to the Hôtel de Ville to see if there is any public rioting."

Half an hour had gone before Fouché came back. Pantin had the scene set for him in his own office: Bérard's prisoner sitting at the table with two men on one side and one on the other, himself standing at one end and holding the party to silence at the points of his bellicose moustaches, Bérard at the other end. Fouché came in with his cap on the back of his head, wiping his forehead and continuously sneezing. He had opened his tunic, revealing the fact that his top trouser button was missing and the next two undone. He dropped into his chair and douched his nose.

"Well, Patin, what is all this, what are these gentlemen doing here?"

"They are under arrest for unauthorized crossing of the frontier."

"Oh dear, dear."

He glanced at the borrowed men. Pantin had got the same ones, they would be all right. He hardly looked at Bérard's prisoner at all, only noting with his passing glance that the man was under-fed and nervous. He took the paper nearest to hand—it was an advertisement for Savon Prunier—and scrutinized it carefully. "Your names: Gustave Voirie? Louis Anquetil? Jean-Baptiste Picard? Joseph Du Bosq? Good. Give me the statements, will you please, Pantin. . . . Now, M. Voirie, you are alleged to have made the following statement immediately upon your arrest. Listen, please. . . ."

The cross-examination proceeded at a leisurely pace, punctuated by Fouché's nasal typhoon. Except for the hay-fever, Fouché was enjoying his morning; M. Galampoix's clerks were doing very well and he was able to put some nice touches of artistry into his catechism. With Picard he was more brief.

"You state that you have recently been employed as a labourer at the irrigation works at Monterrubio? (You have made inquiries, Pantin? Oh, the statement is confirmed? All right.) Yes, your statement is confirmed. And you left France last year? Why? Well, never mind, we needn't perhaps inquire too closely into that. You have returned, you say, for patriotic motives, you intend to join your brave countrymen at the front? Well, that alters the aspect of the case, that alters it considerably. Technically your conduct has been most irregular, but in the present crisis we make certain allowances for those who show themselves true patriots ——" Bérard had coughed gently. "Yes, Bérard? Of course, yes, there is the question, M. Picard, of your cowardly assault on the garde here. I am afraid you will not escape without a fine—though allowance will be made, of course, for the patriotic motive. . . . And now you, M. Du Bosq. Your case seems to me rather more serious. . . ."

He had opened the drawer a little way; the photograph lay just inside. ——? One couldn't be sure. He douched again and proceeded steadily with the cross-examination.

When it was finished the deputy superintendent paused to deliberate. He tilted back his chair and stretched his arms, exhibiting the vast extent of soiled blue shirt across his stomach, the shining stubble on his throat. He cleared his nose again with a series of little snorts, splashing the papers on the table. He seemed to be puzzled.

"I confess," he said, "you have put me in an awkward position. At the present time our country needs every available man in the firing-line. Each of you professes his intention to take his place immediately in the ranks of our gallant forces. So far so good. But here we have a special duty, becoming still more onerous and vital in war time—nntzz! the salts, Pantin!—that of protecting our frontier against the infiltration of hostile nationals. I should be gravely neglecting my responsibilities if I allowed a single man, one single man, to find his way across that part of the frontier which lies in my district without making myself quite certain of his intentions." He was tilting back farther and farther, with his eyes on the ceiling; Pantin thought he would be over at any moment. "Now if I were to get each of you men to sign a statement solemnly avowing your patriotic intention, I might feel that my responsibility had been discharged. Would you be willing to sign such a statement, M. Voirie?"

"Yes, Monsieur."

"And you, M. Anquetil?"

"Certainly."

"You, Captain Séverin?"

"Yes."

Fouché smiled. He picked up the telephone.

"Give me the Dépôt du Dix-Huitième, the bureau of the commanding officer."

*

Captain de la Bouheyre was not to be outmatched in politeness by any deputy superintendent of police. He thanked M. Fouché. He congratulated M. Fouché on his apprehension of a notorious deserter. He thought—if he might make so bold as to say so—that M. Fouché had followed exactly the right course in referring the matter at once to the nearest military authority. Perhaps M. Fouché would add to his courtesy by sending the prisoner to Captain de la Bouheyre under proper escort, together with the relevant memoranda, at his earliest possible convenience; Captain de la Bouheyre would then deal with the matter, and in due course M. Fouché would receive in official form the expression of the authorities' keen appreciation of the high services he had rendered. . . . No, Captain de la Bouheyre very much regretted that it was not possible for him to attend at M. Fouché's office and examine the prisoner there, as M. Fouché suggested. At that moment he was somewhat preoccupied with the business of drafting troops to the north-east; M. Fouché had no doubt heard that military operations of some importance were being conducted there. Captain de la Bouheyre would be exceedingly grateful if M. Fouché would send the prisoner as he had suggested, otherwise Captain de la Bouheyre might be obliged to discontinue his interest in the matter.

He hung up the receiver and said, "Damn the arrogance of all policemen!"

*

He had to go to Oloron, where there had been confusion over the transport of equipment, and was not back till four. The thing had gone right out of his head, and he was immersed in correspondence when Sergeant Huppé reminded him. He said: "Of course, yes! Have you got the budget? I'll just read it through. Where is the prisoner? Very well, you can go straight away and get him."

When Pierre came in the officer was sitting in the window with his back towards him.

"Is that the prisoner?" Bouheyre asked without turning round. "All right, Sergeant, you can leave him here. Just take off the menottes, they won't be necessary. No, do as I tell you and clear out. . . . And now, Captain Séverin—excuse my back, I have rather a lot of work these days——"

"A mistake has been made," Pierre said dully. "A well-meaning polidiot, having this Séverin on his mind——"

"I'm sorry," Bouheyre said, "but your coining of that word is enough to identify you by itself. It was always a habit of yours." He turned round. "Yes, at the Parc de Vernon, I thought you would remember. Sit down, won't you?" He took the chair opposite and pushed his cigarette-case across the table. "Irregular, I know."

Pierre said: "No, thanks. . . . Well?"

Bouheyre examined his thumbnail. He said presently: "You know, Séverin, you're a bit of a fool——"

"That's enough of that," Pierre snapped. "I don't want to hear that sort of chat, Bouheyre. I'm not in the mood."

He had automatically taken a cigarette and lit it. A moment later he flipped it away, belching. Bouheyre saw how it was. God! The man was like a ghost.

"When did you last feed?" he asked.

"About two days. Oh, I've had chocolate since. I don't really want anything."

Bouheyre shouted for Huppé. "Huppé, go and find some cheese or something, will you? And send someone to my quarters for a bottle of cognac—there are three bottles in my truckle-chest. Hurry. . . . I've got something here I must do. We're busy, you know, with this war they've started for us. I'll be back soon."

He collected a batch of company-estates and went across to the empty quartermaster's office, where he worked for half an hour. When he returned there was a plate on the table with nothing but crumbs, and a glass, empty. Séverin looked more human, he thought.

"I wish you'd tell me," he said, "why you did it?"

Pierre shrugged his shoulders.

"I don't see why I have to satisfy your damned curiosity. It makes no difference."

Bouheyre nodded. "I suppose not." Then, "What do you suppose I'm going to do?"

"——? I suppose you'll send me to Bordeaux. And I'll hang about there till they've collected the whole dossier. I don't suppose the army's any quicker now than it ever was."

Bouheyre nodded again. "No, it's not. And they won't be very pleased with you at Bordeaux either. They've plenty else to do. I think I mentioned this war we're running. It will be a nuisance, all the paraphernalia of court-martialling a man and shooting him. Of course it will all be done in proper order, we are the best-organized army in Europe, we pride ourselves on that sort of thing. But it wastes time rather. . . . I do wish you'd tell me why you sneaked away from Sigumbe."

Pierre was smoking now. He blew a cloud and watched Bouheyre's face through it as it rose. "——? Well, if you're so damned interested! Only you won't believe what I tell you, I don't really ask you to. You've never done colonial service, have you? No, I thought not. It used to be amusing in its way. A little less formal than"—he swept the dépôt with a movement of his head—"this sort of thing. But it's been getting—well, bargain-basement. The riff-raff of the eighty-nine departments. Second-class and dull, astonishingly dull. I was under a man called Le Rochais; very amiable in some ways, a kind of Cæsar's concubine. We did outpost manœuvres. We hid in the woods, occasionally a Bisquort popped up and we sniped him, then they would collar two of ours. In time it becomes tedious, that kind of thing. . . . I don't want to bore you. No? Well, it reached my ears that there was going to be this war of yours. I thought that that would be more amusing, I asked for transfer. No, you won't find that in your dossier, they haven't reported that little item, you can take that for granted."

"I haven't anything here," Bouheyre said, "but the police memorandum."

"Ah, well, it doesn't matter either way. But I did ask them. I asked several times. But oh, no! Captain Séverin must be a good boy and keep on sniping the Bisquorts, that was much more important than a hypothetical war in Europe. . . . Well, I got tired of asking. Yes, I recognize now that it was temerarious; and you'd never believe how unpleasant in the actual operation. Still, I did get through to France, you'll grant me that. And I'll just mention for your information that it isn't all that simple for a deserter to find his way from Africa to France without anyone's hook in his nose-ring. The boast, however, is idle, my dear Bouheyre. The gods do as they will. My grand adventure has ended in the arms of a country policeman." He closed his eyes and put his head down on his arms; for a moment Bouheyre thought he had fainted. Then, fiercely, "My God, Bouheyre, if you'd lend me your Mauser half a minute I'd waste precious little more of your time!"

Bouheyre got up. He said "Wait a minute," and left the room. He went across to his quarters and lay down. His head was aching. He cursed Séverin, putting him through this, just when he was up to the eyes. But the guts of the fellow! No one but a madman like Séverin would ever have dreamed of such an escapade. And now they would shoot him for cowardice. Yes, it was inevitable; the fact that France was pitting its forces against those of a nation twice as large, that bravery was worth everything that the professors of Saint-Cyr had ever written in the text-books, that an experienced officer who didn't give a damn for all the bayonets in Flanders was to be had for the asking—that would count for nothing against the formal conception of military discipline, the system, that dogma of obedience which kept Bouheyre at a writing-desk in the Pyrenees, signing travel warrants for scared and under-broken poilus to the very gun-swept fields where he ached to give his brains, his burning heart to France. Yes, they'd keep Séverin and question him and maul him about, they wouldn't listen to a word of his explanation, they'd parade his peccadilloes once again before the bulging eyes of the proletariat and then with appropriate pantomimery they'd put half a dozen bullets in his chest. Séverin himself was right: it would save everybody's time if Bouheyre was careless enough to leave his Mauser on the table.

He went back to the office. He asked rather wearily:

"What did you mean to do, if they hadn't pinched you at Eaux Chaudes?"

"Why do you keep me hanging about here?" Pierre demanded. "Is it just your half-baked sense of humour? Why can't you send me on to Bordeaux or wherever it is and be done with the business? I personally want to get this particular execution over."

Bouheyre bit his lip.

"You seem to forget, Séverin, you're my prisoner. You'd do better to behave yourself and answer my questions. *What did you intend to do?*"

"What the devil difference does that make? I meant, if you must know, to go to Toulouse and be recruited there."

"Had you got money?"

"About ten pesetas."

"You seem to have forgotten, we don't use pesetas here. We use this sort of thing." He took two hundred-franc notes from his pocket and passed them across the table. "If you're so damned ignorant about French currency you'd better keep those to remind you." He shouted. "Huppé! . . . Huppé, I want you to take this man, have him escorted by someone reliable to the station and put in the train for Pau. No, no, he is no longer under arrest. . . ."

★

There was just a note of dwindling patience in Bouheyre's voice when the deputy superintendent telephoned in the evening.

"M. Fouché, yes! Yes, acting-commandant speaking. The man you sent me? Oh, yes, I meant to ring up and tell you, but I've been so busy. Yes, I examined him, but I discovered that he was not the officer whom you thought. What? Well, he was in rather an exhausted condition, no doubt you observed that, and he may have misunderstood you in some way. Oh, yes, he has satisfied me that his story is substantially correct, though I'm afraid he may be rather a streaky customer. What? Well, it happens that I formerly knew the Captain Séverin who is missing, we were in training together at one time, so I can hardly have been mistaken. What do you say? You want him back? Charge of brutal assault? But, my dear Commissaire, I had no idea. . . . Indeed, I must apologize, it never occurred to me that there might be some additional charge. . . . Yes, I had him escorted to the station, he was put on the train for Bayonne."

XXXVII

THERE was still no telegram from the Ministry of War. "They are busy there," Madeleine said, "they have so many details to deal with at the present time that more important matters are being put on one side." "I suppose so, yes, I suppose so," Eugène would answer. ". . . but at present things cannot be very serious, General Caudebec said he would send for me as soon as things took a serious turn." "No, no, my dear fellow," he said rather irritably to Tischer, "things are not very serious yet. I have private information from the Ministry, there is no need for any alarm. . . ." A notice signed by the mayor had been posted all over the town and a copy flapped from a single nail now on one side of the scaffold-poles:

The sacrilegious invasion of our soil is being met at every point by the gallant and obstinate resistance of our armies; but the people of Baulon are advised that the safety of their persons and property can no longer be guaranteed. Everything possible will be done to facilitate the exodus of those who are in a position to leave the town. Citizens are warned, however, that the exigencies of military traffic will render the transport of the civilian population increasingly difficult, and that the opportunity for withdrawal may at any time be closed.

There had been a little crowd round the notice when the man had nailed it up, and for half a day anyone who passed through the

Square would stop to read it; but soon everyone knew what it said, the children were reciting it gaily like a school lesson, it was absorbed into the scenery and no one observed it any more. The copy delivered to the house had been brought to Madeleine, and she had shown it to Thérèse. "Eugène must see it," Thérèse said firmly, but Madeleine obstinately refused. "No, no, it would only worry him; no, he's not to see it. . . . But you, Thérèse, there's nothing to keep you here, surely you will go now. If you will let me I will make arrangements." "Thank you, Madeleine, but if I decide to move I can make arrangements for myself." Presently the notice reached Eugène by the hand of Gaston, in an envelope which Thérèse had addressed. It disturbed him. "This, Madeleine," he said, "have you seen this notice? It's curious, I never thought . . . But of course, it's only signed by Becquet the ironmonger; they like to parade their importance, little men like that. Becquet wants everybody to be as scared as he is himself—it's amusing, this pompous notice of his."

The rumble of artillery that went on all day had become a little louder, and puzzling in its direction; sometimes now, as you faced north-east, you seemed to hear it simultaneously on your left and right; occasionally it rose to a sudden anger, heard like a volley of beats on a tenor-drum, disturbing taut nerves, making a teaspoon tinkle in the saucer. "Those children of Pierre's," Eugène said, "they make a great deal of noise." *Le Petit Baulonnais* had begun to print a sketch-map in which Baulon showed in a white bay with shaded capes on either side; the capes seemed to reach out farther every day. But Eugène had his own maps to occupy his time, and he was by no means satisfied of this perfection. He was afraid, now, of being caught unready; he found that his power of concentration had slackened, he was constantly nervous lest something important had been overlooked. "Madi!" he called: it was after midnight. "Madi, are you awake?" She turned in bed, and he waited impatiently for the end of the inevitable coughing. "Madi, I want to make sure—I'm not quite certain if I placed a battery at Vigne-aux-Bois." She was reluctant to move. "To-morrow," she said wearily, "surely we can put that right to-morrow." But she knew already that he could not wait, that he would toss and worry till his doubt was satisfied. He sat up and fidgeted with the bed-clothes while she put on her old riding-coat and woollen stockings; his eyes, intense and brilliant, rested on her as she lit the gas and followed her as she moved across the room and took the maps from their drawer. "No, no, Madi, not that one!" He was still unbroken to her dullness. "It's the second regional map, surely, you must know." Her movements at this hour were awkward; the shawl she had gathered round her shoulders slipped, the sleeve of her coat caught the corner of the sheets, it took her a long time to find the place. At last, "Yes, it's marked there, at Vigne-aux-Bois, two batteries of the Sixteenth." He nodded seriously, pleased that he had not overlooked that point of strategy. "Yes," he said, "that should be enough." But the next day he would want it altered.

"If any of you are frightened," Eugène said every morning, "you can go away. There's no need whatever for any of you to stop here. For myself, I am not much alarmed by M. le Quincaillier's classical proclamations. But a soldier, naturally, has a different attitude to danger. I don't want to keep anyone here who is frightened and would rather go away."

It was difficult for the Abbé Vignaud to maintain his fund of conversation. He came, never failing, each afternoon; it was a comfort to Madeleine to see his figure appearing at the corner of the Square, his head poked forward like a tortoise's, his face sewn with the exercise of gravity, his greening cassock trailed over the dust; he sat in his usual chair and stirred his coffee with the dainty regularity of a kitten washing its forepaw; he smiled with economy, as if the charm of Mme Séverin forced him, his eyes lighted with the cherished task of recollection when a phrase of hers, a name she mentioned, sent him to rummage in his storehouse. But Paris had lost its charm altogether, he could no longer hold her attention with his stories of the eccentric Comtesse de la Perouaille; and for the rest, what was there, now that everyone in whom the Abbé had the faintest interest had left the town? "I want you to tell me," Madeleine said, "how things are in Baulon. I don't go into the town now, Barbier does the shopping. I want you to tell me frankly how things are going on." And what could he say? Like many who walk with their noses scraping the ground he noticed everything, and a man far stupider could hardly have given the scene a genial interpretation. It was true that the mass of working Baulonnais was oddly calm, with the optimistic fatalism bred of prolonged uncertainty: they saw their squares filling with the dreary caravan of refugees, the Parc Rousseau turned to a vast encampment; but those, they seemed to think, were the unfortunate, country people who had chosen rather foolishly to live out there when the war was going on; in any case it was worry enough that Louis and Marcel and Henri had been swallowed up in the grey procession and might be dead already from the bullets of those swine; and what could you do?—you had your workshop here, your tools, your furniture; you waited to see if anything would really happen. But those a little better off were crowding in the central station where they would wait from dawn till sunset on the suffocating platform in the hope of a place on the single west-bound train. The Ramigny road was cluttered all day long with gigs and motors, which the lorries hurrying back with broken soldiers pressed against the verge. You risked your life in trying to cross the rue Join-Lambert, where motor-cyclists leapt like fleas at any gap between the wagons. On the west side of the town, a little short of Ramigny, a thousand men they said were wiring and digging by night and day. "I want you to tell me frankly, Abbé, how things are going on." He had been visited that morning by an elderly musician, a pianist in one of the café orchestras, who had told him simply, "I have come to confess, Monsieur, I have strangled my wife and my two children. It was the only way to save them from those ravishers, it was the only thing to do." The pianist's face, like that of a child who without intention has done something naughty, was still too lively in his mind; by no device could he make that happening an amusing story. "In Baulon," he said reflectively, "there is a great deal of military activity. It appears that the town is being made a base of operations. But of course it's all a mystery to me, I should never have the brains to be a soldier. I spoke to one of the officers this morning; I asked him if it wouldn't be more sensible to rest the soldiers in comfortable billets and send off detachments at reasonable intervals, instead of having them always on each other's heels and marking time for hours at the crossings? But he seemed to think that a very foolish question. I'm afraid there is a general shortness of temper. I remember talking to General Bazaine once on that very subject. . . ."

No, she would not listen, he had lost the power to hold her fascinated by the slow grimacing of his plastic features. "But why do you stay here?" she asked impatiently, "you must know it isn't safe, you can see from that map in the paper——"

He turned his head on one side and looked at her sadly. Another of the volleys sounded, followed by the mutter of falling plaster, but he did not appear to notice it.

"But where should I find so good a listener?" he said tenderly. "You know, I'm a very prosy old man, hardly anyone cares for my stories now, I belong to a dead world, no one has any patience with me any longer. No, dear Mme Séverin, it is easy enough to part with one's other possessions; my books and pictures, even my Chilly manuscripts, those I can give up if necessary. But one does not part so easily from old friends. . . . Unless you too are getting tired of me——?"

She was instantly moved to tears. "Dear Abbé," she said, "you won't go, promise me you won't go away! I'm so lonely here, I'm all alone."

He shook his head reassuringly and folded his hands.

"But you, I should be so much happier if you would leave Baulon for a while, if you would take a little holiday."

"A holiday?" She was looking out of the window, she had partly recovered her self-control. "You don't seem to understand, none of you understand. It may come at any moment, Eugène's great hour. It is just now that France may need him. How could we go away?"

★

So far the Square was free from soldiers; it had kept aloof, with something of its old exclusiveness, from the turmoil of the town. But it could not escape the echo of the town's uncertainty, something besides the shiver of the windows had infected its insolent houses with the scent of danger. The door of 17 was always shut, guarding in the hall the habitual smell, the moist stillness. And the inward noises were unchanged, the hum of blowflies, the creak of a loose floorboard under Barbier's limping step, the rub of Mme Séverin's dress as she passed from the bedroom to the salon; sometimes, when the salon window was open and a little breeze came in, the scrape of a picture swinging. The children's promenade was limited for safety to the boulevard and the wood-market, and except for Barbier no one went to the centre now; but he, without intention, would drop a crumb of gossip in the kitchen—"They say there'll be no meat soon, there's none coming in but what goes on to the soldiers"—and the morsel was enough to carry the germ. Joséphine went through her work without the smallest deviation; she dragged her pantoufles up the many stairs, shuffled along the corridors with trays and cans of water, scoured the floors persistently and fiercely. The weather seemed to make no difference; her wrinkled forehead shining with sweat, she discarded not one garment; but her face was angry, her movements rougher than before. With growing obstinacy she would do the drawing-room in one of the few hours when Madeleine was there; at a word of protest she would drop her broom on the floor and slouch away, slamming the door behind her.

"Joséphine, why do you behave like this?" Madeleine demanded in a moment of exasperation.

Faced with that sudden assault, Joséphine said nothing. She stared for a second time at Mme Séverin, then turned her back and went on with her work, picking up two heavy books and smacking them together. But Madeleine was roused and would press the attack while her heat lasted.

"Stop that, Joséphine, turn round, listen to me! I'm tired of you and your temper, you're more trouble to me than you're worth." She stopped; Joséphine was staring at her dourly, and from that point she could not see her way. "Yes," she said with ebbing courage. "if you don't feel inclined to behave like a good servant you can go away. I'm heartily tired of you, I shouldn't in the least mind your going."

Joséphine nodded, went as far as the door, and turned round again.

"And Gaston?" she asked. "I suppose you want him to stay, you want someone to look after the old bitch upstairs? You think it doesn't matter, because Gaston's funny, but Gaston's no more funny than that child of Madame's Pierre, he feels things just the same as you or I. And now that the Prussians are coming——"

Madeleine stamped her foot. "Stop it, Josephine!" she said furiously. "I don't want to listen to you, go away."

The clash resulted, as Madeleine knew it must, in a visit from Barbier. He was pitifully distressed. He stood at the door of the salon in deep confusion. "I can't understand," he said, "Joséphine tells me that we are dismissed from your service, I've told her she can't have understood you, I'm sure you wouldn't turn us away just because of something that Gaston's done, as Joséphine says——"

"It's nothing that Gaston's done," she said wearily, "it's Joséphine herself—but it's no good, I can't explain."

"But, Madame, you don't want us to go?"

She was confused now. She said: "No, but you must do as you think best, Barbier. It isn't safe—they say that Baulon isn't safe now, I keep hearing that noise, the Colonel says it's the thundery weather but it worries me—if you have somewhere else you can go to we ought not to keep you, I would write you a recommendation——"

"But the work?" he said in perplexity. "How would you get the work done?"

"I don't know," she answered. "I suppose we should have to manage somehow, we could all do something. And it won't be for much longer, we shan't be here long."

"You mean—you are going to Paris?"

"I don't know. But something will happen soon. That map which they show in the paper——"

He nodded. "I know. You ought to get away from Baulon. I've said before——" But he saw that he was only hurting her, and she looked so ill.

"What is it I owe you now for wages?" she asked distractedly.

"I don't know, I can't remember. . . . But, Madame, you must understand that we can't leave you and the Colonel at this time, it's not to be thought of. Joséphine, you see, she talks roughly sometimes, she's a country woman, she worries about that boy.

But she doesn't mean what she says, you must realize that. How could we leave you now . . .?"

She was grateful, moved even to tears by Barbier's kindness; but she was glad when he left her alone. She locked the door then and knelt down with her arms circling her head on the little nursing-chair, trying to gather her tossing mind into the attitude of prayer. But she could not submit herself to God's will and compassion, her heart would only clamour fiercely for strength and patience, for power to resist the opposers of her will. They wanted her to side with them, Tischer and the rest of them, to surrender to her own alarm and play her hand against Eugène. So: the struggle that had started all those years ago was still being waged; she was short of breath now, sometimes faltering, when Eugène so needed her and the game was still at hazard. He had grown so old since his return from Paris, his face was cut with the thorns of disappointment. His mind, she thought, was swift and brilliant as it had always been, but sometimes stumbling from its own too-reckless vigour; hers was a feeble arm, but he had to have it near him. There was still no telegram, perhaps it would never come; but surely he answered them, the men who had traduced him, by his defiance of danger. They could write as they liked about Viboire, and the truth might never be known; at least they must say that in his old age nothing had frightened him away from Baulon. She prayed, "More strength, O God, more courage!"

*

A telegram came next morning, brought by a scared woman in a yellow dress; but it was not from the Ministry of War. Louis was sending his motor; the whole family could just be fitted in; he implored Eugène to use it and get away while he could.

Eugène took the message very calmly. "It is kind of Louis," he said, "he's a thoughtful fellow. I've been thinking, it would be better for Renée and her children to go away somewhere, now that Baulon is hardly safe. And Marianne, she had better go too; and Thérèse, if she wishes." The decision seemed to stimulate his old capacity, he put his maps aside and talked about it all the morning. "The driver had better be told to take them to Paris. It will be quite safe there. No doubt Louis will make some arrangement for them. They ought to take clothes and things to last a month, they may be away as long as that. Of course, I don't regard it as very serious, this talk of Baulon being in danger; I should have had special warning from General Caudebec if anything was likely to happen, he would have wanted me to inspect the town's defences; but it's much better, at a time like this, to have women and children as far away as possible. You will tell them, won't you, Madi, that they must take some clothing; enough for a month, I should think;

and they had better take some warm things, there may be cold weather coming. And, Madi, will you remember to tell the driver when he comes to be sure that he has enough spirit for his motor; I've heard of motors running out of spirit and people being stranded. . . . Yes, it will be a great relief to me, I have been in considerable anxiety about Renée and her children."

But like Thérèse, Marianne had already made up her mind: she would not leave her parents. She knew—for she scrutinized her own emotions with a scientists's cold eyes—that she neither loved nor was any use to them. But her father's resolution found response in her dry spirit, she would not show herself less obstinate than he. "There's no need for you to stay," Madeleine reiterated. "Your father has to stay because he is under orders from the Ministry, but there's no need for anyone but me to look after him." "I know," she said bleakly, "I know he doesn't want me. But I have no wish to go." She chanced to meet Renée on the landing and stopped to speak to her: "I hear you are taking the children away?" Surprised, Renée answered slowly: "Yes . . . Sophie will miss you." Marianne turned away. "Do you think so? . . . Yes, she can come up this afternoon if she wants to." They spent the afternoon in their usual way, the child sitting on Marianne's knee and spelling out *Les Bébés de Lauriant* with indulgent prompting. When it was time for Sophie to go, Marianne said: "You know you're going to go away and leave me?" But Sophie did not seem to grasp her meaning, she gave her usual kiss and jogged away. It was idiotic, Marianne thought, to concern oneself with a child so stupid and so shallow in affection; Sophie had never cared for her, never regarded her as more than a quietly entertaining person. But the thought came back: *Day after day, no Sophie.* She locked her door, and called to Barbier when he came that she wanted nothing more to eat to-day.

Renée was glad to have Sophie out of the way while she did the packing. So, they were going at last, they were leaving Baulon. But her mind was listless and it hardly seemed to matter. "I shall be glad to have the children somewhere safe," she had said to Mme Séverin. But why, what for? She wandered between the cupboard and the chest of drawers, her thoughts in confusion; she snapped at Armand when, trying to be helpful, he got in her way. There were two summer frocks of Sophie's besides the one she had on; one was too small, the other wanted patching; she could not decide which to take or whether to take them both. . . . If Pierre should come and find her gone? But at least she would have Armand safe, and that was what she had set herself to do for him. Armand: he was sitting down now on the trunk she had finished, watching her with his serious eyes; and almost in the same glance

337

she saw her own face in the little mirror on the door, the dull, plain face of a spiritless woman, the ragged hair sprawling on its forehead. Yes, it was Armand she had kept for him, kept faithfully. She was stupid to-day, she was constantly hunting for things she had packed already. And throughout the long, close afternoon the sky rumbled without intermission.

*

The car did not arrive until late evening. But Diard the driver was ready to start off again at once. He was an old servant of Louis's, and he stood very respectfully at the door of the salon, where Eugène sat in his dressing-gown.

"You'd better wait till the morning," Eugène said. "You're tired, I can see that; it must be tiring, driving those things."

Diard admitted that he was tired. "But if I may say so, Monsieur, we had better start off to-night. In the morning we might not get through. You can't tell, the road's getting worse all the time. I didn't think I should get here, I was held up for two hours on the other side of Ramigny."

If a younger man had said that, Eugène would have pooh-poohed it; the fellow had stopped to pass the time of day at a café and was making excuses; but he knew Diard, and Diard was perfectly calm.

"You mean," he said, "there is a great deal of military traffic?"

Diard made a gesture. "Yes, Monsieur. You're closed in."

Eugène nodded seriously. He called for Madeleine, who was in the bedroom.

"Diard says, my dear, that there is a great deal of traffic on the roads; the journey is likely to take a long time, he thinks it would be better to start to-night. Is Renée ready?"

"I think so. I'll just——"

He called her back. "One moment! I've been thinking, my mother ought to go if she's fit to travel. I don't like the idea of her being here if there's any danger. She's a very old lady, one ought to think of her. Do you think my mother could stand the journey?"

She did not know, and his calmness only fluttered her. Gaston would tell them.

They sent for Gaston, but he did not seem to understand them. A journey? Yes, he would get Mme Nadya ready. Fit? He didn't know, how could you tell?—she was always the same.

"All right," Eugène said, impatient at the boy's silly grin. "Go on, you must get her dressed and bring her down here. You, Diard, you can go to the kitchen now and tell Barbier to give you a glass of wine. And then you'd better see that your machine's all right, with plenty of spirit. . . . Tell Renée, will you, Madeleine, that she's to get all ready and come down here? I shall want to see her before she goes. Wait one minute. Send Barbier, will you, to get hold of Tischer? I should like Tischer to see my mother before she starts."

★

Thérèse made one more journey to the salon; she said that she wanted to bid good-bye to the children, and Barbier brought her down. Her chair was put near the window and she sat very still there, wrapped about with her blue Zaragoza shawl, only her eyes moving like the eyes of a wolf in a toothtrap. Eugène had grown tired of waiting and gone back to his bedroom. But Madeleine was there, nursing a pile of old letters which for weeks she had meant to sort out and destroy, and Marianne, on pretence of fetching a book, had come to catch another sight of Sophie.

"A cigarette, Madeleine, if you have one. . . . Marianne, perhaps you will light it for me."

One of the windows was open, but it made no difference to the weight of the room's air, which was like the air of a wash-house, pressing in throat and temples. To-night the guns were quieter, the constant thunder of the afternoon had dwindled to what felt like silence, only at intervals a rally of double-beats, *dr-bmm*, published a brief reminder against too large security. In Thérèse the claps of warning stirred no answering tremor; she regarded Madeleine's shaking hand with a wondering patience. Her eyes swung round to Marianne, and she asked herself if it were only the poor light of the broken mantle, which increased her ordinary pallor, making her look so old, so sickly wretched. Surely it could not be that Marianne was frightened.

"I suppose you have finally decided, Thérèse, that you are not going?" Madeleine's voice was unexpectedly steady; rather aloof, as if she spoke to a servant to whom she had refused a rise in wages. "I see no reason for you to stay; or you either, Marianne. Perhaps, Thérèse, you do not feel equal to the journey?"

"I am perfectly able to travel if I want to, Madeleine. But I have decided to stay here. Surely we have discussed that already?"

"But you don't think, surely, that Eugène needs you?"

"Do you mean that you find me in your way?"

Joséphine flung open the door. "The man says the motor's ready. You've got to get ready quickly, whoever's going."

"All right, Joséphine. . . . I should be very much happier, Marianne, if you at least would go. It would be nice for Renée to have someone to help her with the children, and there's nothing you can do here."

Marianne sighed. "You don't understand, Mother. You don't

339

realize how we feel about Father. You seem to think that we can leave him without feeling anything."

"You're quite right," Madeleine said, "I don't understand you, I wouldn't pretend to. You've never shown the slightest . . . You, Thérèse, is it just affection for Eugène that keeps you here?"

Thérèse raised her hand slowly and pushed her fingers up through her moustache. "It is a little difficult to explain," she said. "It is really a family affair. We do not for one moment doubt that you are able to look after my brother, to do everything needful for his comfort. It is a pity, perhaps, that neither of us has ever been permitted to take our share of the burden, but——?——it is not worth discussing that." The drub of artillery came again, she waited with faint annoyance for the interruption to be over. "——But you see, Madeleine, we have in our family, we Séverins, a certain sense of loyalty. I myself think—as you know—that my brother is making himself highly ridiculous by his obstinacy; but it has always been useless to argue with Eugène, and so long as he persists in staying here—well, I find it would be rather undignified to leave him. After all, he has given me the shelter of his roof for many years——"

Marianne broke in.

"You think, Mother, that he only belongs to you. And you want to be able to say that you were the only one who stayed with him——"

"I'm very sorry," Madeleine said, "but I don't understand. I don't understand the language in which you speak." The heat of emotion started her cough again; but, fighting it back, she went on speaking. "To me it means nothing, this language of the Séverins. Loyalty? That is an instinct, I suppose, or else an attitude that has no meaning. You don't pretend that you love Eugène? No, that is a language that you on your side have never learnt." The cough broke loose, she gave it a few moments' liberty and caught it back again. "It nourishes itself, the thing I speak of. You give things, you work, you watch him when he is ill and when people hurt him, you are patient. You find then something growing inside you as a child grows; and it belongs to you as children do not always belong. If you had ever——"

The tempest in her lungs would be held no longer. She was huddled in a paroxysm of coughing when Eugène came in, and she did not immediately see him. Marianne was sitting on the arm of his usual chair and he took his stand in the hearth, his hands clasped behind him, leaning back against the mantel as if he warmed himself at a fire; stooping a little from the shoulders, but with his legs straight; it was not the attitude of a sick man.

"Marianne," he said, "can't you get your mother some water? Perhaps that window had better be closed—you, Thérèse, isn't it dangerous for your rheumatism . . .? As you wish, then. No, it does not affect me." He smiled pathetically. "How much easier it would be for me, if I could cure my illness by keeping out of draughts!" Waiting while Marianne went to get the water, he looked compassionately at Madeleine and Thérèse in turn; and when Marianne came back he included her in his kindly regard. "Marianne, she looks done-up," he said to Thérèse. "She works too hard. It's tiring, isn't it, teaching children all day?"

"It's holidays now," Marianne told him.

"Holidays? Of course." He was marking time until Madeleine had finally mastered her cough. He wanted a quiet audience.

"You, Marianne," he asked, "are you not going in the motor?"

"No, Father."

He smiled faintly. "Some young man, I suppose, some pretty fellow who stays in Baulon with a scratch on his arm when he should be doing his duty. . . . You do understand, don't you, what the danger is? Diard has confirmed what I said a fortnight ago, it will very soon be impossible to get away from Baulon—oh, yes, my dear, I have known the position for a long time. Naturally I have been reticent, I didn't want you to be alarmed. But General Caudebec would never have left me here unless Baulon was a key position and he thought it essential to have an officer of experience on the spot in case of dangerous developments. Yes, I am expecting to receive special instructions at any moment." He paused, and his voice became very grave, very mellow. "I don't want to alarm you unduly, it hurts me very much to give you anxiety, but I ought to say plainly that Baulon is as dangerous a place at this moment as any in France. You are offered a chance of getting away; it is probably your last chance. You know what my own feelings are, what a heavy weight would be lifted from my mind if I knew that you were safe. Yes, Madeleine, you especially. Of course"—he was very gentle now—"of course I can't force you. No man can use any force, not even his spiritual strength, against women who are dear to him." He whispered: "That's all—that's all I can say."

*

It took Gaston a long time to get Mme Nadya ready. Renée had brought the children down, dressed for the journey, in their winter coats. They had been to bed in their clothes, they were very sleepy now, puzzled and rather frightened, as Madeleine had seen them as their first arrival. Eugène took Sophie on his knees, where she closed her eyes and dozed again. He made Renée put her chair beside his, so that he could hold her hand. "I wish I could go with you," he said. "I'm afraid it will be a tiring journey, I should like to be there to look after you. You will take care of my mother, won't you, until you get to Paris? It will be a strain for such an old lady." Armand sat on the floor at his mother's side, his head lolling against her thigh. "He is sleepy, Armand," Eugène said. "Poor boy, he reminds me so much . . . I am sorry not to have seen more of your children, Renée. But of course, an old man can't do much to amuse them." He bent to whisper in her ear, gravely, "You mustn't tell him about his father, my dear. He must never know that. I want Armand to be a brave man, it wouldn't do for him to know about his father."

She was too tired to frame her answer. It was a relief to her that at that moment Dr. Tischer came in and Eugène at once transferred his attention to him.

"You look rather fluttered, Tischer—have the Germans been after you?"

Tischer said closely: "No. No, not the Germans."

They were used to seeing him hot and tired, but to-night he was worse than that. He had lost his hat, the carefully guarded silk hat which he would carry at his breast into every room and lay so tenderly on the dressing-table. He had neither gloves nor umbrella, his hair was disgracefully untidy, he was quite out of breath.

"What is it, Dr. Tischer?" Madeleine asked. "What's the matter?"

But he would not tell her. "I have been—subjected to some annoyance," was all he said. He stood and panted like a fish— he refused to sit down as long as Marianne was standing—and for some time he seemed unable to say anything at all. Then he addressed Eugène.

"I have been meaning to visit—to visit you before this, to offer my congratulations."

Madeleine looked up sharply.

"Congratulations?"

"——to offer you my congratulations on the gallantry of your son."

Eugène, feeling the violent tremble of Renée's hand, leaned forward.

"My son?—I don't understand you."

Tischer gaped with astonishment.

"But surely, M. Séverin, you must have heard! Your son has been decorated for gallantry, the ceremony was in the Hôtel de Ville this afternoon, M. le Maire made the presentation——"

"But, Dr. Tischer," Madeleine said, "we didn't know that Pierre was in France."

"Pierre? Oh, no, not Pierre. It was Raymond."

"Raymond?"

"What has the boy done?" Thérèse asked acidulously.

Tischer, like a street orator whose audience begins to shuffle away, said lamely: "I'm not very clear, I have only had an account of it from Mme Brunat. . . . It appears, M. Séverin, that your son was on duty as agent-suppléant at the East Station. Some civilian, a foreigner I understand, attempted to interfere with the troops passing through. Your son came to grips with the foreigner and overpowered him. Afterwards the man had the impudence to complain to the Sureté, that is how the authorities learnt of the affair. M. le Maire, I am told, spoke very highly of your son's brave action. . . . It was a great pleasure to me, M. Séverin, to hear of the honour done to one of your family——"

"Fancy Raymond!" Marianne said.

"Was it a very big man he knocked down?" Thérèse asked languidly. "To be decorated by M. le Maire—how Raymond must have enjoyed it!"

Only Madeleine seemed to take the news ungratefully. "I can't bear to think——"

But Eugène's quiet voice was overriding them all. "He has always had plenty of pluck, that boy, though he does dress and behave like a ninny. If it isn't immodest to say so, he has something of the Séverin in him, Raymond. . . . Do sit down, Tischer, you look like a plucked hen standing there, why are you so winded?"

Before Tischer could reply the door was violently shouldered open and Gaston came in with Mme Nadya in his arms. He put her on the ground, where she stood for a second only and then collapsed like a tent with a broken centre-pole. Tischer ran to pick her up and she clutched at him with her gnarled fingers.

"Who is this?" she asked faintly. "Andryev Fyodorovitch! Where have you brought me? Tell me who this is!"

Gaston, giggling behind her, said nothing. Tischer coaxed and half-lifted her on to the sofa, and she crouched there on her hands and knees, shaking with terror. Eugène watched her calmly, without moving; Madeleine tried to take her hand, but Nadya pushed her aside. "You, I don't want you! Andryev, send her away!" The children stared with solemn wonder at the old woman crouching at bay, her head poked forward as if she would force her smudgy yellow eyes to see what lay about her. "Take me back, Andryev," she sobbed, "take me back to my own room! I don't know this place, all these people."

Eugène got up then and came to her side. "It's all right, Mother," he said, his hand on her shoulder. "No one is going to hurt you. I've arranged for you to have a little drive, Louis has sent his motor for you."

"I don't want a drive," she said, "I want to go back to my own room. Andryev, take me back! Andryev darling, where are you?"

She pulled herself away from Eugène and rolled on to the floor; right over, with arms and legs sprawling, till she lay on her stomach. Then, gathering her limbs beneath her, she began crawling towards the window. Eugène went back to the fireplace and turned his back on the room. For a few moments no one moved or spoke; horrified, they watched Mme Nadya as she groped about the carpet trying to find her way to the door and whimpering for Andryev Fyodorovitch to help her. "Is no one going to do anything?" Thérèse asked bitterly. Madeleine moved round to the door and opened it, signalling Renée to get the children out of the room, but Nadya was right in their path and they refused to stir. Marianne gazed coldly at her grandmother, trying to detach herself from the scene's indignity. It was Tischer who made a move.

"Madame," he said, stooping to raise the old woman, "if you will allow me, I will conduct you to your room."

But she recognized his voice. "I know who you are," she snapped. "You're the doctor, I know you!"

He was behind her, supporting her with one arm round her body, the other hand holding her elbow.

"It's all right," he said soothingly, "you're all right with me. Yes, it's Dr. Tischer, it's only the old doctor."

She leant back against him, pushing her heels against the floor. "Where are you taking me? Let me go! Where are you taking me?"

Eugène, recovered from his temper, came to stand at Tischer's side: "Dr. Tischer's only going to take you for a little drive, Mother," he said.

At once her body was rigid.

"I know!" she shrieked. "To the Petite Maison!"

She struggled frantically and got herself away, she lay hammering the floor with her heels and screaming. "Get hold of her!" Eugène said wildly, dropping on her legs, "you, Gaston!" Tischer was kneeling on the floor and trying to grasp her by the arms. She twisted round and bit his wrist with her hard, sharp gums. Gaston had stopped laughing. "Shut up, you old fool!" he growled, but his voice was drowned by the pandemonium, in which Madeleine's clattering cough and Sophie's frightened wail ran side by side. "Shut up!" Gaston roared, pushing Tischer out of the way. "Here, let me!" He got her firmly with one long arm, she bit him like a puppy and for every bite he slapped her face. "Eugène, stop him!" Madeleine called, revolted by his cruelty. Eugène said: "Gaston!

That'll do!" But Nadya had given up the struggle, she was limp in Gaston's arms and only crying like a beaten child. "Where?" Gaston asked, with a flash of triumph in his smile. "Down to the motor," Eugène told him.

When Renée brought the children down Mme Nadya was huddled on the back seat of the car, quiet and passive, while Gaston chattered to her with idiot amiability through the window. As if to remind them of the need for hurry the guns were in voice again, answering versicle with antiphon from north to south across the sky's wide haunches. From the salon window the three women looked down to the pool of light on the pavement, waiting to see the car go away. their last escape destroyed. But something was going wrong, Renée was in the motor already, pushing Sophie in front of her; but as Armand stood on the running-board the lamp which Eugène held gave him a glimpse of Nadya quivering in the corner, and he would not budge. "No!" he whispered. "Not with her!"

"All right, you little funk!" Eugène said between his teeth. He put the lamp down on the kerb, pulled Armand roughly away from the car and slammed the door. "All right, Diard, off you go!"

Inside the car it was quite dark. Renée, busy arranging Sophie on the seat, did not realize what had happened until they were turning into the rue des Suisses; it was Sophie who asked her then: "Where's Armand?" She shouted to the driver to stop, fumbled for the handle of the door, found it; the door swung and she pitched on to the road. She scrambled to her feet and saw, as she ran breakneck towards the house, that a group was forming on the pavement. Madeleine was there, and Tischer, with Mme Poupoulet behind. Armand was struggling and screaming in his grand-father's arms.

*

Under Eugène's orders Gaston carried Mme Nadya back to her room. "You can put her to bed," Eugène said tersely, "the motor won't be going to-night."

Nadya lay quite still on the bed while Gaston took off her boots, and would not move an inch to help him as he tried to work her arms out of her coat. "You're cross, you silly old thing," he said, his voice mocking her tenderly. "What's the matter, old girl, what's wrong with you? You're cross with Gaston because he hit you, that's what it is. But you mustn't bite see, I won't have old women biting me, you've got to learn your lessons. D'you hear me? Come on now, don't be silly, pull your arm out, come on now, silly old darling." But she wouldn't move. He turned her over and she stared at him with her ordinary, unmeaning stare. He bent and kissed her lips. "Come on, old silly, I didn't hurt you, stop being cross with Gaston!" He took her hand, the little claw that was left of it, and stroked the almost naked finger-bones, hurt and puzzled by her obstinacy.

XXXVIII

"No," Corporal Soudry said when he had got a new cigarette alight from the last one, "no, I haven't the faintest idea where we're going." He pushed himself back a pace to get well under the platform roof; it was sulkily raining, you saw the thin rain falling through the dabs of yellow light on the farther platform, and a few drops from the roof-edge had blown back on to Soudry's cheek. "And a hell of a lot I care!" he said. It was the same man who had asked him again, the lean fellow with the voice of god-knew-whom. They would be content, the rest of them, when the train came in and they could huddle in the dry wagons; the train could take them where it liked, it made no difference. "You'd think I was his nursemaid," Soudry said, and encouraged by their laughter at his wit he let his imagination dance; "No, you wouldn't, you'd think I was a tourist agent. That's what he thinks, our friend here, he thinks the war's got up for his special benefit, he thinks I'm going to arrange a nice tour for him so that he won't miss anything. Any part of the front you like to see, gentlemen, seven-fifty!" The lean man stared at him with gentle insolence; "I want to know," he repeated, in the tempered voice of a practised café orator driving a feeble adversary into argument, "what part are we booked to? You know all right." Much as Soudry disliked the man, there was something in the tone which prevented him from giving the obvious answer. "If you must know," he said with artificial indifference, "it's Soissons. But if the order's changed five times before we get there you needn't go blaming me, M. Poussenez." "That's all I wanted to know," the man said quietly.

They had been on the platform for an hour now, and before that for two hours in the station yard. The jokes were all used up. On the other side the platform was just as crowded, a dark mass of uniform in which pricks of flame appeared as occasionally a cigarette was lighted, the shape of separate men seen only in the orbit of the sallow lamps. They were glum and bored, but hardly impatient; at least they could stand still here, there was no space for anybody to drill them or to demonstrate the use of the rifle-grenade; besides, they had got accustomed in the last twenty-four hours to waiting at stations. The war was like that, they understood; you waited and waited until something you wouldn't care for was sprung at you. They were tired, standing there with their packs and great-coats, trying to support their weight on the least convenient thing in all the world, the service rifle; but it didn't matter, you were sleepy, you no longer cared. Only those at the edge of the platform, feeling the drips from the roof, with the smell and pressure of their fellows not so close about them, were depressed by the rain's incessant whisper and the lightless, gloomy sky. "The train's gone off without us on another line," someone said, "the driver's lost his way." Nobody laughed. They didn't mind, they were all right here, but they might just as well see what the war was like and get that over.

The train came at last, the engine backing into the station with some sixty wagons on its tail. It was nearly one o'clock. The engine shunted back and forth as if it liked to keep the couplings jingling; it came reluctantly to rest, a man went down unfastening the padlocks on the wagon doors, the battalion transport officer appeared from nowhere with his lamp and train-sheets and started counting in the men It went with surprising speed: *dix-sept—huit—neuf—vingt*—the twelfth wagon was done, the lower half of the door swung-to and fastened. Soudry, having secured his place near the door (but forward of it to avoid the draught—he knew), took out his section-muster to call the roll. They had one lamp standing on the floor between them and he couldn't see black from white in his book; but he knew the names and numbers off by heart, and somewhere this conscientious man remembered seeing in his manual that the act of military entraining was not complete without a section call . . . 047 *Labarre*, 048 *Jouveau*, 049 *Tolmer* . . . good, they were all there. He returned the book to his breeches-pocket, dropped his drill-ground manner, jostled with his shoulders to get a larger space and settled himself in the nearest he could find to comfort on the floor. "And now, good night, my children! Let your sleep be deep and pure."

They were tyros in that mode of travel but they settled by degrees, a man's head on his neighbour's stomach, another curled with his cap beneath his hip, his ear in the crook of his arm. Before the train showed any will to move the greater part was dozing, the rest aware in the lonely darkness only of their own discomfort; some of them already snored. The boy Varnier who had been thrust against the farther door was still awake, nursing the miseries of homesickness and headache; but even he was drowsy. A man who had been moving cautiously across the prostrate forms placed a careless heel on his belly and the boy came back to consciousness. "Here! What——?" "Keep quiet," the man said. Varnier watched with curiosity the man's dark shape against the faintly lighted wall, and realized presently that he was fumbling with the fastenings of the door. But nothing further happened, Varnier was growing more sleepy, the man kept still. A long time had seemed to pass, and Varnier thought he was wriggling on the hard bench of his schoolroom at Châteauroux, when the wagon jumped forward as if a giant had kicked it. His chin jerked against the button of his tunic, Varnier opened his eyes. He caught sight of a gas-lamp moving past and a splash of rain came in his face. He was awake now, he knew that the train was moving and that someone had opened the door. The lamp in the wagon had been doused and a rectangle of grey was let into the darkness; there he saw for an instant a man's bulk, like a sack rolling over. "I say!" Varnier called sleepily. "Keep quiet or I'll shoot you!" the man whispered, and the door shut again. Well, it was none of Varnier's business; and in a moment he was back again at Châteauroux, where old M. Guigant with his spectacles pushed up above his eyebrows was shaking him by the shoulders and furiously demanding the names of the chief battles in the Peloponnesian War.

*

A train stood on the other line but it did not extend for the whole length of the platform. Pierre hung against the side of the wagon, grasping the hitch-rail with his right hand and keeping his body quite still, until the first truck covered him. He dropped then, as neatly as he could. His shoulder, catching the edge of a standing truck, gave him a moment's vivid pain and he fell on his face, dizzy; but the shoulder was only bruised, he pulled himself together and before the last of the moving trucks had passed him he was crawling under the other train. On all fours, with a lemur's action, he made a decent progress, counting the trucks as he passed beneath them; about sixteen, he guessed, would bring him clear of the platform; but it seemed in his anxiety to be a lengthy voyage, and his hands on the cinder-beds between the sleepers found painful going. No one, he thought, had seen him. He reached the twentieth truck; that would be enough for safety; and stood erect beside the coupling. Yes, he was well past the platform, and on his left was another line; beyond that he could see nothing. He would have liked to rest there and take a few seconds to consider the next step; but the train might move at any moment and he couldn't be sure that he had not been seen. He ducked under the buffers, glanced both ways, darted across the nearest rails and tripped against another. He saw that he was in a shunting yard, with nothing but the pain-streaked darkness to hide him; but there was no sign of pursuit. His eyes clearer now, so that he could mark the rails and hop them, he ran with his back to the station, cut between two lines of timber-trucks and reached the shadow of a

348

loading-shed. He stopped there, short of wind, and smiled. He hadn't thought it would be half so easy.

But as he relaxed, the warming flame of excitement flickered ou t He was returned now, after so brief a respite, to the state he had endured through all those weeks; and like a man brought back to prison from a few days' freedom he smelt familiar air with weary hatred. He had begun the first adventure buoyantly, finding an acid pleasure in his thirsty march across the Nsoka valley, the desperate scramble through the Kabils; those days were sweetened by the taste of liberty, by pride in his recklessness. But the episode had been too far drawn out, its savour wasting, the bravery of struggle dwindling to a sour endurance; he had felt too long the cold alarm of outlawry, he only longed for safety. On the platform over there he had been so safe; so safe in the confinement of the crowded wagon. There the whole of his existence had been brought to a sweet simplicity; he had only to obey some stupid orders, to march, to run, to lie down as they told him; there was nothing harmful they could do except to put him where a casual shellburst would divide his body into unconscious particles. Well, it was gone, that close security: no use regretting.

He was moving along behind the shed, he came to a wooden fence, climbed over easily and found himself at the end of a narrow cul-de-sac. So, there was no choice of direction. He hung on the fence again and looked abroad to be certain no one followed; then, reassured, set off along the street. Yes, they would have him there, in the end, he was ready for that; but not just yet. Two days, that was all he had asked for at Toulouse, two days to put his affairs in order: and even that had been refused. The war couldn't wait, they said; and the adjutant's sour face had made it plain that the man didn't trust him. A good soldier, yes, they knew him for that, and that was all they wanted; but a man appearing from nowhere with so thin a story—you had to watch him. So! They hadn't watched quite closely enough. He reached a main road, and guessed from its direction that it went to Auxerre. As far as he could see both ways it was empty. He did not know the town, but a sense of position told him that the road he wanted must radiate farther north. He crossed the tramlines and hurried along the continuation of the street he had left, glad of its darkness. It was raining harder now.

He was very tired; the evening ration had been taken standing, and the weakness left by fever seemed to have returned with the need for considered action. His brain had been quick enough as he stood on the platform; it was dull now, and he felt afraid that in these dark streets of a strange town he would forget his purpose. Baulon: he had got so near: but the thought brought greater terror than excitement. The picture which had been so dark, his blurred conception of a scared and wretched woman, had grown more lively in the air of Europe. The misery of parting had receded, he could scarcely see the shadowed outline of her face at the carriage window; but here between French houses and within the smell of France his mind sketched vividly a Renée waiting. The features rested indistinct, twisting his curiosity, and brought a hunger for the smell and warmth of her, to feel her body solid against his breast, only to have her close to him, drowning his loneliness. They could do as they liked with him when that had happened; but, like the vertex of the final peak to a climber sick with struggling, it still seemed so remote, the chance of such fierce contentment.

The gush of tenderness had blurred his sight, the violence of desire had set him running. He stumbled on the broken surface of the road, he turned to right and left at hazard, losing all sense of his direction, till by degrees the weakness of his legs, the nagging pain left in his shoulder, brought back his old sobriety. He had come to a broader street, and in the muddy light of a lamp a hundred paces off he saw two men approaching. He meant to ask his whereabouts, and realized only just in time that the men were officers in uniform. He saluted and passed them quickly, he thought he heard them stop and turn about; they were doubtless wondering where a solitary private should be going at that hour, and he worked at fever-pace to get a story ready. But they did not call; he turned at the next street and increased his speed.

When he had walked another quarter-mile he stopped to listen and look back. No one was following. Here the street lamps had been turned down, no light showed in any window, the sombre houses leaned above him lifeless. A man's rough voice, loud in the haunting silence, said close to his ear, distinctly, "*Non, je regrette, ça ne se peut pas!*" He gasped as if a hand had squeezed his stomach, he stood transfixed, afraid even to look across his shoulder. Only when a woman answered, "*Eh bien, ça se verra demain,*" did he realize that the sound came from a room above his head. He went on his way, shivering, and had hardly recovered from the quick alarm when a figure emerging from a passage startled him again. He controlled his step, marching at soldier's pace and without looking back; but the man who followed walked quickly and he felt him gaining, drawing level. "*Temps d'enfer!*" the man said cheerfully, and never stopping to look Pierre broke into a run. He ran the whole length of the street and under the railway bridge, he chose the narrowest, darkest of the leftward openings and ran again. Until the stretching pain of his chest forced him to ease the pace he never glanced behind. The street was empty then, but

still, when he walked, he heard, the footsteps following, kissing
the wet road in measure with his own.

★

When the light came, showing drearly through the fine-spun,
floating rain, he had got some ten kilometres out from the town
on the Piednoël road. Long before they reached him he heard
a convoy of lorries coming up behind, and when they wallowed out
from the mist he hailed the leader. The driver, crouching over his
wheel with tired eyes fastened to the road, either failed or refused
to hear him; and he watched dejectedly as the rest went by, his
voice no use against the corporate growl of their engines. Another
came alone, and in answer to his hail the driver shouted "Soissons!"
Soissons: everything seemed to go there. "No use!" he shouted
back. The next, ten minutes after, ignored his call, the next was
bound for Epernay. Two more passed by, and when the third
appeared he stood in the middle of the road, daring the driver to
ignore him. The lorry stopped with a jerk, the driver opened his
door, leant out and called without rancour, *"Que diable——?"*
"Where are you for?" "Ramigny, if I ever get there." "All right,
that's mine," Pierre said.

He climbed to the driving-box and gratefully dropped his
weight on the narrow wooden seat. The driver, southern by accent
and complexion, gave him a cigarette and asked no questions.
With the engine stuttering rebelliously they jogged ahead. The
screen was misted, and before him Pierre could hardly see ten
metres of the white, straight road. "The war," the driver said,
nodding forward, "you seen it yet?" Pierre said sleepily, "No, not
yet." "You won't be in such a hurry," the man said, "when you
have." A skirt of drizzle swept the road, blotting out everything;
but the driver held his course with his foot hard down, seeming to
keep the road by a supernatural vision. Two of his cylinders were
constipés, he said, but he'd get her as far as the war all right.
Ramigny, yes, he thought he'd make it. For the present that was
enough.

XXXIX

THROUGH all the confusion a single name, constantly and devoutly
repeated like the name of a Patron Saint, brought comfort to
Baulon: Joffre, Le Père Joffre, he was their man. No one had ever
seen him and no one knew where he was. But Papa Joffre, they
said, he had the whole thing in hand, Joffre knew what he was
doing, he was crouching to spring. They were closed in now;
nothing came along the roads except military traffic, supplies that

the wholesalers had ordered weeks ago might be on the sidings outside Paris or they might have been commandeered; it was no good trying to telephone, the trunk lines had been taken over. But that was only a temporary situation, you had to have patience. The guns had grown furious, at night it was difficult to sleep, children were frightened. Riberpré the pianist wandered about the streets all day, crying, with his fingers stuck in his ears; enduring, he said, a long-drawn crucifixion. But the war was still over there, close, but outside the town; presently Joffre would strike, the battleground would be pushed away to the east and they would breathe more freely. There was nothing to do but wait. If you had a conveyance and horses you might still get through to Ramigny. But that sort had gone long ago. The rumour persisted that a train would start this morning, at ten o'clock, for anyone who wished to leave the town; and about that hour a motley crowd would gather at the central station, only to learn that no civilian would in any case be allowed upon the platform. It became a legend: "Where is Marie this morning?" "Marie? Why, it is ten o'clock, she and the children will be waiting for the train." They worked. With Jean-Auguste away—over there at the war— you had to do the odd jobs that belonged to him, to fetch all the water from the pump at the corner, fix up the broken wheel of a market barrow. There were women driving the trams, old women for the greater part, hard-skinned, who clanged the bell with a constant fury and swung the brake-handle with impatient strength, their lips set dourly, contemptuous of such paltry labour. The cobbler in the rue des Prêtres had gone, but his tools were moved into the front room and his wife would sole your shoes as decently as ever he did. Shopping fell to the older children, who foraged in companies; it got about that there were turnips selling in the rue Amédée-Dormoy, or herrings in the old market, and thither the mob would chase, descending like locusts on the stall, bargaining with corporate violence. So there was no time over to watch the curiosities, which had ceased besides to be either new or curious. The refugees still trickled in, the Lord knew where they came from or how they came; those were the unfortunate, the war had run them over, you pitied those poor country people, but then——? ——someone presumably would feed them. As for the soldiers and their monstrous paraphernalia—the wicked-looking guns, the squealing wagons—the Baulonnais were tired of seeing them. They wondered vaguely what could be happening to so many men; why, when such a weight of steel and uniform was being poured into the battlefield, the war remained so close. But Louis-Michel wrote from somewhere in the north that he was well, with all the girls and cigarettes he wanted, that "the Boche is sticking his dirty muzzle in our trap, the lieutenant says"; and he should know. Presently Joffre would strike.

Away from the river and the centre streets the traffic had dwindled. You seemed never to hear a man's voice, or the high voice of women quarrelling; the children were oddly quiet. That was the difference, that sabbath stillness, with its thundering background; for the streets looked the same, with only a subdued air, and it was curious on a still, warm evening to sit at your sewing in the doorway with the houses and the lamp-posts, the shadow in the alleys, as you always saw them, and to listen to the shaking and tearing of the tranquil, green-lit sky. That noise, the incessant, wavering tumult, when once the nerves had learnt to tolerate its violence, became an anæsthetic to their sensibility. A man's holiday clothes hung in the corner of a bedroom would not be wanted any more; the news had arrived yesterday, the boche had got him: the shock of that was blunted by the high wind of the war's uproar, you could not feel a grief to be so poignant in a world of dulled reality, And to them, dwellers on a volcano slope, it was after all their heritage. They had watched it coming and now it seemed to be here, the war they had heard of from their childhood. Its presence differed from the picture they had formed; it was more immense and more continuous, it had not come like a hail-storm, suddenly and blinding, but had gathered its weight above them like their own familiar fog; they could not be quite certain yet if this was the actuality or only its *mise en scène*, but the question was not worth asking. They were content to find their nerves hardening under the battery of noise and fear. It was better to know, as they did now, that there was positively no escape. The news was common that the neck of the bottle where Baulon lay had narrowed and that for the time being they were surrounded. So: they had not to make a decision, they could only wait and see what happened. Those who might have gone away were for the most part glad they had stayed; they preferred, at such a time, to be in a town they knew the smell of, to go to the wine shop that they always used, walking on footpaths where the shade and tilt of every kerbstone were familiar. To be at such a place as Ramigny, where the people were peculiar, where the shopkeepers would not know you and could talk of nobody you knew—that would have been a heavy price for safety. In secret they were a little proud of their inflexibility; they were people of a short, coarse speech, the Baulonnais, inclined to be sharp with strangers. And now they thought contemptuously of those others who were squatting back there, reading in their newspapers of the war which the Baulonnais had like a hungry wolf on his doorstep. In other towns they wished God-speed to the soldiers and forgot them; here the soldiers crowding in the centre streets were at one with the population, filling the Café of the Maréchal Soult, eating their food. For the soldiers it was a thing you had expected, the war: it came along like the period of service, it was the service over again, harder pressed and rationally developed, brought to the bloody reality. The Baulonnais had captured something of their spirit: like the soldiers they were already tired, and a little bewildered; sourly hopeful, having nothing to hope for but the chance of keeping head and shoulders joined together; unheroic, nourished by a common fortitude, a corporate valour. Things might go wrong: Joffre, and Our Lady of the Sovereign Mercies, might let them down. You could only wait, stiffening your body till it became a rock of senseless patience. To-day had gone through and everything was just the same. You put the children to bed now and heated up the coffee to sip it while you mended frocks and trousers; then there was the broken panel of the door to be repaired, a petticoat to iron, the nesting-box for M. Brille that Jules had left unfinished. In the last sunlight a bony old woman shuffled along the pavement with her market bag and turned for a moment to say in her rasping voice: "They are noisy to-night, those swine!" That was Joséphine Barbier.

"Eh bien, ils s'amusent, quoi. . . ."

*

"For the present you will wait here," M. Séverin said to Diard. ". . . Yes, it's unfortunate that you couldn't get off directly you arrived; as you say, there may be difficulties now; but Mme Pierre does not seem ready to travel yet. Yes, I should like you to stay where you will be within reach, and to have your machine in good order. At present our plans are uncertain. I am expecting a telegram. . . ."

*

Arriving to take his duty at the East Station, Raymond saw that the traffic had changed its direction. It was two in the morning. Yesterday, when he had been relieved at six o'clock, things had been as usual, perhaps a little slacked: loaded wagons singly or in batches of three or four, staff-cars, infantry detachments, guns and limbers, all going east; casualties and the other traffic inwards had been diverted at Ochy-Lebecq to the lower road. Now, as if a wheel were turned the other way, everything was coming back into the town. "What's happening?" he asked the man he relieved, "has something happened?" "I don't know, no one will tell me, nobody seems to know. They're coming back, that's all." It was raining. Beneath the accustomed thunder of the guns no one heard the rattle and squeak of camions, the clatter of heavy wheels grinding on the pavé. As usual, Raymond thought, they are fast

354

asleep, the Baulonnais. And he himself was sleepy. He watched with detachment the throng passing; not a procession as it had been on the outward march but a rabble of vehicles and men, men slouching in straggled files beside the lorries, with bent knees, heads flopping, drunk with fatigue; drivers nearly asleep at their wheels, horses making their own pace with reins drooping on their quarters. "Tell me, what's happened?" Raymond said to a man who stopped to light his cigarette-end. But he got no answer, it was like talking to the dead. They didn't know what had happened, they didn't know and they didn't care where they were going.

The sky's light was screened with heavy cloud, there were no lights in the street, the men could feel and smell the closeness of the houses, they knew they were passing through a town. But no one welcomed them, there were no lighted windows, no one was watching. Only in the place Talleyrand, where nothing could be seen but the rain falling through the flashes, Eugène sat by himself at an open window, shivering, listening to the guns.

*

Tischer knew nothing of what had happened, as he made his way home in the early morning. He had been up all night with Marie Dardel, whose seventeen hours' labour had finished at five o'clock, assisted by a midwife of preternatural incompetence who to allay her terror of the guns had drunk herself to drowsy intoxication. Passing now through the empty streets of Ste Estelle he was happy. It had been a struggle. Godefroy had said with the dogmatism of her long experience that it was useless trying to save the child, and yet he had done so: a boy; the exhausted mother had glanced at the child with weary indifference, but it was a gift, he thought, to man-hungry France. He swayed a little in his walk; he had taken no food except a bowl of tepid coffee since an early supper on the previous evening; his ears were singing, and he hardly noticed the noise of the guns saluting with ecstatic salvoes the birth of another day.

He had meant to go straight home, but when his eye caught the name of the rue Faucon he remembered that old Julie Gâtebois was quite alone in her cottage there and that he had promised to visit her last night. He knew that he was fit for nothing, but the pressure of work in the last few weeks had brought his nerves to such disorder that he could not rest with a job undone. It was just as he had turned the corner that his ears were stunned by an explosion in the next street.

He stood for a moment quite still, dazed. Then he ran back into the avenue Vautier. He looked up and down, still uncertain where the noise had come from. There was nothing to see. A child who had been gathering horse-dung stood a hundred yards away limply holding her box and shovel, paralysed with fright; except for her the street was empty, desolate under the dull sky, the drab familiar houses silent and still. He had started walking to where the child stood when a second explosion sounded behind him, so close that he seemed to feel the whole force of it inside his chest. He swung about and saw at a stone's throw a fountain of smoke and rubble standing on the roadway; and a shower of dirt and stones fell at his feet. He didn't stop to look. The child was shrilly screaming, he turned again and ran towards her. She was running now, away from him, as if the devil were after her. He shouted hoarsely, "It's all right!" but she was too far off to hear him; and the next explosion, following quickly, crashed down upon his cry. Just where the child was, the wall of a house had fallen outwards. He saw it leaning over the street, unbroken, and it seemed to stay like that for the whole of a second before it crumpled and dropped on to the road, a confusion of tiles and broken tables sliding after. A cloud of dust rose, spreading a curtain across the avenue. When it had fallen everything was still again.

He ran full tilt, but before he reached the place where the wall had fallen everyone was in the street, they were clustering round the ruin like flies on a cowpat. "Go back!" Tischer shouted. "Get back indoors!"—but they paid no attention, they appeared insensible to danger. A fourth explosion shook the air as he pushed his way between them. It was some way off, they took no notice. They watched with senseless curiosity as he broke into the débris, burrowing with his hands and throwing chunks of plaster over his shoulder. Only when he picked the child's body from a heap of splintered wood and brick-dust a woman shrieked and rushed at him and tumbled insensible at his feet.

Somebody took the woman indoors, the rest stood still. It was quiet again; the tentative bombardment was over. Tischer still held the child in his arms. "Get something I can put her on," he said at large, "a blanket or a coat or something." There was a cut on the white forehead, nothing else that he could see; the child's life might by a miracle have been preserved. "Where's my case? Find it, somebody. You, get me some water, will you, quickly?" He found then that no one had moved; the shock had pulled their nerves tight, they were stultified. "Hurry!" he said sharply. "Don't all stand there goggling!" That seemed to slacken their tension, but in an unexpected way. "You!" a dormer-breasted woman said, someone he didn't know, "you give me that child!" Another came to her help, and before he realized what was happening they had got the child away from him.

"Here, what are you doing?" he shouted. "You can't——"

Their common fear united them. Aother woman, foul with liquorice and garlic, came between to hold him off; a man, explosively angry, caught him by the arms. "You let her alone!"

"Who did it?" someone asked, and another man—it was Félix Dumont—answered sullenly, "The Germans."

"And who's a German?"

Tischer found that the man on his shoulders was too strong to be shaken off; he was a fettler from the Bouju foundry, the husband of the woman who had taken the child; a stupid, melancholy giant in a yellow temper.

"Let me have that child!" Tischer called again, frantically struggling. "Don't you realize——?"

"Who's a German?" the voice repeated, and someone on the outskirts said: "He talks like one!" "Who does?" "That man, the doctor." "Who is he?" "Tischer. That's his name. He's not a Frenchman."

"You all know me——" Tischer said wildly, twisting and tugging. "You all——"

A hand clapped over his mouth. The crowd was breaking on one side. The child's mother had come round, a woman led her sobbing into the middle of the crowd. "Who did it?" she screamed, clutching the limp, small body.

The fettler jerked his head towards Tischer. "Him!"

Seeing his wife, the fettler had loosened his hold for a moment. With a desperate twist Tischer got free. He ducked, saw where the margin was thinnest and cut through. He started to run, but he was no runner, they were round him again before he had made twenty paces. Someone tripped him up. The fettler, roaring like a drunkard, sprang on his back. The road was covered with bricks and the fettler had got one. The crowd hardly realized what was happening till it was finished. The rain was starting again.

★

The rain did not come to much. It was a quiet, grey day. After an hour or so an agent-suppléant arrived and mounted guard where the house had fallen, "for fear," the Estellois said, "that someone might run off with the plaster." The agent-suppléant was a timid and feckless old man who would not go near the body lying in the ruisseau, and it was a long time before anyone came to take it away. Amongst the scattered débris it was not conspicuous, and many passed without noticing it at all: a very old frock-coat and a shabby pair of trousers with the legs spread, a little curdling stream of brown which flowed to the gutter from the mat of grey, untidy hair. But a teacher of the violin stopped out of curiosity and bent to regard the face; and the face, he said, reminded him of Titian's Christ.

An hour after the first shell had fallen the niggardly bombardment began again, and throughout the forenoon continued spasmodically, the shells coming in groups of five or six, with long intervals between. The firing was poor and erratic. A flying-machine circled over the town and constantly ran along the line of the Maréchal Soult, wheeling low over the Enfants du Roi like a wasp above a jar of marmalade. But the gunners could or would not respond to the spotter's directions. They found an empty warehouse by the river and put a shell or two in the river itself; they destroyed half a street of houses in the Vieux Marché quarter, where no one lived but artisans; in the western archivolt of Ste Gudule they shattered the heads of four apostles which had no tactical importance; they obstinately failed to drop a shell in the narrow, troop-choked, seething rue du Chais. It served, this desultory destruction, to increase the town's alarm. They watched from their windows the tired toops pouring towards Ramigny; there was no exchange of greetings, no cheering now, there was nothing anyone could say. And when they were gone, what then? It was said that you could still get through to Ramigny by the road which crossed the river and turned south a Cher-les-Arches; dangerous yet feasible; but Ramigny, how would you find things there? And they had not learnt to believe that there was any real necessity to get away from Baulon. Sometimes when one of the wagons stopped, held up in the boulevard, a girl would climb on to the tail with water for the men inside. Those girls, white and sick when they climbed down again to the pavement, knew better than the rest what sort of thing the war was. But they did not say much, they kept it to themselves.

In the place Talleyrand they heard the explosions, first near, then distantly. "What does it mean?" Barbier asked when the Abbé Vignaud came. "Tell me, please, Father, what is happening now?" But the Abbé, hardly suppressing his habitual smile, was non-committal. "I don't know, Barbier. There seem to have been some explosions—with so much cordite about it is hardly surprising. You, Barbier, you're an old soldier, you're used to this sort of thing. I don't mind confessing that I find it impossible to read with any comfort, with all this noise going on. . . . Madame is in the drawing-room?" "No," Barbier told him, "Madame is in bed to-day."

"Madame is a little scared by the explosions, she has decided to remain in bed. It is quite all right, I myself will do everything that's necessary": that was what Eugène had said to Barbier. But Mme Séverin was hardly alarmed at all; she was too tired to be frightened. A fit of coughing, more severe than usual, had taken her as she started dressing and had gone on for a long time. Finding herself exhausted she had got into bed again, meaning to give herself perhaps five minutes to recover. She had passed then into a state of lethargy, where her body seemed deaf to the voice of her intentions. Presently she would get up again and dress and get out the plans for Eugène and give Pierre some help with his homework. But she had to lie still for five more minutes, five more minutes, just five more, till the pain in her chest had gone. Eugène had dressed himself completely. It was a long time since he had put on all his clothes and his boots, but he was strong this morning, glad that the light had come, wide awake in spite of having spent almost the whole night at his window. When Barbier brought his coffee he sent for Diard and had a talk with him. "I am a little anxious, Diard, about the situation. . . . It would be possible, would it not, to get through to Ramigny by way of Cher-les-Arches? I was talking to Barbier yesterday, and he understands that that would be quite possible. I shall probably send Madame Pierre and her children away to-day, I should be happier if I knew they were safe. I want you to have the motor ready, with enough spirit and all that. You had better have it in the rue le Brochet—you know, at the back there, the one that goes down to the river—it will be out of the way there. And you yourself must stay in the house so that I know where you are. Yes, that's all, thank you, Diard, you can go now." He went back to his desk then and took out a bundle of papers which he kept in the middle drawer. He called, "Madeleine!" but she did not answer. He knocked at the door and went into her room.

He was very much surprised to see her still in bed. "Do you realize," he asked gently, "what the time is? It's nearly half-past nine." She answered without opening her eyes. "I'm so tired, Eugène. I'm sorry, I'll be up in a minute, but I feel so tired. It's my chest." "No," he said quite firmly, "you must stay where you are. It will do you good to have a day in bed, you'd much better stay where you are."

He did not know quite what to do for her, but he did what he could. It came to Marianne's ears that her mother was ill and Marianne wanted to see her, but Eugène forbade it. "No, Marianne, it's better that she should not be disturbed. I myself will do anything that's necessary till Dr. Tischer comes." He sent Joséphine for fresh coffee, and when it came he took it into Madeleine's room. "There, Madi, I've had some fresh coffee made for you." But she wouldn't drink it at once, she seemed unwilling to sit up. "I'll leave it for you there," he said. "Wait, I'll get another pillow." He was not content with that. He poured out the warm water that was left in his own jug and brought the basin to her bedside. He soaked the sponge, squeezed it out, and bathed her face very tenderly. She was sleepy, she hardly smiled, she only whispered very faintly, "Merci!"

He went across to the drawing-room and for a long time looked out of the window, expecting to see Tischer appear from the rue des Suisses. The Square was empty this morning; in ten minutes he saw only one man and a few children passing through. The day was infinitely dreary. When half an hour had gone he went back to Madeleine's room. "Do you still feel bad, Madi? Is there anything I can do?" "No, Eugène, no, thank you. I shall be up soon." Troubled, he returned to his vigil.

When the shell fell at Vieux Marché a builder's board which had stood for twelve months on the scaffolding crashed down into the place. Eugène got up then and went out into the corridor, where Joséphine, bent like a fish-hook, was creeping back from the tide of dirt and water which advanced beneath the sweep of her wasted arm. "I want you, Joséphine, to tell Barbier that he must go and find Dr. Tischer. Dr. Tischer should have been here by now." She went on scrubbing and did not even look up when she replied: "Barbier is not to go. I won't have him going out, with these bombs. Or Gaston either." He stared for a moment, always surprised by Joséphine's temerity. But he would not argue with her; Joséphine he always considered as Madeleine's servant, and he blamed her shortcomings chiefly to Madeleine's leniency. He went at once to Madeleine.

"My dear, Joséphine——" But he saw as soon as he came near the bed that Madeleine was fast asleep. It was better to leave her so. A knot of ribbon lay between her temple and the pillow; with cautious fingers he snatched it away, pulled the top sheet straight and drew the duvet up to her shoulder. Gazing at her with timid interest he wished that Tischer would come. Madeleine, he wasn't used to seeing her like that. There had always been that cough of hers, sometimes she seemed to be poorly, as if the Baulon air did not suit her, but she had never before given way to these malaises. Tischer of course was not a good doctor, he was far too old-fashioned, too fussy. But at any rate Tischer, directly he came, would have to assume the responsibility. . . . It would pass, she would be up and about again before long. But it was queer, he didn't care to see her like that. He stooped, his hand resting on the bed-head, and kissed her hair. She did not wake.

He was in his own bedroom when the bell rang. That would be Tischer at last. But when he went to the top of the stairs he heard the low, bubbling voice of the Abbé Vignaud.

*

How very quiet, the Abbé thought as he drifted up the stairs, how very still the house was; how little in twenty years it had changed. The colour of the walls was slightly more faded, the paint chipped here and there, the treads of the stair-carpet worn nearly to the wood; this morning a red plush rabbit lay at the turn of the stairs, belonging he supposed to one of those grandchildren who were always in the house and whom one saw so rarely now—that was a startling incongruity, which surely Mme Séverin would never have permitted, a child's toy lying where any visitor would see it. But to-day when the town lay in a chilly fever he felt it curious to find this house so undisturbed; to sniff its familiar odour, damp and rather stale like the smell of a house lately deserted, as if he were back again in a life that never altered. Mlle Marianne had passed him, dressed for out-of-doors, as he stood talking to Barbier in the hall: she had bowed to him rather perfunctorily and hurried away; but that was only her ordinary manner, brusque and shy. Barbier; seemed to have some idea what was going on in Baulon: but on the first landing Vignaud caught sight of Josephine kneeling beside her pail and harrowing the floorboards with bristles worn to the roots; nothing had changed.

He found M. Séverin in the drawing-room, actually dressed and shod. He said: "I am very sorry, M. Séverin, I am really very much upset to hear of Mme Séverin being indisposed. . . . I hope it is nothing at all serious?" Eugène, standing near the window with his hands behind his back, bent a little at the shoulders, his face preoccupied, answered: "No. . . . No, I don't think so, I thank you, M. l'Abbé, it's not likely to be anything serious."

It was a long time since Vignaud had seen M. Séverin out of bed, and he regarded him—his practised eyes appearing to point another way—with lively curiosity. He had forgotten that Séverin was so tall, and it was surprising that he had kept so good a figure; the waist still slim, the knees controlled so that his grey trousers—good cloth, Vignaud could see that—went down to the knuckles of his toes in a smooth and gentle outward bend, kinked only at the ankles. You could see from the mouth, the slacked and broken lips, that it was an old man; but there was no great age apparent in the drawing of the splendid head, the lovely eyes. You had said it was a handsome boy, deftly but unsuccessfully disguised to play an old man's part. And yet—— "He has become so old," Mme Séverin said again and again, "it frightens me to see him such an old man."

"Mme Séverin would perhaps like to see me in her room?" he asked.

He was surprised by the firmness of Eugène's answer:

"No, I'm afraid not. At present my wife is asleep; and I should prefer in any case that she should not be disturbed before Tischer comes. Tischer will be able to say what's wrong with her—he is not a very good doctor, but he should be able to do something."

Vignaud scratched his lip. He said reflectively: "Tischer? He was the most distinguished student of his year at the Institut Broca—so Georges Debaillon always told me. I remember——"

Eugène was not listening. "Tell me," he said, "——pray sit down! you will take a glass of wine, of course?—tell me, have you any news as to the situation? In Baulon, I mean. I have been expecting some information from the Ministry—General Caudebec promised to send me a telegram—but nothing has come through yet, I fear that communication with Paris may have been interrupted. These explosions—I have heard explosions this morning—do you know if any damage was done?"

Vignaud hesitated. To Mme Séverin's questions he could always find an answer, but with Eugène he did not quite know where he was. Séverin had turned his head away and was waiting for his reply as if for a blow on the ear. "They have damaged the west front of Ste Gudule," Vignaud said cautiously. "Some of the figures have been destroyed. Of course, they were very old figures, they were quite out of date. None the less, one regrets these military necessities, one has a certain affection for the things to which one had grown accustomed. . . ." He realized that Séverin was already thinking of something else, and he let the subject slip away. ". . . . I can't help being sorry that you were unable to take Mme Séverin away before this trouble began. I should have been so much happier——"

"This damage," Eugène said abruptly, "who is responsible?"

Vignaud was not much surprised by the question. He had worked himself round so as to get the light on Eugène's face, and he began to see what Mme Séverin meant—"He has become so old."

"One presumes it is the Germans," he said quietly. "Though there is always the possibility that our own gunners may be firing short—you will know more about that kind of thing than I do——"

Eugène had brought his wandering eyes to focus on Vignaud's face. "You mean," he said seriously, "that the town is being bombarded?"

"A little," Vignaud agreed. "It does not seem to be a very serious affair. . . . But if I cannot see Mme Séverin I ought not to be wasting your time——.."

Eugène turned to both sides as if he were looking for something with which his time should be occupied. "No," he said distractedly, "no, don't go. Tischer will be here soon, surely you can wait till he comes. I don't want to be all by myself—it's lonely for me, with Madeleine ill like this." He had begun to walk about the room, picking up things that he saw, a book of memoirs, Madeleine's embroidery. "I don't suppose you understand," he said suddenly. "Madeleine was at liberty to go away just when she liked, I begged her to go. I myself had to stay here, it was my duty. . . . But it's quite impossible now, I couldn't possibly move her, you can't take a sick woman on a journey like that. . . . Besides, it would hurt her to be taken away from you—oh, yes, I mean that, Madeleine's nature is deeply spiritual—I have always realized that —your visits are always a great comfort to her. I should not like her to be without your—your guidance."

Vignaud said nothing. He had taken out his snuff-box but he put it away again unopened. He crossed his legs the other way and nodded comfortably, his eyes on the carpet.

"I have never been a very happy man," Eugène went on. "You know, probably—yes, you're old enough to remember—what happened to me in early life. My friends turned against me, they accused me of cowardice——"

Vignaud was nodding more energetically. As if he had been waiting all along for this very opening, he began to speak now.

"It is very hard to forgive a falsehood like that," he said deliberately. "So much harder, I have always said, than to forgive any other kind of injury. . . . And yet, I have always wondered if a man can really be damaged by a falsehood. I mean, damaged in himself. Wouldn't you agree—or is it only a crotchet of mine?— that a man's virtue hardens, becomes more precious and larger and more splendid, when it is calumniated? Of course, we should not have thought like that when we were young; but you and I, we have both reached the age of clearer vision now, we are able as younger men are not to assess the real importance of things which have hurt us. Don't you feel now, looking back over that ocean of bitterness, that your courage became more precious to you, that it received a finer temper, because you knew that it had been impugned falsely?"

Eugène stopped with his back to the window and shook his head. "I'm afraid, my dear Abbé, you don't understand. To you it would mean nothing to be called a coward, to you——"

"I agree, my dear M. Séverin, it would mean nothing at all as long as I knew it wasn't true. But——"

"I tell you, you don't understand what it was like, to stand in that court, to hear my fellow-officers, one after another. . . . You who have been all your life a priest——"

"——I agree, yes, it is different for me. As a priest, you see, I have had so little to bother me. What matters to so many men— to you, perhaps—is what their friends think about them, what other people think, what all the people in all the streets in every

363

town and village think. It is so much simpler to be responsible only to God. Then you know, when everyone is saying what a dreadful old charlatan the Abbé Vignaud is, that God is just laughing at them over your shoulder. So comforting, I always find that. Wait! You must not misunderstand me. We have to remember—we who have chosen to have God as our single arbiter—that He is very clear-sighted. If you take snuff during Lent—as I do sometimes—you can conceal it from your servant, even from people in the same room (I'll show you the trick some time), but God always spots you, He won't let it pass. But you have an advantage there—that as time goes on you learn not to try deceiving Him. In a way your life becomes easier then, you have not the trouble of keeping up pretences. . . . I must apologize, my dear M. Séverin, you have got me on to my hobby-horse."

Eugène had sat down at last. He said absently: "It's very interesting, all that. . . . Yes, I can well believe that there is a great comfort to be found in the devotional life. My wife, I believe, has always—lived a life of that pattern. It means a great deal to her, her spiritual outlook. . . . But for me"—he laughed half-heartedly—"if I were to try and put my case before God in the way you suggest, I should have a long distance to go back. I'm afraid He would be rather tired before I had finished, if He were listening at all."

Vignaud curled himself farther into his chair and took his eyes away from Eugène altogether.

"God does not ask us for very elaborate explanations," he said meditatively. "He really asks for nothing except to hear of things that worry us, that we are not quite certain about. . . . As for listening, the Church had provided us with an instrument which I believe to be very helpful—her priests have been taught to act as God's ears." A volley of thunder-claps, coming in quick succession, broke across his words. The window-frames were rattling. He went and stood by the window, looking out into the Square. "To some men," he said, "it makes a great deal of difference, that surrender of old secrets. I was talking yesterday to a man who was going up to the line. He was a shopkeeper in private life, the whole of his fortune had been built up on some money he had stolen when a young man. He had hidden that from everyone, he had tried to hide it from God. But he couldn't go into the battle like that, he had to get rid of that burden. If only——"

"You'd better not stand near the window," Eugène said. "What were you saying? A man stole some money?"

Vignaud had not moved.

"I really wanted to know if I could be any use," he said boldly. "There may be something you want to—to get rid of, some mistake that may have made your life more difficult: I don't think you would trust me less because I am your wife's director?"

Eugène, standing in the middle of the room, looked at Vignaud's forehead as if it were a long way off. "But how could I remember?" he said vaguely. "I've always done what I thought right, I've never tried to revenge myself. I may have made mistakes—I don't remember, at my age you forget things. No, it's no good, you would never understand what kind of life mine has been. . . . I wish people wouldn't bother me all the time, I have enough to worry about, I may at any moment have to assume great responsibilities. That noise just now—tell me, Abbé, where do you think it came from? Was it very close . . .?"

★

When the Abbé had gone he rang for Barbier. "Barbier, did Joséphine give you my message? I want to you go and find Dr. Tischer, yes, at once, and bring him here. He should have been here a long time ago. Tell him he must hurry. . . . No, Barbier, I do not think there is any danger except in Joséphine's imagination." He was rather sorry he had let Vignaud go. Madeleine was still asleep and he had no one to talk to. Vignaud had really been rather impertinent; he had been after something—perhaps Madeline had put him up to it; but you could not be angry with an old gentleman of such delicious manners, who spoke with the accent of the Empire. It crossed Eugène's mind that he might have taken the Abbé at his word and made use of him, there was something not quite clear in his memory which he had sometimes thought of discussing with some disinterested party, someone on whom he could rely and whose moral judgments were not the sharp, jealous ones of the women who surrounded him. But the opportunity had gone; and it was dangerous, after all, to give anyone the chance of interfering with the plan on which you lived. Besides, it was difficult, so difficult to remember. . . . He was lonely, he must find someone to talk to, and almost without volition he made his way upstairs.

On the second floor he paused, puffed and rather dizzy. It was months since he had been out of bed for such a long stretch, and the effort of climbing a flight of stairs had cost him more than he expected. But the giddiness passed. He went along the corridor towards the children's day-room and found, to his surprise, that the door was unlocked. He opened it cautiously and went inside.

Renée was seated at the table, where a sewing-machine stood amid a tumbling ocean of coloured silks. Her forehead had dropped on to her crossed hands, she did not stir even when he called her name. There was no sign of the little girl; but Armand was standing by the window, pulling the feathers out of a pillow. Armand saw him as he came in, but gave him only a glance and went on with his play. "What are you doing?" Eugène asked, but the boy didn't answer.

Eugène went to the other end of the window, so that he could see Armand's face, and for some time gazed at it acutely. Once before—he could not remember how long ago—he had watched Armand's face as he did now, intently and without interruption. But then—it was clear, that picture in a small frame—the child's eyes had been tight shut, the light too hard for a proper view. Certainly he had never before seen Pierre so closely copied in Armand's features: the touch of obstinacy in the delicate mouth, the Séverin mouth; the high, flat cheeks, the clever, twice-protruding forehead. Pierre had been just like that in childhood, reserved, wrapped up in himself, refusing to pay attention to anything you said if he had found some trifle that caught his fancy. . . . Pierre, what had become of Pierre? For a moment it escaped him, and then he remembered what they had told him in Paris. He had tried to put that right out of his mind, but it was always coming back, generally in the hour before light came, when he turned from side to side and his mind struggled in a bog of confusion: that one fact that could not be argued, that everyone seemed to know: Louis's silly, windy little voice, *I was so sorry, I was terribly upset, to hear of Pierre's desertion from the Army.* They said that you could tell a coward from his eyes, and he wondered now what Pierre's eyes had looked like; but no, he could not see them, he could only see Armand's eyes, which were cast on the pillow he was plucking, remote and dull, dull like the eyes of the loutish Gaston. He said sharply, "Armand!" and the boy looked up, suddenly alert, coming towards intelligence. Yes, perhaps those eyes were like Pierre's now; he would have said they were oddly like his own.

"Your mother—is she ill?" he asked.

Armand would not answer. He began to retreat, edging into the corner.

"Armand!" Eugène repeated softly. "Come here! You're not frightened of me, are you? Surely you're not frightened?"

Enraged by the child's stupidity and fear, he took a step forward. But something in the room had moved; not Armand, Armand was quite still, shrunk behind the stove; it was Renée's foot. He stopped, and his anger melted into weariness. He had been up all day, he was tired, he didn't want a fuss. Leaning against the table, breathing heavily, he looked at Armand once again. Like an animal the boy was, like a creature caught and baited by children. If only they had given Eugène a chance, let him handle Armand, bring him up in his own way! Things had gone so wrong, so wrong. He saw as he moved towards the door that Renée was still in the same position; a negligible being, a little, dark, untidy woman slumped in that wilderness of colour, like a rusty trowel left on a bed of flowers.

*

Below, on the dark landing, a woman stopped him; that woman who was always loitering about the house but who did not appear to be a servant, whom he had never quite identified. She was overwhelmed, she said, to hear that Mme Séverin was indisposed, could she give any assistance, might she wait upon Mme Séverin and offer a few flowers? She was very anxious not to trouble M. Séverin, but might she be so bold as to ask him if it were true that the town was being abandoned, delivered over to the Germans? He answered her with abbreviated courtesy: Madame was very kind, but no, Mme Séverin's illness was not at all serious, she was only staying in bed until the doctor came. The town abandoned? What nonsense, what extraordinary rubbish people invented! He bowed to Mme Poupoulet and moved away.

Hearing no sound from Madeleine's room, he went back to the salon, and sat by the window on the little chair which Madeleine generally used, turned so that he would see Tischer directly he came round the corner. The window was open, but presently he closed it; the day seemed to be warm, but he found himself shivering. The town abandoned? What had that foolish woman meant? He opened the window again, just a little way, to listen. The rumbling which he always heard now was still going on, and louder to-day: he had supposed that the noise was chiefly in his own head, and due to a slight nervous disorder, since Madeleine seldom mentioned it, but to-day there was a quiver in the walls and furniture which could not come from his imagination. And those explosions: what was it that Vignaud had said about them? He turned a little and saw that it was smoky over the town, as if the wind were blowing south from the factory quarter. While he watched, the smoked grew thicker, reinforced by dirty floccules which oozed from the middle distance. Presently he could distinguish within the clotted smoke the flickering, ruby glow of flame. The fire must be a good way off, but the smeech already carried to his nostrils. He rang for Barbier, but no one came, and he remembered then that he had sent him to get hold of Tischer. A group of women—those pauper folk who lately infested the place Talleyrand—had come out of their houses and stood in the middle of the Square, watching the smoke and feverishly chattering. He could not hear what they said, he was quite cut off from everyone, sitting all by himself up here. He wanted something to occupy his mind, and he fetched the battle-plans from his own room; but when he had spread them on the floor they meant nothing to him, they

367

seemed to wobble under his eyes. Madeleine perhaps had muddled them, so that they lay in the wrong order, and he called out from the door. "Madeleine! Are you awake now?" but there was no reply. He went to the top of the stairs and shouted for Joséphine, but she did not seem to hear him. There was nothing for him to do but go back to his place at the window, to sit and watch the brown smoke wreathing into the mournful sky, wondering when Tischer would come; to listen to the shuddering insistent clamour of approaching battle with reluctant but enchanted ears, as to the shuttered strains of distant, dreary music; to try and control the trembling of his hands, to persuade himself that it was only an old man's weakness, that nothing could really frighten him, that he had never been frightened.

*

At five o'clock, by the watch of an *agent* standing at the gate of the Jardin des Indes, two howitzer shells fell 'almost simultaneously' in the boulevard MacMahon; the first failing to explode. The second burrowed obliquely under the footpath, toppled one of the robinias on to its branches, picked up two quarter-sections of the ornamental grating underneath and flung them whole and spinning like samaras against the wall of the Caisse d'Epargne some thirty metres down the road. A puppy nosing among the flowers in the garden was killed by a falling standard from the broken fence. That was the only major damage. In the bank, the nearest building, not one pane of glass was broken; but curiously, in the houses on the northern side of the rue des Suisses hardly a window escaped. In the place Talleyrand the sound of the explosion, leaping in the trap from side to side, was heard like several separate reports. Here it was a few windows facing east which suffered, most of the rest escaped. On one of the roofs a tile came loose, and having waited till the echoes died slid noisily into the gutter. For a minute after that there was nothing to hear but a baby which had been woken and was crying.

Madeleine did not know what had roused her, but she found that she was sitting up and shaking; she vaguely fancied that the house had been struck by lightning.

She had no idea what time of day it was; from the colour of the light she felt it was late evening; and for a few moments after waking she did not remember the familiar neighbourhood of war. It came as a slight relief, that recollection: the shock that had occurred, the headlong tumble of her dream, was nothing but a part of that war which raged all day and night about the town and to which she had grown accustomed. In the morning there had been explosions; she had supposed, hearing them drowsily, that they came from the firing of some novel gun—Eugène might be able to tell her when he came. It was plain, now that the mist of sleep was parting, that a similar explosion had occurred just now. Disturbed, she called for Eugène, and as he did not answer she got out of bed.

The few hours' idleness seemed to have weakened her, and she had to hold the bedpost with one hand as she drew on her stockings. Her toilet gown was somewhere out of sight, and she pulled a blanket from the bed to throw about her shoulders. The front of her hair must be very untidy but she had not the patience to find her bedroom cap before she stumbled into Eugène's room. It was empty. Calling again, "Eugène! Eugène, where are you?" she went across to the salon. The salon smelt of a cigar he had smoked, but only Joséphine was there, muttering some Gascon nonsense as she drove her mop under the writing-desk. "Where is the master, Joséphine?" "How should I know? Where's Barbier, can you tell me that? They've got him, likely, those fornicating swine. . . ." Madeleine was leaning against the bookcase; she had started to cough, very painfully, without any phlegm. She gasped. "Joséphine, a chair." Joséphine straightened herself and pushed up a chair behind her. "Thank you, Joséphine!"

She was doubled up, her elbows on her knees, her knuckles cupped in the pits of her eyes, when a noise like the flash of a crimson flag pulled the air apart and the weight of the sky falling drove bodily against the windows. In the second that followed she knew only one thing: that, as if the animal which danced in her breast had been smitten down, her cough had stopped. And now she was trying to cough again and the cough wouldn't come. She did not hope to see the light any more, she thought that everything had finished. But her head rose of itself and her eyes opened, she saw the pieces of glass lying all over the floor and then the blue and yellow smoke drifting like a dancer's skirt across the jagged window. A bell was ringing. She heard Joséphine, a statue of fury by the window, say under her breath, mechanically, "Mademoiselle." She thought: Thérèse, all by herself up there, unable to escape.

The smoke followed her into the passage, but when she reached the stairs it drifted away. She accomplished the first flight clutching the banisters, and took a moment's rest on the landing. Somewhere a woman was monotonously screaming on and on as if she were paid to scream for a certain length of time; but the noise came, she thought, from outside the house. She started on the next flight, and lacking the strength to mount it upright dropped on her knees; she hoped that no one would see her, crawling up the stairs like that, with the blanket constantly slipping from one shoulder. The screams had come to an end at last. One of the stair rods was out of place and she stopped to put it right.

In the corridor Marianne caught her up; she was in her outdoor clothes and breathless. To her mother's "What has happened?" she answered in her cold voice, rather impatiently, "It's the house where the Allards lived. . . . Yes, smashed like an old hat." They entered Thérèse's room together.

Here the smoke had come in thickly, adding its smell to the close, soiled odour of a sickroom badly kept. Thérèse had managed to get into her chair and wheel it to the window, where she sat with her back towards them, her feet bare, her shoulders uncovered, staring down into the lane. She seemed not to hear them when they came in; even when Madeleine spoke she took no notice, and she did not move or say a word of thanks when Marianne put a shawl round her back. Madeleine leant against the bed, panting. She was dizzy, she could not breathe very well in this smoky room, Marianne's voice sounded far away. She said feebly, rather stupidly, "I only came up, Thérèse—I thought you might be frightened. I thought your bell rang." If Thérèse said anything it was covered by the drum-beats outside the house, where somewhere, they were too deaf to tell how far, another spray of shell had dropped from grey invisibility across the shaking houses. Thérèse made not the slightest movement. It was Marianne, standing beside Thérèse and following her eyes' direction, who beckoned. "Mother, look!"

Madeleine reached the window and knelt there, too far tried to stand. Then she saw what the others had seen: Louis's motor. A man stood talking to the driver; at the first glimpse, from that strange point of vision, she did not realize who he was; but as he climbed into the motor she saw in a grain of time his troubled face and recognized Eugène. The motor drove away.

The women gazed into the street, where the smoke of the car's exhaust joined the sleepy smoke still drifting on the languid air, as if the car were still in sight. A long time passed before anyone spoke.

"The telegram," Madeleine whispered.

Marianne started to giggle. She had her mouth tight shut and her hand clapped over it, but the giggle came through her nose as if she were crying. Thérèse, it seemed, was still unconscious of the others, though Madeleine's hand was touching hers on the pushing-wheel of the chair. Her brilliant eyes were pointed fiercely where the motor had disappeared, her lips had tightened dreadfully into the Séverin shape. She breathed deeply, steadily, with a little rustle in her nostrils, and her lips moved as if she had something to say. But she said nothing, nothing at all.

XL

At eight o'clock that evening the stragglers were still passing the East Station in considerable number, goaded forward by the howitzers, which so long as the town was known to be occupied by troops would continue periodically to send reminders of their impatience. The two main bridges at Champs-Muscradin had been destroyed by the covering party: a makeshift job; no one wanted, at that time and place, seriously to annoy the Germans. A certain Kapitän Boetnerr, a man of eccentric optimism, had been ordered to press as far as Dêchy along the road which dropped into Baulon from Chinon-les-Austes, and finding himself unopposed, the bridge at Chinon in immaculate condition, had supposed that Baulon was already open. His company sauntered into the town through the Porte St. Grégoire, and a skirmish took place in the streets of that quarter, an affair of three machine-guns and some hand-grenades used without much science, watched by civilians crowding recklessly at every point of vantage. The captain was saved no small unpleasantness when a fleuron from the house just behind him was broken off and struck him on the left temple.

The rumour was in circulation then that the Germans were already in the town, that Baulon was a prize to them. But the flag of France was still curled round the mast above the Hôtel de Ville. A little before the time of sunset the sun appeared for a few moments, yellow and feeble. The cloud joined again, and the day slipped off as it had come, drably. In the boulevard the traffic of camp-followers had noticeably dwindled as the day went on; there a driver could now use his next-high gear. But the western bottleneck, the rue du Chais, was choked as always, and the weird equipage which Ernest Mauger conducted, a hooded flour-wagon painted streaky-grey with a scurfy gelding lolling in the shafts, made no worse progress than the auto-camions. It was half empty, this wagon of Mauger's. At almost every kilometre on the journey from Poël-Foix a man had pulled himself over the tailboard, on which the words *Défense absolue aux soldats de monter* were painted in red, and squeezed through the after-screen; but inside, in the lysol-scented twilight, they could not resist their curiosity to examine the oblong bundles, wrapped in ground-sheets, which had been hastily loaded at Eugency; and each, with a regularity which Mauger found sufficiently amusing, at once dropped off again.

Mauger sat on his box and made little noises, encouraging Georges Clemenceau to go faster, although the nose of Georges was pressed against the drop-board of the lorry ahead. He was happy; for after a period in which, completely lost and very frightened, he had seemed to be at the beck and call of everyone, a ferocious lieutenant at Eugency had given him plain orders: he was to take this load to Ramigny and report at headquarters in the place Galliot, then he would receive further instructions. That was quite simple. He had had no food to speak of for some time, and he was rather tired. But that did not matter. All that he wanted, Mauger, was to be told (as the farmer Goigoux had always told him) exactly what he had to do. They had travelled very well, already they had left behind the region where things were constantly exploding right into your eardrums, sending Georges into a sweating frenzy. Comparatively, Baulon was the seat of eternal sabbath, and Mauger could resume that contemplative frame in which life appeared so easy, so harmonious.

He was angry, in his mild way, when a long, dirty fellow called to him sharply from the pavement. "You! What's your name?" At first he wouldn't answer, but the man shouted again, and he told him then, "Mauger."

"Mauger? You're the man I want." Before Mauger could protest the soldier was on the box beside him. "See here, the captain sent me to tell you you're to pick up some stuff of his in Baulon."

"What captain?" Mauger asked stupidly.

"Who gave you your present orders?"

"Why, it was the lieutenant, the one with the moustache, I didn't hear his name."

"It was Lieutenant Lhonoré. He's sent me to tell you where these things of his are. You go to the right here——"

"But the lieutenant told me——"

The passenger leaned across and pulled on the near rein. "I don't care what he told you——" They were half-way round the corner when something tumbled into the street they had left, perhaps a hundred metres forward. At last the howitzer had got the right direction. The horse, at the sound of the explosion, went off at a furious gallop; the men behind him saw nothing of the mess but the underside of a lorry rocking in the smoke and a wheel spinning through the air towards them. The horse galloped the whole length of the rue Claude Lorrain, across the place Tonnerre and into the rue Fromentin. "You see," the passenger said, "it is always wiser to do what I tell you."

It was getting dark, Mauger did not know the town and had no idea where he was, he was miserable. He said feebly, as they jogged over the river, "I'm sure that wasn't the name of the lieutenant. . . . He didn't say anything about loading things here,

I'm sure he didn't. He said I was to get these"—jerking his head
—"to Ramigny as quick as I could. 'I can't deal with them here',
he said, he was all bleeding, he'd got something in his shoulder,
'you take them through to Ramigny as quick as you can, there's a
good boy,' that was what he told me. You know, I suppose, what
it is I've got in here?"

"I know you're three-quarters empty," Pierre said dryly, "and
that's all I care about. . . . You turn left here."

*

It was Gaston who opened the door. Pierre had no idea who
he was. When he said, "Tell me, where is Madame Pierre, which
is her room, tell me quickly!" Gaston only grinned. Pierre took
his arm and shook him violently. "Pour l'amour—— What d'you
mean? She's not gone?" Gaston, frightened, broke away and set
off up the stairs, with Pierre close on his heels.

Pierre would have shouted, not minding how his voice might
shock her. But his voice would not shout the name, it would
only whisper it. When he tried to shout, a tide of phlegm came up
with the sound from his chest and stifled it.

*

In the long, long room where at night he came so often, the
hollow, windy room, Armand made his way cautiously, stepping
backwards, watching the two holes where the two eyes observed
him, ready to spring aside if the door between them opened.
Occasionally he had to glance behind, for if perchance he reached
the farther wall before he expected it would grip him as a magnet
grips a needle and a thousand times more powerfully; but these
glances had to be irregular and swift, done so neatly that the eyes,
if they saw, would not have time to use their advantage. If the
eyes knew, for only half a second, that Armand was not watching
them, the catch would be slipped and the door jerked open by the
mighty spring controlling it; and instantly the sword, the long thin
sword like a river of steel, would sheet from the opening and pass
excruciatingly through Armand's body. Then for year after year,
for all the years that were to come, he would stand there skewered,
unable to move or to cry out.

It came so easily that he was not surprised, he felt as if he had
waited for it all along: a sudden loosening of his limbs, a pleasant
tilting of the world so that, looking along the room to where the
eyes were, he was looking downwards, hung dangerously above a
deep and deeply shadowed cavern. And it seemed to be natural
that a hard voice said behind him, 'No, I won't see them, I don't
want to see anyone. . . . Yes, bring his things, we'll dress him as
we go along.' Right at the bottom he saw a strip of yellow light.

373

He fell slowly, the light increased, he saw the banisters passing. He knew from the change of smell that he had reached the hall and he found himself sitting on the sofa there with a blanket all round him. The street door was open and a man stood on the threshold, but it wasn't Diard, he knew perfectly well what Diard looked like. He couldn't see Maman. Sophie was there in her nightgown holding her fire-tongs and singing quietly her little song about *Madame Alphonse se fait bonnet;* and Gaston was shuffling about with a trunk on his back, cursing amiably at Angèle, who had stretched herself in the very middle of the hall and lay there moaning and would move for no one. There was a great noise going on; Armand recognized it now as only the banging which you heard all the time. He was sleepy, he closed his eyes. When a man came to lift him he struggled and cried out, realizing instantly that they were trying to get him away from Maman. They had tried before, they wanted to get him away so that he could not protect her. He kicked and wriggled free, but as he lay screaming on the floor he saw, looking up, that it was only Gaston. "It's all right, you little fool-cub," Gaston slobbered kindly, "you're going for a ride, with a horse in front." And Maman was kneeling beside him now, holding his hand, whispering, "It's all right, Armand!" A long way off a voice called faintly: "Josephine! Joséphine, what's happening?"

He slept again, and when he woke he was in a smelly tent with a floor of rough planks bumping under his shoulder. There was hardly any light, he called "Maman!" and her hand came out to stroke him.

*

At the Pont de Broussais the wagon filtered into the main line of traffic, and on the west side Mauger was formally challenged by the picket; but there was no examination. They made some seven kilometres without a serious stoppage, walking and trotting by turns; but at Colza, where a heavy traffic sloped in from Cher-les-Arches, they found the road jammed so that the villagers, if any were left there, could hardly have squeezed out of their cottages. There were two waits there, the first lasting an hour, the second, at the farther end of the village, for thirty-five minutes. It was not quite clear why no one could move at all, the night was cloudy and you could see no way ahead; a rumour came down that two heavy lorries, one trying to overtake another where the road would not permit it, had each got two wheels in one of the ditches, leaving an aperture through which two pullets could not have walked abreast. No one much minded, it was part of their routine, this waiting. A triplet of shell from one of the howitzers which had been pressed in to Binard l'Evêque fell in the village, but well away from the main road. "It's all right, you silly bastard!" Mauger shouted to his horse, standing up and leaning back on his reins. "If you'd just keep still, you son of a constipated hinny, they'd never see you." Some men had been killed, it was said, some men sleeping in one of the farms; and among the soldiers packed in the little steet there was some indignation that the war should have pursued them so far. At about four o'clock, by Renée's watch, they were moving again.

*

"Pierre, what is going to happen to us?"

"I don't know yet, I can't see ahead. We must get clear first. Don't think ahead, don't worry."

"Pierre . . . you understand about Armand? I couldn't help it, I did everything I could. He's all right really, there's nothing really wrong. . . ."

"Wrong . . .? It was me, chérie, I didn't realize, I didn't think. Your letter, it was like a slow fire burning inside. I couldn't think, I didn't know what I was doing."

"I like to hear your voice like that. . . . Pierre, Pierre chéri, did you look at me, when we were in the light? Did you see my face, had it altered much?"

"It was tired, chérie, but it hasn't altered. Wait. Lift your head, lift it up a little so that I can get farther under. There, isn't that better?"

"It's perfect . . . Pierre, what are all those things?"

"I don't know. It doesn't matter. Renée! Renée, are you asleep? Renée, what did you think, when you got that news?"

"I had your letter. I knew you were coming to me. . . . Yes, I always knew."

She wanted to talk to him about Armand, she was still not sure if he understood; to explain, to make him see how difficult it had been, why she had not done better. She wanted to hear his voice, his sad, careless voice, whatever it said; to make him go on talking. But Pierre was sleepy, dead beat; he had tried to sit up with his back against the tail-board, her head supported on his thighs, and already he had twice fallen sideways, and now, falling again, he stayed like that, with his head in the crook of his arm, till she moved it just a little and put one of Sophie's coats behind it. Armand was sleeping peacefully, she thought, curled against the load stacked forward; and Sophie, humming eternally the air of *Madame Alphonse*, was quite contented. She thought: To-morrow? and already it was breaking, for she could see the light at the join of the after-curtain; but Pierre had said that she was not to worry. She turned and hunched herself against his coat, pressed her face into his stomach, and then she was all surrounded by the feel and

375

smell of Pierre. Perhaps he had not understood about Armand; but he had not blamed her. He wasn't ready yet, and perhaps there would never be the time for him to hear the whole burden she had kept within herself, waiting till she could pour it out to him. He was tired, Pierre was, and at present he only wanted to have her near him, to draw upon the strength which seemed to flow afresh in her as the drain upon it grew.

So thin his wrist felt, as she pushed her fingers up his sleeve and stroked the hair of his arm. She stretched herself and he rolled until his head was lying on her neck and the weight of his shoulder pressed into her side, hurting her. But the fear she had, and the hoarded trouble which had grown like a rust upon her spirit, were balsamed by her own fatigue as she became more drowsy; and as her reason yielded to the power of sleep the tide of happiness swept over all resistance. She slept, but not remotely, not carried far from waking life. From sleep's warm chamber she could look abroad through a narrow fissure of awareness, and all she knew was Pierre's reality, his rough skin pressing hers, his live breath blowing upon her like a summer wind; time overhauled and conquered. From that fresh spring of happiness she drank slowly and with lingering ecstasy, feeling the strength that flowed from its depth and sweetness. Her head was on the bare floor, and shaken painfully; but the pain, acutely felt, served only as measure of her contentment. God had not been satisfied to give her back Pierre. He had quickened the spring of life in her again.

*

Himself half-asleep, Mauger kept his tired horse at a lazy trot. The road was clearer now. He had been through Feuvillers just as it began to grow light and he hoped in spite of everything to make Ramigny by seven o'clock. Not that it mattered. It was raining a little, but Mauger did not mind. This part of the road was quiet; the guns, when he heard them, sounded a long way off; and he could fancy, despite the martial shapes ahead, that he was on his old job, taking a load for the market at Marchiennes. Inside the wagon the day had come to nothing but a twilight, and the children were still asleep. Renée had got a loaf from Gaston just as they were starting; she and Pierre shared a portion of it now, sitting on one of the bundles and eating in silence. Pierre called to Mauger, "Where have we got to?" but Mauger did not seem to hear him. When Sophie woke she was surprised but not displeased to find herself in a place so unusual; it amused her that she could not easily stand on the shaking floor. She accepted her father without surprise or fear; she kissed him on both cheeks and hoped that he was well. But Armand would not come near him; he bowed and murmured something and turned the other way. Sophie went across to him and they dropped into one of their private games, played solemnly with one hand lying open on the floor and the other rapping. Pierre found and lighted a cigarette. They could not remember yet the jokes they had formerly shared, and while an hour passed none of them had much to say.

Pierre found a chink in the canvas and looked out.

"We're getting near," he said. "At least, I think so."

"Where are we going?" Sophie asked, and Renée passed on the question: "Where are we going, Pierre?"

He said, "Ramigny. . . . We're lucky, I didn't think we'd get through. Not as easily as that."

They came on to the pavé and through his spy-hole he saw across the drizzle the dirty houses passing; a poor place, Ramigny. He would have to think now, to make a further plan of action; and his mind was so tired. He turned and saw the children still playing, each munching a piece of bread which was laid on the floor when out of use; Renée sitting on one of two valises they had brought, deep in her thoughts. The wagon stopped and he heard Mauger in amiable cross-talk with the picket, while somewhere a telephone rang and rang. "Yes, twelve of them. . . . No, I didn't want to, I was told to. No, I can't help what the regulations are, I've got to hand them over in the place Galliot, those are my orders. What d'you think I'm going to do with them? Take them back to Eugency? . . . Well, if you'd see how things were you wouldn't ask why they didn't bury them. Bury them? At Eugency there wasn't time to bury a baby. . . ." The wagon moved on.

"I want you to turn into a side-street," Pierre called, "and put us down there."

"I'm not under your orders," Mauger replied. "I don't know who you are, anyway. I've got to take this load to the place Galliot." But he knew that it would only lead to more trouble if he arrived in the place Galliot with this ridiculous supercargo, and the fellow inside was not to be trusted. He turned at the next corner and presently stopped.

Pierre lifted down his family and the two valises. "All right," he said to Mauger, "you can go on now. Wait! Here's a Caporal for you. It's my last, but you deserve it."

Mauger fingered the cigarette doubtfully and shrugged his shoulders. "A thousand million thanks," he said. "For myself, I don't smoke cigarettes when they've been overlaid, but perhaps Georges Clemenceau will like it." He brought his whip down sharply on the horse's quarters and the wagon rattled away, leaving all along the street, its faint, foul odour. The children sat demurely on one of the valises, as if they were on a railway platform.

This street led only to an area of orchards and would never have borne much traffic; but it showed Pierre how things were with Ramigny. All the houses seemed to be empty, from many the curtains had been taken away. Things lay in the road, soaked by the night's rain; a woman's hat, a towel-horse, a trickle of anthracite that had leaked from the sack as it was carried off. Some of the doors had been left wide open, showing a carpet rolled up to be taken away, a plaster cast of Mercury lying on a sofa. Farther down there was a gap in the row of houses where one of them had squatted down, covering half the roadway. Pierre, climbing over the ruins, looked out on an area as large as a parade ground which appeared to have been swept by a cyclone. So! They were as near as that; and they had treated this place less politely than Baulon. He scrambled down again, and as he walked back to where he had left Renée and the children the guns were opening up; not, as he expected, on this side, but from the south-east. The thought occurred to him: what would happen to Mauger's load, would they make the poor wretch take it on again, on and on till he got to Paris? The odd smile that he had not used for a long time came to his mouth. "What is it?" Renée asked him, and he stopped smiling. "We're between the pincers," he said, "we shall have to move on."

He thought he could carry both valises himself, he had forgotten what a ghost of a man he had become. Renée helped him with one of them and they moved swaying and lurching along the wet street, the tall unshaven poilu and his little dishevelled wife, with the big valises yawing and swinging about their thighs, the little girl with the fire-tongs clinging to Renée's free hand, the boy with the wandering philosophic eyes shuffling along behind. They arrived like that in the place Galliot.

The square was choked with vehicles and soldiers; as fast as it emptied on one side it was refilled from the other, so that there seemed to be no purpose in its feverish animation. An orderly stood by the statue of Charlemagne holding four horses; his mouth was open, he looked bored and apathetic, as if the war did not concern him; the men trying to manœuvre a gun team into the Cézy road roared at him to get his animals farther back but he refused to move; it wasn't his affair, these antics of the artillery. A party was throwing wires across the rue des Dames, which was barricaded already by a tangle of carts and furniture, and opposite, the upper windows of the Hôtel de Ville were being packed with sandbags. The men on these fatigues seemed to be unmoved by the stir behind and below them; they were earnest tradesmen, who worked as if they had promised to have the whole scene ready by a certain time and would carry out their word precisely. A few civilians, somehow left behind, stood beneath the trees on the west side, quietly anxious, wondering what to do, getting in everybody's way. They were casually and continuously cursed, but no one did anything about them, they were no one's responsibility, no one had any time. The Café de la Paix was open. All the tables had been moved inside but two, and at one of these, beneath an orange umbrella, watching with interest and quiet approval the desperate confusion of the square, murmuring 'Tsch tsch!' when the vibration shook his arm, an old man with a strew hat sat sipping his bénédictine.

In the brigade transport office the duty-corporal sat on the pommel of a sofa with his feet against the china cabinet and shouted into the telephone: "I can't hear, there's a hell of a row going on in this place, I can't hear a word you say, you'd better ring me again, we may be quieter later on. What? No, no, I've told you already, we've nothing at all, we haven't even a wheelbarrow. . . ."

"And you," he said to Pierre, "what do you want? Stop, I'll tell you. A shave, that's what you want. (Fortin! Find out if there's something wrong with this accursed telephone, get on to Communications and tell them it's come unstuck somewhere.) What? You've been detailed to get three civilians out of the town? Great God on high, and what d'you expect me to do about that? I suppose you'd like the war stopped for a few hours to make things easier. Who are you, anyway? What? Become detached from your unit? Yes, you look like that. You look as if you were a bit detached from your brains. . . . What's that, Fortin? All right, give it me. . . . Yes, yes, Lepicard speaking. No, we have not so much as a wheelbarrow. I can't hear a word you say. No, we haven't even a wheelbarrow. . . ."

Pierre went slowly down the Loucherie staircase with one hand on the carved balustrade, the other searching his breeches pocket for a cigarette. The orderlies tearing up and down the stairs crushed past him violently, the life of the town was quickening, he was the only man in that building who moved leisurely. He dawdled on the bottom stairs, he was rather faint now, he didn't know what to do.

He found Renée and the children where he had left them, alone in a parlour-room where the walnut chairs were covered with miscellaneous pieces of uniform and equipment, with form pads and rifle-bolts and pull-throughs all over the round table. "The fellow won't help me," he said with a gesture of hopelessness, "I don't know what to do." Renée had got a thread from somewhere and was cobbling a tear on the shoulder of Armand's coat as he knelt with his face in her lap, crying. "Surely you can leave that!" Pierre said impatiently. "What's wrong with Armand?"

"The guns," she said, "they frighten him a little, he hasn't been well. You remember, I told you. . . ."

She finished off and bit the thread.

"The guns?" Pierre said.

He hadn't realized, but he realized now, that they were louder; that the table he sat on was jumping, jumping, as if someone in the street outside swung a mighty hammer on to an iron wedge. He looked about the room idly, like a bored man searching for something to pass the time. "I don't know what to do," he said.

Renée got up, wiped Armand's eyes and pulled down Sophie's dress. It did not seem to her to matter what they did; she had Pierre there, she was drunk with happiness. "We'll go outside again," she said, "we may find someone to give us another lift, perhaps we could find that man with the smelly cart again." Sophie had lost her tongs, but they found them under the sideboard. They picked up the valises and struggled out to the square.

The sandbag party was doing the lower windows now. They still worked carefully, and with professional pride, making a neat, tight job at every opening; unconscious, it seemed, of the increasing uproar. There was in their nonchalance a certain courage. But it was out of date; for the war, of a new-fangled kind, an affair of machinery and masses, was driving on to Ramigny like a spring-tide, and before that inundation there was no place left for private virtues. Everything seemed to have been arranged, though no one knew quite who had arranged it; everything was according to plan. You could handle your bayonet with unheard-of bravery and cunning; it was not much good against the people, whoever they might be, who had a hurricane between their thumb and finger.

By skill and sweat he had got a seven-inch gun on to the very summit of Tête Rouge, one Sergeant Beuloh of the Jesterburger Artillery Corps; a man on the roof of the Hôtel de Ville could see it through his glasses. Carrying out precise orders, Beuloh fired four shells at five past eight o'clock, keeping a constant direction and increasing the elevation by regular jumps. The second of his shells made a rubbish heap of the barricade in the rue des Dames; the third, pitching almost in the centre of the place Galliot, kicking up the cobbles like a dog's hind leg, drove men and horses, strips of carts and motors, in a flying, shapeless, bloody litter to the steps of the Crédit Nord. Beuloh put down his telescope. That was all right.

The children, paralysed, were watching the men bolting in all directions. They were quite deaf, they didn't hear the shouting or the screams. Pierre barked, "In here!" but they didn't hear him, he had to take Renée with one hand and Sophie with the other and almost hurl them through the doorway. "Down those steps," he shouted, "down into the cellar!" and tried to push them in front of him, but the men flying from the square jostled between and drove them apart. Renée had one idea: Armand.

She was pushed back against the wall, she clung to a door handle and the men drove past her. For a moment the inrush slackened, she squeezed herself back to the doorway and saw Armand standing all by himself between the trees, the side of his face towards her. The men were still running in, she couldn't get past them, she stood helpless, grasping the door-frame, watching Armand's face. The child was white with terror, but even as she looked his expression altered. She saw his mouth tightening, the Séverin mouth; a curious resolution in his sleepy eyes. He shook his head as he always did when she roused him from a reverie, she saw his body stiffen, she thought that he smiled. He began to walk, upright, his hands in his coat pockets, with a callow semblance of the Séverin dignity, to where the shell had fallen. She fought and freed herself and ran after him.

Pierre, with Sophie in his arms, had reached the cellar before he realized that Renée was not in front of him. Forcing his way back, barging ruthlessly with elbow and shoulder, he had nearly reached the door at the moment when Renée ran. He could see her over the shoulders of the men in front, he shouted furiously: "*Renée! Come back! They'll get you!*"

They got her. The fourth shell dropped and landed a few yards from the last one. Comparatively it did not do much good, but the shrapnel whipping across the square must account for anyone fool enough to be in the open after such a warning.

And yet there was no bodily injury that Pierre could see, either to Renée or to his son. They lay face to face, and so close that their fingers touched, as if they understood each other. He did not look at them for long, he could not manage that. He went slowly into the Hôtel de Ville, and found an officer there, and told him that he had twice deserted from the army. But the officer was frantic with anxiety and would pay no attention. Pierre went up and down the great staircase, stopping anyone he could, shouting out to all and sundry that he was a deserter. But the suddenness and precision of the new bombardment had caught them by surprise, they were far too busy to take any notice of Pierre. A little girl followed him like a dog, complaining that she wanted to blow her nose and couldn't find a handkerchief. But he didn't answer her, he had no idea who she was.

*

In Baulon it was quiet now, and the sun had come out. The Baulonnais had closed their shutters, but through the chinks they gazed curiously at the soldiers, the strange soldiers, who in good order and at an odd, slow pace, marched up the boulevard Maréchal Soult and into the place des Enfants du Roi.

Norwich—Birdlip—Worplesdon.
1934–6.